Love is a taboo, a mere fantasy—
foreign, unreachable, and dangerous.

Raised in a society where women have no rights, seventeen-year-old Thia Clay holds little hope for a bright future. When her parents sell her into marriage to elite member William Fox, Thia slowly gives in to despair. William is nothing but a cruel, selfish young man with no other interest than to serve his own.

Born illegally and forced to hide from the authorities his entire life, nineteen-year-old Chi Richards is an active member of the Underground—a rebellious group seeking to overthrow the government.

Chi only has one goal—to rescue his parents from the work camp they were forced into.

Meeting Thia was never part of the plan, and neither was falling in love with her.

If caught in their forbidden relationship, Thia and Chi could face a death sentence, and when devastating secrets surface from Chi's past, Thia has to rely on her instincts to make a choice that could save her or destroy her forever.

D1562964

Under Ground

Book 1

Alice Rachel

For you to enjoy

and ponder

If we should let them destroy

while we wander.

Chi

UNDER GROUND SERIES

Recommended Reading Order

Under Ground
(Book #1)

Losing Ground:
A Stephen Richards Novella 1

Standing Ground
(Book #2)

Holding Ground:
A Stephen Richards Novella 2

Common Ground:
Kayla and Taylor's Novella

Dangerous Ground:
Tina and Chase's Novella

Breaking Ground
(Book #3)

<u>PART 1</u>

"I hope never to see that boy again.
He had trouble written all over that impish smile of his.
I don't need this kind of temptation in my life."
Thia Clay

<u>Chapter 1</u>

"**During the meeting,** only speak when spoken to and don't ask any questions," Mother snaps at me coldly.

"Yes, Mother." I roll my eyes.

Why does she have to remind me to be quiet? I'm only allowed to talk when someone addresses me, and questions from me are never welcome. This situation will no different from any other circumstance in my life. I want to grunt something back at her, but I swallow the snide remark quickly and try my best to look obedient.

"Don't look at William too insistently. Don't say anything stupid that could make him or his family feel uncomfortable." She keeps going on and on with her demands. Mother has been instructing me in proper manners for years; it's hard to focus on her words.

"Thia, I know the Foxes have accepted your engagement to William, but remember that nothing is formalized yet. Your father and I have gone through great lengths to prepare for this wedding. You have to be on your best behavior during the entire dinner."

In one week, William's family will come to our house for our official meeting—a crucial reunion that will finalize our engagement or break it apart. His parents will gauge whether I'm still worthy of their son or not. Mother is anxious, worried I might make a fool of myself.

I rest my head against the windowpane and try to block out her words as they echo against the walls of our private compartment. The train is moving at full speed. My mind keeps drifting while the landscape passes me by like a blur, going too fast for me to stop or breathe.

There are just a few bullet trains in New York State, all of them reserved for the upper-class. They ride through the mountains, between the different towns, and into the metropolis, Eboracum City, where Mother is taking me to try on my bridal gown.

"Your father spent a lot of money on your dowry, Thia. We offered the highest amount we could afford to make sure the Foxes wouldn't turn you down."

As if that family needs any more money. I grit my teeth and inhale deeply. I was promised to William exactly four years ago, on the day I turned thirteen. That's when I became a piece of merchandise sold in a trade to benefit my parents. My marriage to William was settled by our two families. I had no say in it; nobody cares how I feel about the whole arrangement anyway.

Mother is still talking when a knock finally disrupts this monotonous torture. The door slides open and a female server enters our private compartment, pushing a tray covered with beverages. She inclines her head and keeps her eyes to the ground in deference to my mother.

"May I serve madam some complimentary tea or coffee?" she asks, her voice soft and servile.

"No, thank you," Mother responds harshly. She hates it when people interrupt her.

Suddenly nervous, the poor woman nods while holding her hands together in front of her. She looks at me and waits for my answer. I shake my head and smile to atone for my mother's rude behavior.

When the server exits, Mother resumes her monologue. She holds her back straight while sitting next to me, and her eyes remain fixed on the wall facing us. Not once does she look at me. I'm invisible, transparent, non-existent. I might as well not be here at all. She has a unique gift for ignoring me while pestering me.

"You will be standing until instructed otherwise," she continues, "so William and his parents can look at you while I introduce you. It is of the utmost importance for you to impress them and give your very best, Thia. Many girls would give everything they have to be matched with a young man like William. It is an honor for us that his family chose you."

Mother sends me a quick glance. A lot remains to be done before the union is complete, and this upcoming ceremony has put her completely on edge, turning the past few months into a real nightmare.

"Your father holds high hopes for this union, Thia. Once you are married to William, your father will get promoted to a higher paying job. Mr. Fox even mentioned the possibility of a whole new career. If we are lucky, he will hire your father to work in his company."

No one has told me what post Mr. Fox holds in this state, but it must be an excellent position for my parents to strive so much to impress him. My marriage is sure to help my family grow their social network and increase their fortune.

I look outside the window at the landscape unrolling before my eyes, and my mother's voice fades into the background. This area is flooded, filled with marshes left over from the rainstorms that pour over New York State on a regular basis.

Mother snaps me out of my contemplation. "Thia, are you listening to me?"

She looks at me sharply. I nod and lower my eyes.

"You know William has the right to refuse you at any given time. Don't give him any reason to do so. You are to obey him and his parents no matter what they may demand of you. Getting rejected would be a disgrace upon our entire family. I do not need to remind you what the consequences would be. This is your only chance. No one else will agree to marry you if William changes his mind."

"Yes, Mother."

"You know the stakes are high since women outnumber men."

"Yes, Mother."

After the oceans rose, claiming their territory and devouring parts of New York City along with other areas in the world, the surge led to a civil war that killed most of our men—husbands, fathers, and brothers falling in a fight that almost destroyed our country.

When it comes to marriage, the demand is high and the supply is low, giving men the power to take and reject women at will.

"Remember this is the only way for us to rise in status. Rank is everything, Thia. So many women strive to get an eligible husband. Most young girls can only dream of marrying such a suitable bachelor as William," Mother reminds me. "He needs to feel that you are unique, one of a kind. If this reunion goes as planned, he will ask to meet you for the pre-nuptial night as well."

I shiver.

"He can cancel the wedding if your physical union isn't to his taste," she continues. "Give him whatever he wants and make sure to please him."

Shudders run all over my skin, and I have to breathe deeply so as not to panic. I hate it when she talks about the pre-nuptial night. It's something I try not to think about, ever.

Thankfully, the train slows down before Mother goes into details, and the city's buildings come into view— skyscrapers copying the ones that used to fill the streets of

New York City. Mother turns around to look at me. She raises her eyebrow; she's judging my appearance. She doesn't care about the emotions and fear crushing my chest. She's more interested in my untamed hair and the loose strands she's desperately trying to pull back into my ponytail. She gives me a disapproving look confirming that my mane isn't complying.

The train comes to a stop. I stand up and gesture for Mother to get out first. She waits in line to exit the car. I follow suit and squeeze my way between her and two gossiping women.

"I heard the governor will not run again next year," one of them says. "I wonder who's going to step up for such a difficult task."

"I know, my dear. Whoever it is, I hope they will finally lift the restrictions."

"Can you believe they refused to let us increase our energy consumption last year?"

"Purely ridiculous."

"Everyone knows the poor are draining all our resources. It's about time someone did something about it."

I try hard not to roll my eyes, and the shallow jabber grows distant as Mother and I finally exit the train. The sounds in the station overwhelm me instead, a rumble of noises melting together like a cacophony inside my head. I follow close behind Mother and make sure not to lose her in the crowd. She doesn't glance back once. She holds her chin high in defiance of the world while I find myself staggering through the pack.

I stumble into the street and look around to admire the view. We rarely come here because our town is located in the Catskills further North. It takes about an hour to get here from our neighborhood, and Mother hates public transportation.

The crowd is rushing through the streets, pushing me along. I have to keep up. The streetcars honk their horns as their drivers scowl at the pedestrians. A few scattered electric cars ride along the avenues. Their passengers belong to the elite, to the richest members of our society.

Someone bumps into my shoulder. I'm not moving fast enough. I catch up with Mother. Her posture is assured, proud. I wish I could say the same about mine, but everything here is overpowering me. My mind is blown by so much life and energy. Mother stops suddenly; I almost crash into her. I look up in wonder. The bridal store is right in front of us. This is the second time I've been here, and yet the beauty of its façade still takes my breath away.

I take in the windows facing the avenue and swallow hard as excitement takes flight inside me like butterflies. Behind the glass, exquisite dresses are displayed on mannequins surrounded by velvet curtains and lights illuminating the gowns from below.

Mother pulls me out of my trance and shakes her head at my lack of composure. She pushes the entrance door open and drags me into the store. We step into a room so big that I can't even make out the end of it. The inside is magnificent. A winding marble staircase stands in the middle, giving easy access to the upper levels. Dresses are nicely arranged on models throughout the store or hanging from different racks. Each outfit is more gorgeous than the next, making it close to impossible to pick one. Upper-class girls from the whole state come to this establishment to choose their wedding gowns. This store is owned by one of the richest families in Eboracum City; it's renowned for its extravagance.

When we first came here, everything was so mind-boggling that I was enthralled with it all. My parents gave me permission to choose my own outfit. For once in my life, I got to make a decision for myself. Despite my profound anxiety, I was thrilled when the seamstress called yesterday to say that my wedding dress was ready for try-on. I was allowed to pick the color, shape, and fabric I wanted. I decided upon a light purple silky gown in the same style I had seen in history books. It's long, with a crinoline in the back.

The dressmaker, whose tag reads "Sofia," walks straight to us as we enter. She's dressed well, but with modesty. She's pretty, with a style that catches the eye. Her hair is red and long, falling in loose curls over her shoulders. She's of average height, and her face is pale and freckled. She's wearing a green dress made of silk, cut below her knees.

She greets us by name and heads to the back of the store. I'm nervous. I hope the gown looks as good on me as the sample did. It has to be perfect, without a blemish or flaw.

Sofia comes back with my dress wrapped in plastic. She puts it on the counter and unzips the bag around it. Then she slides it out gently and holds it in front of me. I gasp in wonder. The dress is so beautiful it brings tears to my eyes.

I try to hide my emotions, but when I look at Mother, I see a flicker of pride and awe crossing her face. She's quick to recover herself though. I sometimes forget that my mother is human just like me. She most certainly has feelings; it's just often hard to believe. She spends so much time hiding them.

Sofia beckons me to a mirror and holds the dress in front of me. For the first time in my life, I feel beautiful. The purple shade of the gown is radiant and bright, shining against the raven darkness of my hair, bringing out the sparkling light reflected in my anthracite eyes. For once, my pale skin does not look sallow and sickly, but merely fragile and spotless, like porcelain.

Sofia snaps me out of my trance by taking the gown away. She leads us to a grand dressing room and asks me to undress. I flush, my cheeks burning with heat rising from my chest to my face as I take off my outfit. I stand in my underwear in front of Sofia and my mother. I want to hold my hands in front of my body, to hide as much of it as possible, but instead I stand as tall as I can and try to hide my embarrassment.

"Let's put the crinoline on first," Sofia says. She holds it in front of me. "Please, step into it."

I do as she says. She pulls on the drawstrings to hold it in place around my waist. I feel minuscule. My petite frame stands out under this massive accessory, and its discomfort does nothing to help silence my insecurities. I inhale when Sofia finally puts the gown over my head and pulls it down. She comes to stand behind me and pulls the zipper up. When the bodice is tight around my torso, holding the gown in place, I whirl around and the skirt flows all around me. The smooth texture of the fabric catches the light when I move. I almost giggle, but I catch myself quickly. I stop, stand straight, and look at Mother. Her face is hard, as always, but I could swear that her eyes creased with tiny laugh lines for just one second.

"Please turn around, Miss Clay," Sofia says.

She traps my chest in an iris mauve corset. Its lace is refined, intricate, woven by hand. Its color complements the wine berry shade of the skirt. Sofia pulls on the strings; I can hardly breathe. The corset brings up my bosom somehow, making it look much bigger than it truly is.

"I will fix the bottom now. I just need to adjust the length with pins." It takes but a few minutes for Sofia to complete the job. When she's done, she looks at my mother. "What do you think, Mrs. Clay?"

Mother comes to stand by my side. Her arms are crossed over her chest, but a flicker of pride crosses her eyes quickly. She approves, and this is all it takes for my heart to leap so hard that my chest burns.

Mother nods her head; Sofia may put everything away now. She releases the corset first and pulls me out of my gown slowly, without dropping any pins. Then she takes off my crinoline and walks away to hang the dress from a rack. I get back into my usual attire and hurry to cover my half-naked body as quickly as possible.

"It will be ready for pick-up in a week," Sofia says. "I'll call you when it's done."

We go to the counter, where Mother has to pay an additional deposit to help cover the last completions. When we walk out of the store, the masses overtake me, pushing me forward as I try to look around one last time. I may not be allowed to come back here to pick up my dress. I want to absorb as much of the beauty of the place as possible.

We force our way through the throng of people, and when we enter the station, I can finally calm down and breathe. Mother and I look for a bench and wait. The train arrives. We get in and find our reserved compartment. We sit next to each other without a word. I should be thankful that Mother hasn't found anything to hassle me about yet, but I'm waiting for a compliment from her, for a miracle I know will never happen. I can't read her thoughts or tell how satisfied she is with me today. She just sits up straight, with her chin held high, ignoring me as always. When the train passes by the store, I steal one last glance at it. I look at the skyscrapers and the crowd scurrying through the street.

The city disappears as the train enters the slums surrounding it. My heart flutters. The beautiful buildings of the metropolis clash with the structures housing the poor— a place falling apart and crumbling down under the weight of our tumbling economy. Tears well up in my eyes at the sight, and deep sadness replaces the flimsy euphoria I felt upon seeing my beautiful dress.

I blink back my sudden grief, turn to Mother instead, and marvel at her profile. I've always been in awe of her. She's gorgeous—tall, with long black hair that is always fluid and loose over her shoulders. Her eyes are dark blue and her nose is straight. Her skin has a sweet olive tint to it, tanned and yet not wrinkled by the sun, and everything about her face is symmetrical. She has an intense beauty that most people find difficult to look away from.

I wish I were as beautiful and confident as she is. If I were pretty, I'd feel more at ease with this wedding. Then there would be more guarantees that William and his family would accept me. But everything I've inherited from my mother somehow doesn't look as good on me. I'm not outstanding. My black hair is long and curly, reaching my elbows, but instead of falling perfectly upon my shoulders the way my mother's does, mine is always untamed. It has to be pinned down to be controlled. I'm short. I have a fair complexion that often makes me look sickly, and my nose, like my dad's, is a bit too long.

I hope William won't find me plain. I met him a few years ago. I haven't seen him again since then, but he was quite attractive at the time. He was tall and lean, with short blond hair. His eyes were green, and he had dimples in his cheeks even without smiling. He didn't seem the type of person to smile, actually. I'm sure most girls would think William to be breathtaking, but there was a profound coldness to him that was unappealing, and the way he looked at me made me so uncomfortable that I squirmed under his gaze.

He's still really young, only eighteen years old, which is quite lucky for me, I guess. I should deem myself fortunate that my parents didn't try to marry me to an older man, but I can't seem to be grateful for such "good fortune." I still hold this insane hope that William might treat me well, but I should know better. I have been raised to accept that no man will ever see me as an equal or treat me as such.

Chapter 2

At eight a.m., our maid Emily walks in and opens the blinds. I groan and pull a pillow over my face. I hardly slept last night, and the little time I spent in slumber was filled with nightmares about the wedding. Someone had stolen my gown and exchanged it with another dress. The replacement was made of plaid, and as I walked down the aisle, the guests started whistling and booing me. Mother gave me a disapproving look, and William just walked away, calling the wedding a ridiculous masquerade. I was petrified. I woke up earlier than I normally do, covered in sweat. It had only been a dream, but I couldn't go back to sleep after that.

When the light comes streaming in through the window, I pull a second pillow over my eyes and try to suppress the pain already pounding inside my head. The sharp ache hammering at my skull will last all day because Mother limits how much medication I'm allowed to take. She claims the system won't allow her to get certain pills or medical supplies. I know it's a lie. Mother probably doesn't deem pain significant enough to "waste" my father's salary on. For sure, my parents' rank gives them access to all kinds of medicine. We are all well aware that people from different classes get different rations of food, medication, and resources. The authorities view it as a good way to force the civilians to strive for a better position in society. Despite our upper-class status, Mother insists that my family is counting on me to help them reach an even higher standard of living. I personally view my parents' attitude as greed, but I would never dare voice my opinion out loud.

When Emily comes to stand by my bed and glares at me, I push the covers away and sigh heavily. Today is Monday, a school day. I always prepare myself quickly in the morning. Every day the exact same routine. I start with a short shower. Then I put on my school uniform—black pants, a black shirt and white tie. The result is extremely manly, an effect sought by the school on purpose. School is not a beauty contest; it's a place where young girls learn how to become proper ladies willing to stand by their husbands without ever showing the slightest amount of wit. They call it "education." I tend to think of it as brainwashing bigotry, though speaking my mind on the matter would be unwelcome, not to say costly.

Boys attend different schools of their own, lest our proximity trigger shameful desires or feelings. We hardly ever see them, except during outings, in the streets, or for social events. Besides my father and brother, William is the only boy I've ever had a true encounter with, and I hardly spoke to him for fear of saying something insignificant, stupid, or boring.

Once I'm dressed, I have breakfast—always on my own—while Emily hovers in my space to make sure I don't waste any food. When I'm done, I join Walter—our butler—on the front porch. It's his job to ensure I get to school safely. After all, it is quite unbecoming of a proper young girl to wander the streets on her own. Walter and I never talk on the way to or from school. I hardly know anything about him. I've tried to engage him in a few conversations, but to no avail.

"It is kind of you to care, Miss Thia," he once told me. "But you should not sympathize with the lower class. It's dangerous and frowned upon. Commoners like me really don't matter."

I've always disagreed. I'm curious about his life, but after that discussion, I stopped asking questions. I don't want to get him in trouble.

Walter seems to be in his late fifties, with a head full of gray hair. His eyes are light baby blue, and he has a big nose and strong jaw. He lives with the rest of our staff in a small house next to ours. He's especially devoted to my mother, at her beck and call all day and night. If he has a family, I know nothing about it.

Walter and I always take the upper-class train. The entire ride is spent in awkward silence, and when we reach our destination, he walks me to school even though it's located only seconds away from the station. Then he reminds me that he'll be picking me up from the platform at four p.m., as if I would forget our daily habits.

My school is an old institution located twenty miles from my house. It's ranked as the best establishment in the state, which is a good sign for me, I guess. The property is a huge estate. Most of its students come from different counties to be boarded here all year. My friend Melissa is one of them. I, however, do not board here since I have the "extreme privilege" of living nearby. Mother always reminds me how lucky we are to have me go to the best school for girls in the state without me having to leave home. I personally would have enjoyed very much the autonomy that comes with boarding, but luck did not strike me that way.

When I reach the gate, I give my ID to the guard, walk through the schoolyard, climb the stairs leading to the entrance of the main building, and find my friend Melissa waiting for me there. Melissa is taller and prettier than me. She has light freckled skin, crystal blue eyes, and long wavy blond hair. I haven't opened my mouth yet, but she's already shooting questions at me. Her smile radiates happiness, the burden of this life never weighing on her shoulders the way it does mine.

"When are you picking up your dress?" she asks.

"Next week," I reply, slightly apathetic.

"I am *so* excited for you." She claps her hands and jumps for joy as if marriage were the best thing a girl could ever wish for.

I try my best not to sigh at her enthusiasm. After all, she's only trying to help me focus on the positive aspects of the alliance. She knows that this coming weekend is the official meeting with William's family and that I've been stressing out about it.

Melissa and I walk to our lockers as I recount my visit to the store. We grab our books and head to class. We always start with cultural studies, a course focusing mostly on the history of matrimony—a subject meant to remind us that our system is the best there can possibly be and that girls should rejoice at their fate, their lack of freedom, and the opportunity to be chosen by a man at all.

"Guess what?" Melissa startles me. She's fidgeting as if she's about to reveal some big secret that might change the world.

"What?" I reply with feigned enthusiasm.

She doesn't catch on to my sarcasm though; she just giggles. "I received my engagement ring on Saturday."

Melissa is lucky enough to have been promised to a boy she knows well, someone her age. He's the son of her parents' best friends. For some reason, they didn't try to match her to a higher position. They simply looked for someone who was familiar. Melissa is carefree because she knows her match is assured. She knows her mate will not back down or turn her away.

"We also set a date for our prenuptial night," she continues.

My stomach flips when she mentions the dreadful topic. The pre-nuptial night is something I never want to discuss, but Melissa always forces the subject upon me.

"In a month from now," she continues. "How about you? Will you set the date when you meet William?"

I squirm. *Can we please stop talking about this?*

"I don't think we'll be discussing that yet," I reply.

At least, I hope not!

"I really can't wait," she adds.

Well, that makes one of us. I could wait forever and never be ready for it, but I keep my snide remarks to myself, not wanting to spoil her good mood.

<u>Chapter 3</u>

No one ever cared to stop and wonder if William might be to *my* taste. Not once! No one gives credit to a silly girl's feelings. I know nothing about William. I may end up never loving him. Love is a taboo, a mere fantasy, a concept too vague to ever take shape in reality. Only the luckiest girls may get a glimpse of it—girls like Melissa.

Today, I am to meet William and his parents. I'm relieved that the meeting is finally happening, but the tension inside me has become unbearable. My anxiety has risen to the point where I'm nothing but a nervous wreck. *What if William turns me down?* I'm not that special. He could find someone better than me quite easily. I've heard dreadful stories about girls who've been rejected and what it means for their families. Most of those girls end up homeless because their parents disown them and kick them out once they've become useless. A chill runs down my spine. I don't want to end up in the streets. I want my existence to have a meaning. But the game that is my life has already begun and the dice are definitely loaded.

For our meeting, we've invited William's family to dinner at our house. This is common practice. It gives the groom's parents a chance to assess our assets and see if we are a good match for their son or not. Mother has gone all out with the preparations. All day long, the staff has been cleaning the place. Each cushion, each sculpture, each painting had to be dusted and placed in the perfect spot, to create a sense of harmony and beauty. I've rarely seen my mother in such a state. Every second threatens to bring on a nervous breakdown. Every word coming out of her mouth is a snap, as harsh and cold as ice.

My hair has been washed, dried, and styled this morning. I now need make-up and my dress. I have to be the epitome of perfection. I'm shaking from all the stress. I need to calm down, but Mother keeps pacing around, walking in circles, trying to catch the smallest details that may have escaped her scrutiny. She's driving me crazy. I want to shake her into standing still, at least for a moment, so I can find my breath. But this pandemonium lasts all day long.

Sounds of pans and dishes pour in from the kitchen— the staff rushing around the house, whispering my name. They are either trying to obey my mother's orders as precisely as possible or avoid her as much as possible. No one wants to be the object of her wrath.

At six o'clock, everything's ready. The table is set with the nicest china, crystal glasses, and silver candelabras. Each cushion is in its place—or at least in a spot satisfying enough for my difficult mother. Everything's perfect, and we still have a full hour to wait. This is going to be the longest hour of my life.

My brother Lance asks if I'd like to play card games, but he gives up on the idea when he sees the look on my mother's face. Her eyes pierce through his like daggers. We are to sit on the sofa and wait so as not to disturb the air, not move a thing.

Lance is twenty-five years old. He got married four years ago to a girl named Marie. Mother invited them both today to expose our family at its fullest for the Foxes to evaluate. My brother inherited my mother's good looks and my father's dirty brown hair. He's my mother's favorite child, and she has always treated him like he was the eighth wonder of this world. No matter how spoiled he's always been, I've never seen Lance be cruel to anyone, and especially not to his wife. I hope William will be just as kind and understanding with me. I don't dare trust that he will, though. Keeping my expectations low will probably save me a lot of disappointment.

By the time the doorbell rings, everyone is quite on edge. I'm dizzy with chaos filling my brain and thoughts spinning over and over again inside my mind: *How should I behave in front of William? What would happen were I to trip on my long dress? And who had chosen such a difficult gown to walk in anyway?* Ah yes, I remember; it was Mother. Only *she* would choose such an uncomfortable dress for such an emotional event.

The air has left my lungs, and my heart is pounding hard, pumping blood all the way to my ears. I have to hold onto the couch as I stand up, for fear I may fall over. The corset of my dress is so tight that I'll be lucky if I don't faint by the end of dinner. Mother thought of everything really except how to keep her own daughter at ease on the most significant night of her life.

We stand in the house's entrance hall. Walter opens the door and William's parents walk in. Their eyes dart all around first; they couldn't care less that it seems more than slightly rude. After all, they are here to judge whether my family is a good enough match for theirs or not. They don't even acknowledge our presence. They just step in the doorway, take in the room around them, and act as though we are just statues standing in their way.

"Good evening, Mr. and Mrs. Fox. It's quite a pleasure to meet you again," my mother says, a bit too eagerly.

Mrs. Fox finally seems to realize that we are here. She glances at my mother with a stiff upper-lip and a slight look of contempt in her eyes. This woman definitely knows her family's place in society. She seems proud and arrogant about it, too. I try to catch a glimpse of William, but he's hidden by his wide-framed father. When Mr. Fox walks into the house, he holds out his hand to my father. Somehow, both men are more relaxed than their wives. This situation is but a mere case of tradition to them, while to both women, this is a matter of pride and prestige.

I stand on my tiptoes, hoping to finally see William. My behavior is both rude and indecent. It's a sign that I don't know how to restrain my curiosity, a flaw one does not wish to see in a wife. I should be more discreet about it, but I just can't help myself.

When William's father finally moves to the side, he turns to the door, puts his hands on his son's shoulders, and pushes him forward. William comes into view; he is so handsome that I forget to breathe. He's even more attractive than I remembered. He's still tall—incredibly so—but more mature, with blond locks falling in curls over his forehead and green eyes scanning the room with intensity.

I don't know what to do with myself. I just want to run and hide in a mouse-hole. For sure, William's parents will turn me down as soon as they spot me. They must have forgotten how plain I look compared to their gorgeous son. William is the first one to put his eyes on me though. When I meet his gaze, his grass green eyes are arctic cold. He looks me up and down for just a second before his eyes shift to the house. He sizes it up, with more interest than he gave me. I'm vexed that he doesn't consider me significant enough to look at any longer. But of course, I don't exist as a person. I'm just here as a formality. I'm not pretty enough to trigger interest in anyone—not even in my future husband. It must be quite a burden for him to marry someone like me. I'm sure he knows what a good match he is. He probably wonders why he should settle for someone so ordinary, and if that's how he feels, the wedding could be called off at any time. I shudder at the thought.

My parents lead the Foxes inside the house, straight to the living room. I follow them, all the while looking at William, who's avoiding my eyes.

His family sits down on the couch and faces my parents while I simply stand there. I'm not allowed to sit down right away. It's protocol for the family to see me standing so they can size up my frame to see if I will be a good child-bearer—as though one simple glance would suffice to tell whether my genes are good enough to transmit to our potential offspring.

I am nothing more than a racing horse being thoroughly checked out before its purchase. Knowing that my thighs are being evaluated for childbearing makes me nauseous, and a drop of sweat rolls down my hairline.

William's mother, especially, looks me up and down, with spite and maybe cruelty in her eyes. The corners of her lips are turned downward as if I have a foul odor.

She's a gorgeous blonde. Her hair is long, reaching her shoulders. She's tall and thin. Time seems to have passed her by miraculously. She has remained untouched by the years. Looking at her gives me no indication of her age. She could be in her early thirties as far as I can tell.

She stands up and comes to me. I lower my eyes. Looking back at her would be disrespectful—a clear sign of insubordination. I am to submit to the will of both my husband and his parents, and I have to play the game from the very beginning. I stare at my feet, but I can feel her eyes on me, assessing my whole body, as she walks all around me.

She faces me, lifts my face to hers, and looks me in the eyes while frowning. Then her gaze shifts downward as she opens my mouth. I try to hold back a breath of shock, but I can't help gasping. I didn't expect her to inspect me like an animal, though I knew she would be examining me. She looks at my teeth with scrutiny. Now, I know for sure that I've turned into a horse somehow. I try to be serious though the situation feels more and more grotesque. I don't know if I should laugh or be mortified.

She nods her approval, and a tiny freezing-cold smile appears on her face. Then she goes back to the couch and sits down. Her husband witnessed the whole scene, but he didn't care to participate. I exhale in relief. I'm not sure I could have taken any more of this humiliation. My eyes shift toward William, shyly. He has watched the whole thing too, but he didn't come to me either. He's just looking at me with a blank stare on his face. I can't read him at all, and it unsettles me.

I'm swimming in deep turmoil, the heat of all the mortification still burning my cheeks. The way Mrs. Fox has treated me so far brings shame into my heart, mixed with rage now compressing my chest. I clench my fists just enough that I know I'm rebelling, but not enough for anyone else to notice.

My mother indicates that I may be seated, and the evening goes on. I'm stuck in a haze of sort. I'm floating through it all like a ghost, a witness with no grip on the actions unfolding around me. Small talk takes place while the staff brings appetizers to the living room. Mr. Fox and my father discuss the latest political news, and Mrs. Fox asks my mother questions about me, my education, my tastes. Not once does she talk to me directly. She acts like I'm a child who can't speak for herself.

When the meeting moves to the dining room, I sit next to my mother. William is on the opposite side of the table, which prevents me from approaching him in any way. Something about him bothers me profoundly. He's mysterious, fairly aloof—illusive even. I wish he were like his father, a bit nicer, a bit more transparent and easier to read. But it's obvious his mother is the one who raised him and he's a lot like her. He doesn't even look at me during the whole dinner, which only upsets me more and more. *Who is this man coming to my house, sizing me up like livestock, and not even giving me enough importance to seek conversation?*

At some point, William's mother pays attention to me, and when I see the look she's giving me, I suddenly wish she weren't paying me heed at all.

"So, Thia, what skills have you been learning at school? Your mother just told me you're good at writing. Quite a useless ability to have if you ask me! What's the point of writing? Just filling our young girls' minds with idle thoughts and beliefs."

I didn't hear my mother refer to my writing, and I'm not sure how to respond to such a condescending comment. *Is she expecting me to agree with her and acknowledge how worthless my skills are?* Writing makes me feel good. It's the only escape I have from this place. In my verses, women are free. They can make a life for themselves. I can live vicariously through them and imagine my future the way I'd want it to be. Of course, no one has ever read those poems. I only show my family and teachers the sonnets that fit our society's narrow-minded beliefs.

"Thia writes poetry," my mother interjects, trying to save face, but burying me deeper instead. "It is quite good. Though writing may seem useless, poems can brighten a tedious evening and help entertain guests."

I wish she would just shut up, but she just plunges the nail deeper, striking me like a hammer, as she speaks the words I've been fearing, "Thia, why don't you read us one of your poems?"

I want to turn into a rodent right now, go hide, and never come out again. *What is my mother thinking?* I'll just humiliate myself even more than I already have. I nod gracefully anyway and ask to be excused from the table. I stand up and try to act normally in spite of my quivering. I walk to my bedroom, grab my notepad, and head back to the dining room as smoothly as I can.

My hands are shaking. I brush them against my dress in a quick gesture to stabilize them. I breathe deeply a few times, praying for the hundredth time tonight that I won't faint.

I hold myself straight, open the pad, and look for the best sonnet I have. I start reading the rhymes. My voice is shaky with tears threatening to emerge. I hope they'll blame my emotions on the nature of the poem. I chose an ode to my grandfather who passed away a few months ago. It's beautiful, I think, and I'm quite proud of it.

When I'm done, I hold the pad between my hands and stare at my feet. I'm too scared to confront the looks on their faces.

"Well, I do hope you'll have other ways to distract William's guests once you two are married," Mrs. Fox says with a snort.

Her comment doesn't hurt my feelings though; it infuriates me. I hold the papers more tightly, out of anger, while trying to hide the frown forming on my face. *Who is this woman to dare judge the poem I wrote in honor of my late grandfather?* I hold the pad tighter and tighter until it twists between my fingers and my knuckles turn white.

I look up. My brother rolls his eyes at Mrs. Fox, just once, before winking at me. Mrs. Fox has returned to her meal and so have her husband and my father. My mother though is staring at me with profound pity. There is something else hiding in her eyes too, pride maybe? She throws Mrs. Fox one quick look of disdain, so fast it almost never was. I'm both surprised and shocked by it. My mother is not one to be sentimental—especially not toward me. The disgust she just expressed for Mrs. Fox, no matter how swift it was, is quite unsettling. It's such a small act of defiance, but the soothing effect on my heart is strong all the same.

When I turn toward William, his eyes meet mine. He's actually looking at me for once, and delight flickers through his gaze swiftly—there one second, gone the next—as if he were proud of me. Then his eyes shift to his mother, and a frosty spark of irritation shines through them before he looks back at his plate.

I resume my place next to my mother, and Mrs. Fox's snotty comments never stop. William ignores me for the majority of the evening, but his eyes keep on narrowing a little bit more each time his mother throws a demeaning remark at me, and the hope that he might like me is now growing inside my heart.

Chapter 4

This morning, my sheets are wet with sweat as I wake to an intense headache and feelings of helplessness and dejection. I've spent all night worrying that the union might not be taking place, all the while hoping that the Foxes might reject me. I don't want to spend my life obeying such an appalling woman as Mrs. Fox. A pang of guilt stabs me upon wishing for this arrangement to fail. I should want it to work, if not for myself, at least for the sake of my family.

Emily walks in right on time, as she does every day. I just want to turn around and disappear. I wish to hide in slumber, escape in dreams, and never face reality again. I force myself to sit up and rub my eyes which are stinging from my lack of sleep. The migraine pounding through my skull is making me sick to my stomach.

As I walk downstairs, Emily follows me while clicking her tongue. I ignore her foul mood and pretend not to hear her disgruntled mumbles. Our cook has prepared breakfast for me already. This time, she has made salted waffles. Some yogurt is also waiting by the plate. The mere sight of this meal turns my stomach and makes me gag. I sit at the table anyway. I cut a piece, take a bite, chew on it, and try to ignore the feeling in my abdomen. I swallow it down and take a few more bites before pushing the dish away.

I tell Emily that I'm done. She sends me a glance filled with irritation when she sees the plate still covered with food, but she doesn't say anything. Wasting food is punishable by law. Any uneaten rations need to be refrigerated and eaten later. Nothing can be wasted; nothing can be discarded. Anyone caught throwing food away will see their resources cut down drastically.

I stand up and the chair squeaks as I push it. The sound alone costs me another glare from Emily—one of the usual signs showing her annoyance at me. She's extremely professional; her snapping words and short, rapid movements are never blatant enough to be called brazen or insubordinate. But the jealousy still shines through her tiny brown eyes while she holds her petite frame straight in disapproval of my attitude.

Emily and I live on opposite sides of the same wall, both trapped by it, unable to understand each other while looking for our way out. She's only a few years older than I am. Her desire to get married has always been strong and plain for all to see. Her situation saddens me, really. I'm sure this was not the future she wanted for herself. I send her a tiny compassionate smile, and when she responds with a frown, I go outside to find Walter waiting to take me to school.

It's a dark, rainy day. Walter and I run to the station. The rain pours down on us until we reach the train. We find our compartment and settle down. I rest my head against the window and watch the raindrops roll down the pane. Walter and I don't talk. The train reaches the school's station too quickly. I wish it didn't. I don't feel like talking to Melissa about the meeting. I gather it didn't go so well; I don't want to acknowledge how I probably ruined my only chance to make my family proud.

When I get out of the train, I sigh and my shoulders slump forward. Walter has an umbrella ready for me. I take it, thank him, and walk to school. I consider just going straight to the bathroom to wait there until the bell rings for first period. But I'm not so cowardly as to avoid my friend. I join Melissa by my locker, and when she sees me, she jumps up and down, waving her arms.

"Thia, hey! Tell me, tell me, how did it go?"

I groan. My migraine is back, just like that. "It went well, I guess."

"Oh!"

She can read right through me. My attitude is enough to describe the situation. No words are needed to imply failure. But I need to blurt it all out, so I let it flow, all the misery, all the shame, out, out, out of me like a river soiled and polluted by those around me, tainting my soul with embarrassment and disgrace.

"It was quite humiliating and painful. William didn't even acknowledge my presence, and his mother had nothing nice to say the whole time," I tell Melissa.

"Oh! That's quite normal, dear."

Out of everything she could have said, I was not expecting that.

"Well, I guess William's aloofness is a bit strange," she admits, "but it's quite natural for his mother to be harsh. They're just testing you, trying to make you crack under the pressure to see how much you really want the union. John's mother never treated me like that, but I've heard plenty of stories."

I sigh in relief, though I don't feel much better about my promised fiancé.

"So, is William still good-looking?" she asks. "I heard Mary-Alice got engaged to a grouch who's thirty years older than she is, the poor girl."

I'm not sure if that's supposed to cheer me up. Knowing that the living conditions of another person might be worse than mine doesn't comfort me at all.

"No. William is actually really quite gorgeous," I reply.

"What's the problem, then?" she asks, not even realizing how shallow her question sounds.

Her words irritate me, but the bell rings just then, saving me the trouble of explaining to her how being handsome does not make a good husband. We head to our behavioral class, where we usually learn how to conduct ourselves like proper ladies worthy of the superior men who reign over our lives.

The day just drags on with a sense of doom looming in the air and rain pouring down, anchoring the overwhelming grief inside my heart. The sadness just stays locked inside, refusing to come out through the relief of tears. And when the day is finally over, I find solace in going home. I head straight to my bedroom and spend the late afternoon sulking while doing my homework. No one comes to check on me, and I'm just glad I don't have to feign happiness. Soon the Foxes will give us an answer, and I will finally know if William has decided to give me a chance or just reject me and ruin my life for good.

Chapter 5

It took two weeks for the Foxes to send us their reply under the form of a letter—two weeks of me dreading a negative answer while hoping for more than a life spent in Mrs. Fox's claws. Apparently, I made a great impression on William and his father. They've decided that I fit their status. This should bring me joy, but instead, it feels like agony. Now I know where my life is heading, and I don't like the direction it's taking.

We've met William's family on multiple occasions since their consent to hold the wedding. Though they appreciate me, each meeting with them brings along its share of heartaches and vexations. I have yet to hear Mrs. Fox say anything nice or hear a single word from William's mouth. He just sits by my side most of the time and observes me without ever reaching out. If he likes me as I had first hoped, he's not showing any sign of it. The cold wind of his attitude just blows my way, and I can never warm up to him.

Today is just a typical day; nothing warns me that it will be any different this time. William has a football game that I am to attend as his promised fiancée. My life is now punctuated by a series of outings and events. I am to look pretty, make William shine, and seem obedient and polite. The whole time, I feel like screaming and hurting myself, but that's just underneath it all. In appearance, I am calm, compliant, and well behaved. The screams of protest fill my head, but they don't ever get out. I won't let them. I just choke on them while my mind slowly gives in to insanity.

I've never been to any of William's games before, and I don't really care for sports. Such events are meant for young socialites and families trying to impress those around them—something I couldn't care less about, but find myself forced into for the sake of my husband-to-be. I have to pretend I'm enjoying myself the entire time. To others, it looks like nothing could make me happier than to be here for William. Inside, I wish I were anywhere else.

Balls, events, and games are the few times girls get to mix with boys. To prevent shameful desires and unnecessary crushes, young girls aren't allowed to be around men. Because of those rules, today is one of the first times I get to be around males that aren't related to me. I never quite understood what the whole fuss was about. I've never looked at any boy. Romantic feelings are completely foreign to me, and my parents never cared to show me love. Though I've always craved my mother's attention and care, I've never expected to receive affection from her, or anyone else for that matter.

The game started about half an hour ago. I'm sitting between my parents, doing my best to focus on the match. My parents are deeply into it, of course. Or if they aren't, the pretense is good enough to make us believe that they actually care. It's the first time they get to enjoy an outing based on their daughter's engagement, and they're going to make the most of it.

William's parents are sitting closer to the field since they're related to a player. Mrs. Fox is wearing a golden dress today, the color of prestige and achievement. It reflects the champagne streaks in her hair. She looks more splendid than ever. My own mother is wearing a purple dress, the color of royalty and ambition. I'm starting to wonder if outings will become a reason for competition between the two of them. It's as if my mother, especially, feels the need to impress that woman. I'm not sure if she's upset at Mrs. Fox's status in society, or if she's holding a grudge at the way Mrs. Fox has treated us so far. But my mother is making quite an effort to show that woman that we can be just as elegant as she is.

To that purpose, she chose my dress again today. Of course, she placed beauty before practicality. It's not a hot day, but the dress she picked is heavy and warm. It's long and blue, the color of loyalty and integrity—the shade that promised brides-to-be have to wear in public to show every man that they're already taken.

Despite the chilly breeze and lack of sun in the sky, this outfit is overwhelming me and I have to put a lot of energy in remaining cool. To others, it looks like I'm engaged in the game, proud at how well William is mastering the ball, outplaying his opponent. But the corset is crushing my chest and the crowd around us is making the air stuffy. Breathing is getting harder by the minute and heat rises higher and higher in my body, with deep turmoil stirring inside me as I hyperventilate.

I try to ignore the unhealthy feelings and fears, but when I look at William, my heart jumps inside my chest, faster and faster, until it hurts so much I feel faint. Our pre-nuptial night is getting closer. I'm still petrified whenever I think about it. I close my eyes and try to breathe. The last thing I need is to have a panic attack in the middle of the stadium.

I study those around me and push away all these negative thoughts that have become my enemies. Everyone is deeply focused on the game, so no one notices me. I study their faces one by one. I have this strange sensation, as if I'm under someone else's scrutiny. I get paranoid that my thoughts have been showing.

I lower my eyes, take a deep breath, and focus on remaining cool and tranquil. But the feeling that someone is watching me doesn't go away. I look up and see him, a boy about my age, observing me. He's staring at me with no impunity, no shame at such a blatant disregard for the rules. It's illegal for a male to covet another man's promised fiancée. Going after the woman of another is punishable under the law by death. It is deemed a threat to our society's good functions. It is not a matter to be taken lightly. Yet, this boy is devouring me whole with his eyes. He doesn't turn his head away when I look at him either. He keeps on eyeing me steadily without blinking, with curiosity and something else I can't quite pinpoint but that makes me feel special, strangely alive. His gaze is intense, piercing through my skull, examining every detail of my face. I feel visible for the first time in my life.

I turn my eyes away and don't dare look back. It's not becoming for a proper young girl to look at men, let alone stare at them. We are not to feel desire for men other than our betrothed. Only one man is to be the object of our adoration. Whether that veneration is faked or not doesn't matter. We are all well aware of the lies, but this façade is the only thing protecting our society and hiding the imperfections of its foundation.

I can still feel his eyes on me though, and in spite of my own will, I glance at him again. I can't help myself; my eyes shift and I look up. He's still staring at me, his lids not fluttering once. And instead of averting my eyes as I should, I examine him, his face, and his posture. His irises are dark brown, almost black from this distance. His hair is dark brown too, falling over his forehead, almost obstructing his eyes. It looks disheveled in a natural way though he probably spent time working on it. His skin is tanned, his nose is long and straight, and his mouth is nicely shaped, his lips full. He's handsome. The thought reaches my mind before I can suppress it. I flush as heat engulfs me, and a flirtatious grin appears on his face.

He has caught me blushing under his stare—an obvious sign that he interests me. I didn't mean to open that door to him; I didn't mean to seem inviting. And now, it's too late to turn back and pretend that I didn't care about his watching me. I hide my confusion by looking at my feet, but I can still feel him contemplating me, just for a few seconds before his gaze shifts away. I look up, but he's watching the game now. A pang of disappointment grasps my heart, a part of me hoping he was still staring.

My heart races when I gaze at him. Everyone around me will soon hear its beat and turn around to judge me. They will see the shameful thoughts printed all over my face in scarlet letters. I cast one quick glance around to make sure no one has witnessed this reprehensible exchange. My parents are deeply enthralled by the game, and everyone else is either chatting or watching the match. No one's paying attention to me—no one but that one boy that is.

His image is now printed in my mind, his face filling my vision. I have this desperate need to look at him again. I know I shouldn't, and it makes me want to do it even more. I try my best to focus on William instead, but to no avail. I can't control this urge inside me. I turn around and study the boy's profile. He's as handsome from the side as he is from the front. That thought alone makes my heart ache with deep longing. I find myself wanting what I know I can't possibly have, and I know it's bad, really bad.

He must have felt my eyes upon him because he shoots me a glance from the corners of his eyes. It lasts but a flicker of a second, just long enough for my heart to jump with frantic joy. I somehow care what this boy thinks of me, knowing quite well that in the end it won't ever matter. This encounter won't lead anywhere; I'll never know anything more about him. I'd better forget it ever happened.

I hold my hands together, take a breath, and watch William for the rest of the game. But focusing on William is a struggle.

And then the game is over, just like that. It has passed me by as I was fighting the mayhem inside my mind. Everyone moves. I look around to find the boy, but he's nowhere to be seen. Disappointment runs through me as I realize I might never see him again. We head down the stairs and join William's family at the bottom. I'm so distracted I don't even understand what's being said. Mrs. Fox is talking, so it's probably nothing I care to listen to. After the match—which William's team apparently won—my parents and I go back home. I walk through the rest of the day in a trance.

I pretend to be aware of my surroundings, and no one says anything to me. It's easy to fake it when no one pays attention to you to begin with. It's Sunday, so I claim I have homework to do. I go to my room and sit on my bed with a book, but my mind is gone. I see him, the boy, in front of my eyes, his face still quite clear. I wish I had never seen him to begin with, because now I know what longing feels like: It feels like misery.

Chapter 6

I can't stop thinking about him. At dinner last night, when my parents were lecturing me about my upcoming wedding, my mind just kept drifting away. I was trapped, caught in a web of my own thoughts spinning over and over again. I found an imaginary refuge in his facial features, a perfect way to block out everything else around me. I tried to envision what his voice and laughter sound like, and I spent far too much time giving him made-up names, wondering which one might fit him the best.

When my mother finally snapped me out of it, I claimed I was daydreaming about my wedding. It was still rude that I hadn't been listening, but it was better for them to think it was because of William than for me to acknowledge the truth. I keep hoping against all hope that I might see him again, a wish both dangerous and childish on my part. I have no rights to try and get to know a man other than William; the punishment for it would not be worth the risk.

"Miss Clay," a voice calls out to me, shattering the picture of him I was drafting somewhere in my reverie. "Earth to Thia Clay," the social studies teacher speaks louder. I sit up, fully awake, my back suddenly straight.

"Would you mind sharing what has captured your attention, Miss Clay? Or would you rather answer my question?"

"I apologize, Sir. I didn't hear your question," I acknowledge, flushing in shame. I lower my gaze as a few girls snicker around the classroom.

The teacher rolls his eyes and just calls for another student to answer. She's quick to respond and prove that, unlike me, she was paying attention. "Attempt at divorce today leads to imprisonment, Sir," she tells him.

I almost snort with disdain. Divorce is only a concern for women. Men, after all, hold all the possessions. If a man is tired of his wife, he can simply have her committed while he holds on to the belongings. Women don't have that luxury. Some of them are desperate enough to choose their own demise and commit suicide rather than remain married. The situation of women is always dangerous and unstable. A woman never knows if her marriage will hold, and her life can be over if her husband wishes it.

Being a woman in this world is anything but enjoyable. The unfairness of our situation makes me mad, but I can never fully acknowledge it, even to myself. In my heart, there is this hidden place where anger is always boiling. I constantly try to quiet down the wrath raging inside me because showing anger would be dangerous, maybe even fatal. I've heard rumors about what happens to those who don't comply, those who digress and break our strict rules, and that has been enough to convince me I have to keep my thoughts a secret.

"Correct, Miss Wilson," the teacher says. "And what happens to the girls who refuse to follow all common sense? To those who transgress?" he asks Melissa, his eyes shifting to me quickly in disapproval.

"They are disowned by their families, Sir."

That's exactly what would be happen to me were I to disobey. My parents would kick me out of their house. I would have nowhere to go. I doubt anyone would be willing to take me in, for fear it might tarnish their reputation.

"Correct. And what happens to those girls?" the teacher asks.

"They become homeless."

"Yes, and rightfully so," he replies.

I have to breathe deeply to remain impassive. I've seen some of those girls before; they roam our streets like wraiths before disappearing into oblivion, so inconsequential that they end up fading away. I think about the boy I saw at the football field and suddenly hope never to see him again. He had trouble written all over that impish smile of his. I don't need this kind of temptation in my life.

***

The rest of the month is filled with classes that do nothing but insult my intelligence, followed by painful meetings with the Foxes on weekends. William ignores me every single time. Thus far, all he has proven is that I'm not worth the effort of a mere interaction. I might as well turn into the brainless decorative plant that he believes me to be. I just take my fate like a pill, swallow it down, and try to digest the multiple offenses I undergo on a daily basis, my fists discreetly clenched in anger, my fake smile hiding my grinding teeth.

I hope today will help change William's attitude toward me though. A ball has been organized at his school. This is our first official date, the first outing involving just the two of us. William is to pick me up at my house. I'm terrified at the thought of being alone with him. I don't even know what he likes. I'm afraid the conversation might run dry really quickly. I have to seem knowledgeable and avoid any idle small talk that would make me sound like a foolish girl. Mother has put a lot of emphasis on all this, and she has put a lot of work in choosing the perfect dress for me, too.

All day long, my heart has been pounding to the point where it might explode. Every so often, I'm able to breathe, calm down, and think about something else. But any time I think about the ball and the car ride to William's school, my heart starts hammering again. Because William comes from a higher part of the upper class, his family owns a car, which is quite rare. Only the richest members of our society are allowed to possess a vehicle. The rest of us must take the trains dedicated to our different social ranks.

The moment William comes to pick me up arrives faster than I expected, and when the chimes ring, my heart stops beating. Walter opens the door. William's driver is there waiting. My mother looks at me one last time and nods. I look good enough that I may proceed to the car. I walk to the front door like a condemned woman on death row. I try to breathe over and over again. Breathe, I tell myself, the trick is to keep breathing and not faint.

The driver leads me to the vehicle. I'm shocked to see it's a limousine. Such luxury implies that William's family is even wealthier than I had realized. The back door is open. The driver takes me to it, and I step inside as graciously as possible. William is there sitting in the back seat. He doesn't turn his head as I get in. He's looking outside the window as if he can't get far enough from me. This promises to be a great date! I clear my throat to indicate that I'm here though for sure he's aware of my presence. He finally deigns to turn his head and look at me. He sizes me up, but he doesn't smile. He just nods his head to greet me.

The car starts and my heart squeezes slightly.

"Are you thirsty?" William asks me.

My throat is dry. I could definitely use a drink.

"We have soda, juice, or liquor," he adds.

I've never been in a car before. I'm surprised there's actual alcohol in it and even more shocked that William is allowed to drink it. I've never drunk spirits before, but I've heard they can confuse your senses and blur your thoughts.

"Juice, please."

He fills a cup for me, hands me my drink, and pours himself a glass of soda mixed with vodka. I'm not sure if he just wants to try it or if he's more nervous than he's letting on and needs the alcohol to relax.

I look at him and find myself stunned by the splendor of his face, his features sculpted with delicacy and refinement. His aloofness is still keeping me at bay though, making him unreachable. It's been close to impossible for me to connect with him. I hope tonight will help improve our relationship and that I'll finally get a bit closer to him. As soon as his glass is full, William just stares outside the window. He takes a sip and ignores me completely. I want to talk to him, but I don't know how. He's hiding behind that wall he has built around himself to keep me and everyone else at a secure distance. I don't know how to catch his attention.

He suddenly turns his face and puts his eyes on me. "Do you often write poetry?"

His question surprises me. I stutter some kind of answer. I sound horribly dim, unable to find my words. I take a deep breath. "Yes, I do."

"What do you write about?"

I don't trust myself to tell him what most of my poems truly involve, so I describe the ones I show everybody else. "I write about things that touch me. The poem I read at dinner was an ode to my late grandfather."

William looks at me as shock and embarrassment flicker through his eyes. "I'm sorry my mother was rude about it then," he says. "Sometimes she can be cruel, just for the sake of it."

I stare at him for a bit too long. *Do William and his mother not get along as well as she would like us to believe?* I want to say that it's okay, to make him feel better, but it would be a lie. It is not okay, and thinking about his mother's behavior just makes me mad all over again. I clear my throat and change the subject.

"Do you sometimes write also?" I ask.

"No, that's not a skill of mine, I'm afraid," he replies before taking a sip of his drink. "I do read a lot though."

I love reading too, which means that William and I have something in common after all.

"What do you like to read?" I ask.

"Science fiction," he replies. "I own a lot of books. My father also has a huge library in his office. If you're interested, I might show you one day."

I nod with enthusiasm, my body now fully turned toward him.

"I also enjoy poetry," he adds, not smiling once as he speaks.

I would never have guessed that William could be sensitive enough to appreciate poetry. Maybe I could grow to love him after all. William and I might get to know each other better tonight. I feel lighter now.

"What's your favorite book?" I ask, truly curious about him.

"*The Picture of Dorian Gray*," he answers, with a tiny smirk. "I find the character truly likable. He's quite an inspiration, really."

"I've never read that novel. Would you lend it to me someday?" I ask.

His left eyebrow rises and he takes a few seconds to study me, his eyes slightly narrowed as if I were an enigma he couldn't quite understand.

"Sure," he replies. His hand reaches for mine, and I accept it more willingly than I thought I would.

By the time we reach the school, I've relaxed and feel more comfortable in his presence. After stopping the car, the driver opens the back door for us. William walks out first and extends his hand for me to grab. I take it and step out. He puts his arm under mine and leads the way. We step under a porch before reaching the courtyard. There, many students are standing around or talking together. There are more boys than girls since only those with a match living close-by could bring a girl with them.

William looks around as if he's searching for someone. Then he leads me toward the gymnasium where the ball is taking place. The outside is decorated with paper lanterns and ribbons. The music is pounding loudly from inside the building. As we get closer, more students appear in my view. Most of them are chatting, with drinks in their hands.

William's green eyes dart around some more before he takes me inside. The gymnasium at my school is big, but this one is gigantic. Posters representing the different teams ornament the walls. I recognize the one for the football team: a blue panther engulfed in purple flames. The floor is covered with confetti. A disco ball is hanging from the ceiling, reflecting lights all around the dance floor. No band was hired for this event. Instead, a DJ has taken the job.

William takes me further in. He doesn't look at me once. Maybe he's simply nervous. He pulls me in as quickly as possible, drops my arm, and finally turns to me. "Do you want a drink?"

I nod and he heads to the punch table to fill two cups. I use that time to study my surroundings and observe the other couples. Some of them seem nervous while some others are familiar with each other. All the girls are wearing blue dresses.

William walks back to me, his head held high with pride. I catch his eye when he gives me my drink. I open my mouth to talk, but his glance shifts right away, cutting me off. I can't tell if he's just extremely shy or truly inconvenienced with having to bring me here tonight. If anything, I should be the nervous one. It is my future resting in his hands after all and not the other way around.

I'm about to reach for him when he says, "I'll be right back." And just like that, he's gone. It's as if he couldn't get away from me fast enough.

His attitude is upsetting me. The boiling anger surfaces, erupting slowly, and I'm not sure I'll be able to contain it this time. I cross my arms and send him a nasty glare as he turns his back on me. The arrogance and rudeness of this family is getting on my last nerve. I didn't ask to be dragged to this stupid ball. The least he could do is act like he appreciates my presence here. I watch him closely as he walks toward his friends. They tap him on the back when they see him. I notice that one guy doesn't though; he just holds out his hand for William to shake.

I'm vexed that William didn't care to present me to his friends. I wonder if he'll have the decency to do so at some point, but seeing how things have gone so far, I don't really count on it. *Am I that repulsive that he's trying to hide me like some nasty little secret?*

I thought we had managed to cross a bridge and reach toward each other in the car. I thought I'd be more comfortable around William. But now, I realize I was wrong. William is not interested in me. I'm just a formality, something he has to deal with, and he doesn't want to put any effort into our relationship. His snubbing me makes my position quite unstable and shaky, and I'm not comfortable with that.

I keep on staring at him with anger. I couldn't care less if he sees me. He's being rude. I wish my eyes could throw daggers so he would fall down on the spot. I'm so mad that my life and future are resting in the hands of such a careless, inconsiderate jerk that I'm shaking at the mere thought of it. But he just stays there, talking to his buddies and laughing as if nothing's the matter. I have a sudden urge to walk up to him and slap him right in the face in front of all his friends. The anger is still rising from within. Something new is taking shape inside my heart. It's not hatred really, but something close to it. Right now, I just truly despise William, and knowing I'll have to spend my life with him just makes me want to throw up.

I'm ready to walk out of this place when a gap opens in the group and he appears—the boy who held out his hand for William to shake. It's him—the boy from the stadium. I stand here, frozen. Of course, his presence at the football field means he's going to William's school. *Why didn't I put two and two together?*

I stare at him a bit too long, and he must have felt it because his eyes rise to take me in, for just one second. It doesn't seem like he has recognized me, and disappointment seizes my heart right away, tearing at it. What I felt during the football game was not returned. This boy is like all the others, and I am nothing to him. But then, his eyes meet mine again and remain there. I can't look away; his gaze is holding mine with intensity. He doesn't smile, and I forget to breathe. I avert my eyes. I'm blushing. I'm embarrassed at how my cheeks keep on betraying me. When I dare steal a glance again, his eyes are still devouring me whole and I get nervous that someone might catch him staring.

I turn around and walk to the punch table. I'm walking on a cloud, as if I were flying. I step as steadily as I can in my high-heels, with emotions rushing through my core.

There's a line at the table; I have to wait. When I finally reach the punch bowl, I take the serving spoon. My hand is shaking. I try to control it as I fill my glass. I need to get a grip on myself. Someone behind me reaches for the spoon, and I extend it to them. When I look up, I see that it's him. I stumble backward and almost drop punch all over myself. He holds out a hand to steady me, but I've recovered my balance already. I take a step back, and a flirtatious grin spreads on his face—the same mischievous smile that he sent me at the game. I find it both irritating and engaging. My cheeks burn under his gaze.

"Hi, I'm Chi," he says while beaming at me.

His name sounds like "shy," not at all what I had imagined all those times I thought about him. He extends his hand to me as he introduces himself. I recoil and scan the room nervously to see if anyone has witnessed this incident. Even though there is still a line behind us, everyone's busy picking up cake or talking to each other. Chi laughs at my reaction.

He bends close to my ear to whisper, "It's okay. No one's watching, and he's not paying any attention to you."

His breath against my skin makes me shiver. His closeness is unsettling, but he steps back really quickly—too quickly. A part of me wants him closer. Of course, by "he" he means "William." He knows. He knows whom I'm promised to, and yet he's flirting with me. The recklessness of it all is both attractive and disconcerting.

He beckons with his head for me to follow him. I'm at a loss what to do. There's this sudden pull inside me and a tempting voice in my ear telling me to go after him. But I'm petrified, paralyzed on the spot. I stay where I am while he makes his way through the crowd. I have to act now before he's too far ahead or I may lose him.

I run after him, but William chooses this exact second to step in front of me. I sigh in relief and frustration. Of course, William would choose this moment to finally show up. I steal a glance at Chi, but he's already far away and he won't turn around. I focus on William and force a smile on my face. Even if he's been rude to me, I need to hide the insane thoughts that have been flooding my mind since I saw Chi.

"I was talking to my friends," William says, "and I lost track of time a little."

I guess that's as good an excuse as it gets when it comes to him, so I just accept it. I search for Chi through the crowd. He has turned around at last, and he's looking at me. When our eyes meet, he shrugs, gives a tiny smile, and walks away. I sigh in relief. I'm not sure what I was about to do, but it would have been a bad idea.

"It's okay. I went for more punch," I reply. "Did you want some?"

"No. Do you want to sit down?"

I nod. I'd rather dance than remain still all evening, but I already know he's never going to ask, so I might as well forget the idea. We find seats. William is fidgety; he's stirring in his chair. His behavior is so annoying that I almost roll my eyes at him. I scan the crowd for Chi again, but he's nowhere to be found. Disappointment crushes me down, and it doesn't take long before William leans toward me to tell me he'll be right back. Maybe I'm just imagining it, but I could swear his breath smelled like alcohol. He stands up and walks to the punch table. This time, he didn't even ask me if I wanted some.

I can't take this anymore. I've had enough. I stand up and walk away. I step into the hall, as far from the door as I can. No one's around, so I finally have space to breathe. I just want to go home, but William's driver is to take me back and I can't just leave without him. I just stand here for a while. When I've calmed down a bit, I head back to the ballroom, but I stop in my tracks when Chi appears at the door. He looks one way down the hall and then turns his head to look directly at me. When I meet his gaze, his eyes shine with recognition and relief. That's how I know he's been looking for me. At least, someone cares that I am here. Chi smiles and walks my way.

"Why aren't you inside with your boyfriend?" he asks.

There's something in his voice. If I didn't know any better, I'd say it sounded like jealousy. But surely I must be mistaken because he hardly knows me. I don't answer his question. I've come here to cool down, not to be reminded of how cavalier William is being.

Chi gets closer, and a voice inside my head warns me to run away right now while I still can. I ignore it. He comes right next to me and leans against the wall. He's not touching me, but his shoulder is only inches away from mine. A shock of electricity courses through my body, and my heart starts pounding upon being so close to him. He lifts his knee and presses the sole of his shoe against the wall. He's relaxed and casual while my heart is racing and hurting my chest. *Why can't I be more serene like him?*

Chi doesn't turn to me. He just looks straight ahead at the posters facing us. He moves and brushes my hand with his fingertips. I gasp and almost pull back when he slides his hand behind mine and slips a piece of paper against my palm. He closes my hand around it, pulls away, and leans close to my ear to whisper, "Just in case you ever get bored with him and this stuck-up, nonsensical life."

A chill dances down my spine. He turns his face toward me and winks before pressing his index finger to his lips in a shushing motion. He smiles and is gone just as quickly as he appeared. *What just happened?* I take a deep breath and hold the paper, twisting it between my fingers. *What is this all about?* I don't look at the note yet. It'd be too risky to read it here. I drop it deep inside my purse and make my way back to the ballroom.

I brace myself and try to find William. He's standing among his friends, with a drink in his hand. He looks intoxicated. I finally understand why he's been avoiding me all night to join his buddies. One of them must have sneaked in some alcohol. I want to tell him I'm going home, but I don't dare. I wait a few seconds while scanning the room for a chair. I find one a few inches from the table. I'm heading toward it when foreign hands grab my waist. I jump and gasp in surprise. Someone kisses my neck. I flinch and push the person back. I turn around; it's only William.

His eyes look dazed. He's completely drunk. I didn't think I could feel any more disappointment, but apparently I was wrong. My aversion deepens as he tries to kiss me. I turn my face away so his lips brush against my cheek before he says, "You look beautiful tonight, you know that?"

This would have felt like a compliment had it been said when William was sober. Instead, his words make me feel dirty. I fear the drive back home. I don't like the hunger in his eyes. I want to sit down and wait until William has sobered up, hoping he won't drink more than he already has. But instead, he utters the words I've been waiting for all evening and am now dreading, "Let's go. This ball is boring."

He takes my hand in his and walks me to the door, then through the courtyard, all the way to the parking lot, where his driver is waiting for us. William stumbles and giggles to himself. His hilarity makes me nervous. If he wanted to, he could demand that our pre-nuptial night be tonight, and I can't accept that. It can't happen when he's intoxicated. We look for his car. William is too inebriated to remember where his driver was supposed to park.

Finally, we find the vehicle. William knocks on the front passenger's door. The driver is about to get out, but William has already opened the back door. He climbs in and extends his hand for me to take. I step into the car, close the door behind me, and clip my seatbelt on. William is eyeing me with carnal avidity. I shiver. I start a random conversation just to take his mind off of his lustful thoughts.

"How did you enjoy your evening?" I ask with a squeaky voice, choking on the lump in my throat.

He closes the distance between us, his lips only inches from mine. "The fun hasn't even started yet," he says.

A tremor courses right through me. I can't move. He kisses me, deeply. His breath smells like alcohol. I cringe, but try not to let it show. This is the first time a boy has ever kissed me, and it has got to be one of the worst moments of my life. I had daydreamed that it would be sweet and that it would taste good. Instead, William is harsh and his breath is repulsive. I'm ashamed that he's kissing me with his driver sitting right there. I steal a glance at him, but the man is looking straight at the road, pretending not to notice William's lewd behavior.

William pushes his tongue inside my mouth and I almost gag. He runs his hands all over me, intrusive and rough. The strap of my dress comes undone. I pull it back up. I want to push him away, but I'm too scared of the consequences. If he is to be my husband, I might as well just get used to it now. After all, love is a fairy tale, a luxury not even the rich can afford. I know that, but I can't help wishing for something other than this. I was still hoping for my first time to be special.

The ride from the school to my house should only take twenty minutes. I hope that won't leave him enough time to do anything. *Please, don't let him take me somewhere else to do other things; not tonight, not like this! Please, don't force me to do this in the car with the driver sitting right there either.*

He keeps on kissing me roughly until he sits back and just stares at me. "I think we should wait. I don't feel like doing it right now. I'm too drunk, and I want to enjoy it."

I'm so relieved, so thankful, that tears rise to my eyes and a sob comes choking me. I wipe the tears away before they can reach my cheeks. William just looks outside the window as if none of this crude invasion has happened, as if none of this matters, and I welcome his disinterest toward me. I'm distraught and utterly disgusted with him. I'm not sure how I'll be able to keep on pretending that this is all fine with me. I don't like what I've seen of him so far, and I can't believe that he might become my husband someday. I examine him and the perfect exterior he wears as a façade, a veneer, to hide a cold heart of stone behind a wall of ice. I shudder and turn around to look at the dark sky. I try to count my blessings, though I can't seem to find many of them right now.

By the time we arrive at my house, a storm has gathered, with lightning electrifying the sky and rain pouring down like tears that were repressed for too long. The driver steps out to offer me an umbrella which I decline. I can't get away from William fast enough. I wish him goodnight, but he doesn't even turn his head to acknowledge me. A perfect ending to a perfect date! I'm so glad the night is over that I don't even take offense. Time spent with William or his family comes with its own range of grief and abasement. I only find relief when it ends. *How can I spend my life with him if I only find peace when escaping him?*

I run in my high heels, open the door to my house with my spare key, and step inside, soaking wet. Everyone's already asleep. I take the stairs quietly to my room, my feet light on the boards. I'm careful not to wake anyone up. I have no desire to talk about the events tonight. I just want to forget the evening ever happened. When I'm finally inside the room, I come crashing against the door and lean against it for support. Tears roll down my cheeks as soon as I hit the wood with my head, with waves of sadness swarming over me and a cloud of melancholy now overcasting my sullen heart.

I pat my way to the bed and take my dress off. I can't stop crying. I put on my sleeping gown and slide under the covers. They are cold and they smell of lavender—a familiar, refreshing, and comforting scent. The weight of the union is slowly crushing me. I have nothing to look forward to, nothing to rejoice about. I'm trapped, chained inside a cage that society has built for me and gilded with gold—the bars closing in on me tightly.

I weep into my pillow for a long time and pray for the coffin that is my life to become real and suffocate me already. The whole evening turns dark and funereal as I feel my last hopes die.

When my tears finally dry, I remember the piece of paper inside my bag. I sit up, bend down over the edge of the bed, and pat around for my purse. When I find it, I pull it onto the comforter and open it up to find the paper hidden inside. I take it out and feel its roughness against my fingertips. I open it slowly. The handwriting on it is smooth. I think of the hand that wrote the note—Chi's hand—and the weight upon my shoulders lessens. I read the words, but they confuse me. I drop the paper back in the purse, and Chi's phrases spin inside my head, like messages on a billboard. They flash at me like beacons of light calling me back to life.

Chapter 7

Terror fills my sleep with nightmares of William forcing his way on me and pinning me down. I'm screaming and pounding my fists against his chest, but he won't stop. When I open my eyes, I can still smell his foul breath against my mouth. I can still hear his loud and cruel laughter, too. I shake my head to chase the bad dreams away, but I know they will follow me all day.

Most nights, I manage to sleep soundly, but only because I never want to wake up and slumber is better than reality. I feel numb—all the time. In the evening, I find myself wishing that I won't arise the next day. And each morning comes with excruciating pain and disappointment as I open my eyes to find that I am, in fact, still alive. I've been having trouble eating as well. I force myself to do so, for lack of another choice, but each bite I take leaves a sour taste in my mouth. Every day, I go through the same efforts to face my life, to prepare myself for a future I did not choose.

This morning, I'm awake long before Emily comes to my room. It's five o'clock, but I have no desire to pull the pillow over my head and go back to sleep. It will only bring more night terrors my way. The fog clouding my mind makes me drowsy. It promises to be a bad day spent trying to stay awake while dreading sleep.

I head to the bathroom, turn on the faucet, and wash my face with cold water. The pounding in my head is insistent, nauseating. I turn around and go back to my bed. I still have about three hours before Emily walks in. Even on weekends, I have to wake up early. Mother claims it helps me fight self-indulgence and laziness.

I grab my purse and take out the piece of paper. I open it and feel its texture against my skin. It's reassuring for some reason. I study the handwriting, and sudden longing fills my heart. The words on the note have ignited a flame inside me, like a promise unspoken. The rhymes sound like rebellion, but somehow, deep inside my heart, I can't help but agree with them. I can't help but wish for it to be true.

When the darkness meets the light, in fear it shall flee.
Not all is what it seems, open your eyes and you will see.
When the chains break apart, the enslaved shall be free.
When the world has changed, a new dawn it will be.

I turn the paper over, where a place, a time, and a date have been written on the back.

Monday, 5.30 p. m – The Arch
Make it happen!

Is this a date? What is this boy thinking? How am I supposed to meet him? My heart races with excitement at the thought of doing something forbidden. I want to see Chi again. Mother has always taught me not to crave what I could never possess. She told me it would only bring me frustration, sadness, and anguish. Of course, Mother is right, but a part of me is now yearning for what I know I cannot have—one simple chance to break the rules and meet the boy with dark brown eyes. The yearning inside me grows, a sudden desire to get to know him, a need so sharp that it cuts through my core. It's taking over, and a part of me just wants to let it devour me whole.

Is his poem an invitation to rebel? What darkness is he referring to? Our world isn't perfect, but for sure, it's not that bad, right? And yet, I can't deny that his rhymes echo something that I have felt inside me for a while now. They express that desire I've had to flee, this wish to hit something so hard it will break. They give resonance to the rage I feel every single day, this anger that is starting to oppress me.

The time of the meeting is not so late that it would be hard to get there. I stay at school occasionally after class to study with Melissa. Chi wants to meet tomorrow though. The date isn't convenient, but I could tell Mother I have a project to work on. I could leave school as if nothing was going on, meet Chi, and return to the station before Walter comes to pick me up.

The Arch is about a mile away from my school. I'll have to walk through the forest and go up the hill until I get there. It's a desolate place in the mountains. The original monument was located close to Washington Square Park in New York City. It didn't get moved; it was simply duplicated. Only the most important monuments and pieces of architecture were relocated to Eboracum City and kept in shape. The Statue of Liberty is one of them.

When the waters started rising, our state had already spent years preparing for the eventuality of a surge. But when Hurricane Vega hit New York City by surprise, people had to evacuate in a hurry to escape, and not everything could be saved. Some treasures were lost forever. It's still possible to see some buildings emerging from the water, or so I've been told. No one's allowed in that area.

The Arch used to be nice and clean. But eventually, the authorities stopped taking care of it. It is now blackened with dirt and intertwined with vines growing along its sides. Hardly anyone ever goes there anymore, which makes it easy to hide and remain unseen for a while. Lance used to take me there to play when I was little. He used to baby-sit me when our parents had events to attend. Lance wasn't supposed to take me out, but he disobeyed anyway and we spent hours chasing each other around the Arch. It will be a good spot to meet Chi.

I've made up my mind. Tomorrow, I'm going to meet him. Elation takes flight inside my heart like butterflies breaking out of their ensnaring chrysalises. This joy feels foreign and exhilarating, bringing a genuine smile to my lips for the first time in years.

Chapter 8

I have trouble focusing at school the next day. I told Mother I'd be working with Melissa at the library, and she took it for granted that I was telling the truth. Lying was not as easy as I thought it would be. The entire time, I felt like the deception would print itself into my skin for her to read. But I've been molded into obeying so well that it'd never cross her mind that I could lie to her. She assumes a mere frown would be enough to keep me in place.

"Are you all right?" Melissa asks me a few times.

I do want to tell her what's going on, but she wouldn't understand. Marriage is not an iron fist asphyxiating her the way it's crushing my throat. I'm worried she might tell on me. I know she would, for what she would believe to be my own good. I can't even trust my best friend with my secret. There is no one I can rely on, no one I can talk to about the doubts plaguing my mind. I'll just have to follow my instincts on this and go wherever they take me.

When five p.m. finally arrives, I leave school in a hurry. Melissa thinks I'm going back to my house while my mother believes I'm with Melissa. Lies like these never end well. You either end up getting caught or in deep trouble with a fate worse than the one you were trying to escape. I know that, but my situation is already dire at best, and when I think about meeting Chi, my mind blurs and my rational thoughts turn to fog.

I walk down the stairs to the entrance of the school and take a few looks around before I cut through the woods and head up the hill. Nature is on my side, hiding me. I walk about a mile, scanning the area with caution the entire time. When I reach the Arch, I step under it to find Chi leaning against the stony wall, with his knee lifted up so his foot touches the monument. The back of the Arch opens to the valley below and the sight is incredible—all shades of green, with trees always thriving and benefiting from the recurring rainstorms.

I'm relieved Chi is here already. It would have upset me if he hadn't made a point of being on time. I'm glad he truly wanted to meet me and wasn't just playing games. He turns around and beams at me. His smile is breathtaking—his teeth nicely aligned, white and perfect against his tanned skin. His grin reaches his eyes, and he looks more handsome than I even remembered.

This is trouble sent my way to test me, and I want to fail so badly. I want to fall, fall so hard I'll break as I hit the ground. I'm drawn to him by magnetism, a strong pull I can't control, and I know I won't be able to turn back now. My insides are in knots, from fear, anxiety, and an urgent need for him to touch me. I wonder what his lips would feel like pressed against mine, and I pinch myself for even thinking such a thing. I don't know what's come over me. I avert my eyes as his proximity makes my body shake. My cheeks burn under his stare and my head spins. I'm sure he can sense my embarrassment, but he does nothing to show that he has noticed anything.

"I'm glad you made it," he says, forcing me to look at him. "I was hoping you'd have the guts to come. I guess I was right about you."

I'm not sure what he means by that. I can't think straight. My heart is beating fast, pumping blood to my head, loud and deafening, jumping over and over again, almost tearing through me. Being here alone with him is terrifying.

I just stand here and hold my hands together so he doesn't see them quivering. I don't dare talk, for fear of saying something dumb. I'm not sure I can keep my voice steady either, and I don't want him to know how much he's affecting me. But he's staring at the valley below us, with his hands in his pockets, his demeanor calm and confident.

"Isn't this view perfect?" he asks.

"Yes, it is." My voice shakes slightly when I reply, and I want to slap myself for it. I try to push the dread away and force my mouth open to speak. "Why did you want to meet me?"

"Isn't it obvious?" he replies.

Well, of course it's not obvious or I wouldn't ask. I just want to tell him that and make him shut his mouth. But it would come out as aggressive and there is no reason why I should be defensive.

"Do I need a specific reason to talk to a girl?"

He fully turns to me now, but I stare at the scenery. I don't want to meet his eyes; I might lose myself in them.

"You looked so sad that day." My heart squeezes at his words. He pauses and I force myself to face him. "Like you were on the edge of a cliff or something," he adds with a shrug. "I don't know. I just thought maybe you could be a part of us."

I can't make sense of what he's talking about. *What "us" is he referring to?* But what he says hits me hard. I did feel miserable that day. And I've been trying to hold on to life for a while now. His perspicacity stuns me into silence. No one has ever bothered to know how I felt. How disconcerting that Chi—a stranger—saw right through my façade! His words disturb me somehow, but they don't explain his interest in me. I scowl at him.

"Okay. Okay," he gives in, holding his palms up before leaning toward me as if he meant to share some secrets. "I also find you really cute and I wanted to meet you. Sound good enough?"

I'm so shocked I stumble backward. No boy has ever been that blunt with me before. It's quite rude, and I want to remind him that I'm promised to William, but I already know he doesn't care. And deep inside, I know that I don't really care either. No matter how poorly-mannered Chi is being, it's flattering in some way. No one has ever expressed any interest in me before.

"What makes you think I'm interested in you?" I reply. I don't want him to think I'm some foolish girl he can just play with, tossing her future away, before running out of her life. I've heard such stories before, and they were quite dreadful—girls who threw it all out the window for some guys who were just playing with them.

"Well, you're here, aren't you?" he says, his lips rising up on one side. "So I'm assuming you feel some sort of interest in me. Either that, or you have some kind of death wish. Considering the situation you're in, I wouldn't be surprised if you did. But I just wanted to talk to you, and I kinda hoped you'd be curious about me too, that's all. Why? Is that a crime?"

His smile spreads across his face as if this were but a joke to him. This guy is so arrogant. *Really, what does he know about the situation I'm in or anything about my life?* And yes, it is a felony for us to meet. *How can he be so nonchalant about it?*

"I'll have you know my situation is not that bad, thank you very much. This conversation is getting quite tiresome, and I might just leave now." I say it without moving a muscle because I truly don't want to go. I actually hope he won't take my word for it and dare me to do it. No matter what he says, I know he's right and I can't contradict him without feeling inside my heart that I would be lying.

"Oh please! Like you want to marry that jerk William!" He laughs, a small, sarcastic laughter that feels like sand against my skin.

"Oh, because I guess you would be a better match!" I retort, increasingly upset.

Chi's face turns sorrowful when I say it, as if my words just slapped him. But I still want to defend William somehow. Though I don't like William much, I can't help myself. Chi's behavior is making me mad. I take a step back and walk away for good, but Chi runs after me and grabs my arm.

"Please, don't go." His tone is apologetic now. "You don't have to defend him, you know. Any girl would deserve better than to end up with a guy like him, trust me. I don't have anything to offer you. I just wanna talk to you. You can leave if you want, but I'm not used to begging and I won't ask you twice. You know, not all guys believe in this stupid society of ours. Not all of us believe you're an object. Now, if you want to leave, just go. I'm not gonna force you to stay."

I stop in my tracks and look back at him. There's kindness in his eyes now, and genuine sweetness. I've never seen such benevolence in William's gaze. Chi's sympathy is warm and comforting—something I want to wrap myself into. But I still know better than to think a man would consider me an equal.

"What are you saying? That you believe women are on the same scale as men? That women should have rights? Who do you think you're kidding?"

"You can take my word for it or not, it's all the same to me. I know I see you as a person and I'd like to get to know that person. You can take it or leave it."

He shrugs as if he didn't really care either way, but something flickers through his eyes, betraying him. He's worried that I might leave without giving him a chance. This is the second time he's given me an ultimatum though. I want to take him up on it and just leave it at that. But I can't. Something inside me is keeping me here and I don't want to walk away. I've already broken a lot of rules to meet him. I might as well listen to what he has to say.

I cross my arms over my chest and raise my chin. "How do I know William didn't send you to test me?"

A laugh rolls in his throat, low at first, and then louder and louder, as if my question were just hilarious.

"What do you take me for?" he asks. "I have better things to do than hang out with jerks like him."

"You were talking to him at the gymnasium," I insist.

"No, I was not. Trust me. I was too busy looking at you," he says while raising an eyebrow. My cheeks flame in an instant and my eyes widen just a bit.

He sits down in the grass, unaware of my discomfort, and asks me to join him. I do so, but only because I need to hide how much I'm shaking right now.

"I'm glad you came today," he says. "Believe me, I know what it took for you to be here. I know the risks. I like that you were brave enough to come."

"I prefer not to think about what would happen if my mother found out."

"Well then, let's make sure she doesn't." He sends me a lazy smile. "You shouldn't leave too late."

"Why did you want me to come today? I mean, really."

"This is bigger than you and me, Thia."

It's the first time he says my name. The sounds roll off his tongue delicately when he pronounces it, "Thah-ee-ah." My heart skips a beat.

"How do you know my name?" I ask.

"I did my research." He locks his eyes on mine. "Anyway, this whole thing is bigger than us. It's finally happening and when I saw you, I wanted you to be a part of it. I heard you were promised to William. I know him, not too well, mind you, but he's not a nice guy. He's a robotic sheep at best. He doesn't have the brains to question anything he's been fed." His voice turns acidic as he says it. "And the way he was treating you at the ball...I don't know, it just pissed me off. I don't have status to offer you, and I can't promise you anything. I just wanna get to know you. It's just crazy, a girl and a guy can't even get to know each other anymore. I saw you and I'd like to hang out with you, if you'll let me. I don't care if others don't like it."

His words sound rebellious, so I change the subject. "Can you explain that poem to me? The one you gave me. What is it about?"

"Things out there are worse than we think they are. And when I saw you that day..." He pauses, his eyes still holding on to mine. "The look on your face, it was heart-wrenching. You just looked so fragile." He takes a deep breath. "And beautiful." His gaze doesn't waver at all when he says it, and I can't stop the somersault in my chest when the last word escapes his mouth.

He catches himself quickly though. "I'm sorry. I shouldn't have said that." But there is no need to apologize, really. No one who truly meant it has ever called me beautiful before.

Chi averts his eyes as his cheeks turn red. I've never seen a boy blush. It's endearing and confusing. I just blink at him, my own cheeks on fire. After a few minutes, he sighs and breathes as if he were inhaling courage.

"I mean, aren't you ever tired of following the rules and doing what they want you to do? We aren't even in control of our lives! I've just been thinking about it, and if I wanna talk to you, that's my own business. I couldn't care less what other people think!"

I look away. His subversive speech terrifies me. But I know exactly what he means. He's given words to thoughts I've had for a long time, but that I couldn't quite formulate.

I turn my head to find him observing me, watching my reactions. His irises are light brown today, with a sweet honey color as the sun reflects upon them. I don't think I've ever felt this relaxed before—a strange feeling to have considering I'm breaking a lot of rules and could pay quite a high price for being here. I hardly know him, but when he starts talking about school, conversation flows easily, and disappointment seizes me when he looks at his watch.

"I guess you'd better go," he sighs. He stands up and I follow suit.

I want to stay with him longer, but I don't speak my thoughts.

"I don't want you to get in trouble," he adds while facing me. "Would you be willing to meet again some other time?" His voice drops with uncertainty, his confidence suddenly gone.

Breaking the rules turns my stomach to ice. I'm scared of the consequences. But as I look at Chi, there is no doubt in my mind that I want to see him again. I nod my consent.

"When can you come back? I guess you can't make it here too often without it being obvious."

"Well, I could be here again tomorrow."

It shouldn't be too hard to lie to Mother again. I shudder at the thought of misleading her like this, but I don't let my fears show.

"Great!" he says. "Same time, same place!"

He smiles and takes my hands between his. The gesture surprises me and I flinch, but his palms are warm against mine and I don't want him to let go. He looks like he wants to say something, but then he thinks better of it. He turns around and walks away without looking back. He stands tall and lean, striding confidently, with the breeze in his hair. My heart squeezes slightly at the sight of him leaving. I don't know if it's a good thing or a bad thing.

Chapter 9

It doesn't take long for me to reach the Arch the next day. When I arrive, Chi isn't there yet. My first thought is that something has happened to him. *Why is this the first thing occurring to me? What kind of a world is this that we should fear so much what may happen if we step outside the line?*

I turn around cautiously when I hear the sounds of footsteps, and I know it's him the second he says my name.

"Hi, Thia!"

I quiver as butterflies take flight in my stomach. He's wearing his school uniform, the same as yesterday, but his hair is disheveled as if he's been raking though it all day. It gives him an unkempt look, so handsome that it hurts just to glance at him. I sigh, a sudden urge pulling me to him.

He comes closer and just stands there, unaware of the effect he has on me as he simply takes in the view without saying anything. After a while, he speaks, his voice clear and calm. "You know, I never asked for your last name. I just knew your first name 'cause I heard William saying it in passing."

"It's Clay. My last name is Clay. And you?"

He exhales deeply. "It's a little bit complicated."

"Okay, Mr. It's-a-little-bit-complicated, what did you want to talk about today?"

"I just thought I'd spend some time with you, that's all." Chi rests his left shoulder against the monument as his beautiful smile spreads across his face.

"How was school today?" he asks casually, his hands slipping in his pockets.

"I don't know. I couldn't really focus."

His smile turns mischievous in an instant. "Too busy thinking about me?"

"You're so cheeky! I never said I liked you!"

"You don't need to say it," he replies, arching his eyebrow. "Your presence here speaks for itself."

I'm blushing again. I hate how my cheeks always work against me. "Why are you doing this?"

"Doing what?"

"Making me feel uncomfortable," I reply. "Using my coming here against me."

"I'm sorry." He's serious now, clearly remorseful for riling me up. "I didn't realize this made you uncomfortable. It was just a joke, Thia."

A flicker of pain passes behind his pupils, subtle and quick. It was only there for a second, but it was long enough to stab me with guilt. I want to take the words back, but it does make me uneasy when he talks about my attraction to him, especially if he jokes about it. His teasing me is highly inappropriate, and I hate how it makes me flush. I don't want him to know that he can affect me this way.

I just change the subject on him abruptly before he gets to say anything else. "Why won't you tell me your last name?"

"Because it's not my real name."

I'm taken aback and don't reply. I'm not sure what he means exactly. I'm slightly annoyed at myself now for revealing my full identity so easily when he obviously means to keep his hidden like some national secret. My lack of cautiousness hits me hard, accentuated by his own personal discretion. He has managed to use his charms to turn me into some foolish, careless girl unable to think before she speaks. I hate it and I won't let myself slip like this again.

"Look, I wanna tell you about me," he says upon seeing my deepening frown, "but I'm not sure I can trust you with that information just yet. Maybe you could talk about yourself first."

He sends me a quick smile, and I squint my eyes at him. I'm not falling for that trick twice.

"Well, you already seem to know all about me," I retort, though not unkindly.

"Just 'cause I know of your engagement to William doesn't mean I know you. That union doesn't define you as a person, Thia."

I take a deep breath. My name on his lips affects me more than I'd like. "Well, I'm not sure what to say. I'm not used to talking about myself."

"What do you do in your free time?" he asks.

"I read, a lot. And I write, poems mostly. I guess it's a nice escape for me."

"Really? What do you write about?"

I want to tell him what my poetry truly is about, but he won't reveal anything about himself. *Why should I expose myself like this to him, spilling things out that could get me in deep trouble?*

"I write about my family, mostly." That's technically not a lie. "And I describe the landscapes and things I see." Boring things.

"Sounds interesting." There is no sarcasm in his voice when he says it. I wonder what he would think if he knew what I truly express in my poems.

"What else do you do?" he asks.

"I don't know. I've had to spend a lot of time focusing on the wedding and getting ready for it."

"I see." His eyes turn dark with anger flashing on and off, gone in a heartbeat. Then he recomposes his face quickly— but not fast enough. I blink at him. *Was that jealousy flickering through his gaze just now?*

"How about you?" I ask. "What do you like to do? You're not part of the team?"

"I don't have time for sports. I have more important things to do, like save the world." He laughs. I never understand his jokes, but his insouciance and humor soothe me somehow.

He lies down on the grass and pats the area next to him, inviting me to sit down. I join him and sparks of electricity run all over my skin at being so close to him. He doesn't seem to notice. He's serene as ever, and I'm slightly annoyed at how easy this is for him. We just look at the sky, without saying anything. There's a light breeze in the air. I take a few deep breaths—filling my lungs with it—and try to be in the moment. He asks me to recite some of my poems and I get suddenly nervous. I remember Mrs. Fox's acidic comments quite vividly the last time I shared the one about my grandpa, but I oblige Chi and recite my verses. I'm surprised to realize I know them all by heart.

"It's beautiful," he says. "Just like you." His eyes sparkle as the words come out. I blink and flush as heat fills my entire body.

"Did you really not think about me at all since yesterday?" he asks, as if truly worried that I might not care about him.

I don't reply. There is nothing I could say that wouldn't incriminate me and reveal more than I'm willing to let on. My cheeks betray me half the time anyway.

"For all it's worth, *I* thought about you, a *lot*." He insists on the last word and extends his hand to caress my cheek with his thumb, his eyes roaming my face. His irises slowly turn dark as his eyebrows furrow. Anguish shifts through his beautiful features, and he turns his face away immediately. I don't understand why his mood shifted so quickly, but whatever it was, the feeling disappeared right away.

He holds out his hand and acts casual as I grab it. He stands up and helps me to my feet. Time has flown by and I find myself panting. I don't want to leave. He looks me in the eyes and I'm mesmerized, caught in the splendor of his face.

"Would you come here on Thursday?" he asks, timidly, as if he expects me to deny him.

I nod and blush. His eyes twinkle. A puckish smile appears on his lips, and he winks at me.

"I'll see you then." He leans toward me, his mouth so close to my cheek I can feel his breath blowing on my skin. "I'll be thinking of you." With that last sentence, he turns around and walks away—leaving me here, winded, unable to find my breath. *What's happening to me?*

Chapter 10

When Melissa and I enter the classroom the next day, Mr. Johnson hardly waits before speaking, "Take your seats. Today, we are reviewing the fundamentals behind our breeding system."

The word "breeding" sends goose bumps all over my skin. He makes it sound like we are animals to be parked and controlled rather than human beings with emotions and potential goals in our lives.

"Why is the lower class no longer allowed to procreate?" he asks.

My face turns down in a grimace of distaste. I try to control the anger rising inside me, but this topic makes me sick. We've already studied this many times before, repetition being part of the brainwashing. I cannot comprehend why my parents insist on paying so much money for me to waste my time learning such nonsense.

A girl raises her hand. "The lower-class lost the right to get married or have children almost ten years ago to help reduce the rate of poverty, Sir. Little by little, the numbers will decrease to the point where there won't be any more poor people."

The very idea infuriates me. I turn my head around to see if any of the other girls share my thoughts, but most of them show blank faces, probably hiding how they truly feel about the subject.

"Correct," the teacher exclaims. "The law was passed exactly six years ago. And how did we prevent the poor from breaking those rules?"

"Strict regulations were put in place to ensure they wouldn't marry illegally, Sir," another girl replies without lifting her hand. "Boys and girls from the lower class also get sterilized at the age of eighteen to prevent them from having children."

The whole concept makes my stomach curl. A sound of disgust escapes my mouth, and I freeze. Mr. Johnson casts me a sharp glance, and I lower my head quickly.

"Please continue, Miss Wheat," he says, with his eyes still pinned on me.

"Couples from the upper class can have two children, and couples from the middle class can have one child, but those from the lower class are not allowed to reproduce," she says.

I swallow the bile rising in my throat, and she continues to talk in that gleeful, high-pitched voice of hers as if this subject wasn't revolting at all. "A lot of people from the lower class rebelled because of the Sterilization Law, but they quickly learned to stay in their rightful place."

I huff out my anger. Mr. Johnson sends me another sharp look.

"Is there something you wish to share or add to this discussion, Miss Clay?" he asks with disdain.

I know better than to share my controversial views on the matter. I shake my head and his eyes slant together slightly. I need to be more careful, but this conversation exasperates me. The lower-class needs the authorities to provide them with food. Food is so hard to find in the slums that when the poor tried to rebel, they were quickly forced to give in, kept in place by their need to survive. Their rations were reduced to the point where they couldn't complain or they would have been forced to starve. Many of them died in the rebellion, too. The upper class is the only one who could have tried and changed things, but they don't care about the fate of those underneath them.

"Why did we create such laws, Miss Wheat?" the teacher asks.

"When the oceans rose, nations throughout the world lost too many resources, and they fought to gain territory over the remaining lands. A lot of states in our country collapsed as well. They tried to force the State of New York to pay taxes for everyone else as well as provide water for the states suffering from drought, which was really quite unfair if you ask me," she replies, with her chin raised high. "After conquering parts of the neighboring states, New York seceded, and our state now fends for itself. Our state's government had to regulate the population to keep control of the supplies. Our marriage and breeding laws are the best ways to prevent overpopulation," she continues, triggering a proud grin from our teacher.

"You are correct, Miss Wheat," he says. "The war also proved that women are weak and unable to care for themselves. This is why men should be in control of everything—to ensure our state survives such difficult times as ours."

I roll my eyes.

The rest of the class passes me by as my classmates throw around more absurdities as common facts to be taken for granted. And when lunchtime finally arrives, I work on expelling all the so-called values these people have tried to shove into my brain. I sit in front of Melissa in the cafeteria and try to force food down my throat, but these classes have ruined my appetite.

"My mom and I had *the talk* over the phone last week-end," Melissa says, her eyes sparkling with excitement.

I push my plate away. They can box my food for me to take home. I just can't swallow another bite.

"Did your mom talk about sex with you yet?" she asks.

I shift in my seat, but there is no comfortable position for me to find anymore. I clear my throat.

"Yes, many times," I reply. I shiver just thinking about how Mother often coerces me into listening while she talks about my prenuptial night. I hate those conversations. I hate everything about the dreadful thing.

"Are you meeting William's family again this week-end?" Melissa asks.

"Yes."

I haven't seen William since he took me to the ball at his school, but his birthday is coming up and his parents have invited mine over for the event. I'd rather stay home and read, but my parents would never agree to that.

"You've been acting strange these past few days. You're always daydreaming. Are you growing to like him?" Melissa asks.

I nod. Yes, I am growing to like him, except that by "him" I mean Chi, not William. But I can't tell that to Melissa, or anyone else for that matter. Chi is a secret I intend to keep all to myself for as long as I possibly can.

Chapter 11

It's been three weeks since Chi first gave me that note. He hasn't touched me since he last stroked my cheek with his thumb, and his obvious respect for me makes me feel increasingly safe in his presence. I meet him twice a week now. Lying to those around me is getting slightly easier, though I always feel a pang of guilt when the words come out of my mouth.

Unfortunately, I'm still forced to meet with William every week-end. His parents invite us to the social events they host, and it takes all my energy not to scream at the hypocrisy surrounding me. I smile through my clenched teeth and let William grab my hand since touching me was a right granted him years ago. Nausea threatens to overtake me every time his palm rubs against my skin or his lips touch mine, and I wonder why it had to be him and not someone nice like Chi. I got my wedding gown a while ago now. It's hanging in my closet; the sight of it makes me sick every time I need to change and am forced to look at it.

When five p.m. finally arrives, I tell Melissa that I'm going home. I leave school and cut through the woods. I walk up the path until I reach the monument. When I arrive, Chi is standing in front of the Arch, with his thumbs in his pockets. He hears me, turns around, and smiles in that debonair attitude that I've grown to enjoy so much.

"Hello, Thia!"

My name on his lips makes me shiver, spreading delightful goose bumps all over my skin. I sit down quickly before he notices my reaction.

"How were your classes today?" I ask.

He comes to sit by my side and spreads out his legs. He leans backward and props himself up with his arms stretched out behind him. "All right, I guess. I'm still getting used to this whole system. It's kinda hard to adapt after being homeschooled for so long."

"You were homeschooled?" I blink at him.

"Yeah, a story for another time. How was it for you?"

I roll my eyes. "Today, I learned how to be a proper lady and show reverence for a man who will never grant me any importance."

Chi chuckles at that. "Is that all they tried to teach you? The usual misogynistic idiocies?"

"No. I also had a music class, which I actually enjoy. Women do need to entertain their guests after all," I continue with a stiff upper-lip, my tone haughty, and my back held straight in a feigned proud mannerism, "for lack of any thoughtful opinion to share about things that actually matter."

Chi lets out a loud breath that sounds like a snort. "You really are entertaining, Thia, you know that?" He shoots me a smile so charming that my breath hitches.

When a flush rises to my cheeks, I shift the course of my thoughts. "You still haven't told me your last name, you know."

"Like I said before, it's not my real name." He shrugs, not caring to elaborate. His eyebrows crease. "Did you ever wonder what happens to children who are born over the number allowed?" His sudden change in subject takes me by surprise. I don't know how to respond.

"No one has children above the number allowed" I reply, matter-of-factly. "It just doesn't happen."

"Doesn't it, though?" he asks.

"No, it doesn't," I assert.

"You may want to think about it before affirming things you know nothing about!" His remark is harsh, stinging like acid. *Is he implying that I'm stupid?* I've never seen him irritated before; his frustration feels like a blow. It angers me too. I want to find some snide response, but I can't think of anything smart to throw back at him.

He continues, his eyes and voice soft now, "Let me tell you something. It does happen. People do have children above the number allowed. I would know. I'm one of them."

His words come like a slap in my face. *How can that be?* Our system does not permit such things. Illegal births never occur. If they did, there would be no point to our laws. It would all become chaos. I have a hard time believing him, but I can't find any reasons why he would be lying.

"But how?" I ask.

"Do you know what happens when a couple has a child they shouldn't have?"

I don't answer. He looks in the distance and keeps on talking, "When a couple has a child that's unwanted, they either have to abort or society takes that child away. The infant becomes a ward of the authorities. No one knows what happens to those kids 'cause the population doesn't know about them. Our government threatens the parents into shutting up about it, or they could face the death penalty."

"But people get sterilized after they've had the authorized number of children. How can they have more than is allowed? And if you're one of them, how come you're not a ward of the authorities? Whatever that means."

"Well, did you ever wonder what happens if someone has twins, or triplets? It's genetic, you know. It can't be prevented. The authorities are keeping track of those likely to have multiple children, and they keep an eye on the medical records. Doctors are forced to tell our government if they notice any anomalies."

"But then, how come they didn't take you away?" I ask.

"I don't really feel like talking about that yet," he replies, his voice forlorn.

He looks away and his jaw clenches all of a sudden. The subject seems painful to him, so I don't insist. I have a hard time believing what I've just been told anyway. If this is true, then I've been lied to my whole life. *What else could I have been misguided about?* I had heard about people having twins centuries ago. *How could I be so gullible as to believe it never happened anymore?* I behold Chi, an Unwanted, someone not even meant to exist. Shudders shoot through my entire body.

"Like I said," he resumes, "most of the time, the parents are forced to abort. The family has to shut up about it. What they did is an infraction. It's not really their fault, but the authorities don't care about that. If they talk, they'll be executed or put in a camp."

"A camp?" I ask.

"Our state is filled with camps where the officials keep the rebels—those who don't comply with the system and refuse to follow its idiotic rules. The authorities even lock up those who have coveted the wives of others, homeless girls, or women who are supposedly insane."

"These people are either put in jail or in mental institutions," I retort.

"No, they are not. Do you think the authorities would really waste money and resources on people they deem detrimental to society?"

"I guess I never thought it through," I admit.

"Well, it seems most people just prefer not to think about it. The authorities keep everyone focused on the importance of status so they don't think about what truly matters. The civilians don't know about those camps."

"Where are those camps located?" I ask.

"Everywhere. But their exact locations are coded and hidden. Apparently, the camps look like regular prisons from the outside. But what goes on inside is nothing short of an exploitation of the human race."

"What do they do in those camps?"

"Those who committed heavy crimes—the murderers— are executed on the spot. The others are used to benefit our society. They make the clothing we wear each day. They grow, harvest, and pack the fruit and vegetables we eat and the food the authorities distribute to the poor. Those who are too weak to work and those who don't follow in line get put down like animals."

"The things we buy are made and sold by corporations," I retort.

"No, they're *not*," he snaps. "Well, not really," he adds, more softly. "People in the camps make those things. Those places are like factories of forced labor. This way, the corporations get their work done for free. In the meantime, the authorities make use of those they deem harmful to our system. Our government is subsidized by those corporations, too. They work hand in hand. They've created a perfect society that benefits no one but those on top, and the civilians don't know where their resources really come from. It's a nicely kept secret."

Each new revelation from Chi makes my blood run cold. I can't believe what he's saying. I don't want to believe what he's saying. If he's telling the truth, that means the society we live in isn't functioning as it should. It means our lives are nothing but a web of lies spun by the authorities to trap us all for reasons that no longer seem valid. *What else did they lie about?* I don't want to believe Chi, but what he says makes perfect sense.

"How do you know about all this?" My heart aches, and a part of me is still hoping that he's just lying.

"I know 'cause my parents were taken there, and I've spent the past two years looking for them."

"What? Your parents were taken away?"

His features reshape with deep anguish. "Yeah." He turns his face away and averts his eyes. "When the authorities found out about me, they came for my family." He doesn't elaborate, and I don't want to push. He simply says, "When the authorities say someone's been taken to jail, it means they're rotting in a camp."

"You mentioned homeless girls. What about them?" I ask. Chi obviously doesn't want to talk about his parents, and I can't force him. The pain in his eyes is too vivid. "Do they also end up in camps?"

"Did you notice how you might see a homeless girl outside for a while and then she's gone, like she just disappeared?"

"Yes, I just assumed they'd found a job."

"No one employs homeless girls. Those girls were forsaken by their families. No one wants them inside their home. Who knows what disease they might bring in? People don't want them to corrupt the minds of their own children. Only the daughters of the lower class get jobs caring for the rich."

I remember that my family had hired Emily after they had received a call from her parents. They were asking for a position for their daughter once she'd turn eighteen. My parents agreed to meet Emily and take her in. She was on trial for a few months before they hired her for good. While the upper class is looking for a potential match for their daughters and sons, the lower class is looking for jobs for their offspring. I knew that, but never really reflected upon it.

"So what happens to homeless girls?" I ask again.

"The officers take them away. They either serve in the camps or in joy houses."

"Joy houses? Do you mean they become prostitutes?"

He nods and I shudder.

"But those girls are upper class!"

"Yes, they are," he replies. "But once they lose their status, they become disposable."

How could I not have noticed that before? I've been too self-absorbed to pay heed to those without influence over my life. Grief fills me quickly, a surge of shame flowing over me. I've been so self-centered for so many years, it nauseates me.

"Do the families know about this?" I ask.

"Most of them don't, and those who do know just don't care. A lot of families have been brainwashed. They believe their daughters have dishonored them. They think they shouldn't have to pay the price for it. After a girl reaches a certain age, the authorities cut down the amount of resources her family is allowed to get. These people can keep their daughter and have a lower standard of living—they need to share their supplies with her and it's often not enough—or they can push her away and keep on living the way they're used to, by not having to feed a useless mouth. I thought you knew all this. Isn't that why you were willing to marry William?"

I don't answer. Of course, I knew that each family was allowed to buy a certain amount of food and resources each week. It's illegal to go past that quantity. I just wasn't aware that the amount got cut once the girls reached the age of marriage. Now I understand why my mother has been so harsh and intransigent. A sudden pang of guilt stabs at me for being here. My wedding isn't just about Father's promotion, it's about our very survival. A tremor of fear shudders through my heart.

Chapter 12

Chi has opened a door to a different world, a place even nastier than the one I've been living in. The terror growing inside me is mixed with anger that's slowly turning into rage. A part of me wants to know more while the other part wishes to remain innocent and ignorant of all those terrible things happening in New York State.

When Chi and I meet that week, our conversations are serious. He's been taking a big risk in meeting me and an even greater one in telling me the truth about our society. I can't believe he trusts me enough to expose himself in such a way. I feel lighter every time I get to see him, but the burden on my shoulders gets heavier as his secrets bring me down under their weight.

"How do you know for sure your parents were taken to a camp?" I ask one day.

Chi's good mood disappears within seconds as sudden pain crosses his eyes. "I know because I was there when it happened," he replies. He lowers his gaze as if to examine the ground. He moves the dirt around with the tip of his foot, and his jaw clenches as well as his hands.

"Mom and Dad weren't exactly what you'd call ordinary people," he says. "They never believed in the system. You see, my father was very much in love with my mom, and their feelings were mutual. He always treated her with love and respect. To him, she wasn't an object or anything like that; she was his equal."

Chi looks in the distance, his memories bittersweet. "Then the rebels appeared and the authorities started hunting for those who were different. I didn't know it at the time, but my parents were part of the rebellion. I never found out what their role was in it. But I know we weren't like other families. I have a brother, you see. A twin."

Looking at him, Chi seems so ordinary. It's hard to believe he's an Unwanted, an illegal born above the amount allowed.

"My mother explained it all to me when I was five years old. I was a second child born in a family only allowed to have one. My parents were upper-middle class, so only one child was authorized. I was born a few minutes after my brother. That small amount of time made me the Unwanted, you see. Mom told me that if the authorities found out about me, they would take me away, and she didn't want to risk that.

"When she was pregnant with us, she knew twins had already been born in her family before, so it was a high probability. Abortion was never an option for her. She simply refused it. She went to see a friend of hers, a doctor from the Underground."

The Underground? What's the Underground? I try to cut Chi off and ask, but he's too caught up in his own story to stop.

"The doctor confirmed she would have twins, so my mom gave birth to us at home and hid me from the very beginning. Because of my condition, my brother and I were never allowed outside at the same time. We couldn't have normal family outings or usual play-dates with friends. Only my brother went to a regular school. I was homeschooled by my mom."

He stops and looks at me, his eyes searching mine for a reaction. I'm stunned into silence, unable to offer any comfort.

"Didn't you have to share resources?" I ask.

He stares at his hand for a while, flexing his knuckles and opening his fingers a few times, before lifting his sullen eyes again.

"Yes, we had to share food and everything. It was hard, but my parents never complained about it. They just seemed happy to have both of us home."

"How did they manage to hide your existence for so long?"

His hand reaches out for the grass next to him and he starts pulling at it while talking, his eyes pinned on that spot, avoiding mine the entire time. "They didn't. When I was nine years old, I'd had enough of being inside one day and I sneaked into the backyard when my brother was already there. Mom was upstairs doing the laundry. The phone rang inside the house, and when my mom came downstairs, she couldn't find me and she freaked out.

"When she found us wrestling on the grass outside, she pulled me back inside. A neighbor had seen me." His voice fills with deep heartache, almost choking him. "It was such a stupid thing to do. I didn't even understand the consequences yet."

"It wasn't your fault. You were just a kid," I try to comfort him.

His eyes meet mine, the sorrow in him pouring through his gaze like a flood of despair. "*It doesn't matter.* What I did cost them too much." He raises his voice with woe. Then he looks away again, the anguish in him still transparent. "My mom called my dad at work. All I heard was, 'they're coming for the kids.' She couldn't talk about it on the phone, and my dad couldn't leave work 'cause it'd be too obvious. My parents had already planned everything in case this ever happened.

"My mom took my brother and me to the car, and then we drove for over an hour. My brother and I had to hide under a blanket for the entire ride. Mom said we'd be staying with some woman for a while—that it was like a vacation or something and that she'd be back for us soon. I didn't understand. I'd never been away from home before. I thought she was abandoning us."

I try and envision Chi as a child—a little boy who never should have been born. Back then, he already knew he wasn't supposed to be alive. I imagine him left behind with some stranger, not knowing what was going on, worried that his parents might never come back. My heart aches for that frightened little boy.

"How come your mom had a car?" I ask, the question gnawing at me.

"I actually never found out. We've always owned a car. My parents probably got one through their relationship with the Underground."

He pauses, as if pondering this puzzle. "I don't know what happened in the meantime, but we stayed with that woman for a few weeks," he says. "When Mom and Dad finally came to pick us up, we had to hide during the entire trip again. We drove for over an hour. My parents had moved us to a different county. We couldn't cross the state line, but we all had new identities. We didn't own a house anymore; they just left our home behind, without selling it. We had to rent a new place. My parents had lost everything because of me."

"You were just a kid," I tell him again.

"That's what I keep telling myself, but it doesn't change what I did. I was old enough to know better."

I want to reassure him, make him feel better, but I don't know how. And he just keeps on blurting words out, in a failing attempt at freeing his chest from all the guilt.

"My dad got a new job, but it wasn't nearly as good. I have no clue how my parents managed to get resources. But I know they had relations in the Underground. They knew rebels who worked for the authorities. You can change your identity and get a new life if you're skilled enough and know the right people."

That's quite surprising to hear. I always thought the authorities kept good track of everyone. After all, that's the only way to prevent overpopulation. If people can pull strings to become someone else entirely, then our system is flawed and there may be no sense or reason behind the way it works.

"My brother went to a different school, and I stayed home with my mom. Our new location was hidden in the woods, so I had a lot more freedom. We lived like that for a good eight years. I don't really know how we made it, honestly, 'cause our resources were cut really short. But my dad started hunting a lot and stuff.

"One day, I was upstairs reading when some officers broke down our front door. The authorities had found us. My mother came to my room. We had already discussed this before, and I knew what to do. I hid in a concealed space in my closet. Mom ordered me not to come out, no matter what I might hear. She wanted me to wait till it was safe to get out. She told me she'd meet me at her friends' house when she could. And like a freaking idiot, I believed her."

He shakes his head before looking away again. A crease has appeared on his forehead and his hands have balled into fists of anger.

"Then a gunshot resonated through the house and someone screamed. It was her, my mother. But I'd made a promise. I couldn't get out. People were coming up the stairs, talking—officers, you know. They wanted me, the child born beyond their supervision—the affront to their authority."

Chi gives a deep sigh, his shoulders sagging. I've never seen a boy so strong and yet so fragile before. The look on his face cuts like a knife. I want to hold him, tell him that everything's okay, but that would be a lie and I don't know him well enough to give him such comfort. Nothing I could say would alleviate his pain. I press my head against his shoulder instead and take his hand in mine, intertwining my fingers with his. He looks at me, shocked, with questions in his eyes, but he doesn't say anything and we remain like that until he's ready to talk again.

He pulls back eventually and resumes his story. The emotions are still flowing through his voice. "I waited for hours in that closet. When everything was silent, I came out. I assumed the authorities would be watching out for me, but for some reason, they had deserted the place. It must have been pretty late 'cause it was dark already. It took me hours to reach the Wilcoxes' house. They were my parents' friends, you know. When I got there, their lights were turned off. But when I showed up on their doorsteps, Mrs. Wilcox just took me in without any questions. I didn't even need to explain; she already knew what my presence meant. I never saw my parents again after that."

I squeeze his hand. "What do you think happened to them?"

"They were taken to the camps. There's no doubt about it. I've been looking for two years and I've finally found their location."

"How?"

"I'm not alone. There's a group of us, in the Underground. There are others looking for their families or simply seeking freedom."

"You mean that you hang out with rebels?" The question sounds wrong the moment the words come out, but it's too late to take it back.

"My own birth was a rebellion, Thia! There's nowhere else I can go. That's where I belong!"

I try to change the subject swiftly. My question obviously stung him and I don't want him to be upset with me. "How did you manage to get a legal status and go to school?"

"The Wilcoxes used to have a son. He committed suicide a few years ago. They never knew why, and it's been a sore subject we've always avoided. They never told anyone about it. They saw it as parental failure and they were ashamed of it. They didn't want to attract unwanted attention to themselves because of their link to the Underground. They didn't want people prying into their privacy, so they buried their son in secret. When I stepped on their threshold, they gave me his name and I became their son."

"No one ever wondered about his disappearance?" I ask, confused.

"The authorities worry more about births than deaths. And their system is far from perfect. It has a bunch of flaws they're not even aware of."

"So, Chi isn't your real name?" I ask, still shocked at how defective the system is.

"No, it is. No one knows it except for the Underground though. But I told you my real name. I guess I just wanted to be true with you. I figured you wouldn't go brag about meeting me in secret, you know, so I'd be safe. I took a pretty big risk now that I think about it. Don't know what I was thinking." He winks and sends me a lopsided smile. I chuckle.

"How did you manage to get the identity of the Wilcoxes' son? What about his ID?" I ask.

"Well, he'd gone to a school outside the city. So, when I enrolled in my new school, no one knew him, or me. His records were changed so they looked like mine for the ID."

"Why are you telling me all this?" I ask. "I could just talk to the authorities, you know."

"Well, yeah you could, but you'd have to explain how you know my story to begin with. It'd be just as risky for you. And I assumed you knew what it was like to have a life forced upon you and never be free. I thought you might understand." His eyes pin me on the spot, daring me to contradict his hopes.

"Yes, I do understand. Your life makes mine look like a party though."

"I doubt that." He sends me a lazy smile. *How can he smile after telling me such a horrible story?* I guess Chi isn't the type of person to cry easily. Maybe he did too much of it as a child. Maybe he decided to just take the pain in and live with it.

"I won't tell anyone, I promise," I reassure him.

"Yeah, I kinda counted on that," he replies and laughs lightly.

Chapter 13

My life has turned into a long, deceitful tale that I craft carefully to fool my mother and Melissa. My friend believes I'm too busy with my wedding to come and study with her anymore, and my grades are good enough to fool my mother as well.

Two weeks have passed since Chi told me about his family. And each time I meet him, he reveals new truths about our society—horrible things that have altered my vision of the world forever. I understand his poem now. I know what the word "darkness" is referring to. It's the obscurity looming over us all, controlling us and suffocating us. The light is the truth that shall set us free.

The time I spend with Chi always goes by too fast. I try to hold on to it, as much as I can, but it's like air between my fingers. I can't grasp it as it flies me by, gone too soon.

Even though I know him better now, Chi still hasn't told me what happened to his brother; it's a subject he seems to avoid. He hasn't brought it up once, and when I can't contain my curiosity any longer and just ask him one day, his face turns to stone in an instant.

"They took him too, that day," he says and pauses. His face is so hard it scares me. "I was frantic when I couldn't find him. I thought they would execute him or use him for war." He stops again and remains a few minutes without talking, his fingers meddling with a thread sticking out of his uniform. "But what they did with him is almost worse. They took him and turned him into one of them." His gaze meets mine, his eyes darkening as his brows narrow close together.

"What do you mean?"

"They took him and brainwashed him into believing our family was an aberration. He'd always hated us anyway, me especially, so I doubt it took much convincing."

Chi is shaking now, and I wonder what has been upsetting him the most, that his family is in a camp, or that his brother is now an enemy.

"Stephen always blamed me. For the life we had, hiding, you know. He could have been born second, but he wasn't. So, in his mind, I was responsible for it all. And then, when we moved, it got worse. He always held a grudge against my parents for so many stupid things. He used to throw tantrums and be such a jerk. He broke my mother's heart, really.

"I did all I could to try and fix it, but there was nothing I could do to make up for his behavior. He was mad he had to share resources with me, too. When the officers came, they took him and made him one of them. He's betraying his own parents and everything they stand for. He's become everything they've always been against. And it makes me sick!"

Chi's fingers wrap around the loose thread he's been messing with, and he tears it off in anger.

"How do you know for sure?" I ask.

"I have my own sources. I've heard what they've made of him. He got a job as an officer. I'm sure he's been on the look-out for me."

"How come he hasn't found you yet?"

"My mother never told him about the Wilcoxes. Because of the way he was acting, she didn't trust him with all the information. I think that, deep inside, she knew what he was. She wanted to protect me, so she didn't tell him everything. If my parents were to be taken, Stephen was to go to another family. A few months after my parents were captured, I heard that something had happened to those people. I'm sure my brother betrayed them. I guess he thought I was with them."

His shoulders slump forward, but Chi seems a bit calmer now, as if he has turned the story over and over in his head before and is now relieved he finally let it out. He places his hand over mine and runs his thumb over my skin, sending electricity through every spot he comes in contact with. I feel strangely alive. Being with him feels like I finally am where I belong—a peculiar sensation to have next to someone I'm still getting to know.

Chapter 14

Chi told me that he still lives with the Wilcoxes and they are part of the Underground. He explained that the Underground isn't a place; it's a group of people working in secret against what they call "the oppression." They're working on a project of importance right now, but Chi hasn't told me what it is yet. The Underground has managed to infiltrate the authorities with spies, but each mission is a risk for the entire group. And though rebelling could cost Chi his life, he doesn't seem to care about death.

"Are you not afraid to die?" I ask.

"I've got nothing to lose, Thia. When you've got nothing to lose, you can do anything you want. Death is something you fear when you care, when you might leave people behind. There are horrible things going on out there, and that's more important than my life."

Somehow, this bothers me. My heart always races when I meet Chi, as if I were growing wings somehow. They spread on my back as the whole world spins under my feet and I finally take flight. Something's been trying to pull free inside of me, and Chi has become the breeze of air blowing right through the bars of my claustrophobic prison. He keeps sparking these fireworks inside me, triggering emotions and sensations I never even knew existed. These past two months, he has slowly annihilated the torment inside me—replacing it with peace, his light shining my darkness away—something I only feel in his presence. The thought of losing him makes me feel empty, and the possibility of him being gone scares me.

"I wish we could meet somewhere else, somewhere normal, without hiding," I say.

"Yeah, me too. I wonder what it'd be like to just hang out with you casually. But I try not to think about things I can't have. Well...that was until I saw you. Then I couldn't stop thinking about you. I knew I couldn't have you, and it was driving me crazy." He breathes deeply and looks straight at me. "It's still driving me crazy."

I swallow hard. This is the first time that Chi truly acknowledges that he might have feelings for me. At least, that's what I believe he's saying. It makes me want to fly right down into the valley and scream for joy.

"Thia..." The look in his eyes intensifies. "This means that I like you—a lot."

He studies my reaction, and I simply smile, though my entire being has caught on fire. He leans toward me slowly, as if he were expecting me to push him back. When his lips touch mine, they are so soft that it could just be air between us. His hand slides toward the nape of my neck, and Chi pulls me closer to him as he kisses me more deeply. His mouth tastes like spearmint. My heart thunders inside my chest like a storm while his touch electrifies my nerves back to life. When he pulls away, my head feels dizzy with sensations. Chi pushes his forehead to mine and his mouth spreads into a playful grin.

"Now, we truly are in trouble," he says, and his smile widens, reaching his eyes.

This is the beginning of the end. Enlightenment swallows me as my entire life suddenly shifts under my feet. And just then, I realize I no longer care if I'm in trouble. I don't care what might happen. I just want him. I know that every second I spend away from Chi is going to hurt and that the longing inside my heart will leave me restless all night and day.

Chi takes my hand in his and interlaces his fingers with mine. My lips rise into a smile. I don't think I've ever beamed and glowed like this in my whole entire life. I've never felt this light and carefree before. I've never been this happy before. Chi lies down on the grass and I settle next to him. His arms reach for me, pulling me to him as I rest my head on his chest.

He buries his face in my hair and asks, "May I kiss you again?"

My cheeks turn red. I look up at him. "Yes, you may kiss me whenever you want," I reply.

He smiles, pulls my chin toward him, and presses his lips to mine, sweetly. He tastes incredibly good. Our kiss lasts, deepening, and when he pulls away, his eyes shine at me as if he can't quite believe that I let him kiss me again. I close the distance between us and confirm his hopes with one closed-lip peck on his mouth. A mischievous grin shows up on his face as he pulls me tightly against his chest. We remain in each other's arms and simply revel in the presence of one another, without uttering a single word.

Chapter 15

All day long, I've been thinking about Chi's lips against mine. How soft they felt. How his spearmint scent has grown on me. How different Chi's kiss was from William's. While William is possessive, cold, and calculating, Chi is kind and respectful. His emotions are always clear and transparent. He doesn't feel the need to hide behind a wall. He can be funny and sarcastic. He likes to test my boundaries, constantly teasing me, so much so that it's become a game between us. There's always this fire inside him, a volcanic time-bomb on the verge of explosion. He feels real anger at the way we treat others in our society, and yet his rage is hidden deep inside him, surfacing only sometimes. I've never met anyone so incensed before, so tormented by the injustices of this world.

Most days, the thought of meeting Chi is the only thing preventing me from crashing down and breaking into a million pieces. The time when I'm away from him is long, and the wait is excruciating. I spend every second thinking about him. I have this craving, this need to be with him all the time. Chi makes me want to fly, William makes me want to die, and my heart is caught in between, both elated and in agony.

Spending time with Chi is refreshing; spending time with William is just suffocating. Sometimes I wonder how wicked fate can truly be that I have to be with someone I'm growing to hate, someone for whom I am barely human at all, when all I want is to be with somebody who actually sees me, someone courteous and civil, someone who treats me like an actual person.

Chi said he'd have a surprise for me today. I've been waiting with so much anticipation that I can hardly sit still in class anymore. Melissa sends me sideways glances that I ignore while my fingers play over my table as if it were a piano, my restless foot tapping the tempo. Chi refused to tell me what the surprise was. He simply said that it was something I would probably enjoy.

When school is finally out and I arrive at our usual meeting place, Chi isn't there yet. I just lean against the monument, take in the view, and enjoy this peaceful environment—the trees blowing in the wind, the sounds of different birds chirping from the branches before taking flight, finding freedom in a world where there is none.

The leaves crunching under his feet reveal his presence before I see him. I lift my head just as he turns around the corner of the Arch. He smiles at me and my heart pounds against my ribcage, hard. I don't know if I'm supposed to approach him, kiss him, stay away, wave my hand, or relax maybe. I can't think.

Chi drops his backpack. He strides over quickly and joins me within seconds. He doesn't touch me though. He's holding something behind his back. I try to catch a glimpse of what it is without making it obvious, though of course he knows what I'm up to. His mouth tilts up on one side at my behavior and I just clear my throat, pretending that nothing's going on and that I'm not dying to know what he's hiding right now.

"Hi Chi," I just greet him, flatly, my vocal cords cooperating with me for once. I manage to say it without my voice shaking or betraying my curiosity. I might be duping him, but I can't fool myself. My chest is breaking apart, smashed open by this quickening heartbeat that won't stop crushing me from the inside out.

"Hi, Thia." He bends over and deposits the tiniest kiss to the side of my mouth. I hold my breath. When I don't push him away, he remains there, pulling back just slightly before his mouth comes claiming mine again. I inhale sharply through my nose, breathing in the scent of him. My mouth finally agrees to obey my commands and return his kiss. His lips are like feathers against mine, making me want to take off, making me fly.

He pulls away and asks me to close my eyes. I shake my head at him and he chuckles.

"Are you scared?" he asks.

"Scared of what?"

"I don't know. Little Red Riding Hood playing in the woods with the Big Bad Wolf." He lets out a laugh. "Just close your eyes. I won't bite or blow your house down, I promise."

I sigh. "Fine." I close my eyes. "You're hardly a wolf, just so you know. You don't scare me in the least."

He doesn't reply or even wait a second before dropping something in my hands. I feel for it right away. It's rectangular, thick, and made of paper.

"You got me a book?" I ask as I open my eyes to confirm my guess.

"Not just any book," he replies, beaming at me.

I take the time to inspect the cover featuring a bearded man with white hair. *The Empire in the Pillory*, by Victor Hugo.

I cast Chi a quick glance and my eyebrows gather in slight confusion. He's smiling as if this is the most exciting thing he's ever come up with. I bite my upper lip and swallow a giggle. I have no idea what this is about. I open the book and read enough to make out some of the content.

"Poems?" I smile. "You brought me a poetry book?" I'm genuinely happy now. This was really thoughtful of him.

"Not just any poems, Thia," he protests. "Hugo was a revolutionary. He wrote those after exiling himself voluntarily."

"I've never heard of him."

But he doesn't explain further. "I think you'll like the poems," he simply continues. "Well, I hope so." He plays with a curly lock that has fallen over my face and pushes it behind my ear. His eyes reflect the sun, shining at me, brightening my world.

"I'll read some tonight." I grin at him again. I can hardly wait. I really want to know what got Chi so excited and why he thinks this book is so special.

"Do not show this to your family," he adds, suddenly anxious.

"Well, I could never explain where I got it anyway."

He relaxes upon my reassuring him, but his first reaction makes me slightly nervous.

"Is this a book I'm not supposed to have, Chi?" I ask.

"Maybe." His eyebrow arches at me, daring me to keep it anyway.

"I'm sure whatever Mr. Hugo wrote won't get me in any more trouble than what I write in my own journal on a daily basis, Chi." My voice comes out bold and superior. I'm up to the challenge. It's not any more dangerous than my being here with him in the first place. This is just a book—a book of forbidden words—something I am now really eager to read because I know I'm not allowed to do so.

Chi pulls my head toward him and kisses my temple. "You are everything I hoped you would be, and more."

My chest shatters under the sudden leap of my traitorous swelling heart. "What do you mean?"

"When I saw you for the first time..." He pauses. "At the stadium, you know. I was hoping you'd be like this. Smart. Willing to resist and question their stupid rules." He smiles at me, his lips lopsided. "You are everything I expected and hoped you would be."

"What if I hadn't been?" I ask.

"I would have been terribly disappointed," he replies, stating it as a simple fact. "I wanted to kiss you the moment I saw you, Thia." He comes closer to me. "I desperately wanted to kiss you at the ball, too." Closer still, his arms now around me, pulling me to him. "And every single day after that." He leans into me, and his lips find mine, showing me just how much he means it.

His lips brush my mouth, pressing with increasing insistence each time they touch me, until we crash against each other. He's stealing my breath. All my rational thoughts are gone—flying through the wind blowing my mind. And at this very moment, I fall, fall for him so hard I come crashing down, hitting the ground and never wanting to stand back up. My heart speeds up. I don't know if I'm scared, terrified, or just plain elated.

When he pulls away, I give him a tiny smile and try my best to remain calm, though I'm now realizing that I'm falling in love with him. And I'm waiting, desperate, wanting nothing more than for him to just kiss me again. I wait. I wait for him to do so, and when he does, I know that I am lost, lost for good, because there is no way I can ever turn around now and find my way back to the boring, stifling existence I used to live.

Chapter 16

In the evening, I read half the book that Chi gave me. I don't notice it at first, but he has left a note on the first page for me.

"For you to enjoy and ponder.
If we should let them destroy while we wander.
Chi."

The message would be unclear to anyone not knowing Chi. But unlike last time, when he handed me the first note, I decipher the meaning hidden behind his words immediately now. Chi is referring to the authorities. It's a clear allusion to the content of the book. The rhymes of Victor Hugo are so beautiful, filling my soul with a desire to change things irrevocably. It's such a cry for justice, as if he had written those words just for me, making my heart ache and concur.

I fall asleep with the book in my hands, resting over my chest and keeping Chi close to my heart. Sometime during the night, I wake up in a panic. *How could I let such an incriminating item lie around so carelessly?* I stash it away in the box containing my journals.

A week passes by before I get to see Chi again. I can't raise my mother's suspicion. I've been pretending to spend so much time at the library after school that I'm wondering how she hasn't caught on to my lies yet.

The moment I reach the Arch, Chi asks me if I've read the book. I smile at him and nod.

"Did you like it?" he asks.

"Yes, Chi. I loved it. Thank you."

He grabs my hand, pulls me to him, and holds me tightly against his chest before cupping my face. His thumbs run up and down my cheeks. They're slightly calloused against my skin. His lips reach for me delicately and he speaks against my ear, "Let's get out of here."

I pull back. "And go where?"

"Let's head down the valley." One of his eyebrows rises in excitement. He retrieves my hand and interlaces his fingers with mine.

"The path is over there to the right," I declare, proud to remember the route I used to take with Lance.

"How do you know?" Chi asks.

"My brother showed me."

"So, I don't hold the monopoly of bringing you to this place, then?" he asks, smiling at me.

"Sorry to disappoint."

He laughs, his voice filled with humor, carrying me to a place I've learned to love, a place both joyful and carefree, a place I only ever enter when I'm with him and wish I never had to leave.

His fingers remain intertwined with mine as he leads the way down the path. It's been left untouched for years. It's hardly visible anymore. The trail is partly blocked by vines and branches. Chi pushes them out of the way and waits for me to duck and pass underneath them before he lets them fly back past us.

"Where are we going?" I ask.

"Have you been to the stream?"

"No. Lance always made us stop a few minutes into the woods."

Chi doesn't add anything. He just sends me a quick smile, simply happy to show me something I haven't seen yet. He keeps on clearing the way for me. The drop is steep. The walk back up will be hard and treacherous. Our feet hit the leaves, kick rocks, break twigs. It's cold out, but not enough to make us shiver.

When we reach the water, I gasp in wonder as I catch sight of some animals running away at the sound of our intrusion. The brook is low, almost non-existent. Chi sits down, and I crush the leaves underneath me when I settle by him. We talk while he runs his thumb over the top of my hand, electrifying me in the process, shooting sensations through my skin.

"What are you doing this weekend?" he asks out of the blue. It takes me by surprise. He's never wanted to know before today. "Is there any way you could meet your friend to study over the weekend? Any chance you may need some private tutoring?" He waggles his eyebrows at me.

"I..." I pause. I spend almost every weekend with William and his family. I force myself to accept their constant insults, their belittling orders, and their demeaning attitude toward me—the girl they've come to own.

Chi sends me a glance, reading right through my silence. "I see." His good mood is gone in a flash. "Do you have to see him often?"

I don't want to reply. I don't want him thinking about William and me when I can't come here because of my obligations. But my sudden stillness and unease speak for me.

"That often, huh?" His irises turn a dark shade that I've grown to recognize as a sign of the torment residing deep inside him but that only rises to the surface when he gets truly upset.

His jaw is tightly set and his mouth has turned into a thin line of disgust. William is a subject I try to avoid, a topic that always threatens to derail the roller coaster that drives Chi's emotions. I search his eyes for a connection, but he's avoiding my gaze. He just bends over to pick up a rock and throws it away, hard. I flinch when he does it, but he doesn't seem to notice.

"I just can't come here when it's not a school day. I made it clear when we started meeting," I try to explain. I know he understands, but it doesn't make it any easier on either of us.

It's already been two months since I first followed my instincts and threw away all common sense to meet Chi here. Since then, my feelings have changed and grown irreversibly while my inner life has been altered beyond recognition. But this situation between us, the impossibility of ever really being together, that hasn't changed. And it hurts my heart so much to think the circumstances will never get any better.

Chi turns toward me. "The last thing I want is for our relationship to get you in trouble, or worse, put you in danger." He stops and sighs. "But I've grown selfish. I just..." He looks away for a second before closing the distance between us, his body so close to mine I can feel the heat radiating through his clothes. "I just wish I could have you for myself. Without all this." His hand flies around as he says it, encompassing all these invisible obstacles that keep us apart. "Without having to share you with *him*." His voice hits a high cord when he says "him," his tone filled with obvious anguish and disdain. And just like that, my heart cracks and breaks.

The pain in his eyes comes to stab at me, puncturing my soul while he wraps his arms around me. His lips meet mine, hard, desperate, showing me how difficult it is for him when I'm not around, how much he hates it when I have to oblige others and please people who don't even value my presence.

He pulls away and looks me deep in the eyes. "Please, tell me that I stand a chance. That one day, you might choose me, over him."

I inhale sharply. Chi stole my heart from William the moment I saw him. That day, he turned my whole world upside down before I even realized what was going on. I fell for him before I even understood what it meant. I don't know how he did it exactly. I don't know why I let it happen, really. But no matter what my feelings may be, I cannot bring myself to let him hope that this will ever be anything more. I want this. I want it more than anything I ever dared let myself dream about before. But the consequences are still holding me back. Chi could face a death sentence if we were found together, if I agreed to be with him and let William know about it too. But Chi refuses to see that. His life and death mean nothing to him. He acts like the outcome is inconsequential, like his demise is nothing in the larger scale, and like being with me just outweighs all the risks. No matter what he might believe, this isn't worth his life and I refuse to be the cause of his destruction.

I don't answer him. I can't. But he reads it all in me without me even saying a word. Disappointment fills his eyes, making me ache so deeply.

"I'll take whatever you're willing to give, Thia. I know I can't ask for more than this. It's wise of you to be scared. I understand that."

He says the words to soothe me, but I know that someday these clandestine meetings won't be enough for him anymore. I can't blame him. Not when I feel the exact same way. I stroke his cheek with my thumb. He closes his eyes and breathes heavily through his nose, a deep sigh of defeat and acceptance.

Chapter 17

This morning, when Mother brought up the gala I was to attend at William's school, it didn't occur to me that Chi might be there as well. If it had, I would have pretended to be sick from the get-go. Instead, Emily prepared me for it, pampering me, and I let her. Mother hadn't told me about the event until today. It was a last-minute occasion for her to put me on display for all to see. I never meant to expose myself with William in front of Chi, but the moment I stepped on the threshold to the gymnasium, Chi appeared in my peripheral vision and my heart skipped a beat upon seeing him. William's hand was tight around mine, making me squirm on the inside. When I turned around and saw Chi, the look on his face cut right through me. The pain shooting through his eyes aimed right for my heart, striking me fast and hard.

That was over an hour ago. I'm now standing by the punch table, and William hasn't left my side at all tonight. He's been sticking to me the entire time, and I haven't found a second to breathe. So far, Chi has stayed away from us. He's been observing me, with his back propped against a wall and his arms crossed over his chest. I glance around every so often, sweeping the room discreetly until my eyes catch his, but the sight of him just plain wounds me. I'm hurting in ways I never even thought possible. Something is screaming inside me, telling me to throw it all away, to just run to him and kiss him right here in the middle of the gymnasium. But the rational part of my brain knows that would be suicide.

A friend of Chi's has been following him around, but Chi doesn't seem to care for him. The short, black-haired boy has been trying to catch his attention all evening, but Chi is saving it all for me. His gaze pierces through mine, daring me to push William away, challenging me to follow my heart and let it win this battle it's been fighting against my mind.

After a while, Chi's friend gives up and leaves, never even noticing what got Chi so absorbed in the first place. Chi's eyes run up and down my body as a flirtatious smile appears on his face. One of his eyebrows rises for a second and falls the next, teasing me from a distance. He's flirting with me, all the way across the room, right under William's nose. The recklessness of it all seems to amuse him tremendously. His teeth come to bite on his lower lip in a suggestive way, and I can't stop watching. My cheeks burn in an instant, and Chi's lips rise in a rebellious grin. He wiggles his eyebrows at me. I stifle an indecent smile and chuckle in my drink.

But this illicit exchange is cut short when William pulls me against his chest to force a kiss on me. My heart falls hard from being so high on Chi. It comes crashing through the ground, shattering, aching in so many different ways. I close my eyes to shut Chi out. I can't look at him. I can't take the sting of his pained expression. William crushes me against him. His mouth devours mine with impure hunger, and I almost choke on a gagging reflex. I hate it. I hate William's lips upon mine. I hate that he put them there, robbing Chi of his rightful place. I hate that he's forcing his mouth where it never belonged. William's tongue coerces my mouth open, and I fight the cringing instinct inside me. My lids tighten together as I try to keep my disgust at bay.

When William has had enough, he pulls away. I open my eyes and can't help but look at Chi. My heart splinters into too many little pieces for me to collect. The sorrow in him is vivid, leaking through the darkness of his irises in torment and the tight grip of his fingers on his button-down shirt. His anger is barely under control. The muscles of his jaw move with fury and his nostrils flare while his eyes bore holes right through William's skull. He takes a step forward and my heart leaps in fear. But he walks the other way, right out the door. My breathing increases and my heartbeat speeds up.

"William," I say, "I need to go to the ladies' room."

He nods at me. I can't get out of here fast enough; I almost run out the door. I head into the hallway where I saw Chi leave. He's walking away, his hands balled with frustration. I call his name and his back stiffens. His entire body freezes. He turns around and looks at me. His features are twisted as if looking at me was stinging him somehow. I take a step forward, but he doesn't move. I take another one and he tilts his head toward the exit, his silent gesture telling me to meet him outside. He heads out and I follow him while shooting a few glances behind me to ensure no one's watching us. This is a dangerous game that we're playing, but I no longer care if I lose. I just can't leave him feeling like this.

I find my way out of the building, but Chi is still walking, now farther ahead. I try to keep up. I chase after him outside the gates, but he's gone and is nowhere to be seen. I just keep walking. A hand grabs mine and drags me into an alcove. I gasp in surprise as Chi pulls me to him. He presses his index finger against my mouth in a shushing motion. Then he wraps both his arms around me, his despair pouring right through the strength of his muscles claiming me to him. His mouth finds my ear as he touches his forehead to my temple.

"Thia, I can't do this," he whispers, his voice filled with tremors. He swallows hard, his chest rising and falling against mine. "I can't take it. Seeing you two together like this. I just can't." He breathes heavily against my skin. "I should leave before I do something stupid."

He tries to let go, but I tighten my grip around him. "No," I whimper. "Just..." I exhale against him. "Just hold me."

He obliges and pulls me closer until we're locked together in an embrace that nothing could ever tear apart.

"Does he...?" he starts and pauses. A breath catches down his throat. "Does he always kiss you like that?" he asks. "By forcing himself on you?"

I don't want to answer. I want to forget that this ever happened. I don't want Chi to rewind and review this scene over and over again.

He breathes deeply against my ear, his eyes closed, his forehead still pressed against my hair. "Answer me, Thia."

"Yes," I will the word out. "Chi..." I pull away slightly so he has no choice but to look at me. "I don't want to be with him. I never wanted to be with him. The only way for him to kiss me is to force it upon me." I don't add the obvious. I don't tell him that William doesn't care what I want, that he's always rough when Chi is nothing if not gentle.

He sighs. "I just want to break his neck so badly right now," he exclaims. "I don't want him touching you. Imagining it has been bad enough. Seeing it for myself is so much worse. The way he treats you just drives me insane, Thia. I can't stand it."

I stroke his cheek, and his eyes close as he leans into my palm and lets me caress and soothe him. He grabs my fingers and holds them together as he pulls my palm toward his lips. He kisses it. His eyes meet mine and both his arms wrap around my waist again, pulling me to him so hard it knocks the wind out of my chest. His lips meet mine and he does nothing to hide the grief eating at him. His kiss is all consuming, deep, filled with distress. And he doesn't stop. He just keeps going until he can't breathe, until he has to pull away for air.

"Thia," he whispers the word and my heart takes flight, breaking from its shackles. The hurt in his eyes isn't gone though, and I can hardly bear it anymore.

Whatever he means to tell me, I cut him off before his words get a chance to come out. "I'll tell him that I'm sick. I'll just go home," I say and drop a kiss on his cheek. "I'll leave." I inhale the scent of his skin, my nose and lips only inches away from his.

He nods, pulls my forehead to his, and his gaze locks me in place. "Please, don't..." He stops and closes his eyes, the muscles of his jaw dancing as he clamps his teeth together, his nostrils shaking with anguish. "Don't let him touch you. I can't take it. I can't even think about you two like that."

"I won't," I reassure him. "If he tries for more, I'll tell him I'm really sick."

He nods again.

"You're so beautiful tonight," he says as he appraises my blue dress in a simple once-over.

I give him a tiny peck on the side of his mouth. "Thank you," I whisper, my cheeks flushed.

He has no idea how handsome he is either, in his black suit and black button-down shirt, his white tie the only thing contrasting with his outfit. His hair is all over the place from his pulling at it all evening, the locks falling into his blazing eyes. I run my hand through it, to comb it back into a semblance of a haircut.

"Chi?"

He doesn't answer. His eyes are still running all over me.

"I can't meet you this week," I continue, trying my best to ignore these embers his persistent gaze has stirred back to flames deep inside me. His irises turn dark when I say it, a brewing storm waiting to strike.

"Mother wants me home every day." I don't tell him she wants us to plan the layouts of the wedding. Some things are best left unspoken. "I will talk her into letting me go to the library on Monday next week. I'll meet you at the Arch then."

His features reshape with renewed sorrow though he gives me a small, provocative smile. He presses his mouth against my ear. "I still like that you chose to be here with me right now, when he's out there waiting for you. These are moments he can never steal from me."

Chapter 18

I run to the Arch that day. I lied to Mother, and she didn't question me even when I flushed upon my duplicity. I couldn't wait any longer to see Chi. Every day, I need more and more of him, like little pieces of heaven that fate grants me as if trying to make up for the destiny it has forced upon me. When I get there, Chi pulls me in his arms and spins us around, my feet leaving the ground.

"I missed you," he exclaims, "so damn much."

His lips are mere inches from mine before he closes the distance between us. I live and die and am reborn under his kiss. His mouth reclaims what has always belonged to him, and I'm far too happy to oblige. We don't talk about the gala. Chi acts like it didn't happen. He just holds me against him, unable to stop, his lips brushing mine insistently until a cracking sound echoes nearby. A shiver of dread raises the hair on my arms.

The distracting noise immediately threatens our peaceful retreat. Someone is walking close by, and we are in a dangerous, illegal position. Chi lets go of me quickly, though probably too late. He tells me to stay put while he goes to investigate. He walks up to the Arch and looks around it. He goes one way, then the other.

He comes back to me, shaking his head. "It must've been a squirrel. No one was there."

I sigh in relief, but the sound was too loud to be a squirrel or any other animal. I'm sure I heard footsteps after the crack. I know someone saw us or heard us. I can only hope it was a homeless person, someone who might not want to cause us harm or trouble. But my instincts tell me otherwise.

I want to kick myself. *How could I be so careless? How could I be so stupid?* For a few minutes, I forget the way I felt when Chi kissed me, and the old anguish is back. This danger feels all too real and much closer than before. There is sudden panic and despondence in my heart. Though Chi seems to relax, the crease between his eyebrows tells me that he's concerned too.

"I think we should leave. It might be a good idea to find a new place to meet."

"Yes, but where?"

"The Wilcoxes live really close to here. Could you meet me here again tomorrow? I don't want to spend too much time without news from you. We should meet here, and you can follow me to their place. You'll walk at a distance so it seems casual. Then you should only meet me at the Wilcoxes'. This place might not be safe anymore."

His words confirm my fear. I feel faint. Terror rises inside me, making my whole body shake. I can't let it defeat me. I take a breath. As if to help me release stress, Chi touches his lips to mine. It takes effect immediately. I relax just enough to gather the strength to get back home and act normally.

"I'll do my best to get here tomorrow."

"Take care, Thia," he says and squeezes my hand before turning around and disappearing.

The walk back to school is a challenge. I keep turning around to check if anyone might be following me. I find relief upon reaching the station. This feels like a test that I was cheating on and almost got caught doing it. I'm still surprised at how brazen I've been lately. I'm not sure how long I'll be able to keep up this charade.

Chapter 19

I can't focus in class today. I can't hear anything my teachers are saying.

"Miss Clay, may I talk to you for a second?" Mr. Johnson calls out to me after the bell rings to end the last period. I walk to his desk and wait, with my heart thundering inside my chest. The other students leave the classroom, and Melissa waves goodbye while making a worried grimace.

"You managed to get yet another A, Miss Clay," Mr. Johnson resumes once everyone is gone. "I can't quite understand how, to be honest. You're always distracted, daydreaming, not to say borderline-insubordinate. I haven't notified your parents of your attitude because your tests always come with exceptional results, but I shall be expecting more attention in class, more participation as well, and fewer snide remarks on your part." His eyes narrow slightly. "Am I making myself clear?"

I nod and bite my lower-lip.

"Don't think I can't hear the words you mumble to yourself on various occasions, Miss Clay. You may want to be careful. One could think you were a Sympathizer. I wouldn't want to see you reported as a potential threat to our society."

I nod again and lower my eyes. I should probably heed his warning, but all I've been able to think about is that someone possibly saw me with Chi at the Arch yesterday. And if they did, Chi and I could be in deeper trouble than even Mr. Johnson can fathom.

"You may leave now, Miss Clay." He dismisses me, and I run out the door.

I dread going to the Arch. *What if someone follows me there?* Chi told me not to go directly to the monument, but to wait behind some bushes until I see him. I scan the area the entire time for any passers-by. When I reach the corner close to the Arch, Chi isn't there. I hide behind some shrubs and wait.

After five minutes, my nerves slowly give in as crazy thoughts fill my head with paranoia taking over. *What if someone did spy on us yesterday? What if nothing happened to me, but Chi got arrested?* I find myself shuddering. I don't know where Chi lives. If anything happened to him, I might never find out. The thoughts course through my brain while fear grasps my heart in its iron fist. I keep looking around frantically and decide to give Chi another five minutes.

When he doesn't show up, I step out of the bushes. That's when I see him—a boy from the back. He turns around and winks at me. It's Chi. I'm dizzy with relief, exhilarated as the adrenaline leaves my body.

Chi is walking away. I follow him from a distance. He doesn't turn around to check that I'm catching up with him. I look a few times behind me, but there is no one there.

After five minutes, Chi reaches a house and opens the gate to the backyard. He leaves it open and disappears inside. When I get to the gate, I step in quickly. Chi is waiting for me at the corner of the house. He beckons for me to follow him. He's holding the key to the back door. He turns it into the lock, walks in, and holds the door open for me. When I'm in, he closes it fast behind me.

He turns around and takes me in his arms. He spins me around and kisses me, tenderly at first, and then more insistently. He spins me around some more before putting me down. He holds on to me tight, his arms around my lower back, my arms around his neck. He leans in, looks into my eyes, and smiles. Eventually, he drops his arms and lets me go. He grabs my hand in his and we enter the living room on the right.

The house looked small and simple from the outside, but the inside is nice and spacious. The furniture is expensive, with leather couches, a glass table, and a flat-screen TV on the wall over the fireplace. Of course, I'm used to luxury at home, but my parents' house feels cold while this place feels warm and welcoming. The mantel above the hearth is covered with figurines. It's obvious Mrs. Wilcox put a lot of effort into the decorations.

"It's really pretty," I say while examining one of the figurines.

"Yes, Jane spends a lot of time finding collectables. It's her hobby," Chi explains. "The Wilcoxes are at work right now. I told them you'd be coming. I can't risk their security without telling them what's going on. I'm not sure Neil was happy about it, but I believe Jane understands."

"Was she forced into marriage?"

"Yes, it was an arranged wedding, but they became fond of each other. They were my parents' friends, remember. They share the same beliefs."

"Yes, of course."

Chi sits on a couch and taps the space by his side for me to join him. I approach him and sit down. I put my head on his shoulder. His long fingertips come to stroke my hair.

"I feel safe here," I say.

"I know. I've been feeling safe ever since I moved here. But there's always a shadow lurking in the dark. I constantly need to watch my back and make sure I don't slip or make a mistake. I have to remember the Wilcoxes are supposed to be my parents. I have to turn around when people call me by their son's name. It took a while before I got used to that."

"What is their son's name? What name do you go by in society?" I ask.

"Their son was named Jordan. At school and everywhere else, I go by that pseudonym. With people I'm close to, I go by my real name."

"Do you sleep in his room?"

"I actually sleep in the guest room. It was too hard for Jane to give me Jordan's room. No one needs to know since no one visits the bedrooms. Jordan's room was left exactly as it was when he had his 'accident.' That's what Jane calls it when she talks about it."

"So, you keep all your things in the guest room?" I ask.

"Well, I don't really own a lot. I lost everything when my parents were taken. Possessions don't matter, Thia. I don't need objects in my life to fulfill me. I'll probably lose it all again soon, so what's the point." He shrugs.

I think about my own bedroom. Despite the lack of warmth in my parents' house, my bedroom has always been my refuge. There are things I hold on to dearly, such as my notepads, my diaries, and my poetry books. I admire Chi for his practicality, but as his words resonate inside my head, they sting me deeply. Chi has nothing to lose, and life doesn't matter as much to him as the goal he has set for himself.

I remember the nightmare I had the other day. Some men were chasing Chi. Gunshots echoed all around me as Chi fell to the ground. "Remember, I have nothing to lose," he said, and as the words came out of his mouth, they shredded my heart. I want to believe I mean enough to Chi that he would care about life. My own craving for death has disappeared. When I met Chi, everything changed and the sadness overwhelming my heart just went away. I no longer seek my own demise. I no longer wish to die. I want to live. And I wish Chi felt the same way too, but his defiance of our system often verges on a thirst for self-destruction.

He catches me in my contemplation. "Excuse me if I don't show you my room," he says with a wicked grin. "I don't want you to get the wrong idea."

I blush profusely. His hint is obvious. Chi doesn't know about my fear of intercourse, and his joke unsettles me. I'm glad he's open enough to laugh about it and that he's not considering it an option yet. But his remark bothers me. I clear my throat.

He catches on to my mood. "Are you okay?" he asks. "Did I say something wrong? It was just a joke, I promise." He lifts his hands up in defense.

I flush even more. The temperature inside me suddenly rises. I don't know how to respond. I don't want to make a fool of myself, but I might as well just come clean about it now. If the thought has crossed his mind, I have to let him know that it won't happen—not anytime soon at least.

"Hum." A ball of discomfort has lodged itself between my vocal cords. "I've never done...you know. I've never done it before."

"Well, of course. I wouldn't have expected you to," he replies, as if it makes complete sense. I'm not sure if I should take that as a compliment or an insult.

He sees the vexed look on my face and explains himself. "Thia, girls aren't supposed to have sex until their prenuptial night. I know the rules. I mean, some girls break that rule, but the consequences are not worth it. I wouldn't have expected you to have done anything yet." He looks at me tenderly as he says it.

"Yes, but I'm not comfortable talking about it either. My friend Melissa, she talks about it as if it were the best thing that could ever happen to her. Whereas with me, I don't know; it just terrifies me."

"Well, everyone's different, Thia." His hand reaches for my chin and his index finger caresses the side of my mouth.

"Haven't you...I mean, with another girl..."

"With whom?" His mouth tilts up, in the tiniest reassuring smile.

"I don't know. You're handsome. I thought that maybe—"

"Thia," he cuts me off, "I've had more important things to do. I mean, really. I've had more urgent issues on my mind. Well, that was until I met you," he adds, his eyes traveling up and down my face. "Now you seem pretty important too, and I've made it my goal to save you." He sends me a mischievous smile before his mood turns sour. "What I mean is...imagining you and William together..." He inhales sharply, and a groan rises in his throat. The emotional tremor in his voice pains me. "When I think about it, it drives me crazy. It makes me want to break his jaw."

"The pre-nuptial night isn't for quite a few months I'm sure, so we don't have to worry about it yet," I try to soothe him.

"I guess not. But don't you though? I mean, don't you worry about it?"

I don't reply. The answer is obvious to the both of us. I avert my eyes and clear my throat. "Where is this going, Chi? What's the point of us meeting? It's not as if we could ever really be together."

"Is that what you truly believe? That this is pointless?"

I lift my eyes just in time to catch a glint of pain shooting through his eyes. Shame squeezes my heart. Of course he believes we stand a chance. The choice is only mine to make after all. It's all up to me. Chi has tried to talk me into joining the Underground, but I'm scared. It would be a big step, a choice that would change my life forever. If I left my current situation, I wouldn't have anywhere to go. I'd have to put all my trust in him. Girls like me can't just roam the streets on their own—not unless they want to end up in a camp or be forced to sell their bodies as prostitutes.

Chi probably takes me for a coward, but he never says anything. He always nods, never wanting to rush me. I still need to think all of this through, and I don't know how to tell him that. I don't know how to confess to him that I'm still terrified. I just know that I miss him every second of each day and that I wish I could be with him without having to make such a difficult decision.

He looks at me, his face serious, unsmiling. "I've already made up my mind and I'm not turning back. I want to be with you. I want to bring you along with me, but I can't force you, and I understand that it's a lot to ask."

His words sadden me. I'm being selfish. Being with me might prevent Chi from reaching his goal, but he won't leave me behind. He had to make choices of his own, difficult ones, but he did it without any second thoughts, it seems.

"The Wilcoxes will be here soon," he says. "They know you're here, but I don't want them more involved in this than they need to be."

Despite his general kindness, Chi's tone has turned cold. He's putting himself in terrible danger just to be with me. I want to tell him that I have chosen already. I want him to know that I've chosen *him*—that I chose him over William the moment I saw him. But I'm too much of a wimp to speak the words and expose the truth hiding inside my heart. I look at him, but there is no joy left in his eyes. He takes me to the back door.

"Will you be here tomorrow?" he asks. His question hurts because it's filled with doubt. He doesn't even trust me to come back to him.

I nod. Once. And then again, emphatically, to let him know that yes, I will come back. I will always come back, for as long as I'm able to.

"I won't be waiting at the Arch. Just come directly here. Okay?" He holds on to my arm, kisses me, and then he lets go.

I walk out and look back, but he has already closed the door and turned the bolt like a lock on his heart.

Chapter 20

I messed up with Chi yesterday, and I want to fix it. I spent all night worrying about him. I haven't made up my mind yet, but I want with all my heart for us to be okay.

Mother snaps her fingers in my face when she sees that I'm not listening. She has brought a letter to the counter where I'm eating breakfast. It's official news; the envelope has been sealed shut with a stamp. It's addressed to me, but Mother has opened it already.

She's holding it in her hands, and there's a huge grin on her face. It can't be good. My mother never smiles. She strokes the paper as if it's the best thing in the world. When she starts reading the content, the words tear my heart apart. The sudden pain stabbing at me is unbearable. I'm breaking apart as complete despair crushes me down. I want to die.

Mother is holding the official pre-nuptial announcement. It was delivered in person this morning by one of William's servants. I am to meet him two days from now for our first night together. It will happen on Saturday. Today is Thursday. I shiver.

Panic seizes me. I want to run out of the room. I want to run and find Chi. I want to feel his arms around me. I want him to tell me it's all going to be fine. But I remain seated. The ache inside me increases and I can't breathe. The spoon falls out of my hand and drops down, spraying milk and cereal on the hardwood floor. I can't breathe. Emily sends me a glance of annoyance, but I hardly pay heed. I can't breathe. My chest heaves. I'm choking. I can't breathe. The air escapes from my lungs. I can't breathe. No matter how much I try, I can't breathe. Dark spots form in front of my eyes and slowly grow into smudges. Darkness swallows me whole, and I fall.

***

When I regain consciousness, I wish I hadn't opened my eyes at all. My head is pounding. I'm lying on the floor, and the light in the room is stinging my eyes. Mother is over me, holding a handkerchief to my nose. There's a strong smell emanating from it. The back of my skull is hurting as if it has shattered from the impact. I must have fallen off my stool and hit my head against the hardwood floor.

I gather enough strength to ask if I may be excused and go to my room. There's concern in my mother's eyes. I don't want to make a big deal out of it. If I don't go to school, I won't have a pretext to meet Chi later on. But Mother is heading to the phone already, to tell the principal that I need the day off. I'm desperate as I try to talk her out of it, but there is no arguing with her. She thinks I'm too emotional and that I need to rest.

So now, I'm stuck at home for the day. I won't be able to meet Chi. He'll be mad at me. I want to tell him. I want him to take me away from here.

I spend the whole day in bed. Mother comes upstairs a few times to talk about the prenuptial night. I pretend I'm sleeping whenever someone walks into my room. I don't want anyone to know how horrible this situation is for me. I'm supposed to be rejoicing about the news. I don't know how, but I know my parents expect me to. I don't want to discuss the subject with anyone. I'm angry and scared. I don't want William to touch me. I don't even like it when he kisses me.

I'm distressed when I think about Chi, too. Our parting yesterday didn't go well. I'm concerned he might think I was letting him down. I don't even want to consider what this news is going to do to him. Having to hurt him this way just makes me want to scream. The charade is falling apart around me, and I'm not sure how much longer I'll be able to hold on to this masquerade. This existence is just slow death spent buried alive under a never-ending list of obligations. I can only breathe when I'm with Chi.

This entire day is pure torment. I manage to fall asleep a few times, for the weight on my shoulders is exhausting me. It's easier to be asleep and away from this place than awake and facing reality. Despite my napping most of the day, I'm still tired enough to sleep at night. My slumber is heavy, devoid of dreams or nightmares.

Chapter 21

I want to throw up the moment I open my eyes. I tell myself this was all just a night terror and reality cannot be that bad. But I remember quite well that receiving the prenuptial letter wasn't a dream. I feel sick to my stomach and run to the bathroom.

Emily hasn't come to my room yet. I make sure to clean everything up before she does. The last thing I need is to be stuck at home another day. I need to get out of here. I need an excuse to see Chi.

I consider skipping school, but that wouldn't be wise. Last night, I had enough trouble convincing Mother that I should stay at the library with Melissa this afternoon, to make up for the classes I missed. Chi won't be home anyway. There's no point in taking the risk of skipping school to find his house empty.

I get ready and go through my usual routine. I go downstairs for breakfast, take the train with Walter, join Melissa by our lockers, and then sit through all my classes while fretting about Chi the entire time. He's probably upset that I never showed up yesterday.

When the afternoon finally arrives, I run to his house. I'm so frantic I'm just careless. I get there and knock on the back door, hard. Chi comes right away, breathing heavily; he must have run to meet me on the threshold. I don't dare look at him. I dread the disappointment and anger that are sure to show in his eyes. But when I lift my head, there is relief on his face instead. He sighs deeply, pulls me inside, and takes me in his arms, holding me so tight it hurts as he kisses my face frantically.

"I was so worried! Why didn't you come yesterday? I wanted Jane to call your house and ask for you. Are you okay?"

"I'm sorry!"

I'm so ashamed I ever doubted him. Of course he wouldn't be mad. After all, this is a dangerous world for girls; anything could have happened to me. I'm touched that he was so concerned about me, and a selfish bubble of happiness suddenly surrounds me and carries me up, up, up. Up so high I almost forget why I couldn't make it here yesterday. When the memories come back to slap me in the face, a sob rises in my throat and a single tear rolls down my cheek. I try to prevent it from falling, but fail.

"What's wrong, Thia? Did something happen to your family?"

Sadness for Chi suddenly fills my broken heart. My tears pour out, and I know I won't be able to stop them. Of course, Chi would think something happened to my family. After all, didn't something horrible happen to his?

He leads me through the hall, all the way to the kitchen on the left. He takes me to a stool by the island and helps me sit down. He grabs a seat next to me and holds my hand in his, so tight it hurts. I look at him with unrestrained tears running down my cheeks. Chi extends his hand to dry the tears with his thumb. There is concern in his eyes where mischief usually shines, and I don't know how to tell him what's going on.

I somehow manage to get it out without choking on the words. I stop crying, but my voice trembles as I speak. "I received the official pre-nuptial letter."

Chi glances at me and blinks a few times. He looks like he's about to suffocate. His eyes are blank for a second, as if he didn't quite hear what I just said. But slowly, a deep coldness appears behind his pupils and his sweet honey irises darken, his eyes flashing with frightening shades reminiscent of a tornado ready to hit. His jaw clenches as hatred flickers through his gaze, disappearing just as quickly.

Wrath overtakes him, and he bangs his fist so hard on the island that it shakes. I jump in my seat and cringe. Chi stands up violently while cursing and calling William a variety of bad names—some of them in a language I don't even understand. I flinch. He's not looking at me as he speaks either. He's just talking to himself.

"That's why he was leering at me all day, that asshole!"

"What are you talking about?"

Chi looks at me now, and the vivid fury filling his eyes stuns me. I've never seen this violence in him before, even when talking about his family.

"William! He was mocking me all day," he snaps, "looking at me with a smug smile on his face!"

"But Chi, surely William doesn't know about us! Why would he be sneering at you?"

"I'm not sure how, but he knows! His whole attitude today tells me that he knows about us. Maybe he noticed something at the gala, I don't know. But he knows!"

Frissons course through my body. If William is aware I'm seeing Chi, he could destroy me. He can do whatever he wants. He could choose to marry me and have me committed later on. He could have me arrested. He could deflower me and then reject me, leaving me to deal with the shame for the rest of my life.

I'm shaking. I need to lie down, but I don't dare tell Chi. The look on his face terrifies me. His teeth are clenched so hard the muscles in his jaw are moving. His hands are still tightened into fists, his knuckles white from the pressure.

"Let's go upstairs and talk. I'm not gonna let it happen. No way! Imagining that jerk's hands on you makes me sick!"

He shakes his head frantically now while pacing around the kitchen. He keeps on cursing, boiling with rage— expletives and oaths flying around without restraint. I don't like him this way. He makes me uncomfortable, and I don't know how to calm him down.

He grabs my hand suddenly and leads me out of the kitchen, and then down the hall to a staircase leading upstairs. He has never taken me there before, and my old fears surface. But he's so mad that I don't dare protest. I just follow him up the stairs. His attitude is upsetting me even more than I was before.

I try to fight the tears, but I've been too emotional since yesterday. This is too much for me to take. I pull my hand away from his and stop, right outside his bedroom door. My body starts shaking harder as a panic attack takes over. My knees almost give up on me as chaos fills my head, making me dizzy. I just want the rage and fears and frustration out of me. I've had enough. Someone has to take the brunt of my anger, and the only person I can take it out on right now is Chi. I know it's not fair, but his behavior is driving me over the edge.

I stand still and look at him. My whole body shudders and wrath comes out as the volcano finally erupts. Heat engulfs me as I yell in his face, "This is not about you, Chi! I came here for comfort, and all you've done so far is curse, offend me, and yell! You're upsetting me! I don't need this. I don't need this!"

I hit his chest with my fists over and over again. I lose my grasp on reality and see William standing in front of me. My mind is playing tricks on me. The panic attack is hitting me hard, and suddenly I can't breathe. I hyperventilate. Chi pulls my hands away from him. He holds onto my shoulders and forces me to look at him.

"I'm sorry, Thia," he says. "I'm sorry! Breathe! Come on, take a deep breath, like this."

He breathes heavily, and I try to follow his rhythm. I inhale and exhale once, twice, three times. Again. Slowly, I find relief as the air rushes to my lungs and brain. I relax a little, but I'm still quivering and feeling faint.

Chi's eyes fill with pain and apologies. He opens the door to his room and says, "Please, come in. You should sit down for a while."

Chi doesn't need someone who's already taken, someone he cannot have. I never want to hurt him, ever. But our relationship has brought him nothing but misery. I want to tell him that. I want to walk away from here for his own good. But the selfish part of me is begging me to stay and find comfort in him, and I let him pull me inside.

I step into his room, look around me, and find nothing to indicate that someone other than a guest has been spending the nights here. The space is still decorated as a guest room; Chi hasn't even tried to make this place his own. I know it's his refuge away from the world. *But how can it be so when there are no traces of his personality here?* The only things betraying his presence are some clothes hanging from the back of a chair and some books on the nightstand table. I walk to them and flip through the first pages. I catch Chi looking at me and I flush, realizing how nosy I'm being.

I'm confused. The books are worn-out copies written in a foreign tongue I don't recognize. Languages haven't been part of our curricula for years. Since it's illegal to migrate to other countries, the need to speak another language has become useless and obsolete. Trade between countries is hardly existent now. Our seceded state, especially, is cut off from the rest of the world; we've had to learn to rely on our own resources. Only the officials speak different languages now, in case they ever have to deal with other communities. *How did Chi get these books?*

I take the first one and look at the cover. The title reads *L'Ecole des femmes* while the second one says *Le Mariage de Figaro*.

"These books belonged to my mother," Chi explains. "I guess I do have a few possessions I held on to after all. I have a few French books from her. I sneaked back into the house to retrieve a couple of things."

"Can you actually read them?"

My question sounds dumb the moment it escapes my mouth. Chi chuckles and I'm glad to see his good mood is back.

"Yes, I can. My mother's ancestors came from France. They spread the language from generation to generation. They believed it was important to hold on to the past and that communication was the best way to create understanding and prevent war. My mom taught me French herself. I can speak, read, and write it. I've lost a bit of it since she's been gone though. It's hard to hold on to it when you have no one to practice with."

"Would you teach me? I mean, if we have time."

"Yes, I'd love to do that. Then I could practice it with you."

I've never heard of these books before. Chi explains to me that the first one is about an older gentleman who wants to marry his pupil. He gets extremely jealous when she starts seeing a young man her own age.

"That sounds familiar," I say, laughing lightly.

Chi goes on to explain that the second book criticizes the privileges of the upper class in eighteenth century France. He says these ideas were controversial at the time and gave a taste of the Revolution that was to come. I stare at him, my face blank. I've never heard of the French Revolution before. He smiles at my reaction, and I forget all about my life for a while. Chi is a deep source of knowledge, a fount of information constantly pouring out, fascinating me.

"Chi?"

"Yes?"

"The collection of poetry that you gave me was translated from *Les Châtiments*. Is that French?" I ask.

"Yes, it is."

"Do you have a French copy of it?"

"No, Thia. I gave you my only copy." He runs his hand over the back and top of his head, messing up his hair.

I frown slightly. "It didn't belong to your mom, did it?"

"Why?" He tries to avoid the subject.

"Did it?" I insist.

"Yes, it did," he concedes, his mouth quirking up in a tiny smile.

"Chi, I can't accept such a gift."

That he would give me something so dear to him when he has so little left from his family is just too overwhelming.

"Thia, I have other books," he protests. "I don't need that one. I want you to have it."

"How many books do you have from her?"

He clears his throat. "It doesn't matter. My mother had a whole library of them, forbidden works of literature, in French and English. I don't know how she got them. I only grabbed those she preferred. I gave that one to you and you're keeping it."

I steal a glance around his room and only see the few books that I had already spotted on his nightstand table as well as a couple more lying on the floor. "Is that all you have left?"

"Thia, the conversation is over. The book is yours."

I didn't understand the magnitude of Chi's gift until now. I knew that it was a present with meaning, a specific message from him to me. But now, it has become a lot more, something that Chi cherished enough that he risked going back to his parents' house to retrieve it when he knew the authorities were on the lookout for him. I jump into his arms and crash against his chest as I wrap my arms around his neck.

He exhales sharply under the shock and chuckles in my ear. "Had I known you'd react like this, I'd have given you the book the first day we met."

I cup his face and kiss him, shushing him. I meet his lips, the side of his mouth, his cheek, his neck, until the memory of what's about to happen this week-end rushes back at me to put a harsh, destructive end to this bliss. And a tear rolls down my cheek, accompanied by an unwanted sob.

Chi has brought me nothing but happiness while being with me has cast a shadow of pain over his life. I don't want to remind him of what's going on. I want my tears to stop falling. I don't want to think about William right now. I swallow the sounds trying to escape my mouth, but I don't fool him for long. And the saddest thing is that he instantly understands what I'm thinking.

"What's the date of the pre-nuptial night?" he asks, pulling away from me.

He's trying to control himself and not show the anger that's emerging again. But I can still see it burning through him as he grits his teeth. There's something in his eyes now that's no longer comforting or jovial. Instead, it's incredibly painful to look at.

I don't want to tell him. What's the point? I don't want him thinking about me when it's happening. I don't want him to go crazy, counting the minutes, wondering what I'm doing. But he repeats his question, more insistently this time.

"It's on Saturday."

"This Saturday? Do you mean tomorrow?" he asks.

"Yes. Chi, I don't want to! I never wanted to, not with him. And now I want it even less! I'm not ready."

Chi looks at me. "He did it on purpose. That asshole! He planned it as early as possible. I can't believe this! You know what, just don't do it!"

"What?"

"It's that simple. *Don't do it*," he snaps, anger growling within each word.

He must have felt the harshness of his tone because he just looks at me with tenderness now. He takes my head in his hands, lifts my face toward his, and looks me in the eyes with pure sweetness and frustration piercing through his gaze.

"Don't do it! You don't have to do it if you don't want to," he pleads.

"Of course, I do! My family will be humiliated if I don't go through with this. If I don't follow up on my obligations."

Chi explodes. I know he's not upset at me, but the detonation of his anger still hits me in the face as his voice comes out harsh and anguished. "These engagements were forced upon you by people who don't care about you. You mean more than that. You are not an object, Thia! You are a person and I wish you'd finally realize that! You may not matter to them, but you matter to me. If you can't refuse this for yourself, at least do it for me! I will not plead with you not to do it. I will not beg! But if you choose not to do it, I will help you. I promise!"

I know that he means it, but I don't see how he can help. The mere thought of being caught with him brings dread to my heart. I've heard what happens to men who steal another's property. I could never let that happen to Chi. I have to protect him from himself and his desire to save me.

I'm scared and worried about Saturday night. But the fear I feel at the thought of facing William is nothing compared to the terror gripping me at the thought of losing Chi or causing him suffering. I'm about to tell him that, but he cuts me off before I can speak.

"I'm not sure I can take it, Thia. I'm not sure I can go through this. Imagining his hands on you, forcing you, it makes me sick! I wouldn't be a man if I let it be."

"You have to! For me, please," I try to reason with him.

He pulls my mouth to his and kisses me, pressing his lips lightly against mine. A tear falls down my cheek. I shouldn't be crying; I'm making it all the more difficult for him. My grief is like fuel adding sparks to the raging flame always blazing through his rebellious mind. I try to contain the tears. I try so hard. But a part of me just wants to cry against him so badly, to keep his arms around me, rocking me. And I want to scream. I take a deep breath and look up at the ceiling to force the tears back inside. Chi sighs and caresses my cheek with his thumb lightly. He holds me for a long time while kissing the top of my head and stroking my hair.

"Come here," he says, leading me to the bed.

He lets me lie down on it before joining me. He pulls me to him. I rest my head on his chest and wrap my arms around him. It's more than I can take. My heart is an ocean of sorrows slowly drowning me, and I let it. I cry without a sound at first and then louder and louder until my whole body shakes with untamed wails coming out of my throat.

Chi doesn't cry, but the muscles of his chin are tight with anger while his eyes flash with deep turmoil. I know right then that he has made his decision, a resolution that no arguments will change. I'm not sure what his intentions are exactly, but I know from the look on his face that they won't lead to anything good.

PART 2

"I wish Chi and I had never met—
not because I don't want to be with him,
but because I refuse for our relationship
to cost him his life."
Thia Clay

Chapter 22

The weekend arrives entirely too soon. I'm awakened by the commotion of people stirring around the house. I pull the pillow over my face to stifle a scream. I'm frustrated with everyone. Someone comes to knock on my door. I throw the pillow at the wall with anger and close my eyes. I pretend to sleep, and I breathe hard to push back the tears. The door creaks open and my mother enters. I recognize the sounds of her footsteps even without looking.

"Thia, are you awake?" she asks. "We have a long day ahead of us, and you need to get ready."

How can my own mother be a part of this? Giving her own daughter away to be tried out like some piece of meat. The thought appears like a shadow in my mind and disappears just as quickly. I don't grasp it for fear a scream might escape my mouth. I look at Mother. Her gaze is cold, as always. She looks back at me, but she doesn't see me. She never does. Her indifference awakens the rage that's always sleeping deep inside me. I want to shake her.

"Yes, Mother, I'm awake." I stand up and sigh, exasperated. Then I let her lead me to the bathroom.

She closes the door behind us. "After your bath, Emily will tend to your hair. You'll change into your dress later in the day so it doesn't get soiled or wrinkled," she says and steps out of the bathroom like a queen after an official statement.

"Emily," she calls, "please, attend to Thia. We won't have much time for preparations tonight."

"Yes, madam."

Emily walks into the bathroom as I'm drying my eyes with the back of my hand. She looks at me. Her gaze drops to my pursed lips, and irritation flashes through her eyes.

"Today is a day of importance. It's a day to make your mama proud. Let's not ruin it with idle fears and childish caprices," she says while looking at me coldly. Her attitude feels like a punch. But Emily knows I won't tattle to my mother about her blatantly rude behavior. I'm used to people belittling me. I don't even care at this point.

"Of course," I reply while straightening my back to give myself more importance. I'm short, but Emily is smaller than me and I tower over her.

She goes to my bedroom and makes the bed while I shower in silence. Then she comes back in, dries my hair, and styles it into a high ponytail. She mumbles to herself when my locks refuse to cooperate. When she's done with me, I walk out of the bathroom, refreshed, groomed, and smelling like strawberry soap.

"Perfect," my mother says with a faint smile when I walk into the living room.

Compliments from my mother are rare. One does not want a girl to think too much of herself. I've grown to crave her praises with such longing in my heart that her words make me feel lighter in spite of the heaviness weighing on me.

The day goes by and it feels agonizing. My chest hurts a little bit more with each passing minute. I'm on the verge of a nervous breakdown. My heart is beating at a rate that can't possibly be natural. I find myself shaking a few times without being able to control myself or calm down. Mother is as oblivious as ever. She spends the day dictating how to conduct myself tonight. Not only is the conversation uncomfortable and highly inappropriate, but it infuriates me, too. I hardly listen to what she has to say. I don't care what she may think of my behavior tonight. Instead, I think about Chi. But that just hurts me even more. I'm bleeding for him on the inside. Though I worry about myself, it pains me to think what this is doing to Chi.

***

Eventually, the evening comes. The day has been dragging on, and yet this moment is here all too soon. I can't wait for it to be over. When William's driver comes to pick me up, my heart jumps so hard that my chest burns. I can't control my shaky legs. Walking steadily is a trial in and of itself. I breathe deeply during the entire ride while feeling my sanity breaking at the edges.

Why am I even here? What am I doing in this car? Maybe I should open the door and jump out of the vehicle. I could get it over with, right here, right now, so I don't have to face what's coming. Maybe if I fall on my head when jumping out, my skull will break on the impact and it'll finally be over. But I just sit here, looking outside the window until the car reaches the hotel in Eboracum City, where William is waiting for me.

His driver opens the door and takes me inside the building. William is standing in the lobby, leaning over the front counter. When I approach him, he turns around without a smile. I feel like everyone is looking at me as if I were a girl of little virtue. I'm deeply ashamed, and hatred suddenly grows inside me for those who are pushing me to do this.

I look at my fiancé, but I'm not scared anymore; I'm aggravated, my irritation growing into fury. A bubble of anger rises in my throat, but I let it pop and the nasty words I wish to shout at William just die on my tongue with a taste so sour I want to throw up. I don't say anything. I look at him and clench my jaw. I let him take me to the bedroom.

As soon as the door closes behind us, William shoves me against it, violently. He presses his mouth to mine. It's not soft like Chi's lips, nor does it feel good. It's harsh and sloppy. I'm disgusted with him and myself.

"You are mine and mine only," he whispers against me. I want to push him away. I can hardly stand his touch on my skin. His hands are on my lower back, up my legs, everywhere, intrusive and repugnant. He wraps his arms around my waist and pushes me all the way to the bed while kissing me.

He takes off his shirt hastily, and terror takes hold of me as his hand reaches for the zipper in the back on my dress. But I can be strong. I can go through with this and honor my family. I have to. I try to focus on William's physical beauty, to remind myself that many other girls would want to be in my place, promised to someone like him. I try to grasp any reassurance I can think of, but can find none strong enough to assuage this painful agony.

My mind shifts as Chi's face appears in front of my eyes. The world is moving around me, spinning so fast I can't catch my breath. I try to hold on to Chi, to imagine that those are his lips against mine. But Chi's lips are soft. His kisses are sweet, and he would never force intercourse on me.

William pulls my dress down, revealing more of my skin, waking me from my thoughts. I almost gag. I have to focus so I don't throw up. He kisses my neck, his weight heavy, pinning me down. A strange sensation seizes me as I leave my body, suddenly watching this scene from the outside.

It's not me on this bed; it's another girl. I am a mere witness to these unfolding events. But then, William's body presses against mine and I know for sure that this is real and that I'm dying. My mind is breaking, slowly cracking to let the insanity in. I pray that I might be relieved from this, and panic seizes my heart. Everything in my body is ready to get up, run, and flee. I'm so tense I wonder how William hasn't noticed anything yet. I guess he just doesn't care. *Why should he?*

And just then, he takes my throat in his hand and pushes my head back. He looks me deep in the eyes. There's something hiding behind his pupils that terrifies me—cruelty. He bends down to my ear.

"I know," he whispers with a voice cold and distant. I must have misunderstood him, but there's a sadistic smile on his face now, too. I'm scared, really scared. I know exactly what he's talking about. He's referring to Chi and me. *How did he find out?*

The sounds...the sounds we heard when we were at the Arch. Those sounds came from him. They came from William spying on us.

What is he going to do to me? He looks at me and leans toward my ear again, still holding on to my throat, choking me.

"I saw the way you were looking at him at the gala, Thia. What kind of a fool do you take me for? I followed you that day you met him at the Arch. I saw you walk past the train station, and I knew something was up. I couldn't believe it. You betrayed me. I could make you pay for that. I don't like to share, Thia. You are mine, do you understand? Mine!"

Chills run down my spine. I can hardly breathe. I'm petrified. I can't move. I want to push him away and run, but I'm frozen on the spot with fear like ice in my veins. William presses his lips to mine again and kisses me hard. I try not to think about his mouth forcing mine open. He tears at my dress, pulling it down my shoulders, ripping it off. There's no tenderness in his movements, no feelings. And right then, I know he won't make this pleasant for me at all. William is going to rape me. The terror inside me grows, overpowering me. I can't move. I can't breathe. I'm a prey in a predator's lair, with no way out.

I regain my senses and try to push him away, but his body is heavy against mine, pinning me in place. My fists hit his chest. He grabs my wrists to keep me still, and his eyes fill with irritation because I'm resisting him. Just then, something bangs against the door, startling him, and I use that moment to push him back. I stumble to my feet. But he reaches out and grabs me by the throat to shove me against the wall. My head hits it hard and black spots fill my vision. My nails find his cheek and I scratch hard, but he doesn't let go. I can't breathe.

"Thia?" The voice comes from outside the room and my heart quickens. Fear and relief flood my heart at once.

"Thia?" Chi's voice grows louder and more insistent. Another blow shakes the door, and a hard kick makes it quake against its frame.

"What the hell!" William drops his hold on me.

He strides toward the entrance elegantly, recovering his composure as though nothing is wrong. Chi kicks the door so hard it gives way. He enters the room, his teeth clenched with a mixture of grief and anxiety. His eyes turn to William briefly and then to me. Chi catches a glimpse of my bare shoulders and my dress undone at the seams before his gaze shifts back to William. The look on his face, filled with hatred and rage, chills me to the bone. Chi is on the ledge of a precipice—a simple push needed to tip him over and break him apart.

"Come, Thia! I'm taking you out of here," he says, his eyes never leaving William.

"No, you're not!" There's such indignation in William's voice it would be humorous were the situation any different. A couple of steps and Chi is standing next to me, extending his hand toward mine. I take it and pull on my dress at the same time, in a failed attempt at regaining my modesty.

"Don't you dare touch her! She's mine!" William shouts with outrage and irritation.

Chi curses, drops my hand, and takes a few strides toward William, fast. He shoves him against the wall violently and presses his forearm against his throat.

"Watch your mouth or I won't be responsible for my actions!" He hisses the words with venom, spit coming out with fury while his chest heaves and he breathes heavily, his body shaking with frenzy.

He lets go of William and turns back to me. "Thia, we're leaving. Now! We don't have much time." He grabs my hand and pulls the dress up over my shoulder; it had fallen down again. His expression is sullen, his upset clearly coming through. The hurt and rage in his eyes pierce my heart like arrows.

We head toward the door, but William reaches for my arm. He grasps at my wrist with so much insistence it hurts.

"She's mine. I don't know who the hell you think you are! You want a girl? Get one of your own. Unless your position isn't good enough for that!"

Chi turns to him, his eyes blazing with wrath. When his fist meets William's chin, he hits him so hard that William stumbles backward and has to reach for the wall for support. William massages his jaw with his fingers, in shock that Chi even dared touch him. He recovers quickly though and comes for Chi, but Chi is too fast for him. He takes William by surprise and pins him hard against the wall. Chi is beside himself with rage, holding William by the throat, his fist raised, ready to lash out at William, but I pull on his arm from behind and plead with him to stop.

Chi looks back at me before throwing William a glare filled with such loathing that William shudders and recoils. Chi drops his grip on William and turns to me. He strokes my cheek with his thumb, just once.

"Let's go," he tells me. His eyes fall on the strangulation marks around my neck. Chi turns to William and takes one step forward, just enough to make William flinch. "Touch her like that again and I'll cut your damn throat! I swear I'll fucking kill you!"

Chi doesn't wait for William to respond; he grabs my hand and pulls me after him. We exit the room and he leads me down the emergency staircase all the way into the street. We run a few blocks before he drags me into a dark alley. There he pulls me to him and looks into my eyes. "Are you all right?"

I nod though I feel anything but fine right now. Something's been taken from me against my will, something precious. But I can't tell him that. The pain in his eyes makes me want to lie. I should spare him my misery, my shame. The tears reach my eyes and I blink them back inside. I suppress the sob rising in my throat, but not fast enough. Chi pulls me hard against his chest, the wounds inside him reopening slowly under the salt of the tears I can no longer suppress.

"It's okay. It'll be okay, Thia," he says and kisses my hair while holding me tight.

I want to believe him. I can't find the strength in my heart to disagree with him. My sanity is slipping away, so I choose to trust him and ignore the little voice inside my head whispering maliciously that nothing's going to be fine ever again.

Chi cups my face with his hands and kisses me with all the despair he has felt tonight. I abandon myself to him, letting him take me to a place of comfort as he wraps his arms around me, protecting me from the ugliness of tonight's events. He kisses my tears away gently and brushes both my cheeks in turn with his lips before wiping them off with his thumbs. His compassion and the tenderness of his touch clash with William's previous callousness.

When Chi pulls away, a sudden flash of reality awakens me. "They'll be coming for us," I say. "They'll be coming for *you.*"

"We need to leave. I know a place we can stay for now while we make plans for later."

He moves his head around the corner, to sweep the alley with his eyes quickly before pulling me behind him in a hurry to escape. We start running, one street after another. Passers-by look at us strangely. It's not common for proper girls to tear through the streets. The last thing we need is to draw attention to ourselves, so we slow down and walk at a normal pace. Chi takes my hand. His eyes are still shifting from side to side, like a prey being chased.

"William must've called the authorities by now and reported you missing," he says, taking another look behind us. "He'll tell them who I am, and when the portrait gets out, we'll need to be far from here."

We keep on walking.

"We can't go to the Wilcoxes' house; it's too dangerous. William knows me, and the authorities will make it there in no time. We'll go to another friend's place. He's part of the Underground. He lives in the slums outside Eboracum City. Everyone goes to him when they need a place to crash. That's his job, to rescue people who need help and shelter."

Chi and I walk for at least a couple of hours, taking nothing but dark alleys, hiding in the shadows when we hear cars go by. It's completely dark outside. The night is like a cloak around us when we finally reach our destination.

Chapter 23

The houses here are made of concrete. They are all falling apart with cracks showing through the walls. I've never been to this part of the metropolis before, but I've seen places like this during my train rides. Everyone in this neighborhood is probably sleeping after a long day spent at work tending to the rich. Guilt seizes me as I look around. I didn't choose where I was born or what class I came from, but I still feel responsible for the way these people are living. Crushed by the wealthy and persecuted like parasites, the poor's access to water and resources has been reduced to the bare minimum needed to survive. These houses they live in belong to the authorities; they are just rented to the poor. Any rebellion can lead to the poor losing lodging and access to food. I clench my teeth and follow Chi through the streets.

When he finds the house we've been looking for, he follows the instructions and code he was given by the Underground. He knocks a few times using the required pattern. An older gentleman opens the door almost immediately, as if he were waiting for us. He's excessively skinny and a bit disheveled. His skin is ivory white and wrinkled. He glances into the street behind us before letting us in.

The house is decrepit, and the furniture is old and worn-out. But the place feels cozy and welcoming, like an old antique shop. The kitchen opens to the living room and dining room area. Oliver leads us to some wooden chairs and invites us to sit down.

Chi explains the precariousness of our situation. "We need a place to stay tonight, Oliver. I'm sorry for dragging you into all this."

"Well, that's why I'm here, aren't I? You guys can stay here for a few days. We'll contact Taylor in the morning and see what he advises us to do."

Oliver looks at me and takes my hands in both of his, holding them tightly in a gesture of comfort. "It's a pleasure having you among us, Thia. Recruits are always welcome and it was courageous of you to run away. Chi told us all about you. We knew it'd only be a matter of time before this happened."

His welcoming warmth dissipates my original fear of being blamed for all this trouble.

"You can stay in the guest room. There are two cots there. They're not comfortable, but it's better than sleeping on the streets."

Chi and Oliver talk for a while longer. It sounds like they haven't seen each other for quite some time.

"Taylor said things are on the move and the attack's going to happen soon. We're still working on getting more man power and weapons."

I'm not sure what attack he's talking about, and Chi doesn't fill me in. Oliver stands up and we follow him to a small bedroom. It's not luxurious, but it has a quaint, homey feel to it. I couldn't care less about opulence right now. I am free for the first time in my life; it's exhilarating.

***

It's strange for me to sleep in the same room as Chi, but his presence comforts me. He fell asleep after just a few minutes, and I've spent the last hour watching him. He's lying on his stomach, with his arms around his head. His mouth is open, but he doesn't snore. He looks so innocent in this position, with his messy hair spread over his forehead and his eyelids closed to bring him peace. I try to stay awake and drink him in for as long as I can, but eventually, slumber takes over and darkness wraps its coat around me.

At some point during the night, Chi comes to lie down on my cot. He pulls the cover back over me; it had fallen to my feet as I was fighting my way through a vivid nightmare. Chi pulls me to him and wraps his arms around my stomach as he spoons me close against him. His lips brush against my hairline and his sweet words pour into my ear. "Shhh, you're safe now, Thia. Go back to sleep."

I nestle against his body, snuggle in his warmth, and sleep soundly for the rest of the night. I only open my eyes when the sunlight comes streaming through the window. Chi is gone. I get up and put on my clothing from last night. I step out of the bedroom. Chi and Oliver are standing around the kitchen counter, along with a tall, handsome man. His features are highly defined and his skin dark brown. His head is shaved, his nose is long and straight, and his plump lips are set in a stern line. His appearance radiates physical strength, and his expression is closed and uninviting.

He looks up at me as I walk in. His eyes pin on mine, observing me with slight suspicion. This man's intensity makes me uncomfortable, and I don't dare move closer.

"I'm guessing you're Thia," he finally says, without introducing himself.

I nod shyly.

"This is Taylor," Chi says, beckoning for me to join them.

Taylor holds out his hand to me. "It's nice to finally meet you, Thia."

Not once do his sharp eyes leave my face. I walk to him and grab his hand. His grasp is straightforward.

"Taylor is one of the leaders of the Underground," Chi explains. "He's in charge of our state with four other leaders. He's also a journalist and a liaison inside the authorities."

I look at Taylor again. His eyes shift between Chi and me. "The news on TV is all about you two and the authorities are on the look-out. We need to be careful. I have a meeting to hold. I didn't want everyone to come here and raise suspicion among the neighbors, so I'm taking you to my house."

"Is it safe to go places if they're looking for us?" I ask.

"We'll ride in my car," Taylor replies.

"You have a car?" I ask, stunned.

"Yes, I'm a journalist, so it's pretty much as if I work for the authorities. They keep a strong grip on the news. So yes, I have good resources and a car—all perks coming with my glorifying job," he says with a hint of sarcasm.

"So, what are we meeting about?" Oliver asks.

"I want to see how we are faring so far, with the weaponry and all that. Let's go. We'll talk at my place."

We head out. Taylor has parked his car in the back of the house. After locking the door, Oliver goes to sit in the front seat, Chi and I in the back.

"There's a comforter in the back seat. When we are downtown, you guys will have to hide under it."

"Nice memories," Chi says.

"Sorry, man. That's the way it is."

Chi rolls his eyes.

After riding for a while, Chi turns to me. "I haven't told you about the attack yet."

Taylor sends me a look through the rearview mirror before shifting his gaze to Chi. When their eyes meet, Taylor acquiesces with a motion of his head. Chi clears his throat while rubbing his neck.

"You remember how I told you my parents were taken away, right?" he asks, as if I could ever forget something like that. I nod.

"The Underground has been working on locating various camps in the state," he continues.

"And you're going to attack those camps," I simply state.

He pauses for a second. "Yes. Our group will target Camp 19. That's the camp where my parents are held. It's the closest camp to us, located between Eboracum City and the Catskills."

I don't like hearing that there is a camp so close to here. Tremors shoot down my back and I bite my lower lip.

"I'm coming," I say.

"What?" Chi's eyes narrow slightly.

"I'm coming with you to get your parents," I explain.

"It'll be dangerous, Thia," he protests.

I shake my head. "I'm not going to stay behind without moving a finger while your parents and all those other people are imprisoned to work in a camp. If you're going, I'm going too."

Chi casts a glance at Taylor through the rearview mirror, his eyes pleading with Taylor to agree with him on this one.

But Taylor's lips are now curled up into a grin, his eyebrow raised at Chi mockingly.

"I like her," he says. "You'd better keep her."

When we arrive close to downtown Eboracum City, Chi and I lie on the backseat. Taylor lives in the suburbs, on the other side of town. After twenty more minutes, we reach his house and he backs his car into the garage. Then he closes the metallic door so we can finally get out. I have cramps from the uncomfortable ride and I'm sweaty from the warmth of the cover. Chi stretches his legs and runs his hand through his messy hair.

We follow Taylor into his house. His job does give him access to nice possessions indeed. His spacious home and the luxurious items here equal those of people with the best status in society. That's how the authorities keep leashes on their journalists and control over the media, by offering them resources they wouldn't have gotten otherwise. Belongings can become addictive. Some people would do just about anything—dreadful things—to live in a house like this.

We enter the living room, where a few people have gathered already—most of them women. They are of all ages, and based on their outfits, from all levels of society.

"All right, we're back, everyone," Taylor calls out to them. "I invited a bunch of you over to discuss the progress in the camps and get your reports back."

Everyone turns toward us. Their eyes shift to me right away; some of them observe me with curiosity and some others with doubt. Chi wraps his arm around my neck protectively, resting it on my shoulders.

"I'm sure a lot of you saw the news already. Our Chi here is quite popular with the media right now, though not in a good way. Just to make it clear, he obviously did not kidnap Thia as the media is claiming. Thia was attacked by her promised fiancé during her pre-nuptial night, and she joined our group willingly. I don't need to explain to you ladies what that's like. But that's not why we're here today. So, let's all welcome our new member Thia and move on."

Everyone is still looking at me, but then someone moves forward, taking the attention away. He's a strong man, with full blond hair on top, completely shaved on the sides.

"Liam says everything's going well in Camp 19. I've met him a few times in the past couple of weeks," the person says. "He hasn't heard anything suspicious. He's rallied a few guards to our cause, and he's trying to figure out how to access the central security system to turn it off when we arrive. He's already managed to free a few prisoners each day. He'll keep on doing that until we arrive."

"Thanks, James," Taylor replies.

"James works for the authorities," Chi explains to me. "He drives the food from Camp 19 to the poor areas. He'll take us into the camp when we're ready to attack."

"Where is Liam taking those prisoners?" a small girl inquires of Taylor before Chi can tell me anything else. She's petite, with beautiful features, long natural blonde hair, and a black uniform reminiscent of the ones worn by the officers.

"I'm sorry, Tina, you know that for our own security, I can't tell you guys everything," Taylor replies, with a sudden cold look on his face. Then he turns toward an incredibly tall and handsome man, whose midnight brown hair and tanned skin are accentuated by sharp electric blue eyes.

"How are we doing with the weaponry, Chase?" Taylor asks him.

"It's been real hard getting the guns from the military houses without raising suspicion. Craig's been modifying the records. He's over-supplying the place to our benefit. The warehouse is holding a nice collection now, plus all the guns you've got here already. We should have a weapon for each person that's going to Camp 19."

Chi pulls me closer to him. "Craig works in the military. He used to live in Chase's old neighborhood in New York City."

I send Chi a quizzical glance. "I thought New York City was completely flooded and off-limit."

He shakes his head. "That's just a rumor spread among the upper-class. Old Manhattan is uninhabitable, yes, but there's a portion of New York City that's still above water. When the rich fled the city during Hurricane Vega, the poor were left behind. The ones who survived took over what was left. The place is deteriorating, but there's still a bunch of people living there."

"How do you know all that?" I ask.

"Chase explained it all to me. I just told you he used to live in those slums."

"Used to? Where does he live now?"

Chi doesn't get a chance to reply because he's cut off by Chase's interaction with Taylor.

"We've got two trucks to carry the prisoners out. We'll just steal more of them when we get there," Chase says. "I've already found a place to hide all the trucks after we hit the camp."

"Awesome!" Taylor replies before turning to a gorgeous, muscular girl. Her skin is dark, her cheekbones high, and her lips full. Her hair is styled in a beautiful mohawk that's falling loosely over her eyes and down her neck, the sides of her head shaved.

"Kayla, babe, are the apartments operational?" Taylor asks her.

Kayla moves forward and wraps her arms around Taylor's waist. She looks up at him with adoration. Her mouth has spread into a warm smile. "Yes. We won't have electricity, of course, but the water tanks on top of the buildings will provide cold water. We've got candles, batteries, generators, food, and all that. It's been tough getting the resources over there, but Jenna's done a great job getting everything ready."

"Great!" Taylor exclaims. "That'll give us a safe place to crash when things go down." He turns to us. "I want everyone to remain discreet. Keep an ear out for anything suspicious. When the camps are free, our correspondents in the media will let the information loose. We need to make a big splash and wake up this drowsy population. They've been asleep for way too long. It's time they found out where their resources come from. It's time they knew where the authorities are keeping their family members. The civilians need to open their eyes and see this system for what it is. Let's expose its flaws once and for all." Everyone around the group cheers at that. "Let's show them how this system has failed us."

Everyone nods enthusiastically. Some people even hoot while some others clap loudly. When Taylor is done talking, he looks at Chi and me. He beckons for us to follow him to a different room. We exit the living room, walk across the hall, and enter a large study.

"Chi, you need to be careful. The authorities are really pissed at you, and we can't afford for them to spot you. Stay put at Oliver's house until this all blows over. Same thing goes for you, Thia."

"Why do they think Chi kidnapped me?" I ask.

"They just made it up to make him look worse. Don't worry about it. Just stay put and don't bring attention to yourselves. I'm glad you met some of the gang, Thia. If anything happens, reach me here. Learn this address by heart. I'll take you guys back to Oliver's place now."

He taps Chi on the shoulder and steps out of the room. Chi pulls me to him, takes my hand in his, and we walk out of the study. On my way out, I notice a girl staring at us. She's the petite blonde girl who was talking earlier. Tina I think her name is. She looks at Chi and averts her gaze when she notices me observing her.

"Who's that girl?" I ask Chi.

"That's Tina. She's an officer working undercover for the Underground."

Chi doesn't explain further. Tina sends him one last glance, and pain flickers through her eyes swiftly before her cheeks turn crimson red.

Chapter 24

This morning, the TV is on in Oliver's living room. It's an old machine; the image is full of static jumping up and down. Oliver is sitting on his old couch, watching the news. We all know the media is full of lies; it's a mendacious device that has been used for years to deceive and control the minds of the weak. Oliver, however, thinks it's important to stay informed. He believes the lies tell a certain truth and that it's up to us to read between the lines.

Today though, the news is different and I can't remain indifferent. It touches close to home and strikes me right to my core. Chi's picture is on the screen, and the words coming through the speakers send chills down my spine. It's as if the journalist is looking straight at me as he points at a picture of Chi. It's silly because, of course, he's not talking to me specifically.

"This young man is highly dangerous. The authorities are looking for him, and any indications regarding his whereabouts are welcome. Do not approach the suspect under any circumstances! I repeat; he is highly dangerous! Call 911 if you see him or believe you may have spotted him. Any information is vital at this point."

I turn around to look at Chi. My heartbeat quickens while he remains calm. He frowns and crosses his arms over his chest, but he doesn't seem to feel the same kind of fear I'm experiencing. The news that follows is like a stab to my heart, and the world around me starts spinning out of control.

"Chi Richards, also known as Jordan Wilcox, has been fleeing the authorities for the past two years. He's wanted for the murder of Willow Jenison. The authorities lost track of him two years ago, and they've been searching for him ever since. It appears Richards was living with the Wilcox family under the false identity of their son Jordan. The Wilcoxes are also on the loose, and the authorities need them in custody as well. They are wanted for harboring a criminal and concealing the disappearance of their son. Chi Richards is also wanted for the kidnapping of Thia Clay. It is imperative for us to find him before he kills her the way he did his previous girlfriend. Any information is crucial and will be generously rewarded."

The words boomerang inside my head: "murder" and "criminal." Dark spots appear and cloud my vision as shivers take hold of my body. I close my eyes, bend over, and breathe deeply. I will not faint!

I turn to Chi. His eyes are still pinned on the TV. They are wide open with fear and anger. He senses my gaze upon him and sends me a look. When his eyes meet mine, they plead with me to understand. He tries to tell me something, but I don't listen. I'm not sure I truly care at this point. I've been misled again. But this time, it's the one person I trusted the most who has lied to me. My heart suddenly cracks at the edges, slowly breaking apart. The fissure widens as seconds pass me by. *How could I be so stupid?* I know nothing about Chi, nothing concrete really.

I'm so disappointed I'm suffocating. I need air. I walk past him so fast I could be running. He tries to grab my arm, but I push him away. I'm surprised by my own strength as he stumbles backward. The small of his back hits a table, and he clenches his teeth upon impact, his eyes darkening instantly.

"Thia!" he calls me as I run for the door.

"Thia!" His voice is louder now, more insistent, but I don't pay heed.

I've had it with the lies. I don't want to hear his voice right now. I'm not sure I want to hear his voice ever again. If Chi didn't tell me about this, it means that the news could be true.

Something inside my heart tells me that it can't be real. But I'm not sure I can trust my instincts anymore. My instincts led me here, to follow Chi. *What if they tricked me into believing something I shouldn't have?* I wanted Chi to be the perfect person he appeared to be. *How foolish of me! Of course, no one is perfect!* But this is a bigger skeleton in the closet than I expected. And then, it hits me: Chi told me he had never been with a girl before. His lies feel like small daggers plunged into my heart. It hurts to think of him with someone else and to know that he lied about it, too.

Chi comes out of the house. He walks to me quickly, just a few strides needed for him to reach me. His eyes are filled with pain, beseeching still, but I ignore him. He's right in front of me and I start running away, but he's too fast. He grabs my arm and holds it tightly. His strength no longer comforts me the way it used to. Now, it just terrifies me.

He pulls me to him and turns me around so I have to face him. He grabs my shoulders and holds on so hard I can't move. I try to fight him, but he's too strong. I press my hands against his chest to push him back. He grabs my arms and holds them together in front of him in a lock I can't loosen. Fear is telling me to run, but Chi is holding me still and I can't move. He looks me deep in the eyes, but I turn my face away.

"Thia, it's all a bunch of lies. It's complete bullshit." He pauses. "Thia! Look at me!" His voice grows louder now, his tone more assertive. "Thia, look at me!"

But I'm not taking orders from him. I will not let him or anyone control the way I think or what I do ever again! I want to tell him that. I want to yell at him. I want to slash his face. I'm so emotional, almost hysterical, that I start crying in anger. I hate myself for it. I don't want him to see me cry. I don't want him to know that he hurt me or think he can comfort me. I don't want him to mistake my reaction for sorrow when all I'm feeling is rage.

"Thia, I did *not* kill that girl," he hisses.

That's too much and I shriek, spitting the words in his face with vitriol. "That girl?' Who was 'that girl?' Did you know her? I saw the look on your face when her picture came up on the screen, Chi."

I'm so mad I stutter and can't keep my thoughts straight. I can't think at all. I just want to hurt him the exact same way he hurt me. I can't touch him physically, so I use my words like venom. "You lied to me, Chi, and you hid things from me. You said you'd never been with a girl before. You said you'd never looked at girls until you saw me. And now, the news tells me about her. I have to hear from the guy on TV that you killed her!"

"It's a lie!" Chi is yelling too now, with rage rising to the surface. "I did *not* kill her!"

"And I guess I'm supposed to believe that! After all your lies, I'm supposed to trust you and believe you!"

I'm still shouting, and my head hurts from the anger boiling inside. Chi blinks a few times as though I've just slapped him in the face. The hurt is back in his eyes, but I don't care. He won't catch me feeling pity for him again.

"You truly believe I could have done that? You really think I could have killed a girl?" His voice is soft now, shaking. His eyes well up and dry just as quickly.

"Why not?" I reply with fury, though I'm not sure what to believe anymore. The news on TV doesn't make any sense.

"Thia, you know me! Look inside you and tell me you honestly believe I could have hurt a girl. They also claim I kidnapped you, and you know that's not true. It's all lies. They're looking for reasons to have me arrested."

The truth is I still don't know Chi that well, but I can't believe the media. I don't want to believe that he could have done something so horrible.

"If you truly believe that I could have hurt a girl—if you don't trust me—I don't see why you should be with me at all. I can't believe you would even think that," he says in a low, soothing voice, but I can tell he's still livid. It's like the calm before a storm. The anguish is still present in his eyes. He shakes his head with disappointment. He's about to let me go, but he seems to think better of it.

"That girl was my girlfriend, yes. But I hardly even knew her. She was an Unwanted, like me. I don't know why my parents even bothered finding someone for me. My mom said I needed someone to rely on because they wouldn't be there forever. She said no one wants to end up alone. Willow was my best option—my *only* option. She was the daughter of my parents' friends. My mom thought I might grow fond of her in time. She said we didn't have to go through with a relationship if I didn't want to, but that I should let time tell what was best. Willow was shy, like you, and extremely fragile. After a while, I took it upon myself to protect her. I thought maybe I could do that. But I never looked at her that other way. I didn't like her like that. She was a friend and that's all."

He sighs. "Then my parents were taken away and I had to run. A few months later, I heard on the news that Willow and her family were found dead at their house. It looked like the authorities had gotten rid of them to use as an excuse to frame me and execute me on sight. Then one day, the search stopped. I didn't kill her, Thia. I don't know who did."

"Why didn't you try to find out?" I ask.

"I can't do everything at the same time! I've been busy trying to locate my parents. I can't do it all! And what's the point? No one would believe me anyway."

"Why didn't you tell me?"

"And what was I supposed to say? 'Hi, I'm Chi. Oh, by the way, I'm wanted for the murder of my girlfriend.' Great intro, isn't it?" He shakes his head in exasperation. "I didn't know how to tell you. I've been scared of losing you. I had no status or future to offer you. I couldn't add the criminal charges to the mix."

"Your parents don't believe in the system. Why would your mom look for a girl for you? That doesn't make any sense!" I exclaim.

"She didn't force Willow on me. She just hoped that magic would do its trick. I didn't have to date Willow. In the end, it was my choice."

He leans his forehead against mine and lets go of my arms to cup my face with his hands. "Thia, I would *never* hurt someone like Willow. She was sweet, and kind, and innocent. Please, you have to believe me."

He holds me tightly against him, his face buried against my neck, and I let him. I want to believe him. I slouch into him, my thoughts in turmoil, and we remain like this for a few minutes, with my chest pressed against his and my treacherous heart pleading for my brain to please give him another chance.

But when the sounds of sirens echo in the distance, our reconciliation ends abruptly. We both freeze. Fear flickers through Chi's eyes, a mirror to the primitive terror filling my own heart.

"Run! Now!"

He grabs my hand and we race toward the door, but it's too late. The police cars are here; they're flashing their front lights at us, the sirens loud and deafening.

"Chi Richards, you're under arrest," the officer's voice comes out of a speakerphone. "Put your hands in the air now. Do not try to run or we will shoot."

Chi raises his hands in the air slowly. I stop. I want us to run as fast as we can, far from here, but it's too late and there is no escape. There are four police cars here now, and we're surrounded. Chi looks calm, but I know he's frantic underneath the surface. His eyes shift around as if he's looking for a way out. Holding a rifle, an officer walks slowly toward Chi, as if he were as dangerous as they claimed on the news. It would be comical were the situation not so dire. The officer approaches him and forces handcuffs on his wrists. Then he shoves him forward brutishly and Chi stumbles. I gasp. The officer pushes him toward the car, with the tip of his barrel pressed against Chi's back.

Chi turns his head and peers at me. He's serious, without a smile poking through. He appears serene, but I know better. He sits in the car, and as the officer closes the door behind him, Chi just keeps staring at me. An urge almost pushes me forward—a need to scream his name, run to the car, and free him. But they'll shoot me on the spot if I move.

An officer comes to me. "Thia Clay, you are to follow us as well."

My heart is hammering hard inside my ribcage. I have trouble breathing. My legs are shaking so badly I might fall, but my limbs somehow carry me as I walk to the police car. I keep my eyes on Chi the entire time, but the vehicle he's in starts up and drives away. Soon, I lose sight of him completely. The officer opens the back door to the vehicle and lets me sit inside. As the car pulls away, I catch a glimpse of three more officers breaking into Oliver's house. They will arrest him too, unless he's heard everything and escaped already. This is bad, really bad! Without Oliver as a liaison, the Underground will be weakened.

I hope the officers don't know about the Underground and that Oliver is simply wanted for hosting us, a terrible offense in and of itself.

I can't believe I was so dumb as to believe Chi killed his girlfriend. Of course the media lied. They do it all the time. I'm furious at myself for triggering a fight between us. And now, it's too late to apologize.

We drive for a long time. I expect them to take me to jail, but then I recognize the road we're taking. I'm not sure if this is better or worse than going to the police station, but the officers are taking me home.

Dread fills my heart. I'm about to face my family. And even worse, I will have to deal with Mother. This reunion won't be pretty. I'll end up homeless. William will reject me after what happened, and my parents will never forgive me. *What am I to become? What am I going to do?*

Then I think about Chi, and my despair worsens. I actually don't care what happens to me. I just want Chi to be okay. I wish we had never met. Not because I don't want to be with him. Not because of how this is sure to ruin me. But because I refuse for our relationship to cost him his life.

Chapter 25

The officer opens the door on my side of the car and helps me out. I take deep breaths—three, four, five, ten of them—but nothing helps me relax. I'm shivering. I try to find my bearing as I set my foot on the ground. I get out of the vehicle, and two officers lead me to the house. One of them rings the chimes. Someone comes to the door—Emily. She calls for my mother. Footsteps rush down the stairs and I start shaking harder.

And then, here she is, my cold mother, except that she's not cold at all. There is relief in her eyes where superiority usually lies, and she comes running to me. She pulls me into her arms and holds me in a strong embrace. I'm confused. I don't understand.

"Are you okay? We were so worried," she says.

I don't get it at first, but then I remember the words on TV. Mother thought I'd been kidnapped. *Is it possible William didn't even tell my parents what really happened? Is it possible that he lied and hid the truth from everyone? But why would he do that?*

"I'm fine. I'm okay," I reply.

Guilt pierces through me for lying and creating so much trouble. But when Chi appears in my mind, I know I'd do it all over again if given the chance. I won't be able to stay here. I have to find him, somehow. I can't just let him rot wherever they took him.

Mother leads me to the living room and has me sit down on the leather couch. The officers follow us in. They'll be here for a while. They still need to interrogate me. I don't want my mother to be here. There are things I have to say and I don't want her to hear them. But she sits next to me. Too bad, because I need to let it out, no matter the consequences. I will be thrown out of this house, but I will not lie. I won't pretend Chi is something he's not. I won't even try to save myself, not at the cost of his reputation.

An officer sits across from me, on a different couch, and he starts with the questions right away. "Did Chi Richards tell you why he chose you? Why he kidnapped you?"

I clear my throat and take a breath. For a while, I say nothing. I don't want to talk, not to these people. They wouldn't understand. But the officer repeats his questions. When I finally answer, my voice trembles at first. But when I remember the way these people have treated Chi, what he had to go through his whole entire life because of them, anger finds its way through my veins, pumping hard, flaring. I speak and whatever I have to say, it won't be pleasant; it won't be what they want to hear.

"Chi did not kidnap me."

"Yes, of course he did," my mother interrupts.

"William Fox reported you missing, saying you were kidnapped by Chi Richards right under his nose," the officer insists. "There was nothing he could do about it."

"No, Chi did not kidnap me."

"But, of course—" my mother protests again.

This ticks me off. I raise my voice now, seriously mad. "No! I'm telling you! Chi did not kidnap me! I told him about my pre-nuptial night with William and he came for me. I followed him willingly. He did not kidnap me."

"But how is that possible?" my mother asks. The sense of betrayal underneath her tone stabs me deeply, but I don't let it take me down.

The officer cuts her off. "So, let me get this straight. You walked out on your promised fiancé, with an Unwanted, on your pre-nuptial night? Is that what you're telling us?"

The self-righteousness and disgust ooze out of him like something putrid, as if I were some excrement he has just walked on, soiling his shoe in the process. I'm boiling on the inside now, but I can't take my anger out on him or I'll get arrested for sure. Assault on an officer is punishable by death. I have to pretend to be the dumb girl I'm sure he thinks I am. I need to keep calm and make it through this until I find a way to get Chi out of this mess. But my tone is short and harsh when I answer. I can't quite help myself. "Yes, yes I did!"

"And how did you meet Chi Richards?" he asks.

"That is none of your concern," I reply, a bit harder than I meant to.

I'm surprised at how bold I'm being. The words come out before I can think. But the way these people have been treating Chi is driving me over the edge. Instead of reprimanding me, the officer sends me a cursory glance of arrogance.

"You do realize that boy killed his promised fiancée, don't you?"

"No, he did not, and she was not his promised fiancée," I snap at him.

He sneers. "Awh, is that what he told you?"

Faked pity rises through his voice. The officer thinks I'm an idiot who got swept off her feet by some lying scoundrel.

"You don't know him," I simply reply.

"Oh, and I suppose you do?" he retorts, snickering at me again.

His snide remark finds resonance inside me this time, and it hurts. After all, it is true I don't know Chi as much as I wish I did. But I believe him. He exposed too many lies used by the authorities to cover things up. I know how they've been swaying people into believing in their perfect vision of the world. I'd rather be on Chi's side than theirs, no matter what. But the officer doesn't stop. He means to break me down.

"Did you know your boyfriend is part of a rebellious group trying to overthrow our government?"

Chills course through my body. They know about the Underground. Fear grabs me by the throat like a tight vise around my windpipe. They leave me no other choice. Now, I do have to act dumb, or I could get arrested for complicity in rebellion. I can't show that I know anything. I have to pretend Chi didn't share any information with me. I'm sure the officers have been trained to see through lies, but my whole life has been a big wide stage, filled with pretence. This isn't hard for me. I hold his gaze, bolder than I truly feel.

"He is not," I exclaim, faking indignation. I let myself fit this role I'm playing: I am a girl who didn't know the horrible truth about her boyfriend and is only just now discovering it all.

"Yes, he is. He is the son of criminals and he is a felon himself."

"He is not!" I protest and start crying.

I want the officer to believe I'm crying out of frustration and fear for myself, but I'm actually worried sick about Chi. I'm not sure I'll ever get to see him again. The officer watches me like I'm truly idiotic, my tears fooling him into thinking what I want him to believe. But then, he insists on telling me how Chi killed his girlfriend, how he bashed her head in and left her to die on her parents' kitchen floor. He explains how Chi's parents are criminals serving time in jail. My mother gasps. All his lies fill me with rage. Chi has spent the past two years looking for his parents. They are not felons. They are ordinary people whose only crime was to refuse to kill their second son or give him away. They wanted to give him a chance at life, and because of that, they were arrested and put in a work camp.

I'm getting riled up. His perversion of the truth makes my blood boil, and the anger inside me grows stronger. But I pretend to be upset at Chi instead. This is the best way to protect his plans.

"You'd better be careful whom you meddle with from now on, miss," the officer says. "Your promised fiancé believes you were kidnapped. It might be best to leave it at that. I shall see you again soon."

The officer is treating me like some dumb girl; that's exactly what I was hoping for. He must believe Chi didn't respect me enough to reveal his plans. But before he gets a chance to leave, I want to know how they found us at Oliver's house. I'm sure my stupid tantrum is what brought attention to us, but I need to make sure.

"Well, I shouldn't give you that information," the officer says, "but someone sent us a tip saying they knew your exact location. I guess the Underground can't trust all their buddies."

This news feels like a knife, and I have to swallow the bile rising to my mouth. The officer sends me a self-satisfied, sardonic smile as he stands up. Mother walks him to the door, but I remain behind. I'm relieved my statement was taken at face value. It's easy to pretend you're stupid and careless when you're a female in this world. Men never give us enough credit.

My mother wishes the officer good night and closes the door behind him with more force than necessary. Her footsteps tell me she's returning to the living room. My stomach flips. I fear her more than I fear the authorities. I sit up straight and prepare myself to face the wrath coming my way. My mother closes the glass-doors to the living room after telling Emily we are not to be disturbed under any circumstances. Mother comes to sit down next to me. She takes both my hands in hers, and I jerk back, surprised by her gesture. I'm not used to physical contact with her. I don't understand what this means.

"Thia," she starts, her voice low, concerned.

I don't dare look at her. I know what's coming, so I bow my head in submission. A tear rolls down my cheek. I'm still conflicted. I feel guilty for bringing this trouble on my family, for being brought home by officers.

"Thia, look at me," she says, but not unkindly.

I force my eyes to face hers. Her features reveal no emotions. I can't tell what she's thinking. This is quite typical of her, ever illusive and impossible to read.

"Thia, what did you do, dear?"

I swallow a sharp breath. My mother just used an endearing term. *Is this a trick? Is she trying to get me to confess?* I'm at a loss what to do, what to say. But I decide to speak the truth. "Those are all lies. Chi is not a murderer, Mother."

"But why did you do it? William was so frantic. He was so worried about you."

"Mother, William knows," I say.

She blinks at me and questions fill her eyes. She's not as intimidating as I thought she would be. She's really calm, her attitude inviting.

"William knows this wasn't a kidnapping," I explain. "It happened right in front of him, and he knows I don't love him. I don't know why he lied to you about it."

"You mean that he knew you weren't kidnapped and he lied to us, your parents, about it?" she asks, surprised.

"Yes."

She seems disturbed by this. Somehow, William's lies upset her more than my running away with Chi. I don't know what's going on with her, but it's quite unsettling.

"He saw me with Chi before," I confess.

"Before?"

She ponders this new information, and her eyes glaze over, lost in the distance. "Yes, of course. I should have known. I didn't want to believe it, but I could tell something was different about you. I just thought you were worried about the wedding, though that didn't quite explain it. When did you meet him?"

"I met him at the ball, at William's school, and then I lied to you. I'm sorry, Mother. I didn't go to the library all those days; I went to meet Chi."

"Yes, of course. How could I be so blind for so long?"

Her shoulders sag as if she has failed me. I've never seen her like this before. She's always so strong and confident. *Why isn't she yelling at me? Putting me back in my place and kicking me out of the house?*

"Do you know how I met your father?" she asks.

"Well, yes, you were introduced to him through pre-marital arrangements."

"Yes, yes I was." She sighs. "That's how it is for all of us, isn't it? It's safer that way, Thia. I only wanted you to be safe."

"Mother, I don't understand."

"You see, before I met your father, I was a lot like you. I was confused and there was this boy in my life. His name was Tyreese Lefort. I think I was in love with him. But of course, we could never be together. It wasn't up to me to choose whom I wanted to be with. And then, your grandparents introduced me to your father. It was difficult at first. I kept thinking about Tyreese every single day, but I didn't have a choice. It's safer to just obey. It's the best way to protect ourselves. I was hoping that by introducing you to William when you were younger, it would prevent this from happening. I thought maybe you would focus on him and never look at other boys. Now, I realize it was quite foolish of me."

"Mother, nothing could have prevented this from happening. Chi is the one I'm supposed to be with. I can feel it; I just know it."

She's not listening though. She's caught in her thoughts, gone to a different place, a different time.

"You know," she continues. "All those years, not one day has gone by when I haven't thought about Tyreese. I've always wondered what it would have been like, had I been able to date him, or had I had the courage to speak up. But I didn't, so I'll never know. Your father isn't a bad man. I can't complain about the life I've had with him. But I still would have liked to find out what it's like to be with a man one truly loves."

I'm not sure how I feel about this. Of course, I knew she didn't really love my father. After all, marriage was forced upon her. But a part of me has always wanted to believe that love was involved as well. It pains me to hear for a fact that it wasn't. This is a lot to swallow. My mother's new attitude is hard to take in. I don't quite understand it, and I don't know what to think of it. I'm not sure I can trust her.

"I believe that William likes you. I truly do. He isn't a bad man and—"

I have to cut her off because I've truly had enough of hearing how William might be a good match for me. "Mother, I am not going back to William."

This is the first time I've stood up to my mother like this. She looks at me as if truly seeing me for the first time, and different emotions pass through her eyes.

"William attacked me, Mother. If Chi hadn't walked in that night, William would have raped me. He knows I ran away willingly, and he can destroy my life whenever he decides to do so. If I go back to him, I will never be safe."

"I tried to protect you, Thia. All those years, I know I was harsh, but I only did it for your own good. I thought that once you were married, you might finally be out of harm's way. But I realize now that it is too late."

This is too much to take in. All those years, my mother never did anything to show that she cared about me. My feelings, my thoughts, they didn't matter to her. My value has always resided in the profit I could provide my parents through an advantageous marriage. I'm wondering if this is a trick of some sort. I want to tell her about Chi, his story and his parents, but I'm worried she might betray me. The little girl inside me wants to believe I can trust my own mother. I want to have faith that she truly did mean to protect me all along and that she loves me. I've always wanted to believe it, but I'm not sure I should.

"If William demands to see you, I believe it is best to pretend for the time being, for your own good."

My heart aches. *Was Mother lying tonight? Did she pretend to care just to protect her own interests, as always?* Of course, she did.

I speak up. No one's making decisions for me anymore. "Mother, I need to find Chi. I'm leaving, and no one else can know about it."

She blinks at me a few times and exhales a sigh of defeat. "I will think about it, Thia. But if you are to leave, I want Walter to escort you. I do not want you walking the streets alone like some vulgar wench. It's too dangerous. I need time to process all this and ponder your request. Your security is what matters most to me. It seems I can no longer protect you and your life with William is deeply compromised. All I ask in return is that, in the meantime, you keep on pretending and that you do not reject him."

Her voice is sweet and I believe she means well, so I comply—for now.

She pulls me to her chest. I'm so baffled that tears rise to my eyes. My whole life, I've been waiting for this—a kind, loving gesture from my cold mother. Then she pulls away slightly, too quickly. I want to hold her longer. She wipes my eyes with the palms of her hands.

"Always remember, Thia, pretense and silence are a woman's only protections in this world."

She stands up and heads toward the glass doors. She opens them, casts one last glance my way, and walks out. She calls Emily and asks her to help our cook prepare dinner. My father will be back from work soon, and I still need to face him. But I know now that what I told the officer will remain between my mother and me. She will act her part as she does so well, and my father will believe I was kidnapped.

Chapter 26

That evening, the news is filled with images of Chi getting arrested. The authorities need to reassure the population that the criminal is no longer at large and that the situation is under control. Everyone celebrates my getting home safely and away from the dangerous psychopath who kidnapped me. Chi is now a pariah. Even if I find him, it will be difficult for us to hide. It turns my stomach just to hear the things they have to say about him on TV. I'm dizzy with thoughts racing through my mind. Someone tipped off the authorities about our location. I thought it was one of Oliver's neighbors, but based on what the officer said, that isn't so. *Was he trying to confuse me and create chaos in the Underground? Or is it possible someone informed them from the inside?*

If the Underground has spies among the authorities, then it's also possible the authorities have spies among the rebels. If so, the attack on the camps could be jeopardized and things might turn sour quickly. I have to get to Taylor and let him know what I've learned.

***

The next day, William calls our house to speak with my mother. He asks if I may come over and see him. My mother acts as if nothing's the matter as she tells him I'm quite shaken and that it would be nice of him to come over here to visit me instead.

It doesn't take long for him to arrive. The doorbell rings and Emily lets him in. I'm sitting in the living room, pretending I'm reading a book, and I don't move. I really don't want to see him, and I don't plan on making much effort. He walks into the living room. I don't want to face him, but I remind myself that I have to pretend.

I look up. His face is expressionless and cold, quite typical of him. Whatever he may be feeling is hidden behind that wall of ice he built between himself and the world. He comes to sit on the couch by my side, and Emily closes the door behind him.

My mother isn't far. I can hear her rummaging around in the office next door. She doesn't have anything to do in there. She's just spying on us, to make sure everything is going smoothly.

William holds my gaze, and a flicker of emotion crosses his eyes—a spark of resentment mixed with relief.

"Are you well?" he asks.

"Yes, I believe I am."

Silence settles in. I can't return the courtesy of his question after what I did to him. And I don't want him to see how affected I am by what happened to Chi. But I don't need to wait long before he starts talking again. And once he opens up, it's as though he can't stop. His words spill out and his feelings start pouring through for the first time since I met him.

"I'm just trying to understand, you see. I'm trying to figure it out, but I just don't get what you see in him."

Out of everything he could have said, I wasn't expecting this. I thought he was going to tell me our union was officially over. But instead, his voice is shaky with obvious jealousy. *Is it possible he may have liked me the whole time? And that his actions were fueled by more than just pride?*

"I just don't understand. What does he have to offer you?" His voice rises. "You are my promised fiancée. We are to be together! He has no right to be with you! Do you understand? What he did was wrong! And I want to know why you let him."

He sends me a reproachful look filled with pain. I didn't know it was possible, but I actually feel pity for him. All this time, I thought I was a burden on William, something forced upon him. Now, it's as though I'm facing a little boy who's been looking for love his whole life but doesn't quite know how to gain it. And I understand how he feels. I remember the cold look on his mother's face. I wonder how much affection he actually got from her. *Is it possible he never got any at all?*

But no matter what William's feelings may be, there is nothing I can do to soothe him. He still thinks of me as his property, and I won't put up with it anymore. He's been influenced by society for too long. He can't see things my way. He lied about Chi kidnapping me and he didn't do it to protect me. He did it because he truly believes I belong to him and he wants me for himself. I'm his thing, a toy he takes for granted, some prize he never made the effort to win and never even deserved to begin with. And this is his revenge against Chi—to be here with me while Chi is locked up. Of course, I wouldn't have expected him to act any differently. His exposing us was the only reaction I could have expected from him, but it drives me crazy to know that Chi is in danger because of him. It infuriates me that William would think I'm his to keep and that I shouldn't be allowed to make a choice for myself.

"I left with him because he cares for me, William. For the first time in my life, someone actually showed me that I mattered. He shows me respect, and he treats me like a person, not like an object!"

"Is that what you want? For me to treat you like an equal? But don't you see? I shouldn't have to! You are mine, Thia, and you owe me love and respect."

And just like that, any pity I felt for him is gone.

"You just don't get it, do you?" I exclaim, my voice rising. "That's exactly what I'm talking about. Chi would never talk to me like that. I don't owe you love! You can't force someone to love you, William."

"Actually I can! And I demand that you show me respect! It's the least you can do after running away with that scoundrel."

I can't help myself; my slap across his face occurs before I can stop it. The sound of it resonates across the room as the marks of my fingers appear on his cheek. William grabs my wrist in a tight lock, hurting me. He forces my arm behind my back as he snarls viciously, "You will show me respect! Do you understand me?"

That's when my mother walks in. William releases my hand instantly, and Mother acts as if she hasn't noticed the marks on his face or the tension between us.

"Oh, William, how wonderful to see you! Thia has been quite shaken by this whole tragedy. I think she might need some rest now if that's all right with you. But please, do come and visit her again soon. It's always such a pleasure to see you," she dismisses him quickly. She's quite rude in her haste to get rid of him. Though my mother is good at pretending and her voice melts like honey, I can hear the scorn grinding behind her teeth.

William nods slowly. His face has recovered its emotionless façade. He takes a step toward me and grabs my hand. He squeezes it hard as he pulls me to him. He bends over and kisses me. I wince as his lips brush against mine. A cold shiver runs through me when his breath blows against the skin of my cheek. He holds me tightly against him and puts on a show for my mother while whispering in my ear, "I'm not giving you up, Thia! Chi will soon be out of the way for good, and I'll make you mine. What you want doesn't matter! Remember I'll always be the one in control and I can break you, just like this!" He snaps his fingers in my face and I cringe.

He pulls away and smiles at me—a grin devoid of any human warmth—before he inclines his head and wishes my mother a good rest of the day. My mother's eyes have narrowed, now shooting imaginary bullets right through William's back as he walks out.

I sigh in relief when he's gone. I'm still shaking and his words spin inside my head. I don't know what he has in store for me, but I can no longer be a part of this. I have to find Chi, and time is running out. I have to act, and I have to do it tonight.

If anything happens to Chi, I will never forgive myself and a part of me will die with him. It has taken me too long to realize this, but I'd rather be homeless and risk my life than live without him. I explain my plans to Mother and her eyes sadden.

"Walter will take you wherever you need to go," she says.

"Mother, I don't need help. I can do this on my own. There is no need to endanger Walter, really," I protest.

"Walter is coming with you, or you shall find yourself locked inside your bedroom, Thia."

"Fine, Mother."

I know she means well. I go upstairs and start packing. Mother will help me. I know I can count on her now. However, I don't want her to get more involved than she has to. I don't want my decisions to destroy any more lives around me.

Mother knocks on the door and walks in without waiting for my answer.

"So, you truly are leaving, then? Are you sure this is what you want?" she asks. "You can always choose not to go. It's not too late. We can still have the wedding if you want to."

A few days ago, I would have taken this to mean that she didn't care about me and that she only wanted to protect her assets. Now, I understand that there is true concern for me hiding behind her cold words.

"Yes, Mother. I want to do this. I've made my choice. I'm leaving tonight."

"How are you going to reach Chi?" she asks.

"I can't give you any details, Mother. I don't want you in danger. For now, I just need to reach the Underground."

"So, it's true then. There is a rebellious group and Chi is a part of it. I'm not sure how I feel about that, Thia."

"Mother, I can't spend my life with William. You may not realize this, but he means to destroy me and he wants Chi dead. I can't be his wife, and we can't trust him."

She observes me for a while longer before heading to the door.

"Please, come join me downstairs for tea when you're done," she says over her shoulder. "I wish to spend one last afternoon with you. After all, who knows when I may get to see you again."

Her words are sweet, but her voice is devoid of emotions. I don't resent her for it. It's the way she's been for years, hiding her heart and feelings in a vault deeply secured inside her chest. I understand; her attitude no longer wounds me like it used to. She walks out the door and closes it behind her.

I open my closet and frustration arises as soon as I inspect its contents. There is nothing inside that I can use. All my clothes are uncomfortable and inconvenient— nothing but puffy dresses, stifling corsets, and that wedding gown I hope never to see again. I do have my school uniforms though—dark pants and shirts. Those will do. I grab my backpack and arrange my clothes inside. I can't take a lot, just a couple of changes. I also pack some underwear, a towel, and shampoo.

I spot my box of poetry on the floor. It hurts to leave it behind. I don't think I'll be able to come back to retrieve it. I know it's silly and useless, but I decide to take just one notepad—the one containing the poem about grandpa. I make space in the backpack and shove it in there, as well as Chi's book, which I can't possibly leave behind.

I hide the backpack in the closet and head downstairs. I must pretend today is a normal day. I go have tea with my mother. The afternoon drags on, but I try to enjoy it. I've never had any real quality time with Mother before, and I don't know if I'll ever see her again after this. I'm anxious and restless. It's hard for me to sit still and hide my agitation. We spend a long time chatting. I tell her everything about Chi while leaving out the parts about his plans and information about the Underground. She listens carefully and acknowledges that he sounds like a decent boy. Letting me go is still hard on her and she's quite reluctant, but this is no longer her choice to make.

***

When it's time for dinner, I try and remain still. Though my heart is racing, I need to enjoy this moment. Grief swallows my heart; I'll never spend time with my family again. How strange that I spent so much time wanting to get out of here, and yet the moment I'm about to do so, I wish I could stay longer.

My mother invited my brother over at the last minute. She used my recent kidnapping as an excuse for him to be here. Only I know what she truly wanted: one last family meal together.

Though she's great at acting and no emotion is apparent to those who don't look beyond the surface, the sadness still shows in her eyes. Her face is impassive and her voice steady, but she keeps on sending me sideways glances. They roll over my skin, and when I look up, the grief hiding deep beyond her pupils is undeniable. It's horrible, but I find relief in knowing my departure is causing my mother sorrow—not because I want her to feel pain, but because it means that she cares.

Dinner goes by quickly. I try to take it all in, but the fog in my brain won't clear and I'm still restless. When it's over, my brother and his wife depart. I want to hug them and tell them I love them, but that would seem peculiar. I restrain myself and just watch them leave. I snap a mental picture of this moment. My father says goodnight; it's even harder to pretend with him.

Everyone's gone now. I can only leave later when everyone's asleep, so I go to bed as well. Only my mother and I will stay awake. I go through with the plans and let Emily close the drapes in my bedroom while I put on my nightgown. I lie in bed and wait. I grow increasingly impatient.

Finally, the clock indicates midnight and I can rest assured that everyone is in their own bedroom. Mother has arranged for me to meet Walter in front of the house in half an hour.

I push the comforter away and put on my school uniform. In the bathroom, I tie my hair up and tame it in a messy ponytail. Then I reach into the closet in my bedroom and grab my backpack. I open the door to my bedroom, take one last glance behind me, and tiptoe downstairs, doing my best to remain as silent as possible, but the boards squeak despite my best efforts.

Mother is already in the kitchen. She's made a lunchbox for me, surprising me with her touching gesture. "That's for tomorrow, in case you get hungry."

For the first time ever, my mother's voice is shaking and a tear rolls down her cheek. This makes my heart ache. But I don't know how to respond. I'm not used to showing my affection for her. She holds out her arms to me, guiding my reaction. I fall into her embrace and hold her in return. We stay like this for a few seconds before she pulls back. She clears her throat as if she just got caught doing something embarrassing, and she walks back to the counter.

"Walter is waiting for you," she says. Her voice is steady again. She's trying to keep it under control.

"Yes. Thank you, Mother."

And then she says it, the one sentence I've been waiting for my entire life. "I love you, Thia."

And as her words come out, they tear my heart in two, like something one has been waiting for, but that comes too late. The words make it to my brain and I register them, somehow. It doesn't feel real, but I still say it back because I've been wanting to say it for so long.

"I love you too, Mother."

The yearning inside my heart finds relief, and she smiles at me. Then she turns to the counter and starts putting things away. She doesn't want me to see her crying, so I walk out the door. I send her one last glance. Her back is still turned to me, but her shoulders are shaking with grief. Maybe someday I'll be able to forgive myself for this. But it is my decision and I know it's the right one. I close the door silently. Walter is waiting for me. He asks me where we're going and I give him the directions. We walk to the train station. It closes at two a.m., so we have very little time to make it to Taylor's place.

Chapter 27

When we reach Taylor's neighborhood, we get off the train and Walter walks me to the house. He's taking a big risk. If anyone finds out he had anything to do with this, he could get arrested. Despite that, he sat right by my side through the entire ride and didn't flinch or hesitate once. We knock on the door and wait a few seconds. No one comes to open it, so I knock again.

Finally, some shuffling and the sounds of footsteps tell me that someone is coming. The door opens on Kayla. I'm worried I might not be welcome here. After all, they must think it's my fault we got arrested and that Chi is being detained. I still feel horrible about our fight and how it caused us to be spotted. Even if someone told on us and gave our location away, I can't shake this feeling that I am to blame for all this. But Kayla smiles at me with warmth as she lets me in.

Walter remains on the steps. "I need to go now, Miss Thia. Best of luck to you."

"Thank you, Walter. Good-bye."

I have this urge to hug him, but I just stand here instead and watch him leave. Kayla closes the door behind me and yells for Taylor to please get his butt down here. Running feet hit the stairs, and Taylor appears down the hall, wearing nothing but jeans.

He stops in his tracks as his eyes lock on mine. "Thia, I'm so glad you're well! I wasn't expecting you to come here tonight. Did anyone follow you?"

"I don't think so. We took the train and I didn't see anyone. I was careful."

"Okay, good."

My stifled emotions suddenly surface. The truth needs to get out of me, so I babble quickly, "Taylor, this is all my fault. I got upset when I saw the news. Chi had never talked about Willow. I got mad and walked out. I wasn't thinking. I screamed at him in the street, and then the police were there. But the officers told me they got a tip about our location."

I'm not sure I make any sense, but Taylor is in front of me in seconds, grabbing my shoulders with his hands. He presses his fingertip to my lips to shut me up. "Thia, I know."

I just keep on talking though, and as I explain what happened, my thoughts and words come out in an erratic flow.

Taylor shakes me. "Thia, I know," he insists on each syllable as he says it, and I finally listen.

I blink at him, surprised. *How can he know? What does he know?*

"Thia, we have men in the police force. When someone gives tips about the Underground and what we're doing, I know about it fairly quickly. It was Tina. She made the mistake of calling them when Bryan Harris was on the job. He's an officer working for me. He advised me of her betrayal almost immediately. We believed she was on our side, but it appears she wasn't."

"Who's Tina?" I ask.

Kayla steps forward and takes over the conversation while leading me into the living room. "Tina was one of our members, a short girl with blonde hair. We never fully trusted her, to be honest. She was here the other day. I don't know if you remember her."

I search my mind for a short blonde girl and remember the one who had spoken during the meeting, asking for the location of the refugees before looking at me strangely.

"I guess she was jealous," Kayla adds. "She's had a crush on Chi for quite a while, but he never really cared about her. He blew her off and told her he had other things going on because he had to find his parents. I guess she got mad when he walked in here with you. Honestly, it kind of surprised us too when he got involved in a relationship. That probably bruised Tina's ego."

"She called the police, jeopardized Oliver's location, and got Chi arrested because she had a crush on him?" I can't believe this.

"Pretty pathetic, huh!" Taylor interrupts. "First rule: You can't trust everybody. You have to put your faith in a few only, and you have to be careful."

"But what about the information she has? She can go talk to the authorities now or any time."

"I'm afraid she can't do that, no," he says.

"What do you mean?" I ask.

"I mean that we have a place of our own for traitors. We can't afford for people to go babbling about our plans. So we locked her up," Taylor replies, matter-of-factly.

"Do you mean that you kidnapped her?" I gasp.

"I mean that she was a threat and we took care of her. She's lucky she's still alive, and she knows it. It's more than she deserves, really. But if she tries anything, we'll have to get rid of her. Nothing can jeopardize our plans. They're too important, and a lot of people's lives are at stake here."

I'm horrified. I don't know what I was expecting. Of course, the Underground isn't all good and they have to take measures to secure their plans and ensure as few casualties as possible. The whole Underground relies on secrecy, so obviously, traitors need to be dealt with. I'm just shocked, stunned by this harsh realization.

I change the subject before I get to dwell on the matter for too long, "Did you just say you knew some officers? Does anyone know where Chi is?"

"Yeah, Bryan saw him. They're keeping him at the main police station in Eboracum City. He's in poor shape right now, and they're going to move him to the closest camp tomorrow. Bryan's not even sure they're going to put him in the work force. He's worried they might execute him."

The blow hits me hard. The threat of losing Chi is real and painful. Fear grasps my heart so hard that I can't breathe. I can't have a panic attack! Not here. Not around these people I hardly know. I take a deep breath, feel my way to the couch, and sit down. Taylor places his hand on my shoulder and crouches in front of me. My legs are shaking. Kayla sits by my side and pats my hand.

"Thia, we're not going to let Chi rot in that place," Taylor says, "and we're not going to let him get killed either. He's a valuable friend. Okay?"

His voice comes out soft, reassuring. Though he means well, he can't quite hide the uncertainty seeping through his tone.

"We know they're taking him to one of the camps tomorrow," he adds, "and Bryan knows the route they always take when they transfer prisoners from downtown Eboracum City to some of the closest camps. We've already planned everything and we've got all the weapons ready. Tomorrow, we'll go, just a few of us. We're going to intercept the police car and get Chi out of there."

He sounds like he means it this time, and relief quickly alleviates the worry inside my heart.

"What about Oliver? Is he okay?" I ask.

Taylor stands back up, and grief passes through his eyes quickly. He shakes his head and a profound hollowness tears at me. Taylor clears his throat.

"Well, not to be rude, but I was asleep when you showed up, so I'd like to hit the sack." He's only changing the subject because this one is too painful for him. "Kayla, can you take Thia to the guest room, babe? Thia, you'll stay here tonight. But tomorrow, after we get Chi, we'll go into hiding. Everything's ready for the attack. After what just occurred, we can't stick around here anymore."

Before he leaves, he turns around one last time. "And Thia, everything will be fine. But you need to harden up. Shit's about to hit the fan. I don't know what's going to happen, but you need to be ready for the worst."

I nod, my heart sinking, and then he's gone. Kayla stands up, takes my hand in hers, and leads me out of the living room, all the way down the hall. She opens the door to a bedroom next to the staircase and turns on the light.

"Do you need anything?" she asks, her eyes shifting toward my backpack.

"No, I'm fine. Thank you for helping me."

"Anytime. And Thia..." She pauses and sighs deeply. "I'm sorry about what happened. But Taylor always holds on to his words. If he says we're going to save Chi, he means it. We're going to do everything we can."

"Sure, thanks."

She pats me on the shoulder and closes the door behind her. I sit at the edge of the bed and hold my face in my hands, stress pumping through my veins. My head fills with images of Chi and what might be happening to him right now. Not knowing is worse than seeing it for myself.

I take my clothes off and leave them on an armchair. I slip into my sleeping gown and turn to the queen-sized bed. I probably won't be able to sleep tonight. I lie down under the covers anyway. The bed is comfortable, but the torment in my head won't let me rest. I toss around and hardly sleep all night.

I finally manage to doze off and fall into slumber as dawn comes breaking through. Eventually, noises and voices stir me awake. I get out of bed and put on the clothes I was wearing last night. I open the door to the bedroom and follow the sounds all the way to the living room. Some of the men I met last time are standing and chatting with Taylor by the fireplace. They don't turn around when I walk in. They just keep on discussing the plans to locate and rescue Chi.

"Chase and James, you'll be in the car with Thia and me. Akio will be in a truck with Kayla. Based on what Bryan said, they always go through Flatiron Street on their way to the camps. Akio, you'll wait with Kayla on Manhattan Avenue. You'll park there. James will page your walkie talkie when the police are on their way. You don't pick up; it'll be your signal. When you get it, you drive in the way of the police car and intercept them. You need to block the path. They'll probably lose control. Make sure they don't hit you. Kayla, make sure you shoot those guys dead, babe. The last thing we need is to get ambushed by them. Chase, you get Chi out of that vehicle. Akio, we'll meet a mile away from New Tappan Zee Bridge. And be careful with Kayla, man. I don't want to have to hunt you down if anything happens to her."

"Yep, I'll protect her," Akio replies. He's a man of Asian descent, standing tall with a stature heightened by a thin frame. His dark eyes shine with intelligence while his beautiful features are so symmetrical that he could have been carved out of marble.

Kayla's narrows her eyes at Akio playfully as she puffs with feigned disdain. "I'll be protecting *you* is what you mean!" she exclaims, and Akio's lips curl up into a smile.

"Wanna bet?" he asks.

Taylor cuts them off, "How about you don't bet on stuff like that. I'm not kidding, Akio. You'd better protect her if you don't want to get your ass kicked."

Kayla's eyes furrow for real this time. "I'll be just fine, Papa Bear, thank you very much!"

Taylor is about to respond when I step a bit closer and they all turn to me. Everyone greets me with a simple nod. Kayla comes over to grasp my hand and lead me to the kitchen, next door to the living room.

"I'm going to feed you! You'll need the energy!"

"I'm not really hungry," I protest, half-heartedly.

"I don't want to hear about it. You look like you're ready to fall over. We have bacon, eggs, milk, cereal, and grapes."

All fancy upper-class food.

"I'll have some eggs, please."

"Do you like omelets?" she asks while looking in the fridge. "With cheese?"

Kayla grabs a pan. I ask if I can help, but she just shakes her head. Her kindness warms my heart as I sit down and watch her prepare a real feast for all of us.

Chapter 28

That evening, I get in the car with Taylor and the others. My heart is pounding with anxiety. Taylor starts the vehicle and drives through the city, straight toward Flatiron Street. The police station where Bryan works isn't far from there, so we know Chi and the officers will be close by. Everyone remains silent through the entire ride. Finally, we reach the street, and Taylor parallel-parks before he turns around in his seat to lay out the plans one last time.

After half an hour, Taylor's walkie talkie turns on. He glances at it. It's the signal from Bryan. My heart speeds up, and things happen at such a crazy pace that I have trouble keeping track. Five minutes after the signal, a police van passes by us. Taylor starts the car and follows the van from a safe distance. I don't see everything that's happening ahead of us, but I can hear gunshots, and the police van in front of us swerves a few times before coming to a stop. Akio's truck is in view now. Kayla is at the window, holding a rifle.

Taylor stops the car abruptly. We step out. Two guards exit the back of the police van. Taylor and Chase grab their guns and start shooting. I'm horrified and stop where I am.

I've never seen a shooting before. It shakes me; the sound is deafening. But I have to act now, or I could die.

I look up, spot Chi, and run to him. He's sitting in the back of the van. His eyes are closed, his head leaning backward. Sirens and shots resound around me. Of course, we knew they'd have the van followed by at least one more car. I don't stop to look around; I just hope a bullet doesn't hit me. I climb into the van and sit next to Chi. He doesn't open his eyes. His face is bruised. He's been badly beaten. His lip is cut. Blood has stained his entire shirt. There's a deep wound on his arm, too.

I'm sickened with worry. Terror courses through my veins. *Please, Chi, be okay!* We may be too late already. I lean over him and shake his body. He doesn't respond.

"Chi, wake up!"

I shake him harder. He winces and a groan escapes his throat, filling me with immediate relief. Chi coughs and opens his eyes. Surprise marks his face when he notices me.

"Thia?" His voice is raw, and a drop of blood rolls down his bottom lip as he speaks.

I press my finger against his mouth. "Shhh, I'm here. Can you walk? We need to leave. We don't have much time."

I put my arm under him as he tries to stand up. He winces, falls backward, and sits back down. The sounds of gunfire echo loudly from outside the van.

"Are you okay?" I ask. "Can you do this?"

He rubs his eyes with the heels of his hands, nods, and replies, "I'm dizzy."

The noises stop. Someone comes running to the van—Chase. He jumps in and helps me support Chi. We pull him up so Chi can finally stand. He's unsteady and about to fall again, but he manages to put one foot in front of the other, slowly. Each step draws a grimace from him, and I wonder how many wounds might be covering his body.

His pain breaks my heart and my nostrils flare with sudden rage. Violent thoughts plague my mind as I think about the people who did this to him. Vivid images of all the horrible things I want to put them through just fill my head while wrath beats right through my veins. I try to ignore the thoughts, but they just keep coming, my blood pumping with furious venom. Whoever did this to him, I want to find them and make them pay.

We are now at the door. We'll have to jump. I'm not sure Chi can do this. Chase gets down first. He puts his hands under Chi's armpits and lifts him up before bringing him down. Chi's forehead furrows in pain and humiliation. His pride is wounded.

A car races our way and the tires squeal as the vehicle brakes. It comes to a stop next to us. Taylor comes out, opens the back door, and yells for us to hurry the hell up. We pull Chi all the way to the car. We help him get inside, next to the door. I get in the other way and sit in the middle by Chi's side. James takes the seat next to me, and Chase sits in front. We hardly have time to settle in before Taylor steps on the gas.

He turns around and heads in the opposite direction. I'm not sure where Akio and Kayla went, but they're already gone. They were supposed to take a different route to confuse anyone who may try to follow us. Taylor is driving like a lunatic, and I have to hold on to my seat because I don't want to fall over Chi. Each swerve makes him wince, and each sound escaping his mouth tears at my heart a little bit more. At some point, he asks Taylor to stop the car. He hardly has time to open the door before he throws up on the side of the road. When he's done, he sits down and leans back, with his head against the seat.

"Damn headache," he mumbles.

Taylor sends me a concerned look through the rearview mirror. Chi's hand reaches for mine. He entangles our fingers together and holds on tight. We don't speak the whole time. Taylor slows down when we are out of the city. It doesn't look like we've been followed. We don't want to bring attention to ourselves; the last thing we need is to get pulled over now.

It takes over an hour to drive and reach New Tappan Zee Bridge. Taylor parks the car by Akio's truck, about a mile from the bridge. He turns to Chase. "You're sure they don't control this bridge anymore?"

"I never said that," Chase replies.

"Yes, you did," Taylor exclaims.

"No. I said they don't check the vehicles all the time."

Chi's hand tightens around mine.

"What the hell, Chase!" Taylor shouts. "You plain told me this bridge was secure!"

"I never said that! You need to listen when I speak, man."

Taylor exhales his frustration and shakes his head.

"I said I've never seen them check the contents of the trucks," Chase explains. "They just look at the drivers' IDs. I thought James was driving us over the bridge. You can just ask him; that's his job. He's the one working for the authorities, man. I'm not the one driving food to the poor areas. James knows better than me if the bridge is safe to cross or not."

"Yeah, we'll be fine," James says while leaning forward, closer to Taylor's front seat. "I know those guys personally. They never ask me anything. Jenna and I brought all that stuff over to the building and the officers didn't even notice."

Chase looks at Taylor pointedly and raises his eyebrow. Taylor just rolls his eyes.

"You really should look into anger management, dude," Chase hisses. "I swear, it's like talking to a rabid raccoon sometimes."

Taylor grasps the steering wheel and glares at Chase. He inhales deeply, but he doesn't apologize. "Okay, let's go," he tells us. He opens his door and sends one last glance at Chase. "You and I need to talk—later."

Chase mumbles something unintelligible that sounds like "pendejo," and Taylor's shoulders stiffen in respond.

"Don't push your luck, Chase," he snarls as he steps out of the vehicle without looking back.

Chi shrugs when he sees my quizzical expression. Whatever slang it was that Chase used, Chi didn't understand it either.

The rest of us exit the car and I help Chi out. My heart aches at the sight of him struggling. I put my arm around him before closing the door behind us, and I force him to lean against the vehicle.

Kayla takes a few steps toward us. "What took you guys so long to get out of the car?"

"Don't ask," Taylor replies while glowering at Chase.

Chase shoots him an ironic smile and Taylor's nostrils twitch in response.

"Okay, so we hide in the truck and just go over the bridge, right?" Kayla asks.

"Yes, James is driving," Taylor replies. "Let's go."

Our car is hidden deep behind some bushes. Taylor takes the license plate off to avoid recognition, and James takes the ignition key from Akio. He sits in the cabin of the truck while Chase opens the back door to let everyone in. He helps me pull Chi inside and closes the door behind us. It's pitch dark in the trailer.

"Does anyone have a flashlight or something?" Akio asks.

"Yeah," Chase answers. "One sec."

The truck moves and a faint light comes on. It illuminates Chase's face first and then the rest of us. I scoot closer to Chi and grab his hand. I'm stuck between him and Akio. Chase is on the other side. Taylor and Kayla are next to Chase. There are two canoes facing us, stacked on top of each other, next to twelve paddles and one inflatable raft.

The truck stops. We've reached the security area. Sounds and voices pour in through the walls of the truck, but it's impossible to tell what's being said. My heart races. Laughter irrupts from outside the vehicle—James sharing a few jokes with the officers. I squeeze Chi's hand more tightly. He closes his eyes as if he needs to throw up again. I caress his cheek and the truck starts, as if on cue.

James drives for another thirty minutes, heading south through an area called Old Bronx. Everyone remains silent for the duration of the trip. Chi's palm is warm against mine. He winces every so often, but doesn't complain once.

When we reach our destination and step out of the truck, the night covers us with a shroud that will hide our whereabouts. I hold on to Chi while Taylor and Akio take out the first canoe. Kayla and Chase grab the other one and conceal it behind a bush. Chase and Akio will hide the truck. Chase knows the area well. This was his home, where he used to live before he joined the Underground. He said some structures around here are multi-level garages. That's where they'll park the truck. Then they'll come back to the river on foot, and they'll canoe their way through the water, all the way to Old Manhattan.

James inflates the raft, and Taylor joins Kayla as she steps in the canoe. He pushes it in the river and settles behind her. I bring Chi to the raft. James steps in first, then Chi. When he sits down, his face contorts under the pain. I go next. Chase and Akio push us down the river as I wave to them. Akio waves back and turns around to leave.

James and I start rowing. We follow Taylor and Kayla as closely as we can, but we are slow compared to them. We can hardly make out anything in the dark. We can only tell where Taylor is from his faint flashlight. We row across the river until we see a building in the distance. Slowly, more and more of them appear, barely visible in the moonlight, a ghostly vision of a time long gone—the rest of New York City, submerged in water.

We head toward one particular place, a skyscraper shaped like bundled cylinders. It's hard to see the differences among the structures, but this one stands out because it's the only building illuminated from the inside. Despite the flood, the building is still standing tall above the water, and its peculiar shape makes it impossible to miss. Jenna was the one supposed to light candles in one specific part of the building to help us locate the place.

When we arrive, she's standing on a balcony, greeting us by waving her arms high up in the air. She's a small girl, with short pixie hair. Taylor's canoe has already reached the building. He throws a rope to Jenna, who takes it and ties it to the rail. Because the balcony is slightly above the water, we'll have to climb over the ledge. I glance at Chi. *How is he going to manage this feat?* If he's concerned about it, he's not showing his feelings.

Taylor and Kayla climb in first, one after the other. They pull their canoe out of the water and drag it inside. Taylor has warned us about patrols already. We can't leave anything out that may raise suspicion or reveal our location. Tonight is the only night we are allowed to use candles and flashlights for convenience. After that, we won't be allowed to have any lights on after dark.

James and I row our raft closer to the building. James stands up first and throws the rope to Taylor. Then he climbs over the ledge of the balcony, turns toward Chi, and holds out his hands for Chi to take. He bends over the railing and helps Chi, who pushes himself up by holding on to the bar. Wincing through the whole process, Chi passes one leg over the ledge and then his other foot. When he's done, James helps him steady himself, and Chi turns around to look at me, his face impassive, expressionless. I climb the railing next. When we're all standing on the balcony, James and I pull the raft out of the water to deflate it.

Taylor, Kayla, and Jenna have already entered the building through a French door. When Taylor tells us to join them inside, I follow Chi in, and we find ourselves in a bedroom completely furnished. When the surge hit, many people were forced out of New York City in a hurry. That's why Taylor chose this place; it's secure, hidden, and nicely arranged. The building hasn't had electricity for a long time, but we should do fine with flashlights.

Everyone turns around toward Chi, expecting him to talk about what happened to him at the police station. I'm glad when Taylor interrupts the invasive gazing.

"I think Chi needs to clean up and rest. Tomorrow, first thing in the morning, you can give us all the details. I know you enough to trust you didn't tell them much they can use. I'm not worried. Just go rest."

He taps Chi on the back and tells Jenna to show us to our apartment. Taylor will be staying in the condo down the hall so he can keep an eye out on the other side of the building. Chase and Akio will be sleeping in the one across the hall from us. James is staying with Jenna right next door to us. Everyone seems ready for bed. Only Taylor will stay up until Chase and Akio make it back here. We wish everyone a good night, and Jenna walks us to the place Taylor has assigned for us.

Chapter 29

Chi and I step into the entrance, and Jenna gives us a tour of the apartment, starting with the kitchen to the right of the foyer and the bathroom to its left. She walks us to the living room facing us down the tiny hall. Though this building was abandoned a long time ago, the luxury of the place hasn't completely faded away. It's beautiful, with a bay window opening on to the sky above and the river below. Jenna opens the bedroom door to the left side of the living room. Taylor explained to us that certain condos here contain up to four bedrooms, but ours is a one-bedroom apartment. That's a lot more than I was hoping for. Jenna has made the effort to clean the place up, too. Her gesture touches me.

I turn to her before she gets to leave. "Thank you for everything you've done."

"Don't mention it; that's my job," she says. "I'll see you tomorrow for breakfast. I stacked all the food in the first apartment you saw. Wait till you see the dining area there; it's huge. We'll have breakfast together. You guys can use the shower. If I were you, I'd enjoy it while you can. Once the refugees from Camp 19 are here, Taylor's going to limit our consumption."

I nod.

"Okay, well, see you guys later," she says.

I wish her goodnight and help Chi into the bedroom. He sits on the edge of the bed, and I can finally give him my full attention. I crouch in front of him and examine his face. Blood has dried on his forehead. It's probably hiding some nasty bruises underneath. One of his eyelids is black and blue from the strikes. I cup his right cheek with my hand and caress it softly with my thumb. He flinches and I pull back.

"I'm sorry."

He shakes his head. "It's okay."

I look him in the eyes. The seriousness of his face is unsettling. I miss the impish grins on his lips, the playful smiles telling me that he's truly fine.

"Chi, I'm sorry. I—"

He stops me, shushing me with his fingertip. I lean forward to kiss him, but he turns his face away.

"It might be best not to kiss me right now." He sends me a glance. "I threw up earlier, remember. That's not really the kind of reunion kiss I wanna give you."

"Chi?"

"Yeah."

"I am so sorry...for doubting you before." I want to bring him comfort and tell him I'm never leaving his side again. I am here for him now, no matter what.

"You came for me; that's all that matters, Thia." His eyes hold mine in place. "Words don't mean anything; only actions matter. You came back for me." He smiles at last—a grin so small and mirthless it never reaches his sad eyes.

"We should wash the blood off of you and clean those wounds."

"Yeah, I guess we should," Chi replies with a deep sigh.

He stares at the door with a look of determination, as though making his way there would be a small victory. I support him and help him stand up. His right leg gives in and he falls back on the bed. He growls as anger covers his face. I'm sure he'd rather do this on his own without my witnessing it all, but he doesn't have a choice. He can hardly stand on his feet; he won't make it to the door without me.

No matter how strong Chi is, he is only human after all— a fact that he doesn't seem so willing to accept. I love him for his weaknesses as much as his strengths, but I don't speak my thoughts. I simply put my arms under him again. This really frustrates him—having to lean on me, the girl he wants to protect. The reversal of our situation does not please him one bit, and he lets it show quite clearly. He leans against me and stands on both feet this time. We walk through the living room, then the entrance hall, and enter the bathroom. I push the door open with my left hand, and it squeaks in its hinges.

The bathroom used to be luxurious, with marble walls, but the whole place is desolate now. Because the room lacks heat or air conditioning, mold has made itself at home on the walls. I'm not sure the faucet is still working either, but we'll just have to try. Jenna said we could use the water coming from the tanks on top of the building. The tub is cracked at the corners, revealing the concrete hiding underneath the tiles. I ease Chi down so he can sit on the toilet seat while I lean over the tub to turn on the faucet.

Nothing comes out at first, and when the water finally starts running, it is so slow that only droplets fall out. It becomes more fluid after a few minutes as a brown liquid streams out, foul and disgusting. I hesitate. *Would it be better to leave Chi covered in blood or to risk cleaning him up with this filthy water?*

I let the water flow for a long time as I observe Chi. He's holding his face in his hands, still in pain and trying to get it together.

"Are you going to be all right?" I ask

"Yes, I'll be fine. I just have a migraine."

I dread some concussion, but I don't speak my fears out loud. I have to convince myself that Chi is going to be okay. Even if he isn't, there is no hospital we can go to. The search for him will have doubled by now, and the authorities will be on the lookout. We have to make the most of what we have here and hope for the best.

"I'll go get some medication."

I cast Chi one last glance and walk out. When I exit the apartment, his image remains printed inside my brain—a picture of him wincing, ashen with pain. I hurry through the corridor, reach Taylor's apartment, and knock on the door. It takes just a few seconds for him to greet me.

"I'm sorry to bother you. I need some antiseptic and medication for Chi," I explain.

"No problem. Please, come in. How is Chi?" Taylor asks while turning his back on me.

"Not great." I sigh.

He grabs a duffel bag from a chair in the living room and rifles through it. He holds out a bottle of pills as well as a tube of antibacterial cream, some bandages, and medical tape.

"Here," he says. "It will be hard to get more of these, so use them wisely."

"Thank you," I say. "Are Chase and Akio back yet?"

"No. It takes a while to park the car and row back here. They should arrive in an hour."

"Okay. Thank you for the medication."

Taylor nods and grabs my arm before I exit the room. The concern on his face is laid bare for me to see. "Call me if there's a problem. Chi was badly beaten up. We need to make sure he's okay. If his symptoms get worse, come to me immediately."

I nod again, thank him, and rush back to the apartment. I make it to the bathroom as quickly as I can. I don't want Chi to have to wait longer than he should. When I walk in, I find him leaning over the sink, brushing his teeth. He turns around and asks if I'm okay.

"Yes, yes," I reply, too quickly. I'm fine, just worried sick about him.

He narrows his eyes at me, but he doesn't push the subject. I approach the tub. The water from the tap is clear now, but it's still cold to the touch, though not freezing.

"So, are you gonna help me undress and step inside?" Chi asks with feigned nonchalance.

A mischievous smile has spread on his face. He's enjoying my embarrassment just a bit too much. I flush as I meet his eyes, his words setting my cheeks aflame, and he chuckles.

"I thought I might just help you clean your face and then you could take care of the rest yourself." I clear my throat, but it's too late for me to pretend his words didn't just set me on fire.

"Right." There's no sarcasm in his voice when he says it. He just means it as a statement.

He comes to sit on the edge of the tub, and I settle down next to him beside the faucet. I let the water run through my fingers and watch it pour down my hand. Jenna has left some soap here for us as well as a couple of towels. I grab a cloth hanging from the wall and pass it under the water until it's soaking wet. I touch the fabric to Chi's face to clean his skin as delicately as possible. I work on his forehead first and then his eyebrows.

Grime and blood smear the cloth right away. I rinse it in the tub, soiling the water, turning it light brown and pink. As I clean Chi's face, a cut appears; it's slashing through his left eyebrow. On his cheeks, some red and slightly swollen bruises reveal themselves from under the dirt covering his skin.

Chi's eyes rest on my face the entire time, watching me closely. He flinches every so often when I touch him, but he doesn't complain once. I brush his cheek with my fingertip, tilt my head to the side, and lean closer to him to ensure I don't miss a spot. When I'm done cleaning his skin, he holds my chin between his fingers, pulls me forward, and kisses me softly. His lips are like the wings of a butterfly against my mouth, fluttering gently.

"Thank you," he whispers against me. "Would you mind helping me take off this shirt?" he asks, his eyes studying my reaction.

My heart races as I help him out of his top. I pull it off to reveal his upper body and arms. His chest is tanned and his frame lean, his muscles beautifully chiseled. My heart stops and something inside me ignites. I swallow a breath, and a part of my inhibition breaks. Chi is just beautiful, even under all the bruises. I let my fingers run down from his chin to his throat to his chest, then down the line of his abdomen, stopping at the rim of his pants. When I lift my eyes to meet his, a tiny smile has appeared on his face again. My cheeks heat up and I glance away. He has caught me staring and detailing his body with my hand. I pull back my incriminating fingers and hold my hands together, as if to chastise them for being so indiscreet. Chi finds my modesty cute, and I couldn't hide my attraction to him even if I tried. I clear my throat and he chuckles—a low rumble rising from deep down his throat. The more I flush, the more he laughs.

I choose to feign indifference, fooling neither of us as I wash the cloth that has grown nasty. Then I work on getting his chest clear of blood. The hunger is growing inside me, so I focus on the task and try to think of it as just that—a job. I ignore the craving and force myself not to stare at him, no matter how stunning he is. Chi pushes my hand out of the way and lifts my face to his. He watches me before kissing me. His mouth presses hard against mine, and his tongue comes grazing my lips gently. My chest is flush against his, my shirt the only obstacle between his skin and mine. I've stopped breathing. His lips soften as he teases my mouth open. And I respond to his kiss in kind. My heart is palpitating under the effort to keep my cool, but I'm thawing, melting under his warmth. When he pulls away delicately, I come undone, short-winded. I avert my eyes, and he pulls me to him to whisper against my ear, "I love you, Thia."

I can feel myself falling over the edge, the elation inside my heart giving me wings. But I don't reply. I can't. The words just won't come out.

"I know." I kiss him, all the while wanting to kick myself for not returning his words.

What is he going to think? How long is he going to put up with me before giving up? There's no disappointment in his eyes though, just understanding. Guilt stabs at me, and I can't hold his gaze for long.

I change the subject. "You're clean now. Are you sure you can do this by yourself?"

"Well, it looks like I don't have a choice now, do I?" he replies, but not unkindly.

A dry laughter escapes his mouth, full of humor and teasing. I blush profusely. I step outside and close the door behind me. I lean against it, lift my eyes to the ceiling, and slap my forehead. I stay there for a while, eavesdropping to make sure he's okay and that he's not falling or hurting himself. Shuffling and water noises come out from inside the bathroom, as well as Chi's barely muffled groans. I have this urge to rush in and help him, but that's beyond my ability right now. This isn't something I can bring myself to do just yet. The thought of Chi naked is just too overwhelming and intimidating.

When his footsteps confirm that he's out of the tub, I walk away from the door and head to the living room, as quickly and as softly as I can. I don't want him to know I was listening.

He steps out of the bathroom and comes to the living room, with nothing on but a towel. The sight of him stuns me into silence. The situation is so intimate, so intrusive to his privacy, and yet it doesn't seem to faze him, my seeing him like this. He's just so handsome I can't take my eyes off of him. Even when he catches me staring, I can't turn away. *Why isn't he wearing any clothes yet?* He smiles when he catches me gaping at him, his white teeth bright against the tan of his skin, and I find that I can't breathe.

When he sees my confusion, he rushes to explain himself. "James brought some of my clothes here a while ago when Taylor decided this was gonna be our hiding spot. But I couldn't put them on myself. I have some briefs on, but I'll need your help with the rest."

He sounds apologetic and his tone makes me feel bad. He's in pain. He shouldn't have to apologize for not being able to take care of himself tonight. He limps his way to the bedroom, and I follow him in as he sits on the bed. That's when I notice that he does have clothes in his hands. He must have gotten them from the closet when I went for his medication.

I can hardly look at him right now. Chi is so good-looking in all his vulnerability that I'm blinded. I join him and take my place by his side while holding the tube of medicine in my hand. I pop the top open and squeeze a drop of cream out. It's cold to the touch with a strong smell to it. I run my fingertips over the wound on his arm. It's deep and painful to look at. Chi flinches when the balm touches his skin, but he doesn't say anything. When I'm done, I wrap a bandage around his injury.

"You know, I can do it myself if you want," he says.

I shake my head at him and just ask him to turn around so I can apply the ointment over the slashes on his back. After that, Chi turns around to face me, and I'm about to touch his chest when he grabs my wrist gently and pushes my hand away. He entangles his fingers in my hair and pulls me to him. He strokes my lips with his, so softly I might expire under his touch. His kiss deepens, my mouth opening to his, until he takes a different route and makes his way up my jaw. He presses his lips against the curve of my throat before reaching for my ear. When he finds the spot behind my lobe, his tongue brushes my skin and I inhale sharply as he sighs against me. He stays there, with his face buried against my neck, breathing heavily as if he's trying to restrain himself.

I clear my throat and he pulls away from me. He hands me his t-shirt so I can help him put it on. Once his arms are inside the sleeves, he stands up and the shirt falls over his chest. He's understanding enough not to take off his towel until his pants are on. I help him by pulling them up, his body so close to mine I can feel the heat radiating from him and smell the soap on his skin. His breath against my cheek tickles me. He drops the towel and I gasp, my mind a mush of senseless needs, all rationality gone. But he's dressed now, already zipping his pants up. He sits back on the bed, and I crouch in front of him to put his socks on, in an act so innocent and yet so personal. We both stand up at the same time.

Chi leans toward me and whispers, "Thank you." He kisses me on the nose while holding on to my shoulders. "Well, I guess it's time for bed."

"Why didn't you just put on your pajamas?" I ask.

He sends me a glance, his eyes shining wickedly. "I don't own any pajamas, Thia."

I flush, crimson red I'm sure. He has dressed up for bed purely out of respect—such a simple move of decency from him, meaning so much to me.

The bed is old. The covers are clean, but sleeping here still seems unsanitary. Chi lies down carefully. He winces as he lifts his legs up. He leans back against the pillows and breathes deeply. I find my place next to him and rest my head on his collarbone, careful not to hurt him. I wrap my arm around his stomach, and he begins to stroke my hair.

"What happened to you when I was gone?" he asks. "They didn't touch you, did they? I was worried sick about you, wondering what the officers might do to you. But you're okay, right?"

"They took me back home," I reply.

He sighs in relief. "They did? How did that go?"

"Surprisingly well, actually. The officer questioned me, but I acted dumb. I think he bought it. I did make it clear that you hadn't kidnapped me though."

"Are your parents aware?" he asks.

"My mother was there. She lied to my father about it, too. She has changed so much. In a matter of days, it's as if she's become a new person."

"Maybe she was like that all along. You just never knew."

"She said she had to pretend for our own protection. It was strange, but it felt nice, you know, to realize she did care all along."

"So, how did you find me?" he asks. "I didn't think I was gonna make it, honestly."

"Mother had Walter take me by train and drop me at Taylor's house. No one knows. My mother is to pretend I ran away."

"So, they'll be looking for you too, then. They'll know you came for me." His stance grows wary.

"Yes. And I don't care." I pause for a minute while he kisses my hair and plays with my curls, absent-mindedly. "Officer Bryan Harris helped us. He told us you were getting transferred and where to find you."

"Yeah, I saw him in passing. But there was nothing he could do for me. He has to protect his cover. He's one of the few people we have inside the police force, and we need him."

"I think they'll be looking for a leak from within though. I hope they don't figure it out."

"We'll have to move fast. Time is running out."

"What did they do to you, Chi?" I ask though the answer is obvious.

"Well, you know, they beat me up and all that." He smiles, but he doesn't add any details and I don't push the subject. I can tell just by looking at him that whatever happened at the station was not good.

"I kept my mouth shut though. They don't know squat. I think they were going to torture me, but then I passed out. After that, I woke up to your face. I thought I was dreaming." He grins at me.

Then he closes his eyes and inhales deeply. I didn't notice it before, but in this moment when he's finally able to relax, the strain on his face and the dark rings under his eyes are clearer. Chi is exhausted. I doubt he got to sleep much, if at all, while he was in custody. Slowly, his chest rises and falls in a steady rhythm; he's fallen asleep. Though I wish I could change out of my clothes, I don't want to wake him up. I don't move.

I just lie there, contemplating him. His mouth is open and his head has rolled to the side. I press my ear to his chest and listen to his heartbeat. The sound of it calms me down. Chi's safety rids my heart of the weight that had been compressing it since he was gone. I'm duped into believing things might be fine after all—a trick my mind is playing on me to help relieve stress. I pass into oblivion, my head against Chi, comfortable and secure, with my arms around him and his around me.

Chapter 30

Loud, frantic knocks wake me from my slumber. Someone is pounding on our front door. I open my eyes and my head starts hurting.

"Are you guys awake?" I recognize Taylor's voice. He's shouting from the hall outside our apartment. "Open up, it's important!"

He knocks harder, loud enough for me to hear him from our bedroom. I should go open the door before he breaks it down. I stand up and eye Chi. He's still sleeping despite this racket. His body must be needing the rest. I rush to the front door and open it as quickly as I can. Taylor is standing there, glowering at me. Something's wrong, truly wrong.

Without any greetings, Taylor dashes through the apartment. I run after him. *What's going on?* When Taylor enters the bedroom and sees that Chi is still sleeping, he heads to the bed and shakes him, hard.

"Chi, we need to talk. It's urgent. Shit happened last night."

I want to push Taylor away, but Chi is already opening his eyes. He yawns and stretches his arms. His body reminds him that he was badly beaten up just the day before, and he winces while shaking his head to push the remnants of his dreams away. He sits up, his eyes on Taylor, assessing him.

"How are you feeling today?" Taylor asks Chi.

"Like I was run over by a road roller, but I'll live. My headache's gone."

"Probably the only good news of the day. We've got a load of shit going on and none of it's good," Taylor says. "They found out about your escape, and they've already linked it to Bryan."

"Crap!" Chi sits up, the news waking him up for good.

"We need to make plans and act quickly. I don't think you can fight just yet, and a bunch of the others still need to train, but we have to launch the attack soon. I don't think Bryan will talk, but I don't know how much he can take before he opens up either. We have no other choice but to stay here. I'll have Chase gather everyone who's coming to the camp. They can't stay home anymore; it's too risky. We can't afford to lose anyone else. We're hidden well enough that we should be fine for now. We're going to practice in the fitness center upstairs. Thia's coming, she needs training."

He turns to me and gives me a look. He's studying me. I can't quite read his expression, but I don't like it. What he says next hits me like a hurricane. The whole world starts spinning around me, a tornado destroying everything in its way. "They found out about your mother."

"What do you mean?" Fear wraps itself around my heart and squeezes it hard.

"They said on TV that your mother helped you run away and that she's tied to Chi's escape. They know she helped you, so now she's an accomplice to the Underground. It's all over the news. They're using her as an example, a scapegoat, to call for witnesses. Anyone who sees you is to call the authorities. Anyone who's helping you will be apprehended. I don't know where they took her, but she's under arrest."

I feel faint. The room is still spinning. Chi takes my hand, but I hardly register his touch.

"The officers are probably going to interrogate your mom for a while. Then they may take her to the camps. If we're lucky, it'll be the same camp Chi's parents are in."

This feels like a kitchen knife stabbing my heart. My mother locked in a camp. I feel numb. I freeze, stunned into silence.

Taylor grabs my shoulders and shakes me. "Hey, wake up. I know it's tough, okay, but stay with us. Your mother needs you, and you can't help her if you're useless."

I do want to help my mother. I try to surface, but I'm in shock. "It's all my fault!"

Chi pulls me to him and holds my head against his chest. He presses his lips against my ear. "She made the choice to help you. It was her decision, Thia. She didn't have to, but she did. She knew it was dangerous, but she was willing to take that risk. You can't let guilt take over and destroy you. You need to be strong so we can find her and save her." He pulls me back and looks me deep in the eyes. "Thia, do you understand me? Your mother needs you to be strong. You are useless to her if you give up."

I know he's right. I nod, but the guilt inside me won't let go.

"How did the authorities find out?" I ask, but before Taylor answers, the truth hits me. There is no doubt as to what happened. Someone exposed my mother, and I know exactly who could have done such a despicable thing. I speak the name at the same time Taylor does, "William!"

"But how?" I ask.

"I don't know how he found out, but the news said he was the one who let them know about your escape and your mother's participation in it. They're rewarding him too, treating him like a freaking hero. They're using him as an example of what to do if anyone spots us."

Anger rushes inside me. It's fast, strong, and intense. It replaces the guilt, crushing it to pieces in its iron fist. The rage that had been rampant, locked inside me for so long, is waiting for an outlet. My mind gives up on me as if I'm going crazy for good. I can't control the wrath building up anymore. Deep hatred consumes my heart. It fuels my energy all the while clouding my judgment.

I push Chi away and lose all control. I scream and let all the rage loose. I want to hurt someone or break something. I need to, or I'll lose my grip and insanity will win. I grab different objects, different things—anything, really—and throw them across the room. I fall to my knees and let the anger out as a panic attack seizes my core. I scream and scream until my voice gets raw and my body shakes and I can't breathe and I'm hyperventilating. I'm losing my mind.

Chi takes a hesitant step toward me and then he stops. He doesn't approach me any further. I'm glad. I want to hurt someone badly, and I don't want it to be him. Hot tears of fury pour down my face, accompanied by more wails of rage. Chi takes another step and crouches down by my side. A hiss of pain passes his lips as he bends his knees, and I look at him. He strokes my hair away from my face.

Then he takes me in his arms and scoops me up while wincing deeply from his own physical pain. I wrap my arms around his neck, trying my best not to fight him back, and he carries me to the bed. He sits on the edge and holds me against him while rocking me.

"Shhh, you need to breathe, Thia. Please, breathe for me." His sweet words soothe my wrath as he runs his fingers though my hair. "Breathe like this."

I follow the rhythm of his chest rising and falling in deep inhales and exhales. I calm down slowly, but my body won't stop shaking. Chi kisses my cheek, my temple, my eyelids, comforting me the best way he knows how. I'm shocked at my own behavior and so ashamed. But Taylor and Chi are looking at me without judgment; they're just concerned for my well-being. I feel slightly better, but the anger is still there. It's giving me focus; it's giving me a sense of purpose.

"I want to find my mother," I say, "and when she's finally safe, I will find William and make him pay."

The hatred and need for revenge are devouring me, and I let them. I know those feelings are blurring my judgment, but I don't care. I don't want to see straight. I don't want to think about the reasons behind William's actions or even try to forgive him. I want him to suffer. I feel sick to my stomach and rush to the bathroom. I vomit in the toilet and my anger dissipates a little. I rinse my mouth and walk back to the bedroom.

Taylor tilts his head toward me. "Are you better now?"

"Yes. Yes, I am." I clench my fists. My jaw tightens. William will pay for this.

"Okay then, let's go. We need to talk and plan. Then we have to practice. Chi, you can just watch and give guidance during the training sessions. You can already fire a gun anyway."

"Sounds good to me." Chi sends me a worried glance and pulls me to his side.

We make our way out and head to the apartment we first came through yesterday. Everyone is waiting for us. They all stare at me the moment we walk in. Taylor has already told them about my mother. I know they heard my crazy reaction to the news, but I don't care what they think.

"Chase, James, Akio, I need you to go ahead and contact the others," Taylor says.

The three men nod and leave. The rest of us have breakfast together. Jenna was right; the dining room in this condo is gorgeous, with bay windows overlooking the river. We still need to wait for the other Underground members to arrive. It will take a few hours for Chase and the others to find a secure land phone and call everyone. Despite the grief filling my heart, I welcome the meal. Joviality fills the room despite the dire circumstances.

Kayla comes to sit by my side. She squeezes my hand. "We will find her and get her out, Thia."

"William is going to regret this," I reply through gritted teeth. Chi casts me a look while Kayla pats my hand.

A few hours later, some people finally show up, little by little, brought here by James through a different route than the one we took, to avoid raising suspicion. I recognize some of them from before, when I met them at Taylor's house. Not all of the Underground is coming though—only those who will go to Camp 19. The other members need to stay put and go to work as usual. Their infiltration is too important to risk and compromise.

Some of the rebels who just arrived have trained for years, practicing combat and doing sports to remain fit. I'm not ready for what's coming. My joining the group might be a liability to them, but I'm not going to let anyone rescue my mother without my help. Taylor knows that, and I didn't even have to explain why.

Even though this apartment is huge by New York City standards, it's completely crowded now. When everyone is here—eighty of us total—Taylor asks us to follow him up to a higher floor. We exit the condo, walk down the hall in line, and take the emergency staircase to climb five flights of stairs until Taylor finds the door he's been looking for. Jenna has replaced the batteries in the emergency exit lights; we don't need our flashlights to see our way through. Taylor opens the door and strides through a long corridor before letting himself into what used to be the fitness center. We follow him inside. The walls are covered with targets. There's a large table on one side, covered with guns, bullets, and silencers.

Taylor goes to stand in front of it. He raises a hand and whistles to catch our attention.

"Hey guys, thanks for coming today. This is it. The moment we've all been waiting for is almost upon us. A lot of you have been training for years for this, and I believe you're ready. Some of you have joined us more recently." He shoots me a quick glance as he says it. "You're the ones who will need to practice today. I've already assigned specific partners to teach you. I have a lot of tasks for all the others too. I don't want eighty people in this room while there's shooting going on."

Everyone nods at once, and Taylor continues, "We have very little time, so I'm going to be honest; you're not going to master all the skills. But you need to know the minimum so you can defend yourselves in the camp. By the time we go, I want you to be able to shoot straight and at the right people. If I feel like you're not ready or serious enough about holding a weapon in your hands, you'll have to remain behind. There's always lots of things to do, even if you don't join in combat."

Akio raises his hand.

"Yes, Akio?"

"Will we be enough people? For the attack, I mean. How many prisoners are we supposed to rescue?"

"Well, remember that Liam has already freed a few prisoners. But he can't keep on doing that forever. And there are too many camps and not enough of us. As you know, those camps are all over New York State. There's just no way we can get to all of them. We don't even know all the locations. We'll free one specific camp, the one located closest to us: Camp 19. There'll be sixty of us going. The rest will stay behind to prepare for our return.

"The other Underground leaders are working on hitting some camps closer to where they live; around the same time we'll do it here. For our own security, I can't tell you which camps they're targeting. We are hoping that when the civilians learn about those camps, the news will shock them enough that they'll react."

He stops and looks us all in the eyes, sweeping the room briefly. "Two things might happen. One: The civilians might not care; they might just fall back asleep the way they've always done. That's the worst case scenario. Two: Our attack could lead to chaos. There could be another civil war, this one confined to New York State. The poor are already restless. All they need is an excuse to riot again. The camp we're targeting shelters over two thousand inmates. We're hoping to save as many of them as we possibly can.

"As you know, the camps are owned by corporations. Camp 19 is one of the camps owned by Agric Inc. The camp is divided into different agricultural zones: sowing and harvesting, animal farming and apiculture, packaging the goods, and loading the trucks. We'll divide into groups and go to the different areas of the camp."

"Why did you say 'as many people as we can?' What about the rest?" Akio asks. "Isn't the goal to save everyone?"

"The goal is to save as many people as we can, yes! But it's already clear we cannot save everyone, and we'll probably compromise the mission if we try. Our goal is to shake up the authorities, wake up the civilians, and rally as many people to our side as possible. The citizens need to see our system for what it is and help us stop all this crazy shit once and for all. Any more questions?"

No one replies.

"Okay then, let's assign your teaching partn—"

"I want Chase!" exclaims a young woman with short chestnut hair.

Seventy-nine pairs of eyes turn to her, and her cheeks flush with embarrassment. A small engaging smile rises on one side of Chase's mouth. He winks at her, and her blush spreads all over her face as she returns his playful grin with a tiny shy smile of her own. Taylor rolls his eyes and shakes his head.

"I am *so* sorry, Courtney," he says, sarcastically and slightly annoyed, "but our dear Chase here is going to teach Thia. You already know how to shoot, and I have another task for you."

The young woman's face falls into a pout as her hopes deflate, and Taylor's eyes narrow at Chase. Chase shrugs innocently and Taylor just goes on as if nothing has happened. He assigns each person a teaching partner or two. By the time he's done, there are about fifteen of us grouped together for practice. He tells all the others to follow Kayla out the door and wait for her instructions.

I am to train with Chase and Chi. When the others are gone, Chase picks up a small gun and a silencer. Then he stands in front of the target, legs apart, with both hands on his weapon.

"Observe closely," he starts, pinning his electric blue eyes on me. "See how I'm using both hands to hold the gun. It's steadier this way and safer, especially when you have no experience. Place it in front of you and keep your eye on the sight, like this."

Chase does exactly that and shoots. The bullet makes it straight through the middle of the target. He puts the safety on and holds the weapon out to me. He shows me how to take the protection off and then put it back on.

"Make sure your safety is always on except in time of action. These weapons are dangerous, and you don't want to shoot yourself or an ally by mistake. Make sure you know when it's on and when it's off. Having the safety on in action could cost you your life."

I nod and practice taking the safety on and off. When I understand how the gun works, I point the barrel at the target and hold myself the same way Chase did. I shoot. The bullet completely misses its goal and lodges itself in the wall. Chi approaches me from behind and helps me position myself better. His chest is to my back and his hands are tight around my lower arms, guiding me.

"Look through the sight and focus. Also, take into consideration the shock that will push your hands backward."

I try and fail again. The weapon in my hands feels foreign and deadly. I don't feel in control of it. The training goes on for over an hour, at which point I'm finally scoring though I'm not even close to hitting the bull's-eye yet.

Taylor tells us to stop; it's time for a break. We have thirty minutes for a snack. After that, we need to get back here and resume practice. Because we're dealing with guns, Taylor is adamant about our being on time. Anyone who's late won't get to come in and won't go to Camp 19.

I follow Chi to our place after picking up some food. We sit on the dusty armchairs facing the fireplace. I open a can of fruit.

"So, what's Taylor's story? Why did he join the Underground?" I had meant to ask for a while, but everything happened so fast that I didn't get a chance to do so.

"Have you ever heard of Karen Jones?" Chi asks.

"Isn't she the one who helped pass the Deviance Act?" I always found it strange that a woman was involved in politics at all. Such a thing is unheard of.

"No, Thia. Karen died before the law was put in place. She was one of the scapegoats. She was Taylor's sister. He became part of the Underground because of her death," Chi replies.

My eyes widen and Chi continues, "Back then, Taylor's sister was promised to some guy, but she met someone else—another girl. One day, her fiancé caught them together and had her arrested. The authorities didn't even put her on trial. They just shot her. That's when they decided to create a law giving them the right to execute all gay people on sight."

I look at him, stunned. "What happened to the guy?"

"Taylor never told me, and I never asked. Some things are best left in the dark."

"How did he get his job at the news station? How come the authorities trust him?"

"He had to suck up to them and prove his loyalty. The authorities used his sister's image for their propaganda. After she died, Taylor had to condemn her actions and help support the Deviance Act. It's still eating him up today, you know—all the horrible things he was forced to say about her. But what Taylor did was the only way to keep his job as a journalist while becoming part of the Underground. After a while, he proved to be such a big asset to the Underground that he was put in charge of the rebels in this area. He had to do terrible things to keep his position in the media too, but he never talks about that. Kayla told me never to raise the topic with him."

"What's his main goal? If his sister isn't in a camp, why does he want to go there?" I ask.

"Taylor hates the system and what it represents. His main goal is to expose what's going on. Then he hopes to dismantle our society and change it completely."

"How old is he?" I ask.

"Twenty-six," Chi replies.

"And Kayla?"

"Kayla's twenty-two and Chase twenty-five."

I nod and eat the rest of my lunch in silence. When I'm done, I ask something that has been bothering me for quite some time. "What about the Wilcoxes? Do you think they're okay?"

Chi sends me one quick glance before answering, "They joined another group. They knew what I was about to do when I came for you, so they were long gone by the time the officers broke down their door."

"But didn't they mind? I mean, their whole life has changed forever."

"They haven't had a life since Jordan died, Thia. They only cared about taking care of me while I needed it. Now they've found a new purpose—helping the Underground fulltime."

We keep on talking, and when Chi is done eating, we go back upstairs for more training. We arrive five minutes early because I've taken Taylor's warning seriously. Everyone arrives on time. Maybe this was a small test of faith on Taylor's part, to see who truly wanted to come along to rescue the prisoners.

Practice goes on for two more hours. By the end of it, I can finally shoot close to the middle. However, Chi warns me that a target in motion is harder to hit than a still one and I'll have to take that into consideration. I'm not sure it truly matters because I'm not comfortable with guns anyway. I've already made up my mind that I won't use this weapon if I can help it.

***

The next day, we learn about self-defense. I'm facing Chase. I'm at a disadvantage since he's a lot taller and stronger than I am. He has trained for years; I don't stand a chance. But Taylor thinks it's essential to face bigger opponents and be ready for any alternative.

The first couple of hours exhaust me, and I hit the floor face-first so often that I'm starting to give up. But Chase tells me to avoid him as much as possible instead of trying to fight him. After that, I try to dodge him, but he's too fast. He knocks me down over and over again. I get better, but I'm still dissatisfied with my performance.

Chi sends me an encouraging smile. "I can't beat Chase either, Thia. You're doing great, I swear."

The rest of the week includes more training, strength-building, general fitness, and running. I get so worn out that my body hurts all over, but the practice did help. Chi now looks a lot better, too. Though he's still bruised, he can finally walk normally and his face is no longer swollen.

Chapter 31

At the end of the week, I ask Chi if we can have dinner together at our place. It's not that I don't want to hang out with the others; I just want to spend as much time with him alone as possible. He understands perfectly and seems to feel the same way.

We bring our meal along with us and say goodnight to the others. Dinner is quiet, pleasant, and peaceful. I observe Chi as he eats, and when he catches me looking, he winks at me. I feel safe here with him, and I wish it could be like this forever. I wish our parents were safe. I wish things were easy and that we didn't have to face so much trouble.

When we're done with dinner, I put the dishes in the sink, squeeze some soap out of the bottle, and use a sponge to clean them off. Chi joins me, pressing his chest against my back.

"Let me help you," he whispers as his hands join mine.

His fingers rub against my skin as he reaches for a plate, and I inhale sharply. His arms are around me, locking me against him, and my heart quickens. His face nestles against my neck as his lips find the spot that always sends shivers throughout my body. He kisses me while his hands focus on the task in the sink. The mood suddenly changes from a simple domestic chore to something else entirely. I freeze and try to control myself when his tongue strokes the area right behind my earlobe. A desperate whimper escapes my throat, and I can feel his self-satisfied smile spread against my skin.

"Thia." My name comes out like a groan rising from his chest. I lean into him, but he returns his attention to the dishes. My heart deflates in disappointment as he withdraws from me.

He rinses the dishes and we dry our hands, but not before he splashes me playfully and I giggle. I find my way under his right arm and attempt to escape, but he grabs my wrist. He shakes his head at me, draws me to him, and kisses me. He backs me against the fridge, his lips never leaving mine. When he pulls back, his eyes travel my body as he props his hands on both sides of my head.

"You're so beautiful!" His fingers brush a strand of my hair away from my neck, and when he buries himself under my curls, his lips meet my throat and my knees buckle from underneath me.

"Your hair is always so wild; it drives me crazy."

My entire body sizzles when he says it. I'd give everything I have to seize this moment and remain like this forever, everything around us superfluous. He pulls away and stares at me so I can't avoid the devouring hunger in his eyes. His irises have turned amber, shining with a vibrant color I've never seen before.

He takes a step back, grabs my hand, and leads me to the couch, our dishes forgotten on the counter. He sits down and pulls me to his chest. We snuggle and Chi traces the line of my jaw with his lips, his touch shooting shivers through my body. His mouth finds my skin over and over again, and it takes all I have not to let myself be submerged by him. Chi cups my face with his hands, pulls my forehead to his lips, and kisses the skin between my eyes. His mouth is soft and moist, leaving a wet spot where he touched me. I inhale his scent, familiar and reassuring.

"I love you," he whispers.

No one has ever said those words to me in such a pure, unconditional way. His love inflates my heart as joy bubbles inside my chest. But the years I've spent longing for my parents' attention have left a scar. I'm scared of any potential rejection. I fear that revealing my feelings for him will leave me vulnerable, always worried that my love might one day no longer be returned.

I look at Chi. His eyes are inquisitive. I kiss him on the lips, softly at first. He pulls me closer, with his arms locked around me like steel, and our kiss deepens. His mouth tastes like spearmint, making my head spin.

Chi takes me in his arms, scoops me up, and carries me to the bedroom. There, he lays me down on the bed gently. He's on top of me in seconds, pulling me to him as I wrap my legs around his lower back. He's urgent and I give in instantly. A surge of love emerges from within as I catch his eyes. The feeling crushes my chest, leaving me breathless. He looks up and down my body and sends me a sultry glance filled with heat that scorches every spot his gaze touches. Deep longing overtakes me. I'm burning hot, scorched by him, my heart hammering, my breath short. I want him so much that my chest heaves under the growing need.

Chi pushes my hair back with his long fingers as he cradles my neck and works his way from my throat up to my ear. Chills of pleasure run up and down my spine when he breathes against me. I can't stop the sighs escaping my mouth as his lips find my earlobe, his teeth teasing exquisitely. I feel safe and warm. The world no longer exists. It's all about him. It has always been all about him.

He kisses the curve of my neck before pulling the side of my shirt down my shoulder, exposing my skin as his lips reach my collarbone. He marks his way down gradually, his mouth now kissing me over my clothes while his hands find their way underneath. His fingertips graze the skin under my shirt, branding me with his touch. He pulls my shirt higher up, revealing my stomach, and he runs his tongue along my hipbones, setting the entire area on fire, right there above the rim of my pants. His eyes catch mine as he does it too, daring me to stop him, his desire flaming right through the amber of his irises on fire as he pulls my shirt over my head. He takes his time to admire the view, too. One second, two, three. I wrap my arms over my chest to hide as much of my bra as possible, and his eyes shine mischievously as he grins and lowers himself down to trail a path over my stomach, his mouth stopping short of my belly button. Chills tingle up and down my spine, and a moan escapes my mouth before I can suppress it.

My body is longing, but my mind is wild with fear. Suddenly, my heart races, my nerves give in, and panic takes over. I want to push him back. I need him off of me, now. I squirm underneath Chi, my legs kicking in spite of me. I'm stricken with fear as thoughts of William flood my mind: William pushing me on the bed in a brutish way; William tearing my dress off with no respect; William forcing me down, intrusive and harsh.

Chi pauses, breathing heavily against my navel. He lifts himself up with both his arms tense around me. When his face reaches my level, his eyes search for mine. He's seeking a way inside my mind. I turn my face away, but he pulls on my chin with his index finger. I can feel his eyes on me, demanding visual contact.

When my gaze finally meets Chi's, I know a part of me broke in that hotel room William took me to. I thought I had forgotten. I thought Chi had mended the pieces. But the cracks are still there, and I'm breaking apart at the worst moment possible.

Bile rises to my mouth. I swallow it down and stifle a sob. I don't want Chi to see my tears. These traitors are betraying my every feeling. They are an embarrassment. A frown appears as his eyebrows furrow. He pulls my forehead to his lips and kisses it, remaining like that for a few seconds, with his mouth against my skin. The tears fall down my cheeks and another sob escapes my mouth, louder this time.

"I can't," I say, my voice shaking.

"I know. You don't need to explain."

He sits next to me, with his back against the headboard, and he pulls me to him with concern. He presses my head against his chest as he caresses my hair, softly. I sigh in relief. I'm not sure I could have taken the blame if he hadn't understood.

I'm tired of William hurting us over and over again. I'm so mad at him that my heart aches. But I'm even more upset with myself. *Why do I let him hurt me so?* Even when he's not here. I just want to forget, to let it go, but the constant rage inside me just won't let me. All the things I wanted to tell him, to yell at him—that I never was his property, that I never gave him permission to touch me, that he had no right to force himself on me—all the words died on my lips before I could shout them in William's face, and now they are coming back to haunt me.

My repressed emotions drive a deep wail from my throat. I lift my face to the ceiling and let a guttural sound escape my mouth, more animalistic than human. I grab my face with my hands and let the tears come out hard, pouring and melting like lava down my cheeks, turning my hopes to ashes. I'm never going to feel better. I'm never going to be okay.

"Shhh." Chi rocks me in his arms. "Thia, we're okay. As long as we are together, we'll be fine." But Chi has repeated this so many times before that I'm starting to doubt it.

"I'm sorry. I am so sorry!" I feel so hopeless. Desolation crushes me like an anchor.

Chi is clearly worried, but different emotions are flickering through his eyes now. I identify them almost instantly: resentment and anger. Chi is furious, and William is the object of that wrath. The line of Chi's jaw is tightly set, his lips pursed with rage. He's shaking his head, his face clouded with dark feelings.

He leans over the edge of the bed to grab my shirt. He asks me to lift my arms so he can help me put it on. When I'm dressed, he kisses the crown of my head and lies down on the bed again, pulling me to him. He looks up straight at the ceiling and doesn't say anything. I snuggle against him. I can't stop weeping. He caresses my hair as I cry myself to sleep.

Somewhere in my slumber, I hear a light murmur in my ear. "I love you so much, Thia. William will never hurt you again! I will kill him myself if he ever tries to touch you again!"

His lips brush my temple in a delicate kiss, just as I whisper "I love you" and darkness takes over for the rest of the night.

***

When I touch the pillow next to me the following day, Chi is no longer in bed. The sounds of running water coming from the bathroom tell me he hasn't gone far. Then footsteps hit the living room floor before he opens the door to our bedroom, wearing nothing but pants. He's put a new bandage on his arm and he's shaved. His chest is still bruised in some areas where he got kicked. His hair is wet, darker than usual, making him look so good that it hurts just to glance at him. His face splits into a grin of mischief and I know it's directed at me. I'm not sure what I did that seems so amusing to him. Last night remains a blur. I had that dream where I told him I loved him.

Chi looks like he has won the lottery. His eyes sparkle at me playfully, and his mouth spreads into a larger smile, beaming, but he doesn't say anything. He just runs his eyes all over me, devouring me whole with renewed force. He's reinvigorated, joyful. I bite on my index finger and smile back at him. A blush rises to my cheeks.

He comes to the bed, bends over, and kisses me fully on the mouth. Then he pulls back and gives me another kiss, a soft one this time. He grabs a duffel bag and rummages through it to find a black tank top that he puts on. It's slightly tight on him, but he manages to look gorgeous in it.

I jump out of bed, grab some clothes, and head to the bathroom. I inspect myself in the mirror. I've lost weight. I look tired, but my face is glowing. I take my clothes off, step into the tub, turn on the water, and grab the showerhead to spray my face. The cold drops make my body tense up. It's been hot in the building for days, so the coolness feels good against my skin. I clean myself and wash my hair.

When I'm done, I get out of the tub, dry myself, and put on one of my school uniforms. When I exit the bathroom, Chi walks up to me. He takes my hand in his, and we head out of the apartment. We join the others in the dining room where we have breakfast every morning. We grab some cereal and some powdered milk—all brought here from Taylor's personal reserve—and sit at the table.

Taylor and Kayla are standing to the side, caught in a heated conversation. They're arguing through clenched teeth while trying to keep their voices low. Apparently, Taylor doesn't want Kayla to come to the camp with us, and she's upset he's being so macho about it.

"I'm just concerned about you, babe. I can't do the job if I have to worry that you'll be in danger," he tells her.

Kayla narrows her eyes at him. "I guess I'm not supposed to worry about you," she hisses, with her arms crossed over her chest. "Double standards much? Every time you leave to meet the other leaders, you're risking your life out there. But my feelings don't mean shit to you."

Taylor frowns at that. "I don't have a choice, Kayla!"

I cast Chi a quick glance. He's eating and focusing on his cereal, pretending nothing's going on. After a few angry words, Kayla pushes Taylor away and storms out of the room. He just stands there, dumbfounded for a second, his arms dropping to the sides of his body. Then he shakes his head, rolls his eyes, and is quick to recover. He acts as if nothing has happened and joins us at the table.

"I think everyone should rest this morning and resume practice in the afternoon," he says. "It's been an exhausting week and we need our strength if we want to make it to the camp."

Chi nods but doesn't respond. After that, Taylor doesn't try to engage in conversation again. When we're done with breakfast, we stand up and head back to our apartment.

"What are we going to do this morning?" I ask Chi as we step into our living room.

"I've wanted to show you something," he says, pulling me to the bay window. "Look, the river seems so peaceful. I like to look at it and relax."

I follow him. When I'm close enough, he wraps me in his arms as I stand in front of him. He rests his chin on my shoulder and kisses my neck. I look outside the window. The sight really is beautiful. The current flows around the building in an everlasting movement. We remain like this, with me warm and comfortable in his arms, and silence surrounds us.

That's how we see it—a motorboat making its way toward the building. *Why would someone come here with such a loud, conspicuous boat?* We watch as it approaches closer, and we wait until we know for sure that it's a civilian and not patrol officers. Then Chi takes my hand and leads me to the entrance of the apartment. But when we open the door, James is standing right there. His presence surprises me so much that I almost topple backward.

"Thia, could you come with me for a minute?" he asks. "There's something Taylor wants to talk to you about."

He's secretive, and when Chi starts following us, James interferes. "It's okay, man, you can wait here. Taylor would like to talk to Thia alone."

Chi's eyes narrow, but he doesn't protest. I look back at him. He shrugs though his forehead has turned into a deep frown. I follow James through the hall and turn around to see Chi closing the door to our apartment, his aggravation clear.

James leads me to a condo I've never been to before. We get in and the scene inside shocks me into standing still. Taylor is upset, with anger visible on his face, almost seeping through the pores of his skin. He's holding someone by the collar, pinning him against the wall. *What's going on in here?* Taylor suddenly pushes the person back, hard. He gives him a shove and the person comes into view—William.

William is here!

I take one step back and lock eyes with him. It looks like Taylor has roughed him up a bit. Good!

Taylor turns to me again, hissing like a snake, "Thia, why the hell is he here?"

I freeze, shocked into silence. Surely he doesn't believe I led William here! I'm so shaken up that I can't speak. But Taylor's voice comes out, harsh. "Thia?"

"I..." I begin. "I don't know."

"I told you. Thia didn't invite me here," William interrupts.

Taylor is out of control; he grabs William by the throat and glares at him with vitriol. "Don't you open your mouth again, or I'll remove your jaw!"

I look at them both, my eyes darting between them. I've regained a bit of control over myself. I don't know why or how William got here, but I want some answers too.

"Please, let him talk, Taylor," I say. "Why are you here?" I ask William.

"When Chi escaped, the authorities knew he got help from the inside and they found the leak really quickly," William explains.

"Yeah, we already knew that," Taylor snarls, raving with rage. "Thanks for the useless piece of information, asshole! We don't have all day. How did you get here?"

Panic crosses William's face. He starts talking, fast, "They linked the leak to Bryan Harris. My family has ties with the authorities. I managed to get an audience with Harris. He was really hard to crack. I had to threaten him, but after a while, he gave in and told me where to find you."

"What?" Taylor shakes his head with disbelief and obvious distaste. "Damn it!"

"He refused to reveal anything else though. I don't think the authorities know where you are."

"Well, he opened up to you. That's bad enough. Is there anyone I can trust in this damn Underground?"

I've had enough of his interruptions, so I kindly ask Taylor to please shut up. "Can I have a moment alone with William, please?"

"Are you fucking kidding me? After what he did to you! After he attacked you and tried to rape you! I don't think so, Thia. I'm staying here. James, get out and guard the door. Don't tell the others anything and don't let Chi in here yet."

I look at William, and wrath wraps itself around my heart upon remembering what he did to my mother. The anger steams through my veins, fogging up my brain. I lose all control.

"You betrayed me!" I yell at him.

He looks like I just punched him in the jaw, and his shock brings me pleasure.

"I could understand your betraying Chi and trying to get back at me," I snarl at him. "But you took it out on my mother! She was taken away! Do you understand what that means? Do you understand what could happen to her?"

I'm fuming with rage now. Everything that William did to me is surfacing. The words I didn't dare speak to him are making their way up my throat, pushing against my tongue to be let out. My whole body starts shaking. I can't help myself.

I take a step toward William and grab his shoulders. I shake him as hard as I can and he just stands there, startled by my behavior. The sweet, calm Thia he thought he knew is gone. Instead, a banshee has taken her place and he doesn't seem to know how to react. He looks at me as though I'm hurting his feelings, and some sick, sadistic joy fills my heart. I want to damage him, so badly he can never get up.

"I..." he starts.

I think he's about to cry, but that would be unlike him. William is a cold person; he doesn't have feelings for anyone but himself. His eyes wet slowly, but I couldn't care less how he feels. I want to hurt him so much that I don't know how I manage to restrain myself from ripping his face off. I've never felt so much hatred for anyone before, and the violence of it scares me. I shake my head and push him away violently. He stumbles backward, and his back hits the wall.

"Go away!" I shout. "Get out of here! I never want to see your face again."

He takes a step toward me, which upsets me even more.

"Go away, you coward!" I scream at him while shoving him again. I turn my back on him and start walking out, but he runs after me. Taylor reacts and stands between us.

I'm holding the doorknob when William speaks again, "Thia, wait! I know how to get into the camps safely."

I stop in my tracks and freeze. I turn around in time to see Taylor gawk at William with confusion and horror on his face.

"What did you just say?" I ask.

"I know how to get into the camps," he repeats.

"How did you know about that?" I ask.

"Oh shit, Bryan told you, didn't he?" Taylor exclaims, shaking his head.

"No, he didn't. I asked about your plans, but he refused to answer. I know Chi's parents weren't put in a regular prison, and I figured that he might be trying to reach them. That's what I'd do if I were him. If I managed to figure it out, you can be sure the authorities have also, and the camps will be harder to break into."

There's a tremor in his voice and something in his eyes; he's lying or not telling us the whole truth.

"How do you know about Chi? And why should we believe you? Why are you messing with us?" I ask.

"I'm not! I promise, I'm not. Please, let me make it up to you," he says.

"Why? Why would you even want to help me? You care about no one but yourself!" I snap at him with frustration.

"I screwed up, okay! I screwed up, and I want to make it up to you. I never meant for them to take your mother away."

"Now, I have seen and heard it all," Taylor says, rolling his eyes. "Okay man, when you're done with your soap opera act, can you tell us something that's actually useful? My patience is running dry, and you'd better talk before Chi gets suspicious and brings his ass over here. Because then, I wouldn't bet on your safety."

Fear crosses William's eyes upon hearing Chi's name and the threat underneath Taylor's tone.

"Look," he says, frantic to explain himself. "The camps are better protected than you think they are. I know you've got guys on the inside, but most of them are corrupted, and the authorities are on the lookout for you. They've already increased security. You're going to need me if you want to make it on the inside at all."

"Thanks, but no thanks! We have it under control," Taylor replies.

"No, you don't! They caught one guard letting some prisoners out yesterday. He's as mute as a clam about all this, but they'll be waiting for you now. Some other guards opened up already and said you'd be attacking the camps in two weeks. They gave out the date, the plans, and everything. They know you're going to use the tunnels that lead to the supply rooms underneath the camp. But I can help you. They won't be suspicious if I'm there. They have cameras everywhere too, but I can deactivate some of them."

"I'm pretty sure we can deactivate the cameras ourselves, thank you very much," Taylor replies. "I don't know what you take us for, but we're not complete morons."

Taylor's voice exudes confidence, but shock is plain on his face. No one had told him some of his guards got arrested.

"You can't trust anyone," William insists. "The guards might act like they're with you, but they're not—at least not all of them. I can help."

"And why should I trust you over the members of the Underground?" Taylor asks with disbelief.

"Taylor's right. You've done nothing but betray us until now. We can't trust you, William. And how did you know about the camps in the first place?"

"I've always known about the camps. My father told me about them years ago," he replies.

He averts his eyes and clears his throat a few times. Taylor beckons me away from William

"I don't know how I feel about this, Thia," he whispers. "But I've only heard back from a few guards, and I haven't heard from Liam. I didn't tell anyone because I didn't want them to freak out."

"What if this is all a trap?" I ask.

"We've been working on this for a long time now, but if the authorities got to some of the guards already, we have no choice but to take them by surprise. This might be our only chance, and I can't postpone the date. I don't know how he got that information, and I need to look into it before we do anything drastic."

"I don't trust him," I reply.

Taylor holds the bridge of his nose and inhales deeply. "Neither do I, but we can't just stop now; there's too much at stake for all those people. We're not giving up now."

"How about the other camps? Will the others get trapped?" I ask.

"No matter what William says," Taylor replies, "the other leaders can attack just about any camp. All they have to do is shoot the men guarding the tunnels."

I sigh. "We should discuss all that with the others and Chi first," I say loud enough for William to hear.

William cringes again when Chi's name comes up, and Taylor sneers. I'm glad William is scared of Chi. He should be.

"We'll talk it over with the whole group." Taylor says before pointing his finger in William's face. "And you still need to account for your actions. You can't leave. You'll be under surveillance the entire time. If you try anything or if this is a trap, you're dead! You got me?" The menace in Taylor's voice is very real. William's pupils widen with renewed dread.

Before we leave the room, I pin my gaze on his green eyes. "I need to know why. Why did you betray me? Why did you give my mother away?"

I realize it's a silly question the moment I ask. Of course I know why. William did it because he couldn't accept my choosing Chi over him. He wanted to hurt me back. I don't know what he hopes to get from this help he's offering us, but I need him to explain himself. I want to know how he knew about my mother. I want to know how he got her arrested.

"I did it because I couldn't take it, all right? The thought of him touching you, it drives me nuts. You're supposed to be with me! Not with him! And to think of you two like that—"

"But, we didn't...We haven't been together like that," I cut him off.

He pauses as if to reflect upon this. I don't know why I care, but it matters to me that he doesn't view me as being easy.

"But I thought, surely you. Surely he—"

I interrupt him, "Chi is not like that, William!"

He shakes his head in disbelief before realization hits him. "Is that why you chose him?" he asks.

I'm sick of this. I don't owe him any justification. If anything, he should be the one explaining himself. I change the subject abruptly and turn the conversation around on him. "How did you know about my mother?"

"Emily," he says. "Emily told me."

This feels like a slap, hard and raw. Of course, Emily has always begrudged me my position. My mother, though, deserved better. My jaw clenches and my eyes harden. I freeze though I'm suddenly burning on the inside.

William tries to explain himself, panic flashing through his eyes and disappearing just as quickly. "She called me. The day after you left. Emily called me and told me you were gone. You weren't in your room that morning. Emily told me she'd overheard your mother's conversation with you in the kitchen. She said your mother acted frantic, as if she thought you'd run away, but Emily knew it was a lie. I was so mad! It was like I had no more control over myself. I told my father what had happened.

"Because of Chi's link with the Underground, the authorities thought your mother was involved in the rebellion. They came to pick her up. I didn't think about the consequences. I was enraged and it blinded me. When I realized what I had done, it was too late. I am so sorry! I didn't mean for your mother to be taken away!"

His words sound remorseful, but his cold, calculating eyes don't lie as well as his tongue does. He's not sorry—at least not nearly sorry enough for my taste.

"Don't you dare apologize!" My voice comes out raw, harsh, gritting against my teeth. My words spray out like acid to sting him in the face. I don't like this person William always turns me into. I don't like how he constantly brings the rage and hatred out of me. I can't stop the sardonic words from coming out, "You sound pathetic! You are a miserable excuse for a human being, and you are not forgiven."

I turn on my heels just as Taylor pulls William's hands behind his back. He pushes him forward in front of him and I follow them. We go to the kitchen, and Taylor calls loudly for James to come back into the apartment. Then he tells him to go get Chi. Terror flashes through William's eyes again. I don't know how Chi is going to react either. He can be unpredictable when he's upset.

When James is gone, Taylor attaches William's hands with cuffs. He's still working on those when Chi walks in. It's obvious he doesn't know William is here yet. The look of curiosity on his face turns feral the moment he lifts his face and notices William.

"You've got to be kidding me! What the hell is he doing here?" he snaps, restraining himself from hitting William in the face.

Taylor grabs Chi by the arm and pulls him outside the room. Their voices pour in through the door and Chi's tone rises. It quiets down suddenly and they both walk back in. Chi glares at William and shakes his head, not believing what's going on. He comes and grabs my hand in his, possessively, his eyes daring William to do something about it.

"Let's get out of here," he tells me. "I'm not leaving you anywhere near that sociopath!"

But as we reach the door, Chi pauses as if thinking better of it. He drops my hand and strides toward William, so fast no one has time to stop him. He grabs William by the collar of his shirt and pulls him close to his face, snarling, "You try to screw us up, or you try to come near her, just once, and I'll kill you with my bare hands! Do you understand?"

William's Adam apple slides up and down his throat as he swallows. He looks like he might soil his pants. Chi seems satisfied enough though the disgust hasn't left his face. He drops William, takes my hand again, and we walk out.

When we are in the hall, he takes my face in his hands. "Are you okay?"

I nod and he hugs me before we head back to our apartment, all the way to the balcony outside our bedroom. I no longer feel safe now that William is among us.

Chapter 32

Chi and I spend the rest of the day together. We don't go to our training session and we don't join the others for any activities. I don't want to see William, and Chi seems to feel the same way. It's eight a.m. the next day when James knocks on our door.

"You guys need to come with me. We've got new information and Taylor wants to talk to you."

We follow James to the meeting room and find Taylor and Kayla sitting at the table. Kayla is holding her arms crossed. She's still mad at Taylor for not letting her join us on this mission. William is there as well. His hands are still in cuffs and he looks uncomfortable.

"Hey, guys. Sit down," Taylor orders.

I look at Chi, but he's clearly avoiding William, pretending he's not even in the room with us. I guess that's better than assaulting him.

"Our friend William here has revealed some new information," Taylor starts. "Like he said when he got here, it seems we can't trust the guards. That complicates things a lot. We have to act without their help. We can't put our lives in their hands anymore. We have to act sooner and take them by surprise."

"What's changed?" Chi asks. "How do you know for sure he's not lying?" He points to William with his head when he says "he," his voice charged with repugnance.

"Well, it turns out William has a family member who's in charge of all the camps." Taylor looks slightly sickened as he says it. "His father apparently owns the company that trains and supplies the guards."

"What? That's impossible!" Chi exclaims.

His eyes shift toward William for the first time since we walked in, and the look he sends him is far from pleasant.

"Well, we always knew the guards were trained by a specific corporation," Taylor says. "I thought we'd managed to talk some of them into joining our cause, but it seems they've been corrupted and threatened into shooting us when we reach the camps."

"That explains your high status," Chi shoots at William. "Your parents made all that money by oppressing the weak and putting them in work camps!" The revulsion on Chi's face is so vivid he looks like he might throw up. "Tell me again why you're supposed to be so much better for Thia than I am!"

"Okay, let's not start fighting like little boys." Taylor grabs Chi's shoulder before the argument turns physical. "You guys will get over your personal grievances until we're out of this mess. I will not tolerate anyone getting injured because of your childish feud! Chi, don't force me to leave you behind, man. If you look like you might jeopardize this mission, I will! Understood?"

Chi's jaw tightens and his hands turn to fists. But he knows better than to contradict Taylor.

"Fine!" he says while throwing William a look filled with daggers. "What other nauseating piece of information did he give you?" His hand reaches out to claim mine in obvious defiance of William.

"I'm right here, you know! You can talk to me directly," William replies, his eyes shifting from Chi's face to his hand on mine before his brows narrow in anger.

Chi snorts with obvious distaste. "Fine," he exclaims. "What other abhorrent news do you have for us, William?" He pronounces his name slowly, each syllable hissed through his teeth with venom. "Is your family also in charge of getting rid of all the corpses filling the camps? Or is that noble task left to some other corporation?"

Taylor sighs and shakes his head as if he's had enough and is ready to give up. "Anyway," he says, "we have to act sooner. I'm thinking tonight."

"What? That's too soon!" Chi interjects.

"I know, but we don't have a choice."

"This is insane," Chi snaps.

"And what do you want me to do about it, Chi?" Taylor shouts back. "Do you want to just abandon your parents and all those people in the camps?"

"Of course not! But I'm not gonna act blindly and trust some dirt bag like him with my life. I can't believe you're just gonna listen to his bullshit and take his word for it," Chi exclaims.

"You want to stay behind?" Taylor challenges him.

"No." Chi's nostrils twitch.

"Fine! The problem's solved then. I'll send out some messages and pretend that everything's going as planned. We'll just double-cross the guards. And William here had better not be lying," he growls while approaching his face inches from William's. "Right, Blondie? Because I'll break your neck if this is some ploy to take us down. You won't make it out of that camp alive if you try to stab us in the back. Having you come along is just another guarantee, but realistically, we don't need you, so don't screw this up for yourself."

"I'm not," William says, his voice shaking. "My father backstabbed me; I don't owe him allegiance." He shoots a quick glance at Chi, but he doesn't explain further.

Taylor sighs. "I'm just glad I didn't trust any of the guards with our location here. I need to contact the other leaders, ASAP. They need to know what's going on. Do you have anything else to add, William?"

"I've been to the camps a few times—especially Camp 19," William explains. "That's where my father keeps his office. He was preparing me to become his second in command. I went through a lot of training that involved supervising each area of the camps, just so I could familiarize myself with the entire process. The guards won't find it strange if I show up in one of the trucks. They'll just think it's part of my training."

Chi's face has paled with disgust, and I'm just staring in shock at William. William's father had seemed like such an honorable man. He had appeared so much nicer than William's mother. The authorities obviously keep this information a secret to prevent personal retaliation against their highest employees. *But how could my parents be so blind as to who these people were?* I remember the day when Mother told me that Mr. Fox planned on hiring my father in his corporation. I shudder.

"I heard Father talk to his associates," William continues. "He said some guards were arrested, but some of them kept their jobs. That's only because Father managed to intimidate them into collaborating. Working for my father comes with a lot of advantages, which most people don't want to lose. Father didn't hesitate to threaten their families as well as cut their resources. That was enough to shift their loyalty back to him." William sends Taylor a look. "So, the guys you thought you could trust? I wouldn't count on them!"

Then William spills out more details about his family's corporation. I don't know what happened between William and his father, but William sounds furious at him. When he's done revealing what we need to know, Taylor calls everyone to the fitness center. I'm standing close to Chi, with his hand in mine. I turn my head when I feel someone's eyes on me, and I notice William staring at us, his eyes veiled with wounded pride. I look away; William's feelings aren't my concern anymore.

"Okay everyone," Taylor calls out. "Some new information was revealed this morning. We have to act a whole lot sooner than we had planned. We're attacking Camp 19 tonight!"

Gasps echo around the room, followed by a rising rumble of voices, but Taylor is loud enough to speak over us all. "I know, I know! It's really soon! But I think we're as ready as we can be at this point. If we want to make it out alive, we have no other choice. There will be no training this afternoon. Just enjoy the day and rest. I want everyone here at three p.m. sharp. I will lay out more of the plans then, but everything remains the same. I have a lot of things to do, a lot of people to contact. I will see you guys later. James, Chase, I need you now. Chi, I want you here at noon."

People disperse around the room while Chi and I go back to our apartment. When we reach the balcony, the wind blows through my hair, and Chi observes me before pulling me to him.

"Tonight's the night. Are you sure you're ready for this?" he asks.

I nod. I'm excited and anxious at the same time. I can't help but hope my mother will come back with us and that we'll all be safe.

Chi's eyes meet mine. "Did you mean what you said the other night?"

"What do you mean?" I pretend not to understand where he's going with this.

"You know exactly what I mean."

I blink a few times, my heart suddenly racing. "Yes. Yes, Chi. I love you. I've loved you from the moment I saw you."

His grin appears and spreads, filling his entire face. He lifts me up so my feet leave the ground, and he spins me around and around while kissing me. Then he puts me down and walks me backward to the rail of the balcony. He takes my hand in his, and I turn around to look at the river. Chi was right; it does look relaxing.

We spend all morning together, snuggling on the bed, resting, and we avoid talking about what's going to happen tonight.

When noon arrives, Chi reminds me he's supposed to meet Taylor.

"You'll be careful out there, right?" he asks. "I can tell you're not comfortable around weapons, but you have to promise me you'll use your gun if you're in danger."

I look back at him. I don't know that I can swear to that, but he's expecting me to and I don't want him to have to watch my back. I hold his gaze and try to sound as convincing as I can. "Yes, Chi. I promise."

He sighs in relief and holds me more tightly against him. I can tell he's worried, and I'm terrified for him as well. I don't know what's going to happen tonight. More than anything, I fear losing him. This mission sounds more and more like suicide.

I follow Chi to the training room. We don't have a lot of time left, and I'm not wasting one second I could be spending with him. Kayla and William are there as well. For three hours, we clean and prepare the weapons while Taylor consults with Chase and James to work out the last details.

When the time comes for everyone to meet, Taylor stands by the large table. There, everyone has to wait in line as he assigns them each a different weapon with directions. My hands are shaking when it's my turn and he hands me my gun, complete with bullets, a silencer, and a holster. I take it all and wrap it around my waist. It's heavy against my thigh, and I instantly hate its deadly weight against me. I would go without it if it weren't for Chi's insistence that he won't let me come along without a weapon.

Chi grabs a rifle, which he carries over his shoulder. He has trained for years and he's not afraid of weapons. This feels more natural to him that it does for me.

Once we're equipped and ready, Taylor finishes with our instructions. Everyone is listening carefully. Some of us look nervous while some others can't seem to wait to get going. After a couple of hours, we all head back downstairs. It will take some time to inflate all the rafts and load everyone on the canoes as well.

Taylor has managed to convince Kayla that she should stay behind. She's furious about it. She pulls her face away when he tries to kiss her goodbye, her every feature creased with discontent. Taylor's lips rise into a tiny smile.

"I love you too, babe," he says before turning around and directing everyone toward the windows.

Little by little, we make our way out of the building, in line, two to five people at a time. When I reach the balcony, along with Chi and two other people, we climb down to the raft and start rowing, heading north. The closer we get to shore, the harder my heart hammers. Anxiety rushes through my blood when I imagine everything that might go wrong. But I can't afford to think that way; I can't let stress control me and confuse my mind.

Taylor starts pacing as soon as we arrive. We're still waiting for a few others to cross the river. He's probably reviewing all the plans in his head for any potential lethal holes or defects. Chase and James are supposed to be waiting for us with two trucks that the Underground stole from the authorities a few months ago.

When everyone is gathered, we head to our meeting point in the parking lot about a mile from shore. When we get there, Chase and James open the back doors of the trucks for us. Everyone gets in, one by one. Taylor and William join

Chase in the first truck while Akio goes to sit by James in the second one.

Everyone is settled and the trucks start moving. The ride gets awkward quickly. None of us dare talk lest we reveal how scared we truly are. Everyone is uncomfortable on the hard metal floor of the truck. We're squished together, hot and slimy with sweat, like sardines in a can. Chase drives us from Old Bronx to New Tappan Zee Bridge. There, he uses his fake ID to trick the officers into raising the barrier and letting the truck cross the bridge. After that, the ride takes us further north, toward Camp 19.

Eventually, the truck slows down and comes to a stop. Each entrance to Camp 19 requires a pass, which James and William own and will use to let us into the tunnel. I hear a metallic door roll open, soon followed by movements of the truck. We are in the tunnels; the truck has gotten much cooler, though not cold enough to relieve our suffocation.

Chi grabs my hand in his as we get closer to the camp. He squeezes it a few times. He's getting anxious too. He leans in. "Please be careful!"

I kiss him on the lips, once. "I will."

The truck stops. As expected, a couple of guards approach the vehicle. I can't hear the shots because of the silencers, but the sounds of the guards' bodies hitting the ground echo from outside the truck, and bile rises to my mouth. From this moment on, the chill inside me doesn't let go. Adrenaline pumps through my veins as the back door opens up to William's face.

I get out and notice Chase from the corner of my eye. He's stripping a guard so as to wear his uniform. He also finds some keys and throws them at Taylor. A few different trucks are parked in the tunnel, waiting to be loaded with merchandise the following morning. We will use them to evacuate the prisoners.

William leads Chase to the room that holds all the controllers to the cameras. Two shots echo from the security room, and my heart squeezes. Two shots, two more deaths. After a few minutes, William and Chase come back out. The cameras in the main yard have been turned off; it's safe for us to proceed. Taylor opens a door on the right, and we walk into the camp in our various small groups. We are to head straight to the different sections of the camp. People here are separated by sex, as well as tasks. William told us my mother was sent to the packaging area. Though it's late at night and it's dark outside, the prisoners are still working.

Strangely, the place looks deserted. It would be impossible to tell that people are held hostage here if we didn't know what signs to look for. The walls are made of concrete, gray and depressing, and there isn't a sound to be heard. The place feels morbidly empty, and it smells like death and decay. We hide in the shadows and spot a few guards on the towers, circling around.

I'm keeping close to Taylor, Chi, and James. William, who's walking in front of us, leads the way to the packaging building. If a guard sees him, they won't suspect anything until it's too late. As we approach the building, a guard notices William. Questions fill his eyes instantly, but then he nods in respect. William's loyalty to his father is just taken for granted. The guard doesn't have time to react when Taylor comes out of the shadows and shoots him straight in the head. I inhale sharply. Taylor looks at me, cold as frost, and presses his index finger against his lips in a shushing motion.

Chi positions his rifle on his shoulder. He whispers for me to get ready to shoot. I obey though the cold metal of the gun feels foreign against my skin. I don't plan on shooting anybody if I can avoid it. I know these are bad people, but I can't help thinking about their families waiting at home for them to return from work.

William opens the door and we are met by two guards, whom Taylor and James take care of right away. A deep pain fills my heart when the bodies fall down to the ground. I remind myself that these people are keeping my mother prisoner for no valid reasons. They chose gaining high statuses in society over protecting human lives. Cold anger grasps my heart and I'm finally ready for what's coming. I need to focus on getting my mother out, and I can't let undeserved pity distract me from my goal.

James grabs the keys from one of the guards and opens a barred gate. Then he works on the metal door to the packaging room. When he pushes it open, Taylor is ready, on the lookout for potential danger. Of course, more guards are keeping an eye on the workers. I look around and see two of them on the balconies facing us, and three more downstairs watching over the prisoners. James shoots one of the guards facing us, but instead of falling backward, he drops over the railing and comes crashing right into the working room. The other guards react instantly as panic takes over among the workers.

We hide behind columns as the guards start shooting in our direction. But Taylor has been training for years. In less time than I have to think, he has already shot two of them. One man tries to run away and sound the alert, but James shoots him before he makes it out of the room.

Only one guard is left now. He calls out to us frantically, "I'm with you! Taylor, please, I'm on your side!"

"It seems no one in this camp is on our side anymore, Charles! I heard about what happened."

"I know. I know, but I'm still with you," Charles pleads. "I want to help! Please, you'll need my help!"

Conflict crosses Taylor's eyes. He sends Chi a look and Chi nods his head twice.

"Okay," Taylor relents. "We need more forces anyway. But you stay with us at all times. I see you run, call out to the others, or move a finger in a suspicious way and I'll shoot you on the spot! I see you point your gun at anyone but another guard and you're dead."

Charles acquiesces with his head, obvious relief and fear showing on his face.

"Help me get them out of here, now," Taylor orders before he calls out to the prisoners, "We're here to help you and take you out. Follow our orders and do not bring attention to yourselves. If you hear any shooting, run. Follow Chi and I to the tunnels and don't look back."

I take a quick glance around, but I can't see my mother. Fear squeezes my heart tightly. *What if William was wrong? What if my mother is working in a different area? What if I arrived too late?* I don't have time to panic. I can't afford to panic.

Chi takes the lead quickly and starts walking everyone to the main entrance. Before going out, he strips the guard and puts on his uniform. Then he opens the door to the outside, surveys the area, and beckons for the group to follow him, in line, hiding in the shadows.

Chi and Taylor are to meet more armed rebels outside the building to help secure the group as they proceed to the tunnels. James, William, and I will move on to the men's building, located farther away to the right. We leave the prisoners to Taylor's care and walk cautiously while keeping close to the wall.

When we reach the gate to the men's area, I catch a glimpse of someone walking toward us. I turn around and relief fills my veins when I realize it's only Chi. But something's wrong, different somehow. James is looking at the towers to make sure no roof guard notices us.

Suddenly, everything happens so fast I have no time to move. Chi aims his gun at me, and before I can process anything, it's too late. He lifts his rifle, pointing it at my face, and shouts for us to drop our weapons. I'm petrified, paralyzed on the spot. When Chi yells his order again, James turns around, aiming his gun at Chi. His reaction is too slow. Chi shoots first; James falls to the ground. When I raise my hands, I'm still holding my gun; it looks like I'm targeting Chi. Something flickers through his eyes and he fires, right at me.

William leaps into the air, and I close my eyes as the gunshot rings in my ears. A heavy weight pushes against me, knocking me to the ground, hard. I'm down; something is pinning me to the concrete. I hurt my elbow when I fell and pain needles are shooting though my entire arm. It hurts so much that my head starts spinning. I force my eyes open anyway. Blood is dripping onto my skin. A drop of it falls straight into my eye. I squint instinctively.

Through my other eye, I can see someone lying over me, but my vision is blurred. Black spots are dancing in front of me. I try to breathe deeply, but I can hardly inhale because of the person crushing my chest. Something wet and sticky is running down my face. I try to focus past the dark spots so I can regain my vision. But when I identify the person pinning me down, I suddenly wish I had lost consciousness entirely. The empty expression on his face makes me sick to my stomach heaving with waves of nausea. I'll choke on vomit if I throw up. I can't lift myself or move.

William is on top of me. His cheek is stuck to mine and his eyes are wide open. There's a hole in his head and blood is coming out of it, dripping down, all the way to my face. A deep scream tries to force its way out, but I bite on my lip to remain silent, and the wails of horror resonate inside my head instead.

I try to push him off of me, but he's too heavy and the angle of his body makes it difficult for me to move. I push harder, holding myself with one arm, but my elbow is hurting so much I can't hold the position. Someone runs to me and gasps. Chi is still standing there, holding his gun on me, but his attention has shifted. He's looking at something above my head. There's a crooked smile on his face, and my heart shatters upon realizing what he's done.

Time stands still. It's hard to breathe under William's weight and all these emotions breaking me apart. I don't want to catch Chi's attention. Suddenly, William's weight is lifted off of me. Akio is standing over me, pushing William to the side. He takes my hand and helps me up.

I look down at William. I'm still hoping to see a spark of light in his eyes, an indication that he's still somewhere inside that body, but he's gone. Despite everything that has

Alice Rachel

happened, I never wanted this. I didn't wish for his death. Guilt stabs at me as I look at his face one last time.

I lift my head to see what's grasping Chi's attention, and the sight greeting me strikes me with horror and confusion. The man pointing a gun at me—this person I mistook for Chi—is still right in front of me, but he's staring at a cloned copy of himself standing farther away to my right. I shift my eyes from one to the other to take them both in.

"I'll be damned! My little brother, right here in our camp! Tsk tsk!" the man in front of me says. "What the hell happened to your face, Chi?" He snickers.

Chi's face is still bruised from when he was beaten up. *How could I not see that?* Chi walks toward us, fast. He stops and points his rifle right at his brother while looking at him with pure hatred on his face. Chi's twin shakes his head in faked disappointment before returning the gesture by moving the tip of his barrel from me to Chi.

He looks like a perfect image of Chi, but a somewhat colder version of him, slightly distorted, more vicious. There's no love in Chi's eyes when he looks at his sibling, just utter disgust marking his features. I've never seen him show such revulsion for anyone before, not even for William. He's watching his brother with caution too, as if he were a deadly predator ready to pounce at any moment.

"So, tell me, brother, what are you doing here?" says Chi's twin. "Looking for our parents, I presume."

"Don't call me that. I'm not your brother and they are not your parents," Chi retorts.

"Well, legally, they are my parents more than they are yours! See, according to the law, I am the only child they have. And you, you're just non-existent. I could kill you right here and it'd be like you never were."

"You are a traitor and a coward! I don't care what the law says, Stephen. You stopped being their son the moment you betrayed them."

Stephen's eye twitches and his jaw clenches upon being called a coward. "Do you know what it's been like for me all those years?" he snarls. "Having to lie through my teeth every moment of my life. Starving to death every second of each day."

"Stop whining, Stephen, it's pathetic," Chi hisses through his teeth. "You're pathetic!"

"Mother and Father deserved what they got, Chi, and in good time, so will you."

At that moment, Chi lifts his gun higher to point it right at his brother's forehead. Stephen imitates him, and my heart races in response.

Chi's twin shakes his head again like a big brother disapproving of his younger sibling's actions. "Tsk tsk! What're you gonna do, baby brother? Blow my head off?" Stephen laughs, a snicker devoid of all humor. "I'll react before you can even pull that trigger. So you're going to listen to me and follow me nicely."

"I'd rather die."

Stephen smirks at that. "Your choice!" He's about to pull the trigger when I scream. He looks at me quickly from the corner of his eye, and a sadistic smile spreads on his face. "Well, well, well. Look what we got here. Looks like little brother got himself a new girlfriend."

Chi doesn't look at me, but he's livid now. "She's not my girlfriend. She's just a member of the group." He shows no emotion as he says it, and I truly hope he's just acting.

"Oh really?" Stephen points the gun at me again, close, the tip of the barrel pressing hard against my forehead. I can't protect myself; I lost my gun when I fell. My heart is racing fast, with adrenaline shooting through my veins, making me weak in the knees.

"You won't mind if I shoot her, then. What do you say? I'll give you a choice—it can be you, or it can be her."

Chi still refuses to look at me. He tries to hide his emotions, but he's getting nervous.

"So, brother, which one is it?" Stephen asks, his voice dripping out like honey.

"I'm not gonna play your little games. Whatever I say, you'll shoot us both anyway. I'm your twin brother, remember. I know what you're thinking, and I know how you're thinking."

"Fine, it'll be her first then. I want you to watch." Stephen presses the gun harder against my forehead, but he still doesn't shoot. My skin rips under the tip of the barrel. Chi looks like he's ready to rip his brother's face off.

"I will shoot her, brother," Stephen teases with cruelty. "I will kill her, just like I did Willow."

This feels like a fist to my guts. Stephen sneers as he says it too, but a swift spark of pain flickers through his eyes as the words spill out of his mouth, and Chi's hands clench around his gun.

"What did you just say?" Chi's voice is frosty with wrath growling underneath, but the faint tremor leaking through his tone is quite audible, as if he's choking on a suppressed sob.

"Are you deaf now, little brother? I said..." Stephen is speaking louder now, articulating every syllable as though Chi is too dumb to understand. "I... will... kill... her... just.... like... I... did... Willow." His voice breaks on the last word, as if her name is too hard for him to pronounce.

"It was you?" Chi's eyes widen in horror.

"Well, of course! Who did you think it was? Obviously, you didn't get the brains in our family, Chi, if you haven't figured it out yet! When the authorities took Mother, Father, and me away, I had to prove my loyalty to the officers. It was either that or get tortured. And I cared more about myself than I did you, so when they asked for your location, I just gave it away.

"I truly thought Mother had sent you to stay with Willow's family. I was hoping that once the officers found you, they would drag you here, or even better, maybe kill you. But I guess Mother didn't trust me enough to share any real information with me. That really hurt my feelings, you know, to realize that Mother lied to me like that."

He shakes his head and his eyes fill with sorrow, as if he is truly sad and disappointed. He seems deeply upset for some reason, and I can't tell if he's faking it anymore.

"So, tell me, brother. Where have you been all this time? Ever cared to look for me? Ever wondered how I was doing?" Stephen asks.

"Why would I worry about you? You've been doing perfectly fine," Chi replies harshly, and Stephen's face turns livid as his eyes darken with pure wrath.

"What about Lila?" Chi yells at him. "She was your girlfriend!"

"Yeah, some poor pathetic girl passed on to me," Stephen snaps back. "Did you ever really look at her? Damn, that girl was ghastly! So I should have put up with the ugly duckling while you would get sweet, beautiful Willow. I don't think so!" True rage seeps through his tone as he throws those painful words at Chi. "And to think that Mother and Father were supposed to stand up for what's right in society." He snorts in disdain. "Claiming to want freedom and equality for all. Right! They didn't hesitate to push that hideous chick on me and rip my heart right out of my chest!" His tone is harsh and filled with pure loathing, sending chills down my spine.

"You were never forced to date her and you know that."

"Yeah, whatever. You're nothing but a blind fool, Chi." Stephen's attention shifts toward me again. I shudder as his eyes run up and down my body, appraising me. I wish he were looking at anyone but me. I feel like an insect entangled in a web, facing an arachnid about to take its first bite.

"Chi did tell you about her, right? Our sweet, beautiful Willow." He smiles charmingly like a cobra mesmerizing its prey before striking it down with venom. A vindictive smile spreads on his face as he strikes the next blow. "Did he tell you about their first night together too?"

I know I can't believe anything coming out of his mouth. He's spitting filth just to hurt me. But his question still cuts like a knife. I don't want to believe it.

"Shut up!" Chi snarls. His knuckles have turned white with pressure from his grip on his weapon. His reaction just confirms everything Stephen has said. I'm not Chi's first girl and he has lied to me. I don't understand why he did it, but it breaks my heart all the same. Chi still doesn't look at me, but Stephen is studying me now, staring me straight in the eyes, his face showing nothing but malice.

"Oh, he didn't tell you?" A sneer appears on his face, and he laughs some more. I know I shouldn't let it affect me. I shouldn't let any of this touch me, but Chi is still wired and he's clearly avoiding my eyes.

"He told me all about it, you know," Stephen says. "I had to listen to him brag about how they did it in the barn behind her house and how soft her skin was." An emotion that I can't quite read fills and leaves his eyes quickly. Every word coming out of his mouth is a slicing dagger. "You need to realize that Chi has spent his whole life living a lie. All he knows is deception. You'll never be able to trust him."

"Don't listen to him, Thia! He's a psychopath! He's just trying to mess with our heads. He's getting at me through you."

Chi doesn't deny anything his brother has said though, which drives me a little crazier by the second. But Stephen is wasting our time. We need to get rid of him and move on. Akio has been standing still the whole time, watching it all unfold like some excruciating train wreck.

"This is getting tedious and I have a camp to guard," Stephen says, sighing as if truly bored with us now. "I'll just get along with this. Chi doesn't seem to think you matter enough for him to step up for you." His gaze shifts to Chi quickly as he says it, challenging him, before coming right back to me. "So I'll just have to shoot you both, I guess. By the way, Chi. Just so you know, there was no need to look for Mother. She passed away last week. As always, little brother, it looks like you made it just a little bit too late." Stephen's lips rise in a lazy smile upon throwing these last words into Chi's face.

Profound anguish passes over Chi's features in response, but he's quick to recover himself. "I don't believe you!" He's impassive, but the doubt and pain in his voice are plain for us to hear.

"Awh, but she did! She got pneumonia. You know how it is these days. They didn't really care to cure her. I would have helped, but I'm pretty busy, you know."

Though Chi is still holding his gun tightly, his hands are shaking. He's trying to control his emotions, but tears still rise up to his eyes before his irises darken, his pupils as cold as ice. "I'm going to kill you, right here, you miserable piece of shit!"

"Oh, no need for name calling, brother," Stephen replies with a pout.

Before Chi gets to act on his words, gunshots echo all around us. The sirens have been turned on and they're blasting through the speakers, deafening us. Chi chooses that moment to grab his brother's arm. He knocks it hard on his knee and the gun falls out of Stephen's hand, with a detonation going off as the weapon hits the ground. I look around me, but no one's hurt. Chi is holding his brother's wrist behind his back, squeezing and turning it around, and Stephen is screaming from the pain.

"Thia, the gun!" Chi shouts at me.

I'm standing here, unable to move. Chi repeats his order, but then he pauses as something catches his attention. I turn around to see Taylor leading a group of prisoners.

They're all running to safety, except for one man standing apart from the others. His resemblance to Chi is stunning.

"Dad?"

"Chi, my son, you've come for me!"

Before anyone has time to react, Stephen head butts Chi in the nose and grabs his weapon. It takes but a second for him to roll on the ground, position himself, and pull the trigger. Everything happens fast. I'm frozen here, motionless, as Chi's father falls to his knees.

He looks Chi in the eyes and extends his hand as another gunshot resounds. A bullet hits him in the chest, bringing him down for good. I turn around just in time to see Chi jump on Stephen, pinning him to the ground. The two of them are holding rifles, but these can't be used for such close range shooting.

Chi is beyond himself with rage now, his pores oozing with sweat. He's screaming as he drops his gun and starts hitting Stephen, pummeling him with frantic despair. I yell his name, but he doesn't stop. He just can't hear me. Stephen's face fills with strange relief, and tears come streaming down his cheeks as if he has freed himself from some invisible burden that was bearing down on him.

Chi doesn't notice any of this though. He's consumed by rage, and Stephen's emotions are shifting so quickly—from relief to shock to profound sadness—that I'm not sure I'm even reading him clearly. A strangled sob rocks his body too, just before Chi grabs the butt of his rifle and hits him so hard in the temple that Stephen loses consciousness.

Chi drops his weapon, but he keeps on beating his brother up, drawing blood with his fists. I finally wake up from the horrific daze that was mesmerizing me. I run to Chi and pull on the back of his shirt as I call his name, but he still can't seem to hear me. Akio joins in and tries to shake Chi into standing up.

And then, slowly, Chi looks up at me. The wrath and intense grief on his face grasp my heart and tear it into tiny pieces as terror seizes me. This is a Chi I've never seen before; the agony in his eyes is breaking me. He doesn't push me back. He stands up and starts kicking Stephen hard in the stomach as tears come pouring down his face.

Stephen is still breathing. He's still alive. I'm not sure if Chi is aware of that, but I can't let him kill his brother. That would only eat him up over time until it destroyed him. I pull on his arm and manage to drag him away from Stephen.

Disbelief slowly replaces the rage behind his eyes. He pushes my hand off of him and runs to his father. Chi rolls him on his back and listens for a heartbeat we all know is no longer there. More shots echo through the yard all around us while the sirens keep on blaring. This isn't safe. We need to get out of here. Taylor is running toward us while shooting at some guards. I pull on Chi's shoulder, pleading with him to let go. There's nothing we can do for his father now.

"Chi, we need to leave. Now!" Taylor yells in our direction.

Chi nods his head. He holds his father's hand to his lips and kisses it before closing his father's eyelids. He stands up, picks up his rifle, and runs with me toward Taylor. He lurches a little, as if he were drunk or wavering under the weight of his emotions.

Taylor yells for us to hurry the hell up. We run to the tunnels and close the doors behind us once we've made it inside. Taylor leads us to one of the trucks and we climb in the back of it. He signals for Chase to start the vehicle.

We came in with two trucks; we're leaving with ten more, each driven by a member of the Underground. The ride back is horrible. Some prisoners are crying in relief while others are grieving over the people they've lost. No one's talking.

I'm holding Chi's hand in mine, but he doesn't look at me once. His head is bent down, and though he's not crying anymore, I can feel his distress and grief as painfully as if he were shedding tears. His silence and lack of reaction are more unsettling than if he were having a breakdown.

Chase goes above the speed limit until we are safe. When the truck reaches the bridge, he slows down and I hear a couple of shots. As planned, Akio has taken down the officers guarding the bridge. Chase proceeds and crosses over. After thirty minutes, we reach the parking lot previously located by Chase. We leave all the trucks behind, hidden from view. We walk the rest of the way until we reach the river. It's pitch dark and everyone's exhausted.

Some members from the Underground were supposed to stay behind to prepare for our arrival. They are now waiting for us on shore, with multiple rafts ready to be loaded. Several trips back and forth will be needed to take the refugees to the submerged building. I'm not sure how many prisoners escaped, but there seems to be hundreds of them here.

We didn't save everyone and the repercussions on those left behind will be terrible. Just thinking about it makes my blood run cold. Taylor stopped somewhere along the way to send a signal to the media. Our allies working in journalism should be at the camps right now, shooting footage incriminating the authorities. I cast a look around the crowd gathered here and search for Mother, but she's nowhere to be found. Disappointment and fear fill my heart. I don't know if the other leaders have managed to free the camps closer to them either, and all this uncertainty is killing me.

Chapter 33

Slowly, everyone rows their way to the building. As calculated by Kayla, there are enough floors left untouched by the river for the refugees to share apartments and fill up the rest of the building. When I get there with Chi, I take his hand in mine. He hasn't spoken one word since we left the camp. I pull him to me and hug him so tight that a sound finally escapes his mouth. I find his eyes, but they are devoid of mirth and filled with misery.

We wait in the dining room for a few minutes as more and more people walk in through the window. It's getting so crowded here that it's hard to breathe. Kayla is standing by the French window to welcome each refugee inside. Some members of Underground are to lead them directly to their apartments, with instructions to keep all lights turned off and to refrain from leaving or getting in touch with their families.

After waiting for fifteen more minutes, holding onto Chi's hand and watching him gradually collapse, I decide it's time to take him back to our apartment. I lead him away, but a tap on my shoulder stops me as someone clears their throat behind me. I turn around. Mother is standing there, smiling. I'm so relieved I almost stumble.

I pull her into my arms and embrace her like I never got to do before. She laughs at my reaction. Then I turn around to see Chi carrying a strange look on his face. *How could I be so careless and inconsiderate? Hugging my mother right in front of him, completely ignoring the fact that he's lost his?*

I look back at her. "Mother, this is Chi. Chi, this is my mother."

"Good evening, Chi! So, you're the gentleman who started it all," she says with a sideways grin.

She looks tired, older somehow. She's chuckling though, something I've never witnessed before. Of course, Mother has always been strong and nothing ever seems to faze her.

"Yes ma'am, that would be me," Chi replies without humor, his voice still trembling from the emotions he's trying to repress. "I'm sorry I kidnapped your daughter," he adds, nodding his head in respect, gloom suddenly clouding his face. "If you'll excuse me." He sends me a quick glance before walking away and exiting the room.

I'm at a loss about what to do. Chi hates for others to witness his weaknesses. Though it's killing me to see him like this, I choose to leave him be—for now.

I turn to my mother. "Are you okay? What did they do to you in there? What about Father? What did he say when the officers came to pick you up?"

"Yes, Thia, I'm okay. I'm actually feeling better than I have in years. And I am so proud of you. My very own little warrior. I can see why you chose Chi. What a handsome young man he is!" She smiles and pulls me into another hug. A tear rolls down my cheek. This is more than I ever hoped for: a true compliment from my cold mother and a sign of deep affection.

"As for your father," she resumes. "He was furious when he found out what I did. He called me a disgrace and told me he'd never take me back even if the officers let me go."

A pang of sorrow spasms through my heart upon hearing this. My mother is now homeless, just like me. She no longer has status in society. But she comforts me right away and reminds me that she is finally free and actually relieved about it.

We talk a while longer before I tell her that I need to find Chi and make sure he's okay. I shouldn't leave him on his own for too long. I let her know where our apartment is located. She should join us later. We only have one bedroom, but maybe she can use it and we'll sleep on the floor.

I go straight to our apartment, but Chi isn't there. I call for him down the hall, with fear in my heart. *Why did I leave him alone?* That was such a stupid thing to do. Chi isn't well; I don't know what he's capable of, or what he might do to himself. I need to find him, quickly. I look for him all over the place until I remember that the river brings him peace. He must be on the balcony. I head back to our bedroom, and now that I know where to look, I finally see his shadow behind the curtains, moving against the moonlight. Instant relief fills my veins.

I head to the French door. He doesn't turn around even though I know he's heard me. He's staring at the horizon, and I'm just standing here. I don't dare touch him. I don't know if he wants me to leave or stay and comfort him.

When he starts talking, his voice is steady though anger is growling underneath. "I knew I might not be there on time, but I still hoped. That was quite foolish of me, I guess." He turns to me and the affliction on his face makes my heart bleed. "I almost saved my dad, Thia. I should have killed Stephen on the spot. If I had, my dad would still be alive."

I take a step toward him and cup his face with my hands. "You can't think like that. You didn't know what would happen. And really, could you live with yourself if you'd killed Stephen? Your own brother!"

Chi pushes my hands away, his eyes as hard and cold as metal. His rejection stings, but I know it's not personal. He just needs his space. He doesn't want my comfort, and I don't know how to help him. "Thia, what my brother said, about Willow…"

I look straight at him, and a mixture of feelings floods my heart in a wave so strong that all my doubts and insecurities wash out of me. I don't care. I don't care what he did with Willow. Chi just lost his entire family. I'm the only person he has left. I don't know why he lied to me about her, but I just simply don't care. It might hurt to think about him with another girl, but this isn't about me. Chi needs help and support; I want to be here for him.

"Chi, it's okay. It doesn't matter."

He cuts me off, loudly, screaming in my face, "No, you don't understand!" He pauses, as if in need of a breath, before continuing, more softly this time. "I can't lose you, Thia. Not now!"

"You're not losing me, Chi."

But he's not listening. He just keeps on talking, babbling with frenzy, "I'm sorry I lied to you. I didn't know how to tell you. You were so worried about our relationship at first, and then sex seemed to terrify you; I didn't want to scare you away."

"Chi, it's okay. It doesn't matter anymore," I try to reassure him.

"No, it does matter! You see, I had nothing to lose before. It was all about finding my parents and I didn't care about the consequences. But now, my parents are gone. And all this time, I thought I could save them, but I was a fool! I was so wrong! I failed them miserably. What Stephen said, he was right. I'm always too late! I can never forgive myself for this. And I can't afford to lose you, too."

Chi stumbles and falls to his knees. It surprises me so much that I don't react right away. He looks completely broken. He grabs his face with his trembling hands as his whole body starts shaking and his shoulders slump downward in desolation. His grief breaks my heart. I take a step toward him as sobs rise in his throat. He's shivering all over.

His pain is excruciating to look at. I can't stand seeing him like this. I wish I could take all his agony and mourning away. I would carry it all inside me. I would take it all, let it crush me and break me apart as long as it meant that Chi would just stop hurting. A single tear rolls down my cheek. I sit next to him and pull his head to my collarbone. He pushes his face against my left shoulder and holds on to me tight as he cries against my neck. His fingers are clutching my shirt, and his sobs are shaking through his entire body. I rock him slowly against me while caressing his hair and making soothing sounds. I don't know what to tell him, so I remain silent. There is nothing to say, no comforting words that wouldn't sound like lies. Though his pain might lessen with time, nothing will ever be the same for him.

Slowly, his sobs subside and he calms down a bit. He pulls his face away from me and looks the other way. He doesn't want me to see the tears in his eyes, but it's too late. I don't know why he always has to be so proud. He holds the heels of his hands to his eyes, as if he means to rub the pain away.

He's still avoiding my gaze when he sighs. It's a deep exhale, an attempt to let all the air out in the hope it might take away the pain as well. He finally turns to me. He kisses me all over my face. His mouth is wet and warm against my skin. His kisses on my lips are hard, desperate.

He pulls back and presses his forehead against my temple. "I had tried to prepare myself for the loss of my parents. I knew it might happen. But with you, it's different. I know I pretend to be strong. I like to claim that I can bear it all, but I could never make it if I lost you, Thia. I'd rather die. You're everything I have left, and I can't let anything happen to you. Please, tell me I'll never lose you."

He looks me in the eye and my chest fills with anxiety. *How could I possibly tell him that nothing will happen to me and that we'll be fine?* I have to beguile him from the fears clawing at him. He knows better, but I can tell he needs to hear it—one simple white lie to allay his worries.

So I say it even if deep inside I don't believe one word of it. "Chi, I'm not going anywhere. Nothing's going to happen to me. Okay?"

He looks at me, with tears still drying on his cheeks. "Okay."

His voice is so low I can hardly hear it. He doesn't believe one word I just said, but pretending that he does is just easier for him right now than to argue about it.

"I don't think it's worth it anymore," he continues.

"What do you mean? What are you talking about?"

"All this. The resistance. It's not worth the costs."

I look at him. I don't understand. Or maybe I do and I can't accept what he's saying.

"If being a part of the rebellion means I might lose you, I'm out."

"But, Chi, that's why we're here," I protest.

"No, it's not. My goal was to save my parents. I failed and I'm done. I'm not letting one more person I love get hurt."

"Chi, you're not thinking straight. We can't just leave now."

"Why not?" he asks, frustration cutting through his voice.

"Because it would be selfish and unfair," I try to be sensible, but he won't listen.

"I don't care if I'm being selfish. This whole damn society is selfish! I just want to make sure you're safe, and I don't care about the rest."

I'm so shocked I don't reply. Chi is the reason why I'm here. He talked me into this rebellion. He truly believed in it. He knows what's at stake. He knows what this means for people who've been oppressed for so long. I can't just turn back and pretend that I don't know, that I couldn't care less about the fate of those around me.

I look at him, but I can't speak. Like that day I told him about the pre-nuptial night, Chi has that look on his face; he's made up his mind already. Though I don't like his decision, I know that no argument of mine will convince him otherwise. But I still try. "Chi, I'm staying. If you want to protect me, you have to be with me."

"Thia, I am not sacrificing you for this!"

"You're not sacrificing me, Chi. You saved me many times over. You don't need to save me from the world."

"No! What I don't need is to save everyone in the world when all I care about is you! I didn't choose to be born second; you didn't choose to be born a girl. I am sick and tired of this self-centered society and trying to save it from itself. Let the others do the job for once." His anger slashes at me, and I have to remind myself that this isn't personal. This is just his anguish talking. I'm sure I can reason some sense back into him eventually.

"Chi, I can't do that. How could I look at myself in the mirror every morning and know what's going on out there?"

"When I saw my brother shooting at you, I thought I was going crazy. It's horrible to say, but I'm glad William jumped in the way, Thia." His despair comes to cut me; it's hard not to give in, just to comfort him.

"I can't let that happen again," he adds. "I can't breathe thinking you might not make it next time."

There's no talking him out of his decision right now. He just needs some peace of mind. Instead of arguing further, I pretend that I'm on board with him. I just nod and kiss him, hoping to bring him solace. I know his heart is broken, and I don't want to add any more conflict to his life.

"I love you, Chi, so much."

"I love you too. Please, don't leave me," he replies, and my heart breaks a little bit more at the pleading sadness in his voice.

"I'm right here. I'm not leaving." I brush his lips with mine and thumb his cheek.

"Good!" A tiny half-hearted smile splits his mouth for a second, gone in a blink of an eye, instantly replaced by painful sorrow.

Chapter 34

Chi and I remain like this for a long time, sitting on the balcony. We're holding on to each other tightly. My mind is frantic with worry about him. I think about the people that we've lost today: Chi's father, James, William, and countless others I never even met and will never get to know.

I don't understand William's actions and I never truly knew him. I always thought he would lead me to my ultimate destruction and be the end of me. But instead, he saved me and sacrificed his life for mine. *Had I known what would happen, would I have acted differently?* I'm not entirely sure, but I doubt I would have.

There's no going back now. And despite what Chi says, there is nowhere we can go or hide. He cannot protect me. No one can protect me. The world is changing. And yet, just like before, Chi and I are outcasts with nowhere safe to run. I'm still pondering this when Chi gets to his feet and holds out his hand to me. I take it and stand up. We exit the apartment and go join the others.

We head to the fitness center. Taylor is there with Chase and Kayla. He sends Chi a glance filled with concern.

"Chi, I'm really sorry—" he begins, but Chi holds up his hand to cut him off. Taylor's brows crease with worry, but he moves on as if he hadn't raised that topic. "Thia, your mom is going to share your apartment. I hope it's not too awkward or anything."

"No, it's fine. I already told her to join us."

"Great," he says before turning to the television.

I hadn't noticed it was there. It wasn't in this room yesterday. It's small, with a huge antenna, and it seems to be running on batteries. The reception is bad, full of static. The news is on, and the videos are shocking, revolting. A reporter is talking while some footage is being filmed from above, probably from a helicopter. Some prisoners are standing against a wall, with their arms in the air and their backs turned to the officers who start shooting. The prisoners fall to the ground, in a growing pool of blood. The guards move forward and drag the bodies through the yard while other prisoners are forced to line up and wait for their executions.

I close my eyes as more shots take the lives from more prisoners. I don't think I can watch this. Chi squeezes my hand and I look at him. His face is grave; he's as upset as I am. More images of the camps appear, showing piles of corpses lying in the courtyards.

I glance at Taylor and try to gather myself before I speak, but I can't hide my revulsion. "This is a failure! We failed all these people!"

A flicker of pain crosses Taylor's eyes. "We saved hundreds of people tonight, Thia. I received confirmation that more prisoners were saved from some of the other camps. We did what we had to do."

"Some members of the Underground were even left behind and didn't make it back," I exclaim, furious.

"Should we have left all the prisoners in the camps, then? Would you have felt better pretending that nothing was going on? Our missions are never free of consequences. People die every single time."

"How can you just stand here and watch this?" I shout at him.

"That's enough, Thia!" he retorts as if scolding a child. Chi flinches against me, and his hand squeezes mine hard, signaling for me to shut up.

"Look," Taylor continues, more calmly now, "I understand what you're saying, okay! What do you want me to say? That I'm sorry we couldn't save thousands of people! We're not superheroes, Thia!"

I shake my head, glaring at him, and his irritation escalates in response.

"You've never seen the authorities kill or torture someone you cared about, have you?" he asks me.

I don't respond. He already knows I haven't.

"Well, let me tell you something, Thia. The rest of us have. Every single person in this room has lost a family member—shot right in front of their eyes. That shit on TV right now, that's what happens to people who aren't from the upper-class and those who resist the rules. You need to wake up from that utopia you've been living in, princess. 'Cause you don't have a clue what real personal loss is or what sacrifices need to be made to change an entire system."

His words punch me hard, fueling the anger in me. When I look at Chase and Kayla in turn, their faces are covered with sorrow. My hand clenches tightly around Chi's.

"We knew that we couldn't save all the prisoners." Taylor won't stop talking. "I plain told you so before we even left for the camp. This is war now. The fight is far from over, and I need everyone to remain positive. We can't stop, and it's a bit too easy to be all self-righteous about the consequences now. All that human loss, it's not on you, or Chi. It's on me and the other Underground leaders. We are the ones who have to live with it. Things will get a lot worse before they get better. I never said it would be easy. You need to choose if you're in or out because I won't let anyone dissuade the others or tell them to stop fighting."

His eyes bore right through me. He's so angry and displeased with me that I just let the issue go. We keep on watching the news for ten minutes until I've had enough and need some air. I pull on Chi's hand lightly and he gets my meaning. We walk out without saying goodbye to the others.

Chi and I go back to our apartment, where I find my mother standing by the window. She turns around when she sees us. She pulls Chi and me to her and holds us both in a tight hug.

When we pull away, she asks, "What do you think is going to happen now?"

"I don't know."

"How long are we going to be able to stay here?"

"I don't know."

She glances at me and smiles a little. "Yes, of course."

Everyone's exhausted. It's time to go to bed. Despite what I had decided, my mother insists that she should take the couch in the living room instead of the bedroom. Even though nothing has happened between Chi and me, sharing a bed with him is awkward when my mother is staying right next door.

I lie down, but I can't sleep. I look at Chi. His eyes are closed, but I can tell he's not sleeping either. The horrible things we saw on TV just keep on rolling in front of my eyes, preventing me from finding peace. After a few hours, my lids finally get heavy and my eyes shut down, closing the door onto this world where more terror is sure to come.

***

The next day, Chi and I head back to the fitness center. Mother decides to remain behind. I'm still exhausted. I didn't sleep well and nightmares plagued my night, waking me up at all hours. Though we didn't have dinner last night, Chi and I are not hungry. We don't feel like joining the others for breakfast either.

When we open the door to the training room, Taylor is standing there, surrounded by many people, most of whom are still wearing uniforms from the camps. They're watching the news. Taylor turns around when he hears us open the door, but he doesn't smile or greet us. He's still mad at me.

"The news is slowly reaching the whole state," he tells the refugees. "The authorities are trying to shut us down, but we're using an Underground transmission channel. I'm afraid this place won't remain safe for long. The authorities will be looking for us. And we are just sitting ducks waiting to be picked off one by one if we stay in this building. We can remain here overnight and rest, but in a few days, we'll need to relocate. They've already found the officers that we shot at the bridge, but they're holding the riots accountable for now. It won't take them long to figure it out and come for us."

I tune him out and watch the news. A lot of things happened while we were sleeping. The camps have been exposed for what they are. Some riots started in Eboracum City last night, and the outrage is spreading quickly through the slums, including the ones in New York City, the ones right next to us. The poor are emerging from their neighborhoods, and it seems that nothing can stop them. They're using whatever they can find as weapons against the officers facing them. What they saw on TV is beyond what they are willing to accept. On some channels, the officers can be seen calling for the population to calm down, reminding them that all resources will be cut if the riots don't cease. But this creates the opposite effect as it ignites more anger and turbulence. The poor refuse to feed off of anything coming from camps of forced labor.

Some members from the upper-class are staying home, sheltering themselves from the violence outside, but some others have waken up from their slumber and taken to the streets, alongside the lower class. The journalists catch them in interviews during which they express their indignation. None of them knew where our state's resources came from. They didn't know about the camps; they didn't know that our food was grown by humans exploited against their will.

"The war has now begun and we plan on winning it," Taylor says. "We need to dig deeper and strike harder. The poor were easy to convince since they've been suffering for years. What we need is for every upper-class member to change their ways. They're finally opening their eyes, but the news needs to spread faster. We want a tsunami; we need this whole system dismantled and broken apart. The Underground needs you! Can we count on you?"

Almost everyone in the room cheers and raises their fists in the air. I cast a glance at Chi. He looks at me, frowns slightly, and shakes his head in such a way that no one knows what he means except me. Chi no longer wants to be a part of this rebellion. His parents' deaths have taken away his resolutions, leaving nothing behind but a shell of who he used to be. Though Stephen is still alive, he is dead to Chi now too, and I know Chi is grieving the loss of his twin brother as well.

Soothing him has become my primary goal. But if he hasn't changed his mind, then neither have I. I will stand my ground and fight among the rebels. No one can talk me out of my decision. I don't know what's going to happen, but at this very moment, a lot of people in this state are rising from under ground—awakening to a reality more dire than they could have ever imagined. The others in the room keep cheering, and Chi's hand squeezes mine ever so slightly. The future is uncertain, but the coffin that was my life is now wide open as the light of freedom finally shines bright on my horizon.

ACKNOWLEDGMENTS

I would like to thank my husband, Christopher, for believing in me from the moment I said I wanted to write a novel. Thank you for always trusting that I could do this, even when I thought I couldn't. Thank you for pushing me to draw each one of my characters too and for listening to my endless babbles and the readings of my scenes. You are my very own Chi, and I love you.

Merci à mes parents et à mon frère d'avoir cru en moi dès que j'ai parlé de ce projet. Merci pour votre soutien et votre amour. Je vous aime.

Thanks to each person who asked to read my book as soon as it was finished: Jennifer London, Jessica Meeker, Stephanie Rinehart, Evelyn Espada, and Kylie Kaemke. Thank you so much for asking about it, for reading it, for encouraging me, and for telling me that it was good even though the first drafts were just plain awful.

Thanks to my parents-in-law, and especially my mother-in-law, Nancy Dupré, for reading the book and loving it from the start. Thank you for taking the time to correct my mistakes and for asking many questions about the story.

Claire Kann and Batool Al-Shaar, thank you for your honest reviews and feedback. I would never have known to rewrite certain scenes otherwise. Thank you for not sugar-coating the truth. I think the book is better for it.

To those who read my book online, commented on it, and supported me at a time when I was losing faith in my writing: Josh London, Sebastian K., Nadège Chrétien, Diya Mohanna and Vera Burris—thank you for your kind comments.

Special thanks to Chloe Berger and Erica Inductivo for being such big fans of the series. Thank you for supporting me and the characters. Your unconditional love for Stephen is very special to me. Thank you for giving him a chance. I know he makes it very difficult... Your endless encouragements just make my day, every day.

Special thanks to Elizabeth Lee for accepting to proofread the book. Thank you for your precious time and effort.

Thank you so much to anyone who bought this book or simply picked it up and spent time reading it. I truly hope that you enjoyed it.

I would like to dedicate this novel to those who see their rights trampled upon every single day. To all the girls and boys in this world who have been denied access to education or the right to freedom. Our thoughts and beliefs are our own; no one can ever change that. Freedom of speech can always be taken away, but our individuality and beliefs can never be destroyed. You are in my thoughts, always.

Additional

Material

ADDITIONAL MATERIAL

PLAYLIST

Theme Song:
"Bring Me to Life" by Evanescence

Thia:
"Under" by Alex Hepburn

"Numb" by Linkin Park

"Play Dead" by Björk

"Shatter Me" by Lindsey Stirling

"Innamoramento" by Mylène Farmer

"Roar" by Katy Perry

Chi:
"It's My Life" by Bon Jovi

"Scream" by Michael Jackson

"Envole-Moi" by Jean-Jacques Goldman

Chi and Thia:
"See Who I Am" by Within Temptation

"In Joy and Sorrow" by H.I.M.

"Always" by Bon Jovi

"Let's Wait Awhile" by Janet Jackson

"Black-Eyed Boy" by Texas

Under Ground

Chi

A Short Story

Alice Rachel

<u>*Chi*</u>

Chi's short story starts two years before he meets Thia. Back then, he was seventeen years old and the authorities had just irrupted into his house to take his family away.

***

I crawl out of the closet. The house is silent. My legs are killing me. I was stuck in that space for hours. I listen, but there's no sound to be heard. I walk to my bedroom door as discreetly as I can. I open it and the hinges creak. Shit. I stop and wait. No sound. I open the door completely and stick my head out. It's dark; I can't see anything. I can't turn the lights on; there might still be some officers lurking around. I head downstairs. The entrance door is wide open. I look around the living room. A pool of blood has dried on the hardwood floor. My heart squeezes. My mom's been shot; she screamed when it happened.

I grit my teeth and clench my fists. *Ces salops paieront pour ce qu'ils ont fait à ma famille.* Those assholes will pay for what they did to my family.

I swallow hard and walk around the house—into the kitchen across the hall from the living room, and then into the bathroom next to the kitchen. My parents are gone. I know that. I'm just stalling, still hoping. My heart's racing even though I knew I wouldn't find them here. I'm scared; I don't know what the officers might do to them. This is all my fault. The officers were here for me. I'm a coward. I just let the authorities take my parents away while I hid in the closet, like a child. I'm disgusted with myself.

I punch the wall and my fist breaks right through the Sheetrock. My hand throbs on impact and my knuckles start bleeding. *Idiot!* The blood mixes with the dust covering my hand, but I won't take care of the wounds. I deserve the pain.

I go back upstairs. I pass in front of my room, but I don't stop. I open the door to Stephen's bedroom and call his name. I walk straight to his closet and look for the entrance to the hidden space. I pat the wall but find nothing.

Where's the hidden space in Stephen's closet?

"Stephen, get out. I can't find the way in."

I stop and listen, but no one answers. I punch the wall again. *Ouch! Idiot!* My knuckles burn from the shock. I grab one of Stephen's shirts and wrap it around my hand to stop the bleeding.

"Stephen, get the hell out," I exclaim, but I already know he's not in there.

Why doesn't he have a hidden space in his closet? Where is he hiding instead?

I look into my parents' room before going back downstairs. I can't see anything in the dark. I keep calling his name over and over again. I'm frantic.

Where's my brother, damn it?

The authorities can't have my brother!

If anything happens to him because of me, I'll never forgive myself. He should have been an only child. I never should have been born. This is all my fault.

The barn!

I step out of the house cautiously. If the officers are still around, I'm dead. But I need to find him. I *have* to find him. I run straight to the barn behind our house, but when I get in, I can tell right away that he's not there.

Terror seizes me. They have him! The officers didn't just take my parents away, they took my brother as well.

He will die. He will die and it will be my fault. I close my eyes. I need out of here. When I reach the door, I turn around and run without looking back.

I run. I run for a very long time. When I see the Arch, I slow down. I walk at a normal pace. My face is hidden under the hood of my jacket. My hair is covering my eyes, obstructing half my face from view.

When I get to the Wilcoxes' house, I ring the doorbell a few times. More than a few times, actually. I've been freaking out for hours now and I'm losing my mind. I can hardly breathe, my hands are shaking, and I'm really close to fainting right here on the Wilcoxes' front porch.

The door opens. Mrs. Wilcox comes to stand in the light.

"Chi?" she asks while blinking.

"Yes."

"Oh no. What happened?"

She pulls me into her house, closes the door behind me, and takes me to her kitchen. She points at a stool. I sit my ass down, and the tears pour out of my eyes.

I've just killed my whole family. They will all die because of me. Because I never should have been born. I'm an anomaly, an aberration. And a coward!

Mrs. Wilcox stands up, pulls me into a hug, and holds me tight against her chest. I don't deserve her comfort, but I still welcome it. I clutch her nightgown and cry into her arms.

"Shhh, it's okay, Chi. We'll find them. Everything will be fine."

***

When Jane drives me to my new school, she tells me I'm no longer allowed to call her Mrs. Wilcox. It makes her feel old. I've been living at her place for two months now. Two months of going crazy, worried about my family.

I'm anxious; I've never been to a real school before. I've always stayed at home with Mom. Jane says going to a regular school will help me learn how to socialize. I don't want to socialize. I just want to find my family.

Jane and her husband Neil are part of the Underground, just like my parents. Jane said she'd introduce me to some of the rebels very soon and that I could train with them until the time comes to get my parents. She said my parents were probably taken to a camp of forced labor—if they're lucky. I didn't even know such a place existed. It disgusts me. I wanna set this whole state on fire. I want to burn it to the ground and see a new state, a new system finally rise and thrive.

"You need to be careful, Chi. You can't just say things like that at school," Jane says while shifting lanes. There's hardly anyone on the road. Most people take trains.

"Why not?" I ask. I don't mean to be difficult. I'm just sick of hiding.

"Most people don't share your beliefs. The members of the upper-class, especially, don't like change or challenge."

I cross my arms and shake my head. Jane extends her arm and strokes my hand with her fingertips.

"I know you want to change the system, dear. But certain things require time, practice, and focus."

"My parents will be dead by then." I huff in anger. I don't wanna wait. I just want to find the guys who took my family and kill those bastards.

Jane sighs. "Your parents know how the system works. They'll know to be careful and do as they're asked in order to stay alive. Just trust me on this." She sends me a quick glance. "At school, you will hear things, terrible things that you won't agree with. Don't react, don't respond. Observe your classmates and try to fit in. The number one rule of the Underground is to fit into society. It's the best way to take it apart from the inside out. Can I trust you to do that?"

"Yes."

I understand the consequences if I act crazy. I've grown and learned. Not like that time I was dumb enough to join Stephen in our backyard and our family had to move because I was so damn stupid. If I make a mistake, Jane and Neil will pay for it. I know that.

I nod again to let Jane know I'll be careful. She parks the car in front of the school, leans toward me, and kisses my cheek.

"Have a nice day, dear. Try and make some friends."

Right. That's unlikely.

***

I've been going to this school for three months now. It's tough. Not the curriculum; any moron could learn that stuff. Stephen was right. He once said his school program was total nonsense. He was right. It's brainwashing at its best. But I just try to fit in like Jane asked me to.

I haven't made any friends since I got here though. *What's the point?* Most of those guys are misogynistic sycophants. I can't speak my mind when I'm at school. I just bite my tongue each time my classmates open their foul

~374~

mouths—like now. William Fox is standing in front of the class, giving a presentation. He's such an idiot. I can't believe the other guys are actually listening to this shit he's trying to sell us.

The bell rings and I shove all my books into my backpack as quickly as I can. I head out, but someone grabs my shoulder.

"Eh, Wilcox." Fox is right behind me. "What did you think of my presentation?"

J'ai pensé qu't'es qu'un pauvre abruti, et j'sais pas si j'ai envie d'me marrer ou d'chialer. I thought you sounded like a moron and I don't know if I want to laugh or cry.

"Yeah, it was good," I reply and walk away.

He follows me. "What part did you prefer?"

Why does he care what I think?

I stop and turn around. The idiot wants an answer, I'll give him one. "You know that part where you said women are too stupid to think for themselves. I agree that a lot of people don't have the brains to see through the lies. They just eat and swallow what society feeds them, and then they brag about how smart they supposedly are." *People like you!*

I look him straight in the eyes as I say it, but the guy's too dumb to hear the insult behind my compliment.

"I know, right!" He pauses for a second and scratches his head as if he's only just realized what I truly meant. "So what's your presentation going to be about?" he asks.

Nope, false alert; he didn't get it. This guy really is something else. I chuckle right in his face. I've crafted the perfect presentation, the ultimate insult disguised as a praise.

"I'm gonna talk about the Unwanted."

He looks at me and blinks. "And?"

"You'll see," I reply.

"Awh, come on, Wilcox, what is it about?"

I smile ironically. "It's about how good the authorities are at tracking the Unwanted, and you know, making sure we don't get overpopulated, and all that. I did a lot of research. You can't even imagine how effective the system is. No one's passing through, you know. Which is good. I mean, can you imagine if unregulated people could just walk among us without us realizing it?" I feign a shudder.

Fox looks at me like I'm just some weirdo. "Wow, you sound like you've spent hours on this. Honestly, the whole presentation is easy homework. You didn't have to study so hard for it."

I brush him off with a motion of my hand. "I just wanted to make sure New York State is doing a good job. We can't have any nasty children born over the number allowed. We don't need to share our resources with those pests. I'm really satisfied with my research. Now, I feel safe for sure."

Fox smiles at me. "Damn right. We don't need those leeches sucking on our system." He slaps me on the back.

"You know, I like you, Wilcox. We should hang out sometime."

J'préfèrerais brûler vif! I'd rather burn alive!

***

Every day after school, Jane drops me at Taylor's house. I've only known him for a week. The guy's pretty cool. I like him—not like those jerks at my school.

I'm standing in his training room. I don't know that the word "mansion" could even describe his house. The place is huge. I've never seen such a big residence before. And it's just him and Kayla living here, too. Crazy! Taylor told me he chose this location on purpose. This way, when the members of the Underground meet here, they see how much the authorities are wasting on their employees while the rest of us are striving to survive.

"First thing you need to learn is how to fight and how to shoot," Taylor tells me. "Chase and Kayla will teach you." He points at the guy standing next to me.

Chase is heavier than me—all muscles. I'm six feet tall; he's probably six feet three. And his arms are twice as big as mine. He's gonna kick my ass. He shoots me a lopsided smile and raises his eyebrow at me. Great! He's gonna kick my ass and he knows it too. Just awesome!

Of course, Taylor's asked Kayla to be here as well. Just great! The two of them are staring at me now. I can't focus. I

~377~

face Chase and he doesn't wait. He swings his leg and hits me hard in the calves. I fall on the mats covering the floor.

"Dude, you're not even trying," Chase says with a chuckle.

"I wasn't ready. And you didn't even give me any instructions. What kind of a self-defense class is this?"

"Come on, Chi," Kayla cheers and claps her hands high in the air. "You can beat him," she shouts with excitement.

Yeah, right!

Chase holds his hand out to me. I take it. He helps me stand up, grabs my shoulders before I can even move, and hurls me to the ground. I fall face first this time. The guy's starting to piss me off.

"What the hell, man!" I exclaim.

"Never trust your opponent," Chase says. He bears his arms crossed over his chest and a mocking smile on his face.

I stand up again. This isn't a class; this is just him showing me how weak I am. Fine, I can play that game too. Stephen taught me how to fight—street fight. I can do this. I lunge forward and slam my shoulder right under Chase's ribs. He loses his breath and I ram him to the ground. I take a step back to let him stand up.

"Dude, the goal isn't to injure me for real. This is just practice," he groans while holding his ribcage

"Sorry." I smirk. He deserved it.

"Yeah, sure. Next time say it like you mean it."

The door opens just then, and a tiny blonde girl steps in. She stands at the entrance and stares at me with her mouth open. *What did I do now? Do I have toothpaste on my chin? Spinach in my teeth? What?*

Chase tilts his head toward her. "This is Tina. Tina, this is Chi."

She stands there for a few seconds before she finally snaps out of it, walks to me, and holds out her hand.

"Hi, Chi." Her entire face turns red.

Everyone is staring at us with their eyes shifting from Tina to me. I clear my throat and give her a handshake.

"Hi, Tina."

Her cheeks flush hard as if she's truly flustered, and her eyes turn away quickly. She smiles at Chase, who's standing behind me. "It's time to go."

"Sure." Chase taps me on the shoulder. "Looking forward to kicking your ass again, Chi."

He laughs. I roll my eyes and he winks at me. He leaves with Tina, who sends me one last glance.

"Well, that went great," Taylor exclaims sarcastically. "To be fair, no one can beat Chase except me, so don't be too hard on yourself."

He pulls Kayla against his side and drops a kiss on her temple. "Let's show Chi our arsenal, babe."

"Yes! My favorite part," she replies, with a fist-pump. "I've been waiting all day for this."

They take me to another room. This is the sixth room I've walked into so far. *How freaking big can this house be?* Kayla spends two hours showing me all her guns ranging from pistols to rifles. She shows me how to take them apart, how to clean them, how to put them back together, and how to load them. By the time we're done, I still haven't learned how to shoot.

"Tomorrow, we get to play with these babies," Kayla tells me while wriggling her eyebrows and petting one of the guns as if it were some beloved puppy.

I nod. Once I know how to shoot, I can take down the assholes who took my parents away.

***

This month's been such a pain. I'm sick of school. When I told Jane that I wanted to drop out, she said, "absolutely not." I tried to argue my point—school isn't gonna help me rescue my family—but I don't want to be a problem to Jane and Neil, so I ended up complying with their rules.

Our school is hosting a football game today. I didn't want to go, but attending isn't an option; it's a requirement. All students have to be there and cheer for their team, or they'll get detention. It's ridiculous, but everything about this school is just moronic. So I dragged myself to the stadium—like I care who wins—and I'm just sitting here, bored out of my mind.

I grab my book. I don't care if it's rude or against the rules to read during the game. Sports just aren't my thing. I've hidden the book under a different cover. The title reads *The State of New York and the New Empire*. Snore! The book inside though is intriguing: *Nana* by Emile Zola, French edition. Jane told me not to bring it here, but I didn't listen. Reading a controversial book in public is the most fun I've had in a while. A guy's gotta get his rush somehow.

I've read this book twice already. I just keep rereading the few books that I managed to grab from my parents' house. My mom loved this story. I know what's gonna happen next in the plot. I raise my head and study the crowd. That's when I see her—a girl carrying so much sadness on her face that my heart aches.

She's wearing a blue dress; she's promised to someone.

Her skin is pale against the raven darkness of her incredibly wild hair; it's like a real mane surrounding her face. I love it. She's beautiful.

I'm staring now. *What a creep!* I can't stop myself though. I gape at her for some time before she even realizes that someone's observing her. She lifts her eyes and catches me gawking at her. Her cheeks redden—a deep pink against her fair skin.

I can't look away. Damn, she's gorgeous. I'm gonna freak her out for sure, staring like an idiot.

She won't stop looking at me either. The red on her cheeks spreads to her entire face. I smile at her and she looks away. Good job, man, now you've managed to creep her out!

Her eyes rise again. She watches me and I smile, but she looks away to focus on the game.

Cette fille n'est pas pour toi, mec. Laisse tomber! This girl isn't for you, man. Just let it go!

I glance at her every so often, but she makes a point of avoiding my eyes. She must be promised to one of the players, to someone from my school. Just my luck! I bet he's a major asshole, too. All the guys here are complete jerks.

When the game's over, I make sure not to lose her. She glances around a few times as if she's looking for someone. I'm standing behind some huge guy walking along with the rest of the crowd. She's standing with her parents at the bottom of the stairs. I stop in my tracks. People walk around me, some of them shouldering me while cursing. I can't move. Someone approaches her—a blonde woman and her husband. And then, he appears—William Fox. He comes to stand right by her side. I swallow hard and my heart skips a beat. She's promised to William Fox—the biggest asshole at my school.

***

Taylor's invited me to his house for practice again. I've been coming here for two years now. It's just Chase and me in the training room today.

"I'm sorry I kicked your ass that first day we met, Chi," he says. "You needed to understand how any officer could use your weaknesses to take you down."

"No problem, man."

"You're a much better fighter now," Chase adds before sending me a crooked smile. "Still not as good as me though." He raises an eyebrow.

"Always so modest!" I reply.

Tina walks into the room just then. "I have an errand to run for Taylor. I'll be right back."

She sends me a glance and blushes. Chase has made it pretty clear that Tina has a crush on me. She's smart, kind, and all that, but I'm not interested.

She exits the room, and Chase slaps me on the back.

"Ready?" he asks.

"Yeah."

We train for over an hour before he asks me if I want anything to drink. I nod and he leaves. But he doesn't come back; Tina does. She hands me a glass of water and sits by my side on the mat. This feels like a set-up. I curse Chase silently.

Tina clears her throat. Her neck and her face are red.

"Do you know Chase's story?" she asks out of the blue.

I take a sip and shake my head.

"The officers killed his entire family during the riots that followed the Sterilization Law," she explains, with profound sadness.

I blink at her. No wonder the guy hates the authorities so much that he's turned himself into a killing machine. Chase could probably take any man down with his bare hands.

"All of them?" I ask.

"Every single one of them, yes." Tina chokes on the words as if the subject is painful to her as well.

"Did you know them?" I ask.

She nods and moves a bit closer to me. I don't know what to say. I open my mouth to speak, but she cuts me off.

"How are you holding on?" she asks. "I mean, with your parents gone and everything."

"I don't think they're dead if that's what you mean." I shrug. I don't feel like talking about them right now.

She clears her throat again. "Uh, Chi?"

"Yeah?"

"*I think* I know where your parents are," she says really quickly before adding, "Well, actually, I *do* know where they are."

I turn to her in an instant. "Where?"

"Camp 19," she says.

"How do you know?" I ask. "Did you see them? How do you know it was them?"

"I just know," she says. "Your father looks a lot like you." She averts her eyes. She's not telling me everything.

"Are they okay?" I ask.

She nods. "They're fine, just working hard, you know."

I nod. "Have you seen Stephen, my brother? Is he with them?" I ask.

"No, I haven't seen him," she answers. She won't look at me. She's lying. I don't know why, but she's lying.

"Is he still alive?" I insist.

"I haven't seen him, Chi," she reiterates.

"I need to know that he's okay, Tina." *Why is she lying? What's going on with Stephen that she won't talk about him?*

"I don't know," she just replies.

Fine! Don't tell me anything. I'll find out on my own.

She scoots a bit closer and turns her head to me. Then she leans forward, but I pull back before her lips touch mine.

"Uh, what are you doing?" I ask.

She flushes crimson red and stutters with shame, "I...I just thought..."

"Tina..." I shake my head. "I can't get involved with anyone right now."

I'm lying. I think about the girl I saw at the football game—the one with the curly black hair—and I know I'd get involved with that girl in a second if she weren't engaged to William Fox. I'm just not interested in Tina. I can't force myself to like her that way.

Tina sends me a sideways glance like I've just broken her heart or something. *Her crush on me can't be that bad, right?* I hope not! I feel like shit now.

"I'm sorry, Tina," I repeat. "I just want to find my parents. That's my only goal right now. I can't get distracted. I'm sorry."

Dude, stop saying you're freaking sorry!

She looks at me again and nods. Then she stands up and leaves the room without saying another word. The door opens a few minutes after she leaves, and Chase comes in.

"Dude, what did you say to her?" he asks.

I sigh. "I can't get involved with her, Chase. And thanks for setting me up, by the way. I feel like a real asshole now."

He scratches his head, messing up his hair. "So, you don't like her? That's too bad, man. She's truly awesome, I swear."

I study him for a few minutes. "Are you interested in her?" I ask.

He shakes his head. "No, she's just a friend. Believe me, she doesn't want a guy like me."

Right! Chase has a reputation. The funny thing is that girls still swarm around him in spite of everything they've heard. I guess status isn't everything in this world after all 'cause those girls sure don't care what social class Chase comes from.

He sends me one of his signature smiles—the kind with teeth so white they could blind the hell out of someone.

"Dude, let's go shoot some targets," he exclaims. "Kayla told me she got some new toys."

***

School is finally out and I'm so damn late. Thia and I have been meeting for two months now. I don't know how I got so lucky as to end up with a girl like her. I finally gathered enough courage to kiss her. I really thought she was going to push me away, but she didn't.

I'm supposed to meet her in twenty minutes. I try to hurry, but Lawrence is standing in my way.

"Hey Fox, come over here," he calls out to William.

William turns his head and raises his chin. "What do you want, Lawrence?" he asks and walks to us.

Great! I can't stand the guy. I don't need him standing right in my face.

I can barely tolerate Lawrence either, but he's always sticking to me like some leech I can't pry off. *Juste un imbécile de plus qui m'insupporte.* Just another idiot getting on my nerves.

"What's up with that chick of yours?" Lawrence asks.

My body stiffens. I close my eyes.

Ferme-la, William, ferme-la! Keep your mouth shut, William. Just keep it shut.

"Her name is Thia," William interjects.

I feel sick when the name rolls off his tongue. He doesn't deserve to say the word.

"Yes, Thia. Whatever. I saw you two together last weekend at that charity event in downtown Eboracum."

William squints his eyes. "Really? I didn't see you."

"Right. I didn't want to interfere. You two were busy, if you know what I mean." Lawrence winks at William and my stomach churns.

My mind goes wild with images of William kissing and touching Thia, and my knuckles clench with a sudden need to hit him.

William smirks smugly and I could just punch his mouth for it.

"Have you banged her yet?" Lawrence asks.

The blood in my veins pumps in response. It rockets straight to my head, giving a damn headache.

"No, but soon." William wiggles his eyebrows, and I close my eyes to shut him out.

Réagis pas, Chi! Réagis pas! Don't react, Chi! Don't react!

Lawrence laughs really loud at that. "Didn't fancy you for a virgin, Fox," he adds, and William's smile drops.

"I never said I was a virgin, you moron," he snaps back.

Lawrence snorts. "Seeing girls on the side, then?" he asks.

My body tenses up.

Dis rien, Chi! Réagis pas! Don't say anything, Chi! Don't react!

William arches his eyebrow suggestively. I just want to destroy his face. I want to break him one bone at a time.

"I could invite you to one of my father's parties sometime. You too, Wilcox."

He looks at me, and I feign a smile while choking on the bile pushing behind my gritted teeth.

J'préfèrerais crever qu'd'aller à une de tes soirées, connard. I'd rather die than go to one of your parties, asshole.

"My father always brings girls over," he adds, and my nose wrinkles in disgust.

"What kind of girls?" Lawrence asks.

William snickers. "The easy kind."

Prostitutes. My blood turns cold. My nails dig deep into the skin of my palm.

"Nice! When's your next party?" Lawrence won't shut up.

"In a couple of weeks. We're meeting Thia's family for lunch first. The party is later in the evening."

Lawrence hoots so loud the sound could shatter my skull. I'm so pissed off I'm getting really close to bursting a freaking blood vessel. I rack my brain for a way out of this stupid conversation. When I come up with zilch, I just turn around to leave.

William calls out to me. "How about you, Wilcox? Want to join the party?"

J'préfèrerais sauter d'une falaise. I'd rather jump off a cliff.

"No, I've got things to do that weekend." *Comme convaincre ta fiancée qu'elle mérite mieux qu'un pauvre connard comme toi.* Like convince your fiancée that she deserves better than some sick bastard like you.

~389~

"Gotta go," I add. I need out of here *now*.

I want to hear what Thia has to say about Hugo's poems. I haven't seen her in a week. I miss her so damn much. It sickens me to know she's spending so much time with William every weekend. It makes me want to shove him against the wall and break his damned jaw.

"Got a girl to meet?" William asks while sending me a crooked smile.

Ouais, la tienne. Yep, yours.

I smirk at him and shrug.

"I doubt it. Wilcox's a virgin," Lawrence interrupts. "He doesn't care about meeting girls. Believe me, I've tried to talk him into it for months."

"Really?" William looks at me like I'm some strange specimen he'd like to dissect.

"Yeah, I don't have time for all that," I reply, trying to cut the conversation short.

"You don't have time for sex?" William's eyes open wide in shock. And that's the guy Thia's parents chose for her when she was only thirteen years old. Wonderful! I roll my eyes.

Those idiots just gave me a migraine, and I'm gonna be late. I never told Lawrence about Willow. It's none of his business whom I may or may not have slept with. It would raise too many questions I can't afford to answer. I couldn't care less what those jerks think about me anyway.

"Wow, I feel sorry for you. You're sure you're not interested in the party?" William snickers.

My jaw tightens. *Connard.*

"Yeah, whatever." I don't care to hide my irritation anymore. The guy's got a peanut for a brain and he's wasting my time. His cheating on Thia just makes me want to drive a knife up his spine.

The only girl I'm interested in is taken by some major jackass. She's beautiful, smart, and overly coy. I've got no desire to rush into anything physical with her or to take advantage of her. And if William touches her like that, I will break him and make him pay for it in ways he can't even imagine.

***

Thia loved the book. She's everything I've ever wanted. I love how she hates this society we live in. I love her poetry. I love how smart she is.

I fell in love with her so quickly it freaked me out. I don't even know if she feels the same, and not knowing just terrifies me. I don't want to lose her. I don't want to share her with anyone—especially not with someone like Fox.

This week-end, there's a gala at my school. I can't even invite her to it. I want to take her there with me. I want to see her wear something other than those stupid blue dresses the authorities force on promised girls like some damn trademark. *Why don't they use a hot iron brand while they're at it?* Granted, Thia looks beautiful in anything she wears, but those dresses are just revolting. Thia's probably going to the gala with William. It might be best if I don't go at all. I don't know that I can watch while he touches her. But attending is mandatory unless you've contracted polio or something.

"How was school?" I ask Thia like I do each time we meet.

She looks at me and rolls her eyes. I shoot her a tiny smile and kiss her hair.

"Did you know that I'm not allowed to vote in the next elections? Well, of course, I knew that already," she says. "After all, women are too ignorant to participate in such important matters as politics. Well, I'm not of age to vote, mind you, but that's beside the point. The point is that I'm considered too dumb to make choices for myself or have any say in my own future. And you can't vote either since you're an Unwanted."

She keeps on talking for about fifteen minutes, ranting about how lame the system is. I don't interrupt her. I just listen. I pull her to me and kiss her cheeks first, then her nose, then both her eyelids, then her earlobes. I close my eyes.

"Thia," I whisper, "you are smart and your opinion matters. Don't ever let anyone tell you otherwise."

I love you. I love you so damn much. I can't stand to watch while other people treat you so badly. I love you. I love you.

"I..." I open my eyes.

She looks at me. I can't tell her how much I love her. Not yet. She has to choose me first. She has to say the words.

I clear my throat. "Someday, a woman will be governor of this state," I say. "Women will have the right to vote, just like they did before the war. Everyone will have the right to live and prosper."

She smiles at me. "Just like in my poems?" she asks.

"Exactly like in your poems," I reassure her.

"You're a bad liar," she says, "but thank you for making me feel better."

She smiles, but her words wound me. I wasn't lying. I truly meant it. I can only breathe if I believe we stand a chance at a brighter future.

Under Ground

William

A Short Story

Breaking her into obedience will be a fun game
and I'm all play.

Alice Rachel

<u>*William*</u>

William's short story starts when he meets Thia for the first time, at age fourteen.

***

"William, please come downstairs," Mother calls.

The Clays are here. Today, I am to meet their daughter. Father said I'm allowed to reject her if she's not to my taste, but he hopes I'll like her because he has already made a deal with her father. I asked him about it, but he refused to say anything more.

I'm wearing a tailored suit with tie, all black except for my green button-down shirt. My hair is short. I don't like it that way. Next time, I'll get the haircut I want. Mother doesn't get to choose what I should look like.

I've never met Thia before. I hope she's pretty. Mother has introduced me to some of her friends' daughters too; I didn't like any of them.

I head downstairs, stand up straight, and enter the living room. My parents are talking with the Clays. I look at them and my eyes fall on the girl. She's short; I like that. Her hair is pinned down and attached into a ponytail, but curly locks have escaped the tie like rebellious strands refusing to obey. She's pale, deathly white, really. I'll just have her join the tanning salon when we are married. I like them with bronzed skin, straight long hair, and curvy bodies. This girl is none of that. She's only thirteen though. Maybe she'll fill out a bit by the time we wed. No matter what, by the time I'm done with her make-over, she'll fit my standards. I was told she was mine, which means I can mold her into being exactly what I like.

I give her a once-over and she blushes. I nod a greeting and keep my eyes on her. She squirms as if she's scared of me. Good! Fear keeps girls in their rightful place.

"William," Mother says, "please, come closer."

I glare at her. I don't like it when she orders me around. I step forward anyway and hold out my hand to Mr. Clay. I don't look at his wife; she doesn't matter. In my peripheral vision, I see Thia studying me, blushing all the way down her throat. I cast one single look at her and smirk. She likes what she's looking at, I can tell.

***

Three years later

It's been three years since I met Thia. I've only seen her once, and I don't even know what the point of the meeting was. Probably just Father checking that Clay is still a good asset for his company before making more plans for the future. I don't know why we haven't seen those people again since then, but Father says the wedding is still going to happen.

Mother has invited a friend of hers to come over today. I'm annoyed with her. I was supposed to hang out with Todd. Now I'm stuck here having to make small talk with those females. The woman has brought her daughter Joy. I've spent a few afternoons with that girl before. She's sixteen years old; I'm seventeen. She's a dimwit; I'm smart. End of story. I asked her questions about politics and she just stared at me with her eyes wide open. She knows nothing about our state's current affairs, nothing about literature, nothing about anything. Her brain is empty. Either that or she's too wary to talk and speak her mind. No matter what, she's a bore and I'm irritated with Mother for forcing another dull afternoon on me.

"William, could you take Joy for a walk?" Mother asks. "The weather is so beautiful today."

I'm not going to take that girl for a walk. I have other plans. I smirk at Mother and nod my agreement anyway. I stand up, take Joy's hand, and lead her up the stairs, straight to my room. Mother is too busy talking to notice where Joy and I are heading. I open the door, let Joy in, and step inside.

I close the door behind me, and Joy looks around for a few seconds. My room is three hundred square feet, with marine blue walls, a king bed, a desk, six bookshelves, a couch, a walk-in closet, and a flat-screen TV on the wall facing my bed. I take Joy's hand and lead her to the couch. She hasn't sat down yet, but I'm already kissing her. When she doesn't protest, I run my hands all over her and push her against the couch. She lies down underneath me. I take my shirt off and then her dress. Things happen fast, and I lose my virginity right here on the couch. I deflower Joy in the process. She makes a tiny sound as if she's in pain, but I don't stop.

When we're done, I ask her to put her clothes back on. If Mother finds out what I did to her friend's daughter, she'll have a fit. Not that I care what she thinks, but I've just ruined this girl for all other men to come. Mother won't be happy. Father will probably give me a congratulatory pat on the back.

Joy sits up and looks at me. Her cheeks are flushed. She bats her lashes and bites her lower-lip. She probably thinks that this is it, that we're getting married. I already have a fiancée. I don't tell her that though. I want to make sure we can play this game again if I feel like it. Make her believe she stands a chance and she'll do anything I want for as long as I want.

I smile at her, and she averts her eyes. I clear my throat, put my pants back on, my shirt too, and watch while she gets dressed. Then I take her back downstairs.

"Be quiet," I whisper in her ear.

I lead her out the back door. I take Joy for a walk like Mother asked me to. We don't talk. She has nothing to say.

Her words don't matter to me anyway. My interest lies elsewhere—right under her dress—and she knows it. I take her hand in mine, make her feel secure. We walk around the block, and I take her back into the house.

Mother stands up when she sees us. "Did you have a nice walk?" she asks.

Joy blushes just a bit. I send Mother a snide grin.

"Yes, Mother. It felt really good. Didn't it, Joy?"

Joy flushes crimson red, all the way down her neck. My smile widens.

***

My father's driver John drove me to school this morning like he does every single day. There've been rumors of a new student joining our class today. I enter the room and sit in the back. Todd joins me and takes the seat to my right.

"Did you have a nice week-end, Fox?" he asks. "I thought we were supposed to hang out; you never showed up. A phone call would have been nice, you know."

My lips curl up. "I was busy."

Todd glances at me. "Busy doing what?"

"I think you mean 'doing whom,'" I reply.

"Ohhh!" He waggles his eyebrows, chuckles, and holds his palm up for a high-five. I give him one and he laughs. "Definitely better than hanging out," he says.

Mr. Sanchez walks into the room, and Todd opens his backpack to pull out his books. The new student is right behind our teacher, and Mr. Sanchez asks us to stand up and greet him.

"Please, introduce yourself," he says to the new guy.

The student's eyes scan the room. He's studying us just as we're observing him.

"I'm Jordan Wilcox," he mumbles as if he can't quite get the words out. "I used to go to school in Syracuse, but this establishment is rated much higher, so I asked to be transferred here instead."

A few students whoop in agreement, and Mr. Sanchez asks them to please calm down. The new student looks familiar somehow, but I can't quite place where I may have seen him before.

"Thank you, Jordan. You may be seated now. There's still a seat in the back next to William. Mr. Fox, would you be so kind as to show your new classmate around the school after class?"

I nod reluctantly. Jordan comes to sit next to me. I hold out my hand to shake his. He takes it with a strong grip and rakes his other hand through his hair. Then he sits down and pulls some fountain pens and papers out of his bag.

During class, I look at him from the corner of my eye. He's going to fail this course. He hasn't written anything down. He's just holding his head up with his hand as if he's incredibly bored or annoyed. He even sighs at times as if he can't be bothered to care. I smirk at the teacher's comment about the poor, and when I look at Jordan, he narrows his eyes at me. Weirdo! I could swear I've already seen his sulky face before.

***

Two years later

My parents have thrown a party for my nineteenth birthday. Every month they invite people over. It's just a way for my family to brag and show off their wealth. However, these are not the parties where my father invites girls over while my mother pretends not to know what's going on. These are real social events meant to dazzle their so-called friends. Tonight is different though; tonight is about me.

My parents have officially accepted Thia as my promised fiancée, so the Clays were invited as well. Thia is standing by the buffet. She's nibbling on some appetizers. I'm glad she's eating; she still needs to fill out—especially her small breasts. She lifts her eyes to look at me, but she doesn't smile. She's not like the other girls I know. She never tries to impress me. She never beams at me with joy so overbearing that it irritates me. And there are times when she just plain ignores me. I've seen her get irritated at Mother's comments too, even if she tries to hide her anger. I like that. Mother always pisses me off. Thia finally showed some enthusiasm when I took her to the ball at my school.

In the car, we started talking about books. I've never discussed literature with a girl before. When I meet a chick, I usually just take her to my room, or some hotel, and hope she'll shut up while I find my pleasure.

I turn my eyes away and notice Joy staring at me. She's standing against the wall next to the door. When our eyes meet, she smiles. I walk up to her and nod politely as if she were just a member of my parents' entourage and not someone I sleep with on a regular basis.

"Is that her?" she asks while looking at Thia.

"Yes, stop staring."

"She's not pretty," Joy adds in a tone that implies the exact opposite.

I look her straight in the eyes. "She's prettier than you. Jealousy does not become you at all, my dear Joy."

Her face twists under the insult. "There's no need to be cruel," she says, her voice breaking on the last word.

"You've just insulted my fiancée. What other response do you expect?"

I cast a look at Thia. Her back is turned to us now. She's leaning over the table while talking to the server. Joy uses the opportunity to run her fingers over my lower arm. I pull away.

"What are you doing?" I ask.

"Nothing." Her eyes carry a very specific message that she sends me every time we're around each other.

My lips tilt up. "Go to my room," I say. "I'll be there in a minute."

Joy bats her lashes twice and nods. When she turns around to exit the room, I steal a glance at Thia. She's talking to her brother now and laughing. No matter how much fun I've had with Joy, I have to break it up. She's tedious and I'm losing interest.

Thia has remained distant though. Not that I've made much of an effort to communicate with her, but she has piqued my curiosity. She's much more interesting than most girls I've met—definitely more intriguing than Joy.

I head upstairs and find Joy in my room. She's not the only girl I'm seeing. Although, apparently, she believes she is. Her feelings for me make her so gullible I *almost* feel bad. It's almost too easy.

Sadly, I can't take my time tonight; I have to rush things up. We can't be up here for too long. I tell her that, and she obliges me like she does every single time. She probably still thinks we're getting married. But when we're done, I tell her this was the last time she was coming to my room. She looks at me and blinks.

"What do you mean?" she asks.

"I mean that I'm done with you. You can go back downstairs now."

"No, I deserve an explanation," she says.

"You and I," I reply, motioning with my finger between the two of us, "are done. For good. You can leave now."

She holds back a sob, but tears come pouring out of her eyes. *Why do they always have to cry?* I hate it. Every time I meet a girl, she takes it to mean so much more than it is. I tell them that I won't marry them—after the fact of course, not beforehand, I'm not that stupid. I tell them that I'm already engaged, and they break down in tears because I've supposedly ruined their reputation for life. I can't stand it. They should have thought about that before joining me in bed.

Joy is no different. She's sobbing so hard now that I have to hold my hands to my ears to quiet the noise.

"Stop crying!" I snap at her.

She swallows hard and tries to restrain herself.

"I gave you my virtue," she says. "No one's going to marry me now."

"They can't prove that you've been touched," I exclaim, exasperated.

Of course, that's a lie. The promised fiancé always checks the sheets for blood after the fact. If the girl doesn't bleed, he will cast her out.

Joy stares at me with her eyes wide open like a deer before the kill. "William," she hiccups, "I love you. I've always loved you. Please, don't do this to me. I gave you everything I had."

Is she for real? I laugh right in her face. I can't control myself. She's just ridiculous. Her features contort with sudden anger.

"Joy, I'm going to marry Thia," I say.

"What does she have to offer you that I don't?" Joy shouts in my face. "She didn't even look at you all evening."

My nostrils flare. I won't allow her to raise her voice at me. I tell her exactly that.

"You've ruined my life. I can raise my voice all I want," she shrieks.

I take a warning step toward her and tower over her. "Do not talk to me like that ever again!" I snarl in her face. "Thia is smart and beautiful. You are none of those things. Now, leave!"

"My parents will hear about this," she threatens me.

I laugh harder now. "Are you going to make this affair public, then?" I sneer. "Joy, if you talk about this, everyone will cheer for me. No one expects men to remain virgins until marriage. And you're not promised to anyone. I didn't do anything illegal. Your parents, however, will tear you apart if they know you've been touched."

She blinks at me. She knows I'm right.

"You are a despicable man. I never want to see you again," she barks.

I smile at her and wave her goodbye. Good riddance!

She puffs out her anger. Her hands have turned to fists on both sides of her body. "I hate you, William Fox. Someday, you will pay for your wicked ways."

And with that, she storms out of my room and runs to the bathroom across the hall, probably to fix her make-up and salvage the little dignity she has left. I shake my head at her when she bangs the door on her way out. Foolish girl!

I grab my tie and put it back on. Then I straighten my suit and join the rest of the party downstairs. Thia is sitting on a chair, looking bored. I head her way, and when I stand in front of her, she raises her head.

"Would you care for a dance?" I ask.

She nods without a single smile and gives me her hand. By the time Thia is wrapped in my arms, Joy has fixed herself up and come back downstairs. I pull Thia into a deep kiss while locking my eyes on Joy's, and I watch as Joy's face contorts with barely contained pain before she turns away to leave the room.

Two months later

Everything is so screwed up! Nothing's going as planned. I'm sitting on the bed in the hotel room I had reserved for Thia and me. The place is ransacked. I got so mad that I took my anger out on everything in this place. The pillows are torn apart, the lamps are broken, and the bathroom mirror is shattered. It felt good to lash out.

Thia will pay for what she did to me. I go down to the lobby, pick up the phone, and call John to tell him to come and pick me up. I tell the person at the desk that I was attacked in my own room. It's unacceptable. He will hear from my father. The man apologizes, cowering so much in front of me that his head buries itself in his shoulders. He and everyone on staff will lose their jobs for letting Jordan Wilcox into the hotel.

I storm out of this place and wait for John on the sidewalk. I pace up and down the street until he gets here. Then I step into the car without greeting him.

"Take me to my father," I snap.

"As you wish, Sir." He sends me a quick look through the rearview mirror and drives without talking.

My father keeps his office in the camp closest to Eboracum City, about thirty minutes away from here heading north. He's always working. He leaves early in the morning and comes home around midnight every day. I hardly ever see him.

When we arrive at the camp, John parks the car and I step out. I head straight to my father's office. I turn the knob and walk in. Father is sitting behind his desk. An officer is standing in front of him. Father's eyes shift from the officer to me with a quick flash of irritation.

"What is it, William? It's called knocking, you know. You can't just barge in here whenever you feel like it. This is a place of business, and I'm having a meet—"

"Thia was kidnapped earlier tonight," I cut him off without apologizing for intruding upon his so-called important business.

"*What?*" Father stands up from his chair. He shoos the officer away with a motion of his hand. "Explanations, William. I don't have all night."

The officer leaves and I explain the circumstances.

"What's that kid's name? The one who took her, do you know his name?" Father asks.

I nod. "He goes to my school. His name is Jordan Wilcox."

Fox's eyebrows furrow. "Wilcox, as in computer security genius Neil Wilcox?"

I shrug. No idea who that guy is, and I don't care.

"Let me check the school's files," Father adds.

He sits back down in his leather chair, logs onto his computer, and accesses the school's records after just a few seconds. His eyes widen.

"Is that him?" he asks me while turning the screen toward me.

I lean over the desk and see Wilcox's face. My hand twitches in response. "Yes, Father."

"I should have had him killed when I had the chance!" Father exclaims, with a punch of his fist on the desk.

"What do you mean, Father?"

He ignores my question, picks up the phone, and dials one single digit. "Bring me Richards, now."

Father's features turn livid when the person on the other end of the line replies. "I don't care that he might be sleeping, Smith. I pay my guards to work around the clock.

Tell Richards to bring his ass up here, *now!* Don't make me ask you twice!" He slams the phone down in anger.

"Father, what's going on?" I ask.

"Nothing that concerns you, William. Just go home. I will find the girl. It's only a matter of time."

"But Father—"

Father's cold gaze cuts me off. There's no arguing with him when he gets mad.

"Fine!" I sigh with irritation. "Good night, Father."

"Good night, son."

I leave my father's office and kick the door on my way out. I hate it when he treats me like a child and hides things from me. Something's going on—something other than what I came here for.

I cross the hall, take the elevator, and go down to the main courtyard. The door opens up automatically and I step out. It's nighttime, but the yard is lit. I walk over to the front gate, and from the corner of my eye, I see someone move just as I'm about to get out. The person is standing just a few feet away from me. His back is propped up against the wall and his arms are crossed over his chest. His eyes are closed as if he's relaxing. And I recognize him right away—Jordan Wilcox. I frown. *What the hell is he doing here?*

No, this can't be right. Of course, Wilcox wouldn't be here. But this guy is his exact replica; he looks just like him. That's why Jordan has always seemed so familiar; I had already seen his twin brother here before. That's why Father recognized Jordan's picture so quickly, too.

I want answers and I want them now. If Father won't give them to me, I will pull them out of this guy. I take a step toward him when someone shouts from across the yard, "Eh, Richards, Fox wants you in his office, now."

The guy opens his eyes, sighs heavily, and mumbles something I don't understand but that sounds like an insult to my father. I take another step toward him, but he shoots me a nasty glare as if I were the one giving him orders. He passes by me without looking back, and I stand here for a few minutes. Father owes me some serious explanations.

***

"We can get you another girl if this one doesn't come back, William," Mother tells me.

We're sitting on the leather couch in my parents' living room. She doesn't understand. I don't want another girl. I can get all the girls I want for goodness' sake. That's not the problem here. Being married to Thia won't prevent me from going around if she's not to my taste. But Thia is mine. She was promised to me when I was fourteen years old. She belongs to me, and I'm not going to let some good-for-nothing criminal take her away.

I saw the look she gave him at the gala. She's infatuated with him and it sickens me. She's *mine*. She had no right to do what she did. Chi is not even worth a quarter of my inheritance. He's a lascivious scoundrel and a murderer on top of that. I will find Thia and she will pay for what she did to me. I shouldn't have to step back and let him get her. I shouldn't have to take a bow and watch him steal what's mine. I simply refuse to let him win.

When I find him, I will make sure Father puts him down. He's just some loser who can't even afford this game he has bet on. He's not good enough to attract a girl of his own, so he had to take mine.

I wanted to break his neck when I saw him kissing Thia under the Arch. She didn't even push him away. She just took it, as if that kiss was his to give, as if it was his right. But it's wrong. All of this is wrong and I won't accept it.

"She's not worth the trouble, William," Mother says. "She's lucky enough that we accepted her in our family. I know your father has high hopes for Clay, but I'm sure he can find some other man to do the job. I have friends who have daughters too, and I can guarantee you that they are a lot more beautiful than Thia. She's not worth the investigation your father is instigating just to find her."

Mother is irritating me. I've spent enough time with Thia to know how smart she is. She's not some half-wit. I don't need some trophy wife who can't align three words. I can get any girl to lay down at my feet or in my bed. That's not what I want. Thia is a challenge I plan to take on. She has rejected me, and I shall prove to her that she can never scorn me like that again.

"Honestly, I pity the girl for getting kidnapped by some low-class criminal, but she's no longer ours to worry about. You just turned nineteen, and you need a wife worthy of your status."

I sigh heavily. I've had enough. Enough of her lecturing me constantly, over and over again about this. It hasn't even been twenty-four hours since Thia left, and Mother is already pushing some ignorant girl on me, just to please one of her friends. I should put her back in her place. I don't have to listen to her, and I'm sick of her malicious comments.

I only respond to Father, and Father is siding with me on this. Thia is to be mine. Father plans on granting her father some prominent position that he won't tell me about. But if I reveal that Thia wasn't really kidnapped and that she actually agreed to run away with Chi, my parents might call off the wedding and Chi will have won. I won't let it happen. He will *never* get what's mine.

***

The officers have found Thia and brought her home. Talking to her just riled me up. *How could she just stand there and look at me without apologizing or showing submission?*

The phone rings in the living room. I head downstairs and answer it. I don't recognize the voice on the other end of the line. She says her name is Emily. I don't know anyone by that name. I hope she's not one of those psychos I've slept with. I should really choose them more carefully. Some of them are so desperate to get married that I can hardly pry them off of me after introducing them to my bed. Seriously, I have better standards than to marry some random half-wit just because she's willing to put out. Thia, though, had the gall to push me away. The girl is feisty. I like it. Breaking her into obedience will be a fun game and I'm all play.

"What's this about?" I'm this close to hanging up on Emily, whoever she is, but what she says next stops me.

"What the hell do you mean, *'Thia left?'*" I shout in the receiver.

Emily explains the situation: Thia ran away to go find Chi *again.* And her mother helped her this time. Thia's betrayal stings somehow. It affects me more than it did on our prenuptial night. The fire inside me grows and turns into fury. I try to tame it. I try to keep control, but I can't. I hang up. My fingers grip the edge of the desk, and I'm suddenly screaming at the top of my lungs. I could just kill her. She keeps shaming me over some low-class rascal. *Does she have no sense of decency at all?* I will break her into compliance if it's the last thing I do.

She's mine. Mine to mold. Mine to touch. Mine only!

I head out of the house.

"John, take me to my father's office, *now,*" I tell the driver.

He nods at me politely, and I climb into the limousine. I'm so angry that it takes all I have not to wreck everything inside this car.

I want him dead. Chi will die for this. If Father doesn't take care of it, I will do it myself. And Thia will be mine whether she wants to or not.

I arrive at the camp and walk straight to my father's office. But when I get there, Father is shouting so loud his voice can be heard through the door. I don't even need to eavesdrop. His words stop me in my tracks.

"Absolutely out of the question," he yells.

Someone else is talking now, saying that Chi needs to be released from custody. *Is he for real?* Father will never agree to this.

"Sir, if I don't help the Underground get him out, my cover will be blown. Richards will not drop the search for his parents. The Underground could be partly brought down when they reach the camps. Let him go and I can guarantee you that they will come right here, Chi included. He's been looking for his parents for a long time. He will come here for them himself."

Chi's parents are in this camp? Father never cared to share that information with me. I thought Father and I were a team. *How am I to take over his business someday if he keeps hiding things from me?*

Still, there is no way he would agree to this nonsense.

"This had better not be a trick of yours. If you screw me over, Harris, I will show no mercy. Take this as a nice warning."

What? Father is releasing Chi? How could he do this to me? He's going behind my back, betraying me, making me look like a fool and letting that jerk out just like that. *I can't believe this.*

"Of course, Sir."

Father dismisses Harris, and I find some closet nearby. I hide inside and leave the door just slightly ajar so I can see the man leaving the office. I want to know where the rebels are taking Chi. I will find Thia myself since I can't rely on anyone and I can't even trust my own father. I study the man and imprint his face into my brain. I've seen him here many times before. He will give me the information I need if I have to torture it out of him.

When he's gone, I return to the limousine. Forget about talking to Father. He can go to hell for all I care. He's humiliating me in front of his officers—in front of everybody.

I find the car and tell John to take me far from here.

"Where should I take you, Sir?"

"The Joy of Life," I reply.

"Is your father aware, Sir?" he asks.

"Does it look like I care," I shout with scorn. "When I need your opinion, John, I'll ask for it. Just drive the fucking car."

I pat around for the liquor that Father always leaves around here, and I drink it right from the bottle. The first gulp burns my throat and fires right through me. I take another gulp, and another. It numbs a bit of my stabbing irritation, but not much.

By the time we reach the joy house, I feel slightly better. I get out and knock on John's window. He rolls it down.

"Don't tell my father about this, John," I warn him.

"I'm his employee, Sir, not yours," he dares reply. Wrong answer! I grab him by the neck and push my mouth to his ear.

"I know where your family lives, John. Don't be stupid." I let go and rejoice in the fear that flickers on and off in his eyes.

"Wait for me here. I'll be back in an hour."

I walk into the house, and the owner Jasmine comes right to me.

"William," she greets me. Her voice is like honey, so sweet it disgusts me.

"To what do we owe the pleasure?" she asks as if she didn't already know the answer.

"Is Lillian here?" I ask.

Jasmine sends me a quick knowing smile. "Yes, of course. Just one minute, please. May I serve you something to drink?"

I shake my head and go wait in the parlor.

After a while, Lillian enters. She's short, with black curly hair. She's not Thia, but she'll do. She's the best there is in this place, too. She knows her job and she does it well. She grins and holds her hand out to me. We don't talk. She knows how I am. She knows what I want. I follow her to the bedroom and push her toward the bed the moment she closes the door behind us.

***

Lillian hardly made me feel better. I'm still angry. I need more alcohol. John sends me sideways glances through the rearview mirror. I flip him off and his eyebrow rises. He's getting on my nerves. I don't owe the guy any explanation. He would never behave like this around Father. Everyone respects *him. Everyone.* But no one respects me—not even my fiancée. My nostrils flare and I take another sip.

By the time we get to my parents' house, I'm completely drunk. Mother is going to flip out like she does every time I come home intoxicated. As if I care what she thinks.

I can hardly find the handle to the door. I stumble out and manage to make it to the house somehow. I get in, and Mother is right there with all her stupid friends. They all look at me; they're judging me. I'm still holding the bottle in my hand. I wave it at them.

"Why did you invite all these unbearable women into our home, Mother?" I exclaim and laugh into the bottle before drinking some more. "To discuss the latest fashions in town?" I scoff at her just to piss her off.

Mother stands up in response.

"William, have you been drinking?" she asks.

"Of course not," I retort while taunting her with the bottle. "Why? Are you going to ground me, woman?"

Her eyes narrow, and her stuck-up friends look at one another in shock. I laugh at them loud enough to be considered overtly rude. I can't stand these insufferable females.

Mother is humiliated and her cheeks have turned red. Perfect! *Why should I be the only one to suffer from embarrassment today?*

"Go to your room," she shrieks in a high-pitched voice.

"Or what?" I challenge her.

"I'm calling your father," she adds while looking at me like I just shat all over her Oriental rug.

"Yes, please call God Almighty, Mother. Let's see what he has to say for himself."

Her face turns quizzical. "I have no idea what you are talking about, William, but you shall go to your room right this instant, and your father will hear about this."

"I don't take orders from you, damned woman," I shout right in her face. "It's time you remembered your place, Mother. But please, do call Father. I have a few issues to settle with him."

I walk right past her and shoulder her on my way out. She tries to grab the bottle from my hand, but I hold it out of her reach.

"Nah uh, that's mine." I chuckle at her dismay.

Father is going to rip me a new one for this. I can't wait for what's coming.

***

Father is standing right in my face, but I'm too inebriated to push him back. I just want to laugh. I want to laugh so badly right now. The fury on his face is just hilarious.

"What the hell is wrong with you, William?" he shouts. His voice is harsh and his face is red with anger. I'm a disgrace to him. I'm never good enough.

"What the hell is wrong with me?" I yell back. "You're the one letting criminals out. You think I don't know about Chi. How could you do this to me, Father?" I bark in his face with spit flying in frustration. "And what's up with that guy I saw at the camp? He looks exactly like Chi. What the hell is going on, Father?"

"Stop acting like some damn child, William. I have valid reasons for doing the things I do. This does not concern you."

I've had it. I'm losing it. I'm literally screaming in his face now, "My promised fiancée left again to find that jerk, and you're going to let him out."

"*What?*" Father pauses. Ah, he was not expecting that one!

"Yes, those people you think so highly of...That woman, Cecilia Clay...She just helped Thia run away last night. She's gone to find Chi."

Father looks at me like I'm too drunk to enunciate clearly, so I repeat myself, louder this time. He doesn't respond. He just turns around and leaves.

I fall flat on my bed. My back hits it, hard, and my head starts pounding as though sledge hammers are striking against the sides of my skull. The thought of Thia and Chi together makes me sick. I throw up right here on the comforter and pass out.

***

"William, this is Amelia."

Mother didn't even wait twenty-four hours. I just woke up with one hell of a hang-over. I showered, and here she is already pushing the daughter of her dimwitted friend on me. My teeth clench. I give the girl one single look up and down, just long enough to know I'm definitely not interested.

"And what do you want me to do with *that*?" I ask while motioning toward Amelia with my hand.

Amelia's cheeks turn red. I never said I wanted anyone other than Thia. Sure, this is the second time that Thia has betrayed me. It's getting just a tiny bit tiresome, and I'm losing patience with her, but she's mine. I don't know how many times I have to repeat this to Mother: Thia is mine.

M.I.N.E!

Mine!

Mother sends me a cold look. "Show some respect, William," she dares scold me. "You owe me for yesterday."

My nostrils flare.

"I owe you nothing," I reply with spite. My nose is mere inches from hers, and I tower over her. I turn on my heels and leave her there.

I have places to be and things to do, quickly. I call John and tell him where I want to go. I will find Harris and he will tell me where to find the rebels. I will help them get into Camp 19. Father has betrayed me. It's time he knew what that feels like. I will make sure Chi doesn't make it out of the camp alive, and Thia will finally be mine.

In the car, John turns on the news. "Chi Richards is still on the loose...Cecilia Clay was taken into custody last night for complicity in his escape...William Fox was a key witness; his testimony helped the officers apprehend the suspect..."

What the hell! Damn it, Father!

I never meant for Thia's mother to be taken away. Father took this whole affair too seriously. *Why the hell did he have to arrest the damn woman?* Nice way to screw up my chances with Thia, thank you very much! I couldn't care less about that woman, to be honest, but she's still Thia's mother. Thia will probably hate me for this. I sigh. No matter, she will love me eventually. She has to. She's mine after all; no one can steal her from me. Not today, not tomorrow, not ever.

Fox's Reaction

This scene takes place after William's death, and it is a prelude to Book 2.

Someone knocked on the door. Dimitri Fox looked away from the window. "Come in."

An officer walked into the office, with his head lowered in submission. The tall, bulky man turned toward him.

"I have news of your son, Sir," the officer said.

"Where is he?" Fox asked with irritation. He had been looking for William for a couple of days now, wondering where his son could possibly be.

"He's in the camp, Sir," the officer replied.

Just thinking about the news he had to deliver made him shake with fear. The repercussions would be terrible for him and anyone else working in this camp.

Fox sent a glance outside the window. In the courtyard, some prisoners were lined up against a wall, with their backs to the officers. Guns were raised. Bullets were shot. The prisoners fell to the ground. Fox smirked.

Then the man's green eyes narrowed. "What is William doing here?" he asked, now looking at the officer.

"I'm afraid something happened last night, Sir," the officer answered quickly before shutting up in cowardice.

"What is it, Smith? I don't have all day."

Smith cleared his throat uncomfortably. "I'm afraid he's dead, Sir."

Fox's face turned into a mask of dismay and profound heartache before he recovered his composure quickly and asked, "What do you mean *'he's dead?'*"

"I am so sorry, Sir. We just found your son in the yard. He was shot. He's not breathing."

"What *the hell* was my son doing in this camp?" Fox's tone turned to ice so cold it froze the officer in fear.

"We b-believe he helped the rebels, Sir," Smith stuttered.

Fox's jaw ground in response. "That's just not possible."

"We have one guard saying he saw your son helping them."

Fox's nostrils flared. "That's a lie. My son would *never* help the rebels," he snarled while running his hand over his face. "Who shot my son?"

"We're not sure, Sir. The cameras in that yard were turned off. We have no footage of it. It appears the rebels came in through the tunnels as planned, but we weren't expecting them so early, Sir." The officer averted his eyes.

Fox's hands clenched. "Idiots! All of you! *Nothing but a bunch of idiots!*" he yelled. "I don't care when the rebels were supposed to arrive or how! Orders are orders! You hardly took any of the them down, you incompetent buffoons!"

Smith didn't dare look at his boss again.

"How about Chi Richards?" Fox snapped. "Did he come for his parents? Do you have him?"

The officer squirmed. "I'm afraid he ran away, Sir. The girl as well."

"That was your job, Smith! I specifically told you that Chi Richards was not to leave the camp," Fox yelled in his face. "I should have done the job myself."

"We weren't expect—" the officer tried to defend himself.

Fox slammed his hand on the desk and Smith jumped back. "I don't want to hear your lame excuses, Smith."

"I'm s-sorry, Sir," Smith apologized, close to tears.

"What about his brother?" Fox's nose wrinkled with disgust. "Did Stephen help Chi at all?"

"Richards was found unconscious, Sir. We're not sure what happened."

"I see." Fox shook his head. "Maybe he isn't the backstabbing slime I expected him to be."

"What about the rebels, Sir?" the officer asked.

"Kill anyone who was left behind. The others won't take long to fall now. The rebels took in the Trojan horse that will tear them apart from the inside out. The disease will take them down one by one. Make sure that Richards is okay. I'm not done with him yet."

Losing Ground

A Stephen Richards
Novella

Her angels fight my demons,
winning a battle I've already lost.

Alice Rachel

Excerpt: Chapter 1

It's almost time. Willow should be here any second now. I shall find relief from this pain any minute now.

I look at my watch. She's late. *Why is she taking so long?* I breathe.

Inhale. Exhale.

Inhale. Exhale.

Breathe. I try to breathe, and fail miserably.

You know she deserves better than you. You'll destroy her. The truth about you will devastate her.

Shut up! Shut up! SHUT UP!

I close my eyes. Breathe. I have to breathe.

The sounds of her footsteps announce her presence. I turn around, and here she is standing in front of me. My sweet, beautiful Willow. She bats her lashes and smiles. She's so shy. Even after all this time, she's still so timid.

I love that she is so bashful, so delicate. She's like porcelain. So very fine. So very fragile.

You will break her.

She comes to sit next to me. Her turquoise blue eyes lock on mine, and she grins again. I pull her to me and kiss her cheek. Soft. Her skin is so soft.

"How was your day, sweetheart?" I ask.

"It was good, and yours?"

Mine was awful, as always.

"It was great!"

I breathe, breathe in her scent—violet and lavender. Her smell is intoxicating, and my mind is finally at peace.

Her long chestnut hair falls over her shoulders in curls, and her eyes sparkle with conspiracy.

"Wanna know what I learned today, Stevie?" she asks.

"Always."

I draw her closer. She rests her head on my shoulder, and I pull her hair away from her beautiful face.

"I learned some more about the flowers filling our forests. Mom knows them all. It's fascinating. Did you know we can eat dandelions and turn them into a nice salad?" She faces me, her eyes twinkling with delight.

"No, sweetheart, I didn't know that." I smile at her.

Peace. She brings me such peace.

"Chrysanthemums can also be eaten or boiled into tea, but those aren't grown here. They're imported from another county. Mom said they're considered a delicacy in the upper class."

How fitting in our society that we should be eating the flower of death! But I don't tell her that. I just chuckle.

"How about you? What did you learn today?" Her big blue eyes shine at me.

What does she want me to say? What did I learn today? Yet again that life is a pile of dung I have to dig my way through. I look at her. *How could I ever tell her the truth?* About me, about this world, about life.

You will destroy her.

"Anything worthy that I may learn, I learn it from you, dear. There is nothing else for me to learn."

"Oh, Stevie."

She pushes her face against my neck, takes my hand in hers, and we don't talk. Not talking feels good.

Her peace quiets the voices inside my head.

Her peace makes all the pain go away.

Her peace makes my life worthwhile.

I cup her face with my hands and look her deep in the eyes. "Willow?"

"Yes, Stephen?"

"I love you."

She doesn't reply. She just flushes in that bashful way that breaks down all my walls and all my defenses.

I kiss her on the lips and breathe. I breathe in the sweet scent of her skin.

Oh, Willow, if you only knew.

She'd be gone already if she knew.

"Stevie?"

"Yes, sweetheart."

"Why are you so sad? You always look so forlorn."

She will leave you when she finds out.

"I'm sad because it's time to go and I don't want to leave you."

She blinks at me with her big blue eyes—once, twice—her long lashes stroking her cheeks.

"I will always be with you, Stevie. Always."

If only that were true, Willow, but I can't afford to believe you.

COMING IN OCTOBER

Standing Ground
Book Two

Alice Rachel

2016!

ABOUT THE AUTHOR

Alice Rachel grew up in France before moving to the Unites States to live with her husband. When she doesn't write, Alice teaches French to students of all ages.

She also spends hours reading books of all kinds (Young Adult, New Adult, Mystery, Horror, Romance, History, Graphic Novels...There probably isn't a genre that she doesn't like). She also enjoys going to the movies, visiting museums with her hubby, taking care of her guinea pigs, and drawing.

Alice loves to interact with her readers (and so do her characters). You can find her on Twitter under @AliceRachelWrit. She also likes to chat through her website at www.alicerachelwrites.com as well as on Instagram, GoodReads, and Facebook. Her drawings can be found on www.society6.com/alicerachel.

33222013R00244

Made in the USA
Middletown, DE
05 July 2016